LEADER OF THE PACK

Red Jordan Arobateau

LEADER OF THE PACK
Copyright c. 2008 by Red Jordan Arobateau.
All rights reserved.

Second in the Series the OUTLAW CHRONICLES.

2nd Edition
1st Printing 1993

This is a work of fiction. Any resemblance
to any person living or dead is purely coincidental.

978-0-6152-0166-5

Published by RED JORDAN PRESS
484 Lake Park Ave. PMB 228
Oakland, CA 94610
USA

Author's Bio & Introduction

RED JORDAN PRESS is privileged to present this reprint of Red Jordan Arobateau's classic dike biker novel originally written in 1993. Now — finally processed, the long sought after 2nd book of that Dike Biker Series, The Outlaw Chronicles, LEADER OF THE PACK stands along with her sisters SATAN'S BEST, TRANNY BIKER, THE BLACK BIKER, & OUTLAWS! Because of lack of support these five are the only ones finished out of notes for ten.

Originally shunned because of fear of being tagged as anti-Semitic, and for its stark portrayal of SM and other variant sexual practices it was rejected for publication by the underground press. However, has been maintained by the RED JORDAN catalogue. LEADER contains material that can be called controversial, but that's not what was intended. Here is a novel about the struggles of lower-income, too-queer dikes of different races & cultures, all brought together in camaraderie in that female gang, the mighty Outlaw's.

There is all too little lesbian literature, to begin with. Many under-class writers, too discouraged to testify to their truths. Non-professional queer writers material has been ignored not simply by a bigoted straight world, but because of failure of the lesbian press, and cold shoulder avoidance of gay men's press. Further, too many are afraid to take the risk of bringing up difficult subjects. After witnessing suicide of acquaintances; and those murdered in degraded circumstances of illegal survival hustling, the accounting of their lives never seeing the light of day, this author feels he has little left to loose but to tell their stories. The Higher Calling would not have us keep silent, but to reach out — to those unspoken too and discounted previously.

So, here is that 2nd biker novel. For the sake of real-life characters who will never be able to write because of lack of materials, because of shame, or fear. It is a novel patterned after the authors limited motorcycle experience and involvement with the leather community of the 1990's. A lot of the biker women's experiences were the authors, in his own voice.

Red is 64 years of age, of mixed-race heritage. His education ended after 2 semesters in Art College. He studies and worships in the Christian & Jewish tradition. And continues doing oil painting, novels, short stores, poetry, plays — plus spiritual focused Journals. His newly released **'CATALOGUE OF BOOKS, 2008'**, lists 80-titles. He was not stopped by the world! --- RJA

'Daddy George was the
Leader of the Pack.
She rode a Harley,
and she wore black.'

Chapter One

'I was on my way somewhere. Wild horses couldn't stop me.

And if it was a horse-drawn Chariot I'd need no whip to make the horses go! They went fast with the Power that drew them for I had chosen the direction. --And I was handcuffed, chained to the Power I chose.

Going foreword! Forces tugged me, but I would not turn. Not to the right side, not to the left, but kept on racing to this place. This white light, this blazing day, these eyes of God.'

    ***

Every now and again she'd stick her head out of her shell like a Turtle and come out.

She had at last a lesbian lover, but in five years of their marriage they had acquired no friends. No community. & dealt with a straight world all day long. She was lonely. Lonely to be among her own kind. To be a hero among her own kind.

Although she had not realized it until now, until she found the gang. --That she must find a community to which she must belong.

Pam had been happy with their kids & to stay behind closed doors and watch TV in the coziness of their home.

Angel would complain and bitch. So often, that finally they would go to the club.

400-women inside. A great majority lesbian. A few transsexuals, many bi's, and some straight.

The music rolling over them in a big sea.

They'd come all the way across the city thru a cold night to be with strangers--and would never touch but a few of them--but came, just because they were her own kind. Even if she never got to know their names.

Of course Angel looked with interest at the girlie girls. Of a nature the same as Pam. Long hair. Dresses, or tight pants & halter top blouses. Which were low-cut revealing naked flesh. Mistakenly might cruise a transsexual thinking she was female-born & get pissed & wonder why the lady was with a man. They were short and tall. Skinny and fat. Asian, black, brown, red and white. All manners of women-mostly young to an early middle age.

'A square person who thinks gays are all a bunch of he-she's or ugly creeps might stray in here, see all these pretty women with earrings, bracelets and fine jewelry; their hair shoulder length, and cosmetics and think, 'what are they doing here? Isn't this a queer bar?'

There's all kinds that seek out the lesbian life.'

A party of gay girls came in; sat on each other's laps. Flirted among themselves. Manicured hands, long red nails touched each other's hips. They kissed. Another wiggled her shoulders, shaking her breasts at her girl. They wore cut-away blouses & short skirts. Femmy fems that liked other ladies. High heel pumps made their feet dainty.

Pam & Angel sat arm in arm watching from the safety of their monogamous relationship to the women clustered in the blazing light of an artificial fireplace. Angel still felt like a stranger on the outside looking in.

'The gay life, the nightlife. I been in it long enough.

In those days I had to prove myself as a lesbian butch. Sex drive pounding in my clit. And my throat; in my chest. And arms and legs week, tingling with need. I had to fuck.

I had to find a willing woman or a lay date. My need neglected for weeks. Needed sex. Horniness had piled up & I couldn't do nothing about it. And you can't go snatching females off the street. ---This is how my early life had been.

Kelly, the 70-year old Ancient Mariner of the tavern had phrased it well. "It wasn't always easy to meet a sex partner. We were fewer and further between. Women In The Shadows. --The Secret Society." It's coming out into the light.

We're so respectable now. Gays live openly. Have good jobs. Walk hand in hand by the light of day. We have more and more stuff that straights always took for granted. Gay boys own restaurants, gay hotels & movie houses. And there's the Suburban Dykes & Their Friends. There's coffee houses. Bookstores. We have our children & churches.

Yeah, we're building a world-a gay one.

With the advent of gay liberation, more and more gays are stepping out into the light.

However, a lot of us were created to be in the shadows.

The human heart has it's secrets. It's cutting edge.

It's party nights.

It's driving force.'

Chapter Two

The first year after Pam's death, visions of her, and pet words they use to whisper in each others ears kept reappearing in her mind. Life-like, framed into consciousness, as if Pam was calling to her from the other side.

A young husband, blond Angel took care of their babies. Changed diapers. And at night they snuggled close & fucked each other's cunts.

As a teen, she had been more or less disgusted with life. Disgusted with the world. Grown up in a square industrial city whose gay life was subterranean-it would not be until age 26 she'd have her first joy with Pam.

She had lived too long a lone butch roaming a straight landscape of honky tonk bars, Mafia joints catering to freaks, whose star was a female impersonator on stage, while b-girls worked the audience. Real women, warm, naked shoulders, big breasts bouncing under satin, round hips in tight dresses, jangling jewelry. Angel stood behind them as they sat at the bar with their johns in 3 piece suits; men talking loud, scornful, drunk. A baby butch, hunting for female companionship, wanting their womanly wetness & warmth. Hanging on beside the hustlers; when she could, paying for their drinks & for some of their time; & baring the degrading hassle of being propositioned herself. Not in her world, but their world. Stood at the bar, mute, hurting inside all night.

She was a lonely person, basically. One who had no power. This was 15, 16, 17, 18.

Sometimes the Mafia'd open a true gay bar for a while before the police shut it down & some of her own could crawl out of the woodwork & they'd dance and play. And laughing femmes had turned a cold shoulder to her. Or once in a while she'd get a girl, and they were good for a night, or a couple of weeks before the horror at what they were doing made them kick her out the back door while some man was walking in the front.

So she'd go over to the straight world-- a dike in their bars, picking up their women.

For the most part, gone on solitary. Lifting weights, riding her motorcycle, earning money at rinky-dink jobs, and jobs that walked the borderline of semi-illegality.

8

By 20, human life seemed valueless. Didn't attach but little value to her own. Life was worthless. In depression thought she would snuff it.

And began more and more to walk on the edge, the danger side -- caring less about life.

By 23 Angel began to get control of her life. A handsome butch entering an emerging gay society in the mid-1970's. Now the times provided her a place to be around women who desired women. And, especially they desired Angel. For her long blond shoulder length hair and her toughness. Her class. Her good taste. And her style of dress--masculine black leather.

Over her young years Angel had learned about the secrets of the heart. How to size-up people.

Angel had turned tough, and become a winner. It was other's now who were the losers. That one, on the other side of the bar. Short hair, swaggering; a butch, styled coarse & hard. Not as smooth as her competition--Angel. She'd become elegant. She learned how to get the girl. Thought about that rude butch, 'She thinks success is to be like a man. Does she let a woman touch her breasts, let her go inside? Does she allow herself to be fucked?' Yes, Angel did. This versatility made women come back, they wanted a butch who was a woman too.

Cruising, idly studied the object of her interest thru blue eyes, wondering about the a girl, how she made love with a woman; asking herself private questions-this one, long hair like herself, but fem. 'She's somebody whose searching, just like me.'

Then she'd stride up, offer to buy the girl a drink, make conversation. Ask all the typical questions; "what's your name? Is your girlfriend here tonight?" And would connect with others that were hurting inside, and they'd go home and make the pain go away with love.

Women stumbling thru the night looking into each other's eyes for the answer.

9

People are looking for something to believe in.

There's a time... Time in a bar when all the house lights go up, you can see everybody for what they are. --Times when the mask comes off all things.

Of all the one nite stands with dikes & with hookers she had paid, or wanted to mostly but didn't have the price;--of straight frightened women she followed in the streets in her 1onliness, who wondered what she wanted of them; trying to talk to them; they that scorned her because instead of having a dick she had a cunt between her legs like they did, which they & the world also scorned....

Now God, or Time, or Fate had thrown gold into the balance, to weight against the pain.

Pam, her wife had come into her life.

And she held her arm. In a red silk blouse & a red skirt. Black leather boots & coat to match Angels own leather zipfront jacket & pants with silver studs. Black leather from head to toe.

The lonely era had passed; to a home with 2 blond kids, & Pam, & now, it was 1993, and Angel was starting over with a new fem.

Had a wife, a friend, a sex partner. Didn't have to worry about going out every Friday and Saturday night to try to get laid. Running all over town all night long and maybe, just maybe if she was lucky she'd score. Crystal was right there within arms reach across the sheets; her hot her sweet mouth ready to service Angel. Didn't have to worry about negotiating with bitches.

Angel had lived so much of life being cautious. Holding herself back, to preserve her life at great cost. Was one of the butches who was still-alive. Gave up liquor and pills for Pam during their five years together. --Being careful, as she Walked On The Wild Side.

10

Even as she rode her motorcycle; cautious. --Aware of everything around her.

Her silver rings were turning a shade of green.

And now Angel saw herself getting older.

Always thought, for so long she had wanted and needed a woman so much, that when she'd have a woman of her own, finally, to be loved, with the woman at her side, that life would be so much better. & God had done it. -- She had. Brought Pam to that location in time & space (which was a lesbian tavern) for Angel to pick-up. But after years, 5 of them together --something had still been missing. & was kind of wondering when her life was going to start and she was getting older. This put a crimp in things--that she was getting closer to eternity.

What to do?

'Even at 16 I had thought--I got to live now! Before I get old! As if that was death. I might die before I get a chance to live.'

Maybe that's why she rode a motorcycle and walked on the wild side.

'Now at 34, I have to live life! *Now*, before I die.'

Chapter Three

The wind in her hair, knees wide, seated on her motorcycle, power throbbing between her legs; air gushing all over them in a bath, ahead, silver rails and cement highway plunge into the unknown.

Bike went thru a weave of straight-aways, curves & arms which is the highway system. Rush here, there, to far parts of the city doing errands. Packages tied down behind them on the saddle of the bike with bungee straps.

Passed a van on the street which was delivering old people & handicapped in poverty to places they could receive medical services & meals. "Now look Angel! There's a dike driving that van! You could get a job doing that!" Crystal yells against the wind, into her ear, clutched tight to her back.

Clouds were dramatic, black billowing. Remainder of the sky was white; coming in from the west so heavy it was on fire below. Hands on the handgrips flip the throttle, accelerating.

Angel and her lady went shopping that day at a costume store. But before they got in, an incident occurred.

They were outside; the broad shouldered blond in black leather had just put the kickstand down on the bike, & as they turned to walk in, threw her arm around Crystals shoulders and left it there.

"FUCKING LEZZY QUEER! FUCKING TRANSVESTITE BITCHES!"

Feels a shove, Crystal screams. Angel turns around swinging her fist. A man backs up & she misses, he stands, tall, bigger build outweighing her by 100 pounds, white. An evil expression on his face.

Angel jerks a knife out of its sheath at her side, and swings it back and forth in front of them, he backs off **"I HOPE YOU QUEERS DIE!"** Crystal had lost her balance, gets off the pavement, and Angel takes steps towards the man swinging the knife, it's glint flashes in empty air. He shouts at them again, **"FUCKING QUEER BITCH!'** Jogs in place up and down, just out of reach. And Angel wasn't going to go running after him. **"WHAT ARE YOU GONNA DO ABOUT IT DIKE!"** And Angel knows she's got a gun to back up the knife, and the man laughs, a sneer on his face, and jogs away.

"I should have shot him right there." The big blond exclaims.

The cold air seemed hot. They had forgot--had embraced in a different part of town, for a moment forgot the rules of a cold society. Angel put away the knife, slammed it into the leather sheath.

They walked in out of the streets in a gust of air.

The clerk in the store stared at them, rude. So Angel starts laughing, and struts down the aisle with her lady like nothing is wrong. But she wanted to scream, 'LEAVE US ALONE! WE'VE GOT OUR WORLD!' Wanted the world to know—'We have our society, our places, our women, our rules!'

They toured the costume shop picking among the clothes. A make-up caked face; drag queen twice their size flitted among the racks, and suddenly they felt better. And that's when Angel made her decision what to buy--hadn't been sure in the beginning. A simple shirt would do. In black and white. Chose two in her size, to stretch over her broad muscle shoulders. Now she too would have a uniform to do a scene.

FUCKING LEZZY FREAKS! The insult still rang in their ears.

Took her hurt home with her woman that evening. In her arms it faded. In her tender love. In her own power.

Sometimes, Angel was just afraid to look Crystal in the eye, she felt so bad, that somehow she was getting her woman into this--'after all, I'm the dike, I look queer & Crystal don't. She looks like a suburban secretary or a shop girl, which in fact she is.'

Down thru herstory the human race has endured all sorts of indignities. Deaths, and living deaths.

This endless hell.

Chapter Four

The downtown area where Angel & Crystal lived was bleak. Tall tall brick buildings of different color yellow, red, brown. And modern ones; cement and steel, formed a corridor in air. Narrow channels thru which, from the pavement view, could be seen white and grey sky.

Their building was older, had ornate scrollwork around its windows; towered in space in the style of yesteryear, its feet planted in a subbasement, among a line of huge steel and glass giants. Traffic weaves to and fro underneath.

The two dikewomen had set up housekeeping. Their hotel had a wide view of the spectacle of grey winter moving in, with a chill.

Soon they'd have to go out thru snowbound streets to duck into the little Chinese food joint to have dinner.

And Crystal had begun to cook meals at home on a hotplate.

Cash was no object. They would go in, make purchases; Angel'd open up a wallet stuffed with $20's, $50's, and a few $100rds for emergencies, and nonchalantly toss a bill onto the counter. She earned good money impersonating police officers in a phoneroom charity scam. But the deal would come to an end in the New Year. The goal was $120,000; of that Angel had brought in $20,000 for herself alone. The charity would derive about $12,000, and be thankful for it, it was more their miserable poverty children got anywhere else. The new deal with a new angle would start in February, and Crystal was coaxing her to square up and change her life.

Her clit had got a good work out these last months since they'd met & begun a relationship. Also her cunt, in heavy sessions, in which the butch allowed herself to be taken as a woman by her sweet lesbian lady. They went the way of all flesh.

Angels big thrill was she liked to be *received.* A woman's arms yielding, open to her; her hips and thighs taking her in, and all that she was, into herself.

That night Crystal took her butch into her arms and romanced her too, "butchy butch, let me love you… oh baby… let me touch you too..."

Crystal's curly blond hair would appear above an open newspaper as she sat up in the bed reading Want Ads. She herself worked in a Department Store a few blocks away. "Here are some baby." She'd read out loud. "Hmmm... All you have to do is be able bodied, have a drivers license and be able to drive a car and you can make $8 to $10 an hour."

Heat steamed from the radiator in the 12-by-15 foot room. Newly painted and upgraded to make a pleasant stopping place until they could get an apartment. Crystal put down the paper, smashing it onto her legs covered by sheets. "I don't want to come home and find out my baby's been hauled off to jail by the police! *Officer Anglin!* God Angel! Impersonating a police officer on the phone! What a scam!"

"Aw; I go in, there's 200 people want that job. Fill out an application, they ask what have I been doing the last 10 years." Angel sez.

"Some jobs you don't need that honey."

"I need *money* Crystal. Not a petty minimum wage job."

"You got me honey—you don't need money. You don't need to be a big spender to impress the girls anymore."

Now Angel stood at the window of their hotel room, on the 13th floor. The sky was blueblack--just before-dawn. 'I'm out here just a little longer then everybody else.' She thought as she viewed the silent city.

They had come home from Oil's; made love, and Crystal fell asleep. Her party shoes and party motorcycle hat tossed on a chair, having worn her lipstick off on Angels cunt, on her knees so Angel could stand over her in motorcycle boots, jacket and cap and feel dominate.

The rush was over.

Sex, hot, liquid, melting thighs and bones and skin and nerve into one soaring colossal burst. And not like it had been with all the other girls in an empty wasteland of rubbed raw sex & sadness after they left. Unlike those nights of illicit love. Crystal, pink skin, soft as a cloud was still beside her, a warm body, giving contentment. -- Happiness.

Angel came back to the bed, got in; pulled the sheets and blanket over her long legs. She felt good.

For just a moment had had elusive thoughts... dream scenes… in touch with mysteries of the beyond. Of womanhood. What it meant to be a carrier of the light of civilization…. pondered about that. And about the club. Where were the Outlaws going? What they were going to do about situations-- wither right or wrong, they were going to Do Something.

So good to be back with a loved one, in each other's arms.

Comfort.

Had noticed when they got home in the wee small hours of the morning she felt buoyed up by a great spirit--bigger then the two of them. It was the peace from being with her own kind; she and her mate, in the bedroom weren't alone; they were part of a greater tribe. 'Monkey see, monkey do. See somebody just like you.'

Angel rolled to her side and embraced the sleeping Crystal, felt her warmth. And heaved a huge sigh of some burdened thought, ---

16

because it deals with a matter of the soul--& not the guts, which are easily satisfied.

'It's like when I was a teen, I'd gaze deep into a woman's eyes, and thought I'd found the end. But, there is a greater mystery of life.

Before, we were just chasing after each other.'

One goal, Angel knew, was to see the face of their Mother God. And the other, to deal with the depths of her own soul.

It was as if being on a journey of sorts. To her there'd been little humor in it, very little lucky breaks. A hard mean world; it makes you tough. Nobody gives help to another because everybody's scrambling, hustling, climbing over each other to get someplace. They don't have enough themselves.

A lot of her problems were rooted in long ago. That's when the big hurt starts. A child in tousled blankets, not tucked in. Crawling in to sleep whenever she chose. Lay there lonely. That's when the pain had begun, after her mother had left her & her father; and she'd had to go live with her step grandmother. & the little girl missed them so.

And now, as an adult, after a frozen teenage span of years began to thaw, in the clubhouse she'd stumbled upon it. A force not realized. Nor analyzed. The exchange of power between women in a sexual situation. Females tending to each others sexual needs--in the scenes the club orchestrated in their shows Angel glimpsed it; her need for a different kind of sex; of dominance, of power.

Chapter Five

One fine day Daddy George & Queen Georgina came driving downtown. **"GEORGIE! KEEP DRIVEN' OVER TO 3RD STREET!"** Her wife commanded. George was behind the wheel; motorcycle cap with the death eagles wingspread, leather jacket with epaulets, and her title; PRESIDENT OUTLAWS MOTORCYCLE CLUB etched on a silver pin on the left side of her chest.

17

'THAT OLD PLACE! YUH KNOW! THAT NIGHTCLUB WHERE I USE TO DANCE!' When they got there she blinked; white face, double chins & heavy made up eyes; "See! It's boarded up!" George looked from under her cap brim; the car idled. "God The owners are so mean, that's why they keep shutting the place down. It's about the 10th time it's changed owners. Their always shutting down. It's shitty."

The couple was on their way to a leather goods factory outlet to get some customized saddlebags for their Harley Davidson motorcycle, --a wide glide Evolution V Twin Harley, --and a few leather toys.

Workers in the sewer in big orange overalls dug clumsily in the mud.

A bulldozer of rusted iron seemed to have a mind of its own plowing the earth.

People in this sector had holes in their shoes, mix-match clothes. Poor. That kind. Or had money to burn & could afford to pay high rents, & eat out in fancy restaurants.

Daddy George had coal black eyes and coal black hair.

Large; a very large he-she, tall and wide also. Georgina was a large white women--and fat. Near 6'2" herself, same as her bulldike husband, and tipped the scales at 400 pounds. Had lots of jewelry, earrings, was a total fem.

"DRIVE BY THAT OTHER PLACE! ON THE CORNER! Let's see if they still have that picture of that bellydancer up in the window--in that club where I worked 3 months--that horrible skinny wench !"

"You didn't see it last time."

"HA! They've cleaned everything out of the windows. Good! They're going broke too!"

18

They hadn't been downtown in two years.

Soon Daddy George found the factory. Rain ran down the brim of her leather bikers cap, over immense shoulders & dripped down on her big boots; proceeded by Queen Georgina under a huge umbrella, nagging her every step of the way.

The two big dikes came to the door of the factory, and George bellowed, **"GODDAMN IF IT AIN'T OPEN I'LL SHOOT MYSELF IN THE FOOT !"** Daddy George hollered and the Queen grabbed the big dikes shoulder with tiny hands, trying to calm her down. George shook the handle of the door furious. **"DRIVE ALL THE WAY DOWN HERE ! *GOD DAMN!"***

George & Georgina went back from under the awning of the factory into the rain, the bulldike stomped ahead, mad. **"WAIT! I CAN'T WALK THAT FAST I'LL FALL DOWN! COME BACK HERE GEORGIE! YOU'LL GET ALL WET! I CAN'T WALK THAT FAST! I CAN'T EVEN KEEP UP WITH YOU!"**

George was henpecked. Made a grunt of air between gritted teeth as a response. Couldn't wait to get to her dungeon and rid herself of the hemmed-in trapped feelings by using sadism with a willing slave.

The two traveled the highways and byways of the city, making checks off on their To Do list. 3. The motorcycle shop. 4. The party favors shop. That days errands also included at the bottom, 5. Lunch with Angel & Crystal.

"Lets go to another leather factory."

"No! We'll be late to the kids house." Sez Georgina. Thick black ringlets of her hair matched dark deep eyes set against pasty white skin.

Angels adventure in the Outlaws club had been hell at first, but a series of good fortune & fluke events had insured her installment in the motorcycle gang, as a full fledged member, and caused an interest in Angel by Daddy George,---The Leader Of The Pack.

She had made pals with good people right away—Comancho the Indian & Johnny the mechanic & their wives. These were old established members & had value to the club. And, Angel had proven herself in battle against a Warlord, one of the group's fierce leaders, which was how she won her girl, Crystal.

It was not often the Leader paid visits to a member's house.

Queen Georgina looked like Royalty. Small silver tiara sparkling diamonds nested in her thick black wavy hair, & a satin dress down to her ankles. A few heads turned as the pair walked across the lobby to the elevator.

George was use to judging weights, and checked the sign on the elevator--it certified they were guaranteed 2,000 pounds carriage. They climbed into the elevator, the metal walls shut around them.

Painstakingly, chains of the hoist creaked to the upper floors.

Inside the young couple rushed around making themselves ready, Angel had doubts about it. So Crystal sez, as she bobs around dusting the butch off, straightening her jacket lapels, "I don't see why you can't wear it! -- All the club members are into this SM stuff, they-wear uniforms--the ladies love nun uniforms. But I've never seen one in a priest collar."

"I'll be original."

Thing about the clubhouse those that did Sadio Masochism put on uniforms and when they went into scenes they could be anything they chose. A cop, a nun, a soldier, a slave.

'Why not?' Angel fingered the cleric collar. And went to answer the door.

20

'Well what have we here?' Thought Daddy George when she saw Angel.

Came in, said their hellos. George felt her weight gingerly on the side of the bed, testing to make sure it wouldn't break. Georgina sat next to her, and Crystal. Angel sat on their only chair.

The four gabbed awhile about nothing in particular, then they hit the road. Before they crammed into the tiny elevator butch Angel appeared very uneasy; but George had no doubts, having read the 2,000-pound weight sign. She thought ahead.

In the street a mixture of common beggars & business people went on their ways in an effluence of perfume, and stench. The city had planted flowers, thru which blew garbage. Millionaires sailed by in limousines. Wrecks of ships-- derelict humanbeings sat dying by the way.

George strode along, tall, heavy, big boots clomping down on the pavement, face tough & knowing. Crystal looked up at her with big blue eyes, walking along at her other side, a smile on her face of appreciation for this bulldike. "Down here, it's muscles that's the final say." George mused aloud for all who would listen. They passed gangs of male workers who talked loud and walked loose, amid pools of secretaries, walking rapidly and circumspect with packages in their arms. "Physical strength. And it's the men got it of course. They strut around, look mean like they hate everybody. Now, up there across the tracks, in the hills where we live, they use economic muscle. --Which is worse? Now I got a gun. You got a gun. We got a gang. We got muscle. Together. Most of us ain't got it alone. Must of us ain't got a lot financially, but together we're strong."

Georgina nods her head, her red lips pursed firmly in agreement. Her white skin was rouged & powdered.

Anywhere else in suburbia in the shopping malls of Amerikkka this quartet might seem strange. --- Only Crystal looked normal. Curly

21

blond hair, trim figure, feminine in a smart leather outfit. Then, a Queen--in a crown & floorlength dress made of iridescent satin & glass like weaves that shone off lights like it was her wedding day. A bulldike who looked the part of a heavy rig diesel truck driver. And a smaller dike dressed in full leathers & a cleric collar like an SM priest. Not many heads turned, and those just with languid interest. They were Downtown. Here, the metropolis one of many oasis noted for their gays, transvestites, interracial couples, artists, they fit in quite splendidly.

Daddy George was a Dominant and had a rude habit of ordering people around. "You sit there!" She commanded Angel, pointing to a red-cushioned seat in the booth of the Chinese restaurant. Angel, tho an aggressive butch was a big enough hearted person to obey, for the sake of avoiding an argument.

They slid into the booth; the outcome was that Angel & Daddy George, the men, sat on one side, and their ladies sat facing them across the table. Queen Georgina being on the outside, as was Daddy George.

If the two immense behemoths had sat together, they would have squeezed each other out of the booth. Angel noticed she was sitting comfortably, with elbowroom, and George was just near the edge of the red-vinyl seat, but had room to spare.

4 of them wedged into the booth and were served glasses of water by the waiter, and menus, which they now studied.

The waiter went around with a soft shoed walk putting plates down on each place setting atop bamboo mats on a pink tablecloth.

Background had statues of their Gods, a waterfall, & a vase as large as a person overflowing with plastic flowers.

It was understood they were all non-monogamous, the four. Tho a lot of biker Outlaws mated for life so it seemed, Rip a Warlord & her wife Debbie; Johnny, Comancho & their wives Stella Dallas and Frosty, George & her Queen as examples; all had sex partners on the side both the fems as well as the butches.

Soon they were chomping on delicious Chinese food, piled high in platters--an abundance of all they could eat. Heat & steam rose from the vegetables noodles and meat.

"I think it's silly. There's a lot of ways to make money, they don't have to do that, they do it because they're fucked up." Sez Crystal, her eyebrow penciled eyes flare & she daintily consumes a forkful of Dim Sum.

"They make big money." Sez George gruffly.

"You can live without big money in this world! You just have to know how!" Sez Crystal her high young voice emphatic.

"She' s right." Sez Georgina as she eats, eyes focused on her plate.

"Comancho's old lady was a stripper for 6 years and never did it."

"You believe that?" Sez George stopping in mid forkful to stare with a glare of black eyes.

"WELL I WAS A DANCER AND I NEVER TURNED A TRICK IN MY LIFE GEORGE!" Sez Queen Georgina, dropping her fork into her plate with a clatter.

"Yeah, I know, and so was Lady, Sleazy wife for years. Yeah, I know, she did, they had their first kid together that way... but they stopped it. Money or no money, that's why things are so rough for them. But they squared up."

Georgina picked up her fork and resumed picking pieces of Tomato Beef and putting then daintily into her mouth.

"Some of the butches even are Go Go dancers, but they don't have to touch anybody, they stay up in those glass booths... You'd think the club was a bunch of hookers and hypes and it ain't true. There's tow truck drivers and waitresses, and construction workers, and women who work in the sewers for the Water Company, & who climb telephone poles, --all kinds of jobs. Yuh know what Hawk told me when I was living with her? She said no lady of hers would ever sell her body. Of course what she did to me was just as bad. But she told me the run down on everybody in the club. It's only a few, about 10% of the girls do that…and it gives us a bad name."

"Like that little slut Dena." Georgina turned to stare at George, black ringlets tumbled down her shoulders, her tiara refracted fire. Dena was George' mistress.

"Yeah yeah." George nods her head.

Later, when the plates were emptied, piled up and removed & the four were full George sat back, hands folded over her big stomach, basking in contentment and reminisced. "I'll never forget how you gave Slave Monique that burial."

"She deserves a burial." Said the Queen, with ambiguous meaning.

"It's perfectly clear to me," sez George, "that you deserve to wear that collar. You earned it. Not like that psuedo cop what killed her."

"Oh the clubs drowning in shit!" Wails Georgina, wringing her fat white ring decked fingers together. "Oh George, I'm so worried about the club, it's going downhill!"

"IT AIN'T GOIN' DOWNHILL! IT AIN'T GOIN' NOWHERE!" George bellowed at her wife, and the Queen shut up. Put a piece of Chinese pastry in her mouth. Wiped a few crumbs daintily off her red lips with the linen napkin. "Boy," sez Angel, "if Chang gets to eat like this every night, she's lucky." Referring to one of the gang's Asian members. And Crystal gave her a look of chagrin, like it's an insult to her home cooking on the hotplate, western style.

Daddy George was good for advice, and the topic came up, -- as the incident was just a day ago & fresh in both women's minds. She was a bulldike who'd had her share of hard knocks for it, --when not a passing woman.

"Tried to pull me off my bike that time. But I fired my gun & that ended it quick." Angel was recounting a battle.

"I don ' t get much of that." George replies. "It's the long hair. Cut your hair, try to pass as a man, or keep on fighting as a woman. That's all I can say. They mistake me for a man, unless it's summer and I let my tits show."

"She likes to let her tits show." Sez Georgina. "She's got nice tits."

"It scares 'em. They think I'm a man whose grown tits.... Yeah, I'm more free these days… It's not like the old times at the steel works, I had 'em thinking I was a man 12 years. Had to bind my tits down. Watch how I talked ... but some began to catch on I think, just nobody never said nothing." A wide smile cracked George's face, amused. "Walk like a man-- *I* do. We should all be able to." Sez Daddy George.

"All I had fear of is the police and gangs. Now, times has changed, it ain't illegal to be gay, or cross dress. We can stand up to the police with the law. --And any other stuff ain't nobodies business. And we got our own gang good enough to fight anybody exempting the US military."

Some are blessed with sympathy for others weakness, not everybody is. George had none whatever in that department, despising weakness. So she simply said, when Angel mentioned the incident at the costume shop,

"Too bad."

George always got mad when she thought dikes were whining; tho she'd learned not to let it show.

"Let me tell you about yer fight Angel." Sez Daddy George. Her coal black eyes studied the younger dike intently. "You had a gun, & a knife, you could have ran after him and made him turn tail and run & show what a coward he really is. Any man who picks on women is a pure coward. But, you stood there hoping he wouldn't come back, and you were scared. You held your ground, but you had fear. Women always have fear.

You backed down because dikes always back down, because they're women and it's a woman's nature to back down, to avoid a fight. --Unless they've been pushed over the edge like crazy women, or women defending their young. If the stake is too great they will fight, but not often enough, & then they get hurt because of giving in.... Does that make you mad Angel?" Sez Daddy George, probing. A little sarcastic.

"Yeah." Admits the blond hutch, eyes lowered to the table top.

"Ego games. Fear & shaking. Dominance. Next time, go after him like you're a mother defending her young-- don't forget your gun! If he turns on you, shoot the son-of-a bitch in the leg! You're a dike defending your life! Don't forget that!

"She's right honey." Sez Georgina, looking at the young couple solemnly, her eyebrows arched, wrinkling her forehead.

"We've fought all our lives --Daddy and me. --That's why we're alive. That's why we got the things we've got."

George grinned down at Angel with an air of superiority. Her short hair slicked back like a man's, pudgy fingers laced, propped under her chin. "Makes yuh mad, huh?"

"Fuck it." Angel said. Pissed at herself for not having run after the man waving her knife, and making him run, turn tail and get out of their lives.

"Good." Sez Daddy George. A smile on her face.

"Goddam it."

"Yes."

Angel pounded the tabletop with her fist so hard the ice water shook. George wasn't fazed. No emotion in her face.

Crystal cuddled up beside the cold restaurant wall, wishing she could hold Angel in her arms.

"A dike, even if she's a puny one, she still has courage. She's going against the grain of society to stand up and be so different--she's fighting the world. So don't be ashamed. You're already brave. You ain't no coward Angel. I just wanted to show you, how to take a step foreword."

"Oh the kids know that George. They've been around. Look at 'em. They're going thru the same stuff we had to."

"It's better now to be gay, yer lucky, but the world is getting bigger & rougher at the same time... Now look at that Stryker, she's just 4' tall look what she did to that guy who followed her into the alley when she went to puke; she kicked his balls off."

"*What* was she doing in an alley?" Crystal wanted to know. George looks across the table at her and acknowledges; "that was the stupid part. Out in an alley behind some gay bar, drunk & sick. Puking."

"Yeah, you got balls Angel. "George sez, awhile later.   "Don't worry. Just walking around town in that get-up." Pointed at her. "Yeah honey." Georgina agrees earnestly;   "Yer' a dead give away." And heaves a sigh from her bosom.

Crystal's pretty face was animated; big eyes, intelligent, curly blond head bobbed, "And he pushed me!" She says to George, so mad at remembering it that she bares her teeth.

"Because he hates women. Yuh just got to realize there's so many men that hate women."

"Yes. Oh yes there are." Georgina sighed, raising her eyes to heaven. Red lipstick, contrast to her white face, and black eyebrows & hair.

"Not even just 'cause yer queer--they really hate females. All females. I think they hate more then how we hate them."

"I'm a total woman dear." Says Georgina. "Total woman, not a sign I'm gay unless *she's* with me." Indicating with a ringed finger the bulldike directly across the table from her. "And I've seen plenty in my day, of men's hate towards straight women. You see it in the clubs where I use to dance. You hear it from their wives in the beauty shop where I do hair. Not all of them, not nearly all. There are some sweethearts, but there are some…" And she shuddered making a terrible face.

George had already begun a conversation with Angel to her side, lifting up her cap brim with the death angel as emphasis's and setting it back down on her head hard. "I kicked the shit out of him. Brought him down. Ha ha ha. What a sight! Now, not everybody's big as me… I tell the girls what's runts… I tell 'em, sexualize it later, in a scene. "That'll do you some good." Daddy George wove her fingers together. "Excellent idea."

All was quiet for a moment, expectant; so Daddy George continued.

"Stabbed him with my knife. Didn't want to kill him & go to jail for assault with a deadly weapon so I just weakened him, the blood gushed out, and then I kicked the hell out of him."

"Yes she did dear." Sez Georgina, bending over the table, nodding her head to assure Angel, then turned to Crystal who leaned beside her against the red cushioned booth, "Oh I use to have a time! I dress so ladylike, and men would follow me in the streets offering me propositions of marriage, & worse! George came into my life and that ended it. But once in awhile some idiot, like this man she's talking about, they just can't get it in their minds to leave me alone, I'm so beautiful, well I use to be."

"You still are." George told her.

Day grew dim outside the windows of the Chinese restaurant.
Angel looked solemnly across the table at Queen Georgina, large &
dainty her tiara glimmering in the red glow lights. "Have any kids?"
"One is enough." Says the dowager Queen, looking at George
knowingly, darkly, then resumed her pleasant demeanor.

Daddy George black hair & black eyes to match seemed to grow
darker. A look of pure evil flickered over her face. Angel saw it, and
it sent a tremor in her guts. Evil. --Or was it just the effects of a little
indigestion--compiled upon a multitude of worries. About their club
the Outlaws, about life.   The he-she spoke in a base voice.

Daddy George was 6'2" weighed 350 pounds, a muscular build
covered by a layer of fat. Not merely female fat, but the fat of
prosperity of years of which she had seen many since youth. She was
now 52. Georgina was the same age, and surpassed her in girth,
standing a full 6'1" and weighing the greater amount. For a moment
the two seemed very big, like two giants at the ends of the table,
bigger then life. "The kind of hassles we got from the start was
because we was female. Just 5 or 6 of us riding in a small motorcycle
gang. Not like it is today, with 80 members. We got harassment
allright, from male gangs, or just men in pick up trucks. Rough
redneck men, whatever. We all liked to figure out why people stay in
a group in a city, when there's so much beautiful country out there,
well, some of it is for reasons of protection. When yer' out in the
country, or a deserted place, you're on your own. We got more
harassment then male motorcyclists would. From simple stuff, to
dangerous confrontations. To begin with, a female motorcyclist, no
matter if they have a Harley Davidson like mine, a $15,000 dollar
Harley underneath them, it don't matter, they're still going to get
harassed by male riders. Because they're obviously figuring that the
women are trying to be equal with them, and what they figure is that a
woman can't ride as fast. And if a woman fights back and harasses
them, it could be a bloody confrontation. It depends on where the
group is. Once we were out in the country, miles and miles of
deserted land, and we come across a gang of bikers, the Devils
Disciples.   There was lots of vans, motorcycles, drunk rednecks
having a party, and we got the hell out of there fast, after we stumbled

on 'em. Uh, there were some women who were with them, but mostly men, about 400 men. And about 8 of us. I guess they saw we were females and they didn't have enough women, so they took off after us on their motorcycles. Peeling rubber, one after another till there was 30 or 40 of them so it seemed, following us down the road. We were lesbians, that didn't make any difference, we knew that. Now in the past we had been sparsely armed. All of us had a knife, some a big knife in a sheath strapped to their side like you got. Then I had this small .32 caliber pistol. We had had by that time enough series of minor incidents to be more leery, and thus got more and more armed, so by the time this happened, we had fully escalated into major artillery.

Of course my knees were knocking against the gas tank; I'd popped the clutch, shifted into gear, let out the throttle and accelerated to a speed where I thought the hair was leaving my head, peeling rubber trying to outrace 'em, thinking it's gonna be death if all 400 take off after us. Nothing but country around, trees, grass, sun shining, and nobody else. One sheriff deputy for a thousand miles, no houses, deserted. But we had anticipated a confrontation, being a dike group in situations before with drunk rednecks, or somebody on drugs who can't discipline themselves who has to spout off about being male & the difference in being male and female on motorcycles, and worse. And calling us fags and queers and dikes, yuh know. Situations like you were just in. Generally I had handled myself in a courteous way to men who were on motorcycles, and speaking from experience, I'd never really seen such a large confrontation. I was more peaceful then, but was always aware that men can really lash out at a woman trying to be a man, so to speak, in their terms. So here we are, doing 80 miles an hour over dirt roads that's winding, and 40 Devils Disciples yelling and howling and chasing behind us. I sez to myself 'we gotta make a stand. We can't keep running. We'll run off the road & one of us'll get killed or hurt & they'll tear her apart.' Time was at an essence, and there was a ridge ahead, a crest in a hill on the road we was traveling. So I gauged it, I'd speed up to 100, make it before the rest somehow, so I wouldn't fall behind, then start to brake into the dirt, and whip out my .32 pistol, and go dig into my saddle bags for my two piece rifle it's an automatic. Once I could get that together we'd be saved, unless they had big weapons, or unless they caught up to me first; and that's why

30

I'd pull out my .32 out of my jacket first, ready to fire. I hoped they didn't have weapons, they didn't want to get us that bad, but if they caught up to us-40 men to 8 women, I was sick at the thought, because I knew the gals were gonna fight. Hawk was there--ha, yer friend, and Rip, and they wuz all packing pistols. And some gals I don't know what ever happened to them. I squeezed the throttle, hit the accelerator, flew out from my pack and up over the ridge doing 100rd. Got into a stretch & pulled further away, then I rode off to the side, breaking slow, trying to avoid any gravel so I wouldn't skid, and immediately my gals wiz by, then the first Devils Disciples, and oh, my God over the ridge I saw 'em come, drunk, beards chains, like savages, more and more of 'em, but going fast, whizzing by me, and I'm going in my saddle bag and got the rifle, lock up the two parts together, shove in a clip and it's good for 60 rounds automatic fire, & then I knew we had a chance. Up ahead the gals had slowed & pulled out their guns, and the Devils Disciples are wheeling around them in the dirt, drunk, & flies swarming on them, & they pull out their pistols too, a few of them, laughing, shooting off a few caps into the air. So I'm at a distance. I fired my .32 in the air 6 shots quick. To make my point, crouching behind my bike, and lowered the automatic rifle with them in the sights.

That's how 8 women do battle with 40 men. **"I'M SHOOTEN' TO KILL." I sez. "I'LL PICK YUH OFF! I MEAN BUSINESS! NOW GET OUT OF HERE AND LEAVE US THE FUCK ALONE!"** And their laughing, but keeping their distance. Circling the rest of the gals. Rip & Hawk & Royal and the others are in a circle; they got two pistols between them. I'm about 50 paces up the road. A bunch of the male bikers peel off towards me, & that's when they notice the rifle aimed at 'em. **"BLAM BLAM BLAM!"** I shot low into the first man and knocked him off his bike, blew a hole in the bike & his leg. I was risking hitting my own people, I was risking them all charging us, but I had to do something. If one of us died, we all died. They're pissed & hollering not grinning no more. **"GO ON!"** I holler to my gang, **"MOVE ON OUT!"** And the gals gun up their cycles and move out of their circle, and the male bikers let them go, they drive further up the road, I hear their bikes going further and further away. The men are picking up their buddy. He's bleeding from a leg wound, bleeding bad, bullet must have cut an artery & his bikes smoken', disabled. They're all cussing and rolling wheels around in the dust.   I'm standing behind my bike, rifle aimed, dust in my mouth. And they're glaren' at me, worried.' Yer gonna be picking up corpses too before it's over, yuh sons-of-bitches.' I'm thinking. And then I saw the sight of my life.   Here's Hawk and Rip come riding back, slow.   Rip's got her sawed off shotgun leveled at 'em, the barrel on the handlebars, finger on the trigger, riding one-handed; and Hawks got her pistol cocked, and holding another pistol in her teeth ready to switch guns & keep firing when the first one ran out of ammo, 'cause she wouldn't have time to re-load.   Well, I guess them damn Devils Disciples wuz glad to be alive.   They threw their buddy over the back of a bike and began to ride.   Ride back off down the road.   It was the sight of my life, when I saw them riding off slow, I knew we were safe--because we were protected.   "The old boys ain't as bad as they look."   Sez one gal, after.

"Yeah, but what would have happened if we wasn't armed and they knew it?"   I told her.   We'll never know.

They had chased us a few miles by that time, and had become separated from their huge club who was still partying down in the valley.   Now I think, maybe they had weapons there, automatics, rapid-fire pump style shotguns.   And I think to myself; 'next time I'm gonna have hand grenades.   More automatics, and guns and ammo for everybody's saddlebags.'   That's how 80 women can fight 400 men whose also armed.

A Word To The Wise."   Sez Daddy George.

"Whew!"   Sez Angel wiping her brow, after the tale.   The glass windows of the restaurant had turned black with night, streaks of neon played reflections on the panes.

"Bikers make good fighters."   Sez The Leader Of The Pack.   We've had fights with Devils Disciples.   Fights with other male bikers.   And fights with the Avengers, --those *pigs*."   The Avengers was a female bikers group.

Orange walls of the Chinese restaurant enclosed them for a few more minutes.   "Well," The big bulldike was pensive, a shock of black hair fell down over her ear. Drummed thick fingers on the table so the remaining silverware rattled; in answer to a question Angel had asked. Georgina laced her gold ringed fingers with red polished nails together. (The couple glittered.) "Reason I started the club... was biker reasons, to find dikes on bikes to ride with me. And for social reasons above & beyond that. Yuh know, I knowed women whose given up being lesbian 'cause they can't find somebody. Face it, you go in a gay bar, either you're attractive, or maybe throw a lot of money around & act secure, and can pull a woman to be with. Pull her out of her upright frigid drawers, and her opinions on who she should be seen dancing with or whatever. If you ain't got none of this you go home alone. You strike out. I know how it is. I know how it was before I met Georgina. --I seen my pals dying on the vine. There's women, even, ladies who are pretty, who, for some reason can't find somebody to even meet them half way. They're tiered of being lonely. Sick of being broke, which a woman is unless she has a partner. So they quit the lesbian life. Some do. Well I'll tell you, our club has a lot of pretty women, a lot of really pretty ladies like your Crystal here. And my baby still turns heads. And we showgirls and models, and we got a lot of dogs too. If a dike can't make the grade, if she don't look good, or is too rude, or is too wild--if she's an Outlaw, & walks the edge where as ordinary dikes don't appeal to her, or she don't appeal to them, then she's got a place in the Outlaws. We'll give you friends. Give you a place. Give you women. Give you back the sense that you are somebody."

"They get sick of dealing with the hassles of this world." Sez Georgina, eyes wide, red mouth pursed, looking into the 23-year old Crystals blue eyes. "So they come into our Clubhouse--to be among their own kind. And then, then, it's not just straights who give them a hard time, *us, us!* We give each other a hard time. You know it's true George! The gals are having fights every other night at Oils! No wonder some just give up and put their heads down on the bar dead drunk!" She turned and spoke sharply to George as if lecturing her. Then turned back to the young Crystal. "They go out in the street, can't find a decent job, bosses exploit them, men harassing them for sex in the streets, then they come in Oils and can't find a friend!"

"We're working on it." Sez George.

And they're ready to go.

"They hate that in there." George said.

"Ought to take it off then." Angel sez, about her miserable clerics collar; as she strode on long legs towards the door.

"Naw, keep it on. They might think it's a joke. Or a priest scene."

"I always wanted to be an alter boy."

"You can still be one." Sez George knowingly, & slapped her on the back with a meaty hand. "Keep the *faith*. --That ' s out of the New Testament ain't it? **Ha ! Ha ! Ha!"**

Chapter Six

When they entered the Clubhouse was dark night. Inside, the walls were painted black, which gave a dungeon like effect.

Women, most of them bikers, many simple and vanilla personalities. Others of a more complex strain. In back many gathered, watching a show.

A dike, she had been made to feel small by the world, & wanted to feel big. Now stood in a black leather jacket with a silver nametag, MASTER, it said simply.

Another wore a teeshirt on which was printed, MOTORCYCLISTS KEEP THE EDGE.

Homoerotic women, 80 of them. Piercings --gold rings in their noses, many in each ear, in their tongues, gold rings in their eyebrows, and pierced labia's, --golden rings in their pussylips.

Shaved heads and tattoos.

And some like the girl next door--with a leather flair, as Crystal, or Frosty the tall, plump showgirl.

I MAY NOT GO DOWN IN HISTORY, BUT I'LL GO DOWN ON YOUR KID SISTER. Read the inscription on another woman's teeshirt, and it was probably true.

In 1950's, & 60's in small towns across the USA, young gay girls & boys grew up with the secret of their queerness locked inside. If it became visible, they were picked on, taunted; or assaulted. They might feel 'I'm the only one.' Out of a school of 2,000, maybe only two or three others, and those they weren't sure about.

Gay liberation came, brings a wave of visible gays to the classroom. It is no longer so, that you are the only one. Gays step into the mainstream. High school teachers are coming out. Gay politicians run for office. Clean cut and gay, --but straight looking gay.

Some of the Outcasts among the Outlaws felt there was absolutely no one like them in the whole world--a different type of gay.

Because it was more then homosexuality; it's not as simple as going to bed with another woman. It is a power homoeroticism beyond the loving lesbian acts. Another power at play, which she didn't understand.

The Outlaws. --They liked group sex, they had plenty women.

More sex with more women. Ronny used it. It made him/her feel more butch, more masculine.

They were lesbian hutch dikes. --And lady lezzies with cock. Having the fortunate ability of not having to strain to rise to the occasion. And could take a tape measure, open up their nightstand drawer and measure their cocks at any time for this information for any lady who might inquire as to their endowments--which could vary depending on which dick they chose.

Angel stood in the tavern, somber, and watched the scene transpire. A figure dressed in black, languid blue eyes, long blond hair.

Woman tied to a rack.

Voluntarily chained, receiving punishment, which she desired.

'I want power.' Angel thought. 'Power. Power over my sex. Power over the world--in my small way.'

She saw it now, it wasn't the cracking whip inflicting pain--red stripes across the buttocks of a slave; 'it is mastery over sex & that a woman would submit to me.

I want to come to power.'

Upon this realization, & the knowledge that this power was now hers for the taking; a kind of spiritual calm filled Angel.

She had several problems & they all were based in how she dealt with pain.

Closely related, those two --like twins. The first was, that she got hurt so easily. So disappointed with life.

The second was, hanging onto that hurt--so that the final result was the rejection of all people, then finally herself.

Angel had come close to the end as a child, abused by a guardian in a home without love, again, thru her teens, then turning 20, in a street life without love. Finally, when Pam had died. The death of love.

Sex seemed to relieve it. Being in a woman's arms--and in an extra woman's arms, above and beyond the wife she had at home.

And the universal pain, the things that complicate our lives. Like being a woman afraid in the streets, of violence, rape, or being murdered. Of gay bashing. Of war.

And the rage that she felt about these things; not being able to save others, maybe not even herself.

Oppression of women all over the world.

Last, in a world that didn't celebrate her butchness, she felt disgusted with herself.

More then anything at times of stress like these, she wanted to be the object of love of women; to sit up like a pimp surrounded by women, beautiful women sitting on her lap or visa versa--and, unlike a pimp have them all to herself, sharing their affections with no one. Laughing, running their blue & red fingernails thru her hair.

She wanted to be loved.
She wanted love from a woman.

So, she had made herself like steel, so as to be received by a woman--in a lace negligee, body warm, yielding, rocking her in motion.

Herself, not soft, nor clinging, but strong.   So the woman would take her love, & her sexual excitement out of love for her.

Because she desired love she must be made of steel.

Now, Angel had love from a single woman--her wife; and still she wanted it from many women. She wanted to be loved. To belong.

She wanted power.
Because she wanted to be loved.

So, maybe she was here tonight in this room, with walls painted black --so as to be gloomy, withholding of joy, -- with these people of serious intent, dressed in black leather, color broken only by the glint of their steel knives, studs and zippers; a pair of handcuffs on one shoulder, because she wanted to understand her pain.

Wanted somehow, somewhere, someone to speak to the raging of feelings inside. Someone to pull close to her, physically grappling, to get close somehow to that ache inside; the hunger that she didn't know what it was for.

Angel & Crystal stood together against a wall and watched Lou's scene. Girl—her bottom-- eagle spread on the rack; wrists restrained by handcuffs up on its crossbeam. And the Master began whipping.

'I want to come to power.'

Had seen The Life, it's hustling, it's dope, for all it's huge spans of bartime.

One after another they came to grief. A drunk partygoer in the street wearing a partyhat and party clothes--come to grief. The transsexuals born male who can't make it as a woman, or born female and can't make it as a man with a woman by their side--they come to grief. Simply, Angel thought; 'I want to come to joy.'

Chapter Seven

The Leader was not poor.

The he-she & wife dwelled in a sprawling ranch style home in two sections, just 3 cement stairs up from the earth in front, and a basement deep drop in back, due to the incline of the land on their one acre property.

The house had become a Mansion, of double width, when the two had purchased the house next door, years past when real-estate was relatively cheep, thus combining the two into an extravagant palace high up on the hill in an expensive neighborhood far above the growing inner city ghetto below.

The Mansion had 15 rooms. 1 master bath, 1 regular and 2 half bathrooms. 6 bedrooms, a den, a dungeon full of playtoys for SM,

(George had established this when she saw it was a way to empower dikes & herself), a sewing room with lacy curtains, a weightlifting room, a monstrously vast living room & dining room which was originally two separate living rooms and dining rooms in two separate houses, now with the wall knocked out between, and connected by a five foot wide addition at the seams—to account for the original space, a driveway which had once run between the two dwellings.

Georgina had control of the Master bedroom where they slept. Her things were everywhere. Her sewing room was to one side, and also a huge walk in closet--which was formerly a 2nd bedroom, within which George had constructed partitions & it had become a maize of hanging clothes, racks & mirrors, resplendent with 450 pairs of shoes--to rival Imelda Marcos, Queen of the Philippians, and make any gay nun disgorge herself, and any transsexual die in a fit of envy at the sight, or a sissy squeal for mercy. Ribbons and bows; and rows, rows, rows of spike heels, thigh high boots, sandals and shoes with pointed toes.

No wonder the gang members never saw Georgina in the same gown twice--and it was conjecture among Outlaw ladies--'what will Georgina wear tonight?'

Over the years they'd assembled these material goods, thru work at honest jobs--and because they'd bought the houses together when they were young & kept making payments for 25 years. They were older then 95% of the gang, so, naturally Daddy George & Queen Georgina were impressive.

George continued to work part time, even after club membership dues were collected, put in her pocket--$1,600 per month--from which great expenses must be doled out, and would sit at the table in the hiring hall with the rest of the men holding her black book union card, & wait for her name to be called and thus pick up an extra $64 for that day.--If she felt like going in at 5am in the morning.

Georgina was a huge woman equal to the size of George plus very fat, outweighed her by 50 to 100 pounds depending on the state of her dieting which was perpetually in flux.

George stood at the stove in their grand kitchen, fumbled, lifting lids of various pots that sat on its marvelous 8-burner range to see what her wife had cooked. George hollered;   "I SEE YER' NOT EATING RICE TODAY?"

"I MIGHT AND I MIGHT NOT!- --Georgina bellows back.

Queen Georgina didn't work much after her bellydancing career, but earned extra spending money doing hairdressing, could make $25 per perm; working in various shopping mall beauty parlors for upscale little white ladies who had no idea it was a lesbians fingers twining in their locks.

Had also a good little business at home doing punk hairdos. Knew all about dyes from her days doing these suburban housewives at the malls of Amerikkka; transferred this knowledge into the lunatic color scheme; pink, purple, garish green; and had learned to do spikes, and weaves and shaving from the youngsters.

"Queen Georgina done it." A young biker might say, as others admired her pink & green Mohawk doo, bald on both sides with huge foot long spikes down the middle. --As a creature from an extraterrestrial landscape.

"How'dja like the way I'm doing the kids hair these days?" Georgina once boasted proudly to Kelly.

"Well," Sez the 70-year old bar owner;   "It's the *bald* ones, how about them? Yuh can't make any money with them now, can yuh?"

"Well!" Exclaims the Queen, "--It's just as bad as you trying to sell 'em liquor & all they do is come in here and buy drugs in the bathroom!"

George strode past the goldfish pond & went to the 2nd deck where she kept a few barbells to work out outdoors. Kept her massive arms and shoulders pumped up by pushing iron.

40

They lived well. Some members did not, as she knew, they had driven them home often enough in their van. When too drunk to ride their cycles, or after a spill had paralyzed their wheels and had to throw 'em both, bike & biker into the back of the van.

The young dikes lived, some, in one room in skidrow hotels with loitering men, felons & dope dealers on needle alley. Amid dragqueen hooker transvestites hungry for a sexchange & dopefiends with a monkey clutching their backs who would for the price of a bag of white powder, do anything.

It was not an uncommon sight to see a youthful 15 or 16-year old biker from the club over at Georges to help Queen Georgina with her wifely chores at minimum wage, or for trade. Bikers in black leather chaps & bluejeans and vests & teeshirts on their fit bodies, and darkglasses & biker caps, or pink spiked hair. Her bike parked in the driveway.

In exchange for labor, Georgina might dye their hair iridescent pink or blue, and prepare a sumptuous lunch for them like a family does.

George had many ladies, sluts, mistresses & slaves. But Georgina was her first and only wife. --Who George had renamed after herself, her original identity being Eleanora, 'Nora' Stewart. She could be both a submissive wife, and a regal queen with power over the rest of the pack.

At club Oils she surveyed the leatherdikes with a matronly eye of discipline. Bikers came to Georgina with their problems more then their mother.

Daddy George was extremely dominant.

Actually, George was a real masochist to keep running the Outlaws.

It takes a submissive to be able to put out all that energy into people--directing them to do this, telling somebody else to go help a member in need, telling another member to drop dead, suggesting another go get laid, getting this fixed, and that changed. Not playing nursemaid, but running the show.

The Boss had great power--both thru personal magnetism, a force emanating thru those black eyes at her powerful height & build & stance, and, as the elected Leader Of The Pack.

Some idea of their domestic tranquility was illustrated when Queen Georgina came in and saw the garbage in metal can collected by a young biker from all the rooms, but still sitting in the vestibule. With one shapely foot in a boot of elegant stiletto heels, made of the finest leather--the pair cost $400 and was stylish, she pressed down the garbage in the can **CRUNCH!** Straightened her colorful dress—a Mumu—then went on back into the recess of their lovely Palace, leaving the garbage for George, and there it sat stinking for days.

Finally, Georgina was consumed with a passion to get rid of that trash. **"You *will* do it."** Sez the Queen looking at her dike husband. **"NO?"** Arched eyebrows; her purple painted eyelids fluttered, eyes rolled in their mascarad sockets, looked up to heaven. Her hands began to clench into fists, and a low tone began to escape thru her red lips and clenched teeth.

And she was liable to keep this up all night.

"ALLRIGHT!" George hollers.

Her tantrums--she could keep on and on for hours, and do it anywhere. George had a choice, either pack up and move out--or put up with it. And she did the latter.

The only person who had any modicum of-control over George was Queen Georgina. They had shared a lot together in times gone by. –Most of it was all the bulldikes fault. And because of legal difficulties in which Daddy G, had been threatened with lawsuits and prison, the house was solely in Georgina's name.

The bedroom was painted pretty pink with golden spreckles on the walls. A custom made XXtra large king size bed. White furniture with gold trim. Lavish drapes, accessories, color TV, Princess phone.

Georgina wore a tiny babydoll negligee of blue & gold trim for sleepwear. Later that night George would take firm hold of her fleshy shoulders and lay her Queen down in bed and love her.

Daddy George & Queen Georgina were life mates. Until the termination of their liner existence, like a couple of ox's yoked together, plodding thru the days.

Daddy's playpen, a wooden affair with bars and wheels was folded neatly against the wall. --Her original pen, from when she was a child; which she kept for sentimental reasons & that it gave her confidence.

"Daddy George in diapers. *That's* a scene the club'll never see."

Georgina sat propped up in bed reading MOVIE REVIEW, while the behemoth mindlessly watched television. "George, it says 25% of American wives report cheering on their husbands, and 60% report thinking about it."

"Thinking about it? Everybody thinks about it! -- The other 40% are liars!" Sez Daddy George.

Queen Georgina never had sex with any fag friends, nor any men in any way shape or form, but had stuck her fist up fags asses. This, in an advanced form of SM assplay, using a latex glove & plenty of Crisco.

Daddy George had much on his/her mind, she had a mind lag. Had dropped Punk & Jody, a couple of butch members off at their new house awhile ago, and for 2 months after they moved still thought they lived there, tho repeatedly had been told different. They were so poor they didn't have a bike, or a car, and George drove them back towards the same house one night, only to be reminded they no longer lived there, but they were thankful for the thought.

People had to tell George something 5 times when her mind .was in lag, otherwise, the only memory she had was the original state of play as first presented to her.

People mistook this; assumed she didn't listen to them. It was not that she didn't want to spend more time, but there was no time to spare--just a few moments to glare at any one person & a grapple with each major issue as it came up--police raids of parties, bails, members domestic battering, the infrastructure. --Then she was on to the next.

Cold winter months when they were snowed in--into cars instead of bikes George had provided for; the couple drove a $30,000 long bed van on which they made monthly payments.

Another insight into the nature of their relationship; George might be in the exercise room, laying on the bench doing presses in her blue sweatpants outfit, a sweatband around her forehead, pushing 300 pounds of iron, when the phone rings; either club business or one of her wife's fag friends **"GEORGINA!"** George bellows. **"GEORGINA ANSWER THE PHONE!"**

The phone is longer then an armslength away, but in the same room. Her wife must come trotting from across the other side of the Mansion, over carpets, stairs, linoleum floors to take care of George. It was a good thing. It kept her from being sedentary. She came at a clip in gold shoes over the gym mat, baring the phone receiver in hand. "Yes Georgie!"

SM was brought into the Outlaws club in various ways.

The bulldike needed help with her flagging sexuality, and sure enough, the scenes helped bring her sex drive back up to its peek.

SM came into the club via different women. Some of the sluts, and even ladies worked in the sex industry, and had been using it for years on their customers.

Some young dikes in boots and sawed off bluejeans were in fact strippers--about 5%-- in local clubs on the Broadway zone. Used it in their acts. And then, there was Rip. An old master at the black arts.

Its time had come.

Daddy George was one lucky bulldike. She hadn't had to feel herself up --alone, since 1950. Nor to squeeze a pillow in her grip pretending it was a woman's breasts, while humping her clit against a rolled up towel smeared with Vaseline. She had everything. A lady to squeeze, lick, fuck, & even to penetrate her own cunt at special times. A lady to play with & fantasize with & be with.

Plus a parade of whores, sluts, SM players, other dikes ladies & assorted freaks.

Everything.

400 pounds of flesh-sweetness weighed in on earth.

"Put on a show for me." Daddy cooed.

"Tickle me and fix my dinner!"

"I always do that Georgie!"

"I don't always get a show!"

George prevailed on the Queen Dowager for a show. --She had gained 150 pounds since her showgirl days.

Their bedchamber was warm. Wall-to-wall carpets, drapes closed, the expensive dresser & mirror set with slips and bras hanging out, and cosmetics mussed around. Shoes here and there kicked off over the plush carpet, and filmy veils littered the velvet-lined chairs. A room about 30 by 35 feet, big as the average living room, with a fireplace—crackling logs radiated heat pleasantly, and fire design flashed up against the walls; for this was originally the living room of the first house they'd purchased.

Georgina began to undulate. Some might mock--due to her large omnipresent size, but not Daddy George. He-she's coal black eyes drank in the familiar sight of her beloved working up a sweat for her. Soon pleasant aroma of her female body began to fill up the room.

They shielded each other in sickness & in pain.

When George was on the rag, bleeding big clots of red blood, discharging voluminous red menstrual tides & suffered severe cramps--they would pass shortly, she'd crash into the warm king-sized bed with Queen Georgina, who cooed; "Poor Baby". Who held her fast until the pills kicked-in.

Bought her drugs exclusively from Rip who had connections. A high grade of codeine straight from the pharmacy in bottles. Didn't even need to bother her doctor.

Jobs in the steel industry had gone.

Since both were legitimate working people they had to get up early in the morning--especially George who worked factory shifts at 7am; had to get up at 5.

They tricked each other to get up, using the same method year in & year out. **"GEORGIE! IT'S 6:30! YUH GOTTA BE AT WORK IN HALF AN HOUR!** And it was only 5:10.

Georgina rocked the behemoth peacefully asleep under the sheets. She was an immense woman, muscled, had done hard labor carrying steel in the yards of long-ago factories. Georgina's arched eyebrows were plucked, almost invisible without cosmetic pencil; her lipstick was wiped off.

But George was outside of human tragedy, in a place past language, and outside of thought. And didn't want to start yet. **"*GEORGE!* IT'S 7 O'CLOCK! YER SUPPOSE TO BE AT WORK!"** Knowing it was actually 6.

"*GEORGE!* WAKE UP IT'S TIME TO GO!" And George slumbers on, her unconscious mind knowing she has 45 minutes.

Morning. A face peers out of the mirror, shaving. Lathered. A razor at her cheek. The big behemoth pumped out enough male hormones to grow fuzz on the side of her cheeks; and somewhere in her mid 40's had developed an almost invisible moustache, then it grew thicker. And she was quite proud of it.

Daddy George slept like a baby. --Nothing disturbed her. Other more introspective types might toss and turn, tense with evils of the day--after witnessing life & death motorcycle crashes, or beatings or murder.

George strode foreword, did what she had to do for the sake of the club, mistake or not. Defended the criminals in her club wrong or right, with loyalty.

True to the code that she believed. And when she slept, it was the sleep of the righteous.

The couple was possessed by a black cat. A male. Satin black, with yellow eyes, named Georgette. To whom when fags came over they loved to talk baby-talk. The Queen would tie a red ribbon around its neck for festive occasions like the upcoming holidays.

Queen Georgina & Daddy George. No Outlaw in the group was a match for George, at 6'2", the big butch. They'd also have to fight the Queen.

In the old days when they were poor they'd hang out in places where rough people partied. When George supported them by working in the steel yard and Georgina did manicuring jobs and danced.

Hillbilly bars, for in those days, in their town there were no lesbian clubs. Even today, they'd prefer a hillbilly bar instead of namby pamby lesbian clubs with their politics and plaid shirts.

"Wouldn't catch me dead in one of them dyke bars." George bellowed.

George thought nothing of it--redneck taverns. The years of her childhood had played almost exclusively with boys, and ran a boys gang, and had camaraderie with the men she worked with at the steel yard.

The couple detested dyke bars because, in them, they were such an oddity. Both for playing butch/fem roles. And because dykes frowned at their attire. Laughed at Georgina in her lady satin evening gown, dangling earrings, as well as her stomping man. What George hated most was lesbians--skinny ones who looked at her funny because of her butch demeanor.

Often Queen Georgina would repeat harrowing tales to the bikers in Oils. In the past she'd had to add her weight to fights. Literally sock men with her ringed hands and sit on them, "Crush 'em, that's what we did honey. We did what we had to do. Oh it was a rough place. Rough people went there, but they always respected George and I because of the way we carried ourselves.

We earned our money & we spent it. We set the boys up drinks, and they sent us drinks. The bartender wouldn't allow no dirty talk around me.

George can crush the life out of a man. When they went wild, drunk, we stopped many from hurten' us, or somebody else."

The redneck bars they hung out in they were respected as a Lady & Dike. As a youthful dancer at finer clubs downtown, where George was not allowed in, Georgina might have found the fast life tempting, but never had a thought of soliciting men for money. She had been approached by a few, because of her exquisite, tho ample charms. Over the long years, the answer was always a flat; **"Go to hell!"** From a redlipsticked mouth, twisting, angry, and accompanied by an upraised ring-fingered fist, & arched eyebrows.

Then, the neighborhood grew more cosmopolitan. A fag bar opened and a gay frontier moved in. Where, from that time on the couple could be seen on nights out. ---Kissed their old redneck men friends goodbye. Queen Georgina & George in the fag bar amidst squealing nelly fags & drag queens.

Many of her fag friends had moved away--to heaven. Died in the Aids epidemic, early in their middle ages. And they no longer went to gay men's bars since they got their club, so had no way to meet new ones.

Was not entertaining royalty any more. Fags, squealing sissies and queens were gone out of her life but for a few dear old (male) girlfriends who had well ensconced in each others bosoms and had become grand old pals.

All thru these transitions was never an empty space in their lives. The boys at the fag bar had been replaced by a pack of Daddy Georges weasel faced biker dikes.

Originally, it was just a group of 7 or 8 with no leader. But George showed an intense interest in building the group into something bigger. And when they officially became the Outlaws, was elected by the group to be Leader. Efficient. Strong. And was the heart and soul of the gang.

Daddy George knew how to talk to people. Had no inferiority complexes or self-doubts. She didn't have any morbid introspections.

In the beginning George reached out and made friends, drew newcomers into the gang, took great trouble to organize meetings, always was dealing with people, made telephone calls. A lot of work to hold it together.

It helped that she was a natural leader, always had been a good friend to depend on, in her childhood and around her cronies in her 20's and 30's.

George was the Leader also because she would do anything that must be done. Wasn't afraid to die, and prison meant nothing if she felt the calling of a righteous cause.

Anybody who had anything to loose was a coward by comparison.

Queen Georgina lay down, head on the pillow. A very strong cunt smell assailed her senses. Where was it coming from? She thought it was her. Embarrassed. --'Haven't I washed up with my rose petal soap?' Then saw she'd laid her nose directly on a pair of Daddy G's jockey shorts. In fact right in the middle of the crotch where her cunt had been all day.

"GEORGE

"WHAT!" Her voice echoed from the den.

"WHAT ARE THESE JOCKEY'S DOING IN THE BED!"

"THAT'S WHERE I TOOK 'EM OFF! NOW LEAVE ME ALONE!"

So, matrimonial life progressed in matriarchal bliss.

George was loyal. This new stuff about leaving your lady and going on to someone else--that was a joke. George was a true he-dike and didn't go in for such foolishness.

After the nights plays of sadio-masochism, all the drinking, gaming and fucking--daylight always saw her back in the same bed in the same place--with Queen Georgina. They'd been together 25 years.

Daddy George gripped the Queens massive shanks with her hands and kneaded.

Whipped one white arm between Georgina's legs, took her panties off, lifted then in air, sniffed them, then buried her nose deep into the soft wet cunt and began to lick

Lick her clit and get her hot and wet and ready to fuck. Lay there down under the covers, between Georgina's spread legs as the Queen read a sex magazine, turning the pages between her fat fingers. Her pompadour head in disarray, wisps of black hair which she dyed coming loose; and penciled eyebrows arched; lipstick wiped off--

50

makeup less. While the lump like a whale under the covers--George-- was savoring Georgina's delicious female taste.

A salt taste came up in her mouth--a desire for sex, so great. Her own clit throbbed. Webs of blood coursed hot lust thru her body.

Her wife was beginning to smell like a humanbeing again & not a bar of fleur-de-lis rose petal soap--all her womanly scents coming out. Usually Georgina smelled so clean, with all human scent erased.

George dived back up out of the covers, sat up & spread her own legs. Georgina wiped the back of her mouth with ringed rednail manicured hand, saw to it that her lipstick was off, and bent to her job. Thru Georges rolling white layers of fat knew where her clit was, had spent the last 25 years finding it, got thru the fleshy folds of flab. Began licking, and soon they would be ready.

Daddy George arose, pulled the drawer of the nightstand open, got out the toys. A size 9" cock. Strapped it on with the harness; from a tube squeezed out a glob of clear lube onto the cockhead which bobbed on its shaft from between her thighs; placed her immense self over her wife, worked the cock into her pussyhole, and proceeded to fuck Georgina into the mattress.

45 minutes of dick driving. That's just how long it took them to cum.

Soon Georgina's head was hanging over the bed, they'd fucked so hard, and had to move back into the center. "Fuck me Daddy."

"It's dark, and I'm reaching under your night gown. How does it feel for your daddy to fuck you little girl?"

"Oh Stop! A little girl like me shouldn't have to do this!"

"Oh but *I* have to!" Sez George.

"No! Not a little girl!

Daddy G. drove her dick harder, faster into her wife's pussy, which lubricated wet onto their thighs.

Daddy George rode Queen Georgina's voluptuous body. Handfuls of her mountianess flesh in her grasp. Big, hairy, bone crushing, hands.

"I MUST FUCK YOU!" Bellowed the big bulldike.

Georgina's feet began paddling like a duck running, then her hips made a full circle around clockwise, uttering a low moan, her hips going around and around in a circle, then her hips started pumping wildly, orgasticaly, as she came.

Chapter Eight

That morning they heard on radio there'd been rioting in the black ghetto which was quite a distance from their house, but only a few miles from where the clubhouse was located.

"The blacks are rioting." Georgina informed George.

There'd been a shooting the night before, of a black by the cops, unfairly. A mistake. The black community was simmering.

So when Daddy George & Georgina went down to the club they had their firearms handy. The places thru which they had to pass might be dangerous, and Oils tho in a neutral zone of mostly warehouses, integrated with artists, gays & multi-races; was on the outskirts of poor minorities, including the rioters.

The rioting had been over for hours. They found it had been sporadic and far from Oils, but both were nervous.

"One of 'em gets beat up, he's drunk, resists the arrest, right? --- *He's* drunk, and *they're* rioting ? Does it make sense?"

Daddy George was stuck --She hated cops and lawless men. Both sides of the spectrum.

Their safe neighborhood fled behind them out of the rear view mirror of the van, as they descended the hill and drove across to the freeway that cut thru the city.

On both sides it could be seen, as they whizzed past. A neighborhood in decline. This fall had begun years back when the bluecollar class took a loss of industrial jobs, and began to move out. George saw this where she had worked as a passing woman. The steel yard had been a causality. And in the hiring hall for warehouse & factory the pool of jobs dwindled. The lots once had been enclosed by short fences 3 feet tall, picket fences that served more as property line makers & decoration. A few, worn and rotted remained from a different era when life was peaceful. Now, most houses were surrounded by 6 foot fences, and had security bars and snarling dogs.

Here, of all places had come dikes, living on the fringe. An area poor enough so they could afford to buy houses or rent, an area so consumed by its own problems that it had no time to challenge the lifestyle of gay women, to combine its forces to try to drive them out, as might happen in a more affluent area. A neighborhood under siege. & here they shared space with other near-poverty class, and minorities.

Jody & Punk had been part of this influx. Two novice bikers. Had rented a house in an area especially heavily populated by blacks, 80%. Other dikes had been suppose to move in & join them and help with the rent, but once they saw how bad the neighborhood was they changed their mind--and so the commune never materialized.

A few bad incidents had happened to the two butches. And they though they were singled out because of the color of their skin-white. 3 break-in's. And other incidents had happened to people of the neighborhood as well. So they decided to move after 6 months.

The owner of the house, a middle class black man who lived nearby was very understanding. Gave them back their deposit & let them break the lease and go.

The dikes were pissed. Had hoped to make it a home. In a better neighborhood all they could afford was a room, not a house. They had lost a fireplace, hardwood floors, washer & dryer, a lot of great stuff. They were mad at loosing a good chance.

Crime, drugs, & civil disobedience was eating the community alive.

"If yer poor yer either gonna be living in a redneck area or a ghetto. A poor neighborhood is where all the people with no money wind up. Gays, bikers, minorities, poor white trash, artists, dopers." Sez Daddy George. "We're lucky we got our place Honey." Sez the Queen.

15 minutes later as they drove off the freeway thru the neighborhood near the clubhouse, they saw a white man standing out in front of his place with a broom in his hand cleaning the sidewalk of broken glass where the rioters had been. "A white man, good." George sez. "I'm glad! Push the niggers out! I'm sick of 'em! They're so ugly and mean and bad! Out!"

"Don't let the black girls in the clubhouse hear you say that honey!" Cautions Queen Georgina.

"**SHIT!** Fuck the Club!" George hollers. Black hair smooth on her head, wrinkles of coarse white skin stretch around her mouth as she yells. A mature bulldike.

"FUCK 'EM! They can suck my dick!"

"Which one of your dicks honey?" Asks Georgina, her little-girl eyebrows arched coyly.

When George had started the whole club thing back then, it was whites only. Them--white, & one Indian, Comancho. That was it. The idea of having blacks in the club had never entered her field of

54

speculation. All of their associates where white—rednecks. Nordics, Wasps.

But that changed. The club reflected the demographics of the greater city to an extent. It had become a veritable cosmopolitan cross section.

There was even talk of transsexuals joining--not just girls to boys like Ronny, but visa versa--males who'd had the operation & who now had pussies. Post-op. Of course, a lot of boys who had it cut off made very good girls. Better then some girls. 'I'd almost rather whip a submissive boy then a dominate girl." George had said upon occasion. And Jews. She was gonna whip one of them in scene one night.

It was early afternoon. Daddy drove the van cautiously, maneuvering narrow streets, white knuckled fists controlling the steering wheel, belied the anger inside. Automatic pistol, a big silver .45 on the seat between them, and a rifle with a 30 round clip underneath on the floor.

"The white man! Race! That's all they talk about!" Scoffed George. "I hear 'em down at the club. Blacks are the kind of people you can hear 'em a block away, even if they're just having an ordinary conversation--they talk so loud."

"Yes." Sez Queen Georgina.

"Rednecks don't talk loud, just when they're drunk."

Kelly, the Ancient Mariner who owned Oils tavern had bought her establishment before the neighborhood had begun its share of problems. And she paid dearly for it.

Lately, the district immediately around Oils had begun to reverse its decline and make an improvement. Artists were renting lofts in warehouse space of business that had abandon the inner city. An influx of peaceful Chinese families, the second generation of immigrants were buying in, and a lot of single women, gays, first time home buyers. But it was still rough.

George looks out the window while at a stoplight at a loitering man. "When you get to know all the thieves and hoodlums & panhandlers in the street, when you recognize all the lowlifes by face & even know their names, it's time to move out." She says sarcastically. "See what they did to our old neighborhood. The Avengers think we're fools. 'Those stupid Outlaws are fools!' That's what they say about us."

"The neighborhood is getting better George, I can tell."

"Ha! It's got the highest crime rate in the whole city---in this one neighborhood! In the whole state!"

Now all those gay gals who live around us, up in the hills--ha, what a joke. Nobody's suppose to know *they're* gay. That's why they're embarrassed by *me*. They're living in a dream world. They think everybody thinks they're straight, and everybody knows damn well they're gay, but they think they're fooling people, so they have to live their lives governing everything they say and do--like they're testifying in front of the FBI every minute of their day or something. And they live up in the hills where it's safe…"

"That's why they get so much money George, from being in the closet."

"Shit, half my gang's more upscale! They got nice jewelry and leathers and fancy bikes! Those dikes in the hills wear bluejeans & pantsuits from Sears!"

"LOOK!" Georgina jabs her finger at a fence--6' tall made of wood, painted a brown color with BUTCH POWER scrawled in uneven letters. Georgina read the sign aloud.

"IT'S *BLACK* POWER! NOT *BUTCH* POWER! JESUS CHRIST!" Bellows George. "Dream On!"

56

Yet, lesbian graffiti had begun to appear in the neighborhood. A ray of hope. A place for us.

"I wanna get away from the niggers." George sighs. "Not black people--niggers."

The wintry sky has wind blown clouds thick; greyblue connected into one massive cloud. Wet air.

The neighborhood looked grim, but here & there peeked a red orange yellow green blue purple rainbow flag--the Gay Flag.

"Since the steel workers left, there's lots of unemployed, so things has reached a point they all settle down on the bottom of the pile fighting it out."

To Daddy George it was moves on chessboard. Someone would loose someone would win.

Chapter Nine

There's everything in the big city-- the sophisticates, & the slimy underbelly creatures. The Junkie parasites and the elegant lesbians of a professional class.

The sick & the slick.

They wake up at midnight-and don't know who to reach for --so they grab their bankbooks & count their money.

So they reach for a whiskey bottle. And it gives them murderous thoughts & angry ideas.

So they sniff up a line of white powder on a glass, up their nose. It confuses their minds so they can forget their hearts.

And slowly cuts the strings, one by one to all humanity, so they don't feel anymore.

High Dam Road.

Locals in the area call it "The Damn Road. Go up the Damn road. Get off at the Damn road." Etc.

Motorcycles raced down to the warehouse district.

It was a magical night in the gay sector of the city. A group of gay girls disappeared across town on their bikes from a Victorian style house that stood 3 stories, that a group of dykes & fags were occupying, included in its basement a way station for women.

Night was full. Multicolor lights, blue green, yellow red from taverns. Laughing voices.

Butch lesbians on each other's arms; a butcher lesbian and a more fem one.

Star had come to crash in the way station for women--for $15 a night, cheaper then any hotel/motel. She was a novice in the club.

Star was big. Powerful. 6 foot tall, 200 pounds. A Scandavian female. A butch, but quite a feminine one. Of all the dikes she was the mildest mannered. Maybe her imposing height and power was the cause. Having never had to scuffle like the smaller women. & her stately quality made her get her way more often, by a natural process, and she didn't have to fight.

And thus wasn't mean.

All the fems were drooling over Star.

She rode a big road-worthy bike; a full dresser with casings, that looked like suitcases on its sides, a fancy bootwrap on the left heel with a chain over that which suggested she was dominant; and was looking for a job. Feminine enough to work on Broadway as a dancer--which was what she had in mind, unless she could find a rich fem to support her while she went back to school.

The big beautiful butch was in heat. Drove down the avenues looking. Eyes ran over every human object on the street. Briefly ran over the length of their bodies. Men she rejected, and most women. She had to watch the road too. Rode down another block & came to a stoplight beside a woman in a car. Admired her, from an aloof distance. Motorcycled gloves holding the handlebars, wind in her long hair & a tiny motorcycle Helmut-the soldier kind on her head. She marveled at how much sensuality could be drawn from them. How much eroticism they contained.

The new almost-fem butch highly attractive strode into the club, in satiny spandex trousers, black leather jacket--the expensive kind.

Bikers arrived, each breath they blew gusts of steam out of their nostrils like panting horses. "It's frightening when you get this much rain, it's dangerous. Wind conditions become bad. Gotta be careful, a storm like that last one. I sure hope it'll be clear for the Run."

Dikes, wet from a small amount of rain that had begun to hit the road; stood outside, by the parked bikes looking at the weather. And wondered how many good runs the club could get in on their cherished bikes before they put them up for winter.

They saw Star go past. "Everybody wants that lady. Butch dikes, femes, dominants, slaves." One whispers. "God she's great!"

& then the Leader Of The Pack's huge shadow darkened the doorway and strode in. Powerful bulk in solid black leather, thick-soled motorcycle boots sweeping up to a cap with the eagle of death spread across the brim. A barrel chest & biceps. Bigger then life. Black boots shone & glimmered pyramid shape studs; with buckles in back and chains wrapped.

Oils was a box-shaped tavern 100 feet in length, by 50 wide. Sofas & tables, as well as red-vinyl barstools. It had a horseshoe-shaped bar. The ceiling rose to a lofty height of 20 feet, it was actually two stories high.

59

The old he-she Kelly, a 1950's drag butch was the owner of this physical property; and had just unpadlocked the door an hour past. Already the place was full of women. Red and blue pools of bar lights & dancing feet.

Kelly was directing the removal of old bottles, the night had barely begun, & she was getting ready for it. A blue bus, the back of it folded down into a lip parked by the entrance and some dikes were carting off empty bottles thrown into cartons in which the beer company had delivered its merchandise off the brewery truck. Green, clear, and brown bottles. Stacked on a dolly 3 cartons high. The Indian Comancho pulled the metal dolly, a headband on her head from which an eagle feather stood up, and medicine beads around her neck. The cases rattled. Their stacks wobbled. She handed the cartons up to Johnny who took each, & threw it into the bus with a clank of bottles shifting together. Occasionally a bottle would fall, CLANK! making a glassy, hollow sound on the pavement, and bounce. "Oops." The Indian muttered. They were very sturdy. But one bottle had broken, & shattered shards over the street, so they got a broom and swept it up. Muchas bottles. When they were through, the entire bus bed was full of cases of bottles--20. 2 cartons high, 4 across, and 5 lengthwise. The drinking capacity of Oils patrons for a week. The two dykes were recycling & had earned about $40.

Inside the cavernous tavern ran a horseshoe shaped bar, amber beer advertisements blinked. Under them a young biker tended to customers on one side, and Kelly, the greyhaired old dike worked the other.

Angel was at the bar. Black leather jacket whose silver zippers glistened like teeth. Studs and snaps & a silver chain wound thru the epaulet on the left shoulder. Zippers cut diagonally on the jackets front marking many pockets, & one silver snap pocket. The jacket hit Angel just above the hips, and leather ran, smooth, sleek down her legs. She moved like a panther; tossed her hair back out of her face and motioned Kelly for another beer.

Angel was a woman of few words.

Queen Georgina began to remove her ermine coat; George pondered, something was different. Looked up and down the long bar to see who was present, then gazed into space to the other side of the tavern to see what was going on over there, stuck one beefy white hand out of the sleeve end of her black leather jacket; an expensive watch glittering on her wrist, to help Georgina off with the fur coat, automatically, not looking at her, but still gazing into space, deep in thought. Georgina slung the coat over the bar.

Queen Georgina dressed up tho they had no place to go but entertain lavishly in their own home & Oils.

"White makes you look bigger." George said absent mindedly, in answer to Georgina's question. "Black makes me look smaller. It's all that light bouncing off your surface that makes you look big." It was true. The Queen seemed even more huge then George tonight.

Within seconds a biker ran up with a problem. Sat down beside Daddy George, and they could feel her hot breath.

Black walls. Red lights streak Oils. Old Kelly directs the removal of the cartons of bottles. And got set to start the night.

When George got to the club she could see it in their eyes around the bar.

Something was wrong.

Daddy George had arrived just to find, on top of everything else, a race riot had broke out in Oils.

Pink faces with mean expressions glowered on their side of the bar.

Soon the big motorcycle king was in the middle of it.

Saundra, a fem, brown skin, slender red-orange natural hair done modestly sat crying on a barstool.

Hawk, a Warlord stood by. Hawk was dressed in a shiny black jacket with contrasting silver zippers and wore purple lipstick--on the side of her face, having been kissed by a punk girlfriend. Mohawk spikes dyed green/pink down the middle of her scalp, with both hemispheres on the sides shaved bald. Hawks big hands dazzling rings held onto Saundra's small shoulders pulling her so close their green & orange hair mixed.

A big ebony biker with a cutaway shirt that said, WANT SOME BLACK LOVE? inside a heart, and smooth satin skin stood next to them, a sour expression on her face.

Daddy George went over to Saundra, put a hand on her like she owned the woman--a thing she did with many bikers in the 80-member club; & remembered her enough to call her by name.

Tears rolled down brown cheeks carrying mascara & her eyes puffed up. Her full Afro lips had worn off their lipstick. George took her hand. A graceful brown hand, slender fingers, and chipped short nails--she had done a lot of poor hard work in her life. Saundra was a nurses aid. In a gentle voice marred by sobs she told Daddy George what had happened.

"Who did it! Who done this to you!" Daddy George demanded to know.

"It was those two punksters --Jody and her friend." Says Hawk.

"Jody! She's a real jerk anyways!" George turned to stare back down at the brown girl. "Jody and Punk? Those two? She's an asshole! Jody 's got her fist so far up her butt her fingers is wiggling out of her mouth!"

Saundra sobbed.

"How'd she hit her?"

"Open hand." Sez Hawk. "Slapped her."

"Uh." Grunts George. "Then what?"

"Then I waded in and broke it up and kicked them in their ass!" The green Mohawk Warlord's eyes glinted.

"She was high on what?"

"Drunk."

'I hate when they beat women. --Not their own women of course, that's natural, but I hate that too.' The giant in black leather towered over them, cap brim on which the Death Eagle spread its wings pointed downward as she listened, and had inner thoughts. Behind them the jukebox music toned, and life went on. 'Women are women because they're naturally more submissive, they're more peaceful; it's a shame to hurt them--unless they're asking for it.' Walls of the tavern, black, shone with a red hue. Conversations, and tinkling glasses.

If one could have been inside George's private thoughts, it might seem strange to hear. --As a Master she had done many sadio-masochistic scenes. But was a careful sadist. Her discipline did not result in broken limbs, or torn muscles or permanent damage--or tearful eyes.

The green Mohawk spikes shake, Hawks teeth grit, silver chains rattle on her muscled arms. "So Saundra just puts her hands up over her face to protect herself and don't try to fight back at all, and so then Punk grabs her arm and twists it."

"Where 's the cocksucker?"

"Been gone."

"Hawk threw her out." Sez Saundra in a soft voice.

"Good." George says with satisfaction. An evil glint in her eye; "Don't let 'em back in tonight --if they have enough nerve to come back." Then the leathered giant turns to look down beside them at the big ebony bruiser-- a lot smaller then George; but still big at 5'9" 200

63

pounds. Eyes narrowed;   "Where were *you* when all this happened?"
As if to say, what kind of man was she?

Ebony wore a mean pout on her thick lips. "I wasn't sitten' here. I
was over there--" Pointing down the bar. She and Saundra tho both of
the same race within a club where they were a small minority, still
weren't exactly friends.   Saundra had turned the black biker down for
sex on a number of occasions. It was a well-documented fact that
Saundra liked to sleep white.

Cap brim pointed back at the brown woman with orange
Afro hair, mussed by the confusion; "Just some fools in this club.
You know what I mean. Too much liquor, too much dope, too little
sense." Her teeth clenched.

Saundra nodded her head.

"Don't forget who the leaders are and how we feel about you,
that's what counts, not what some lame brain thinks.... I'll have a talk
with them...."

About 20 minutes earlier these events had transpired. Reeling with
events of the race riot out the public sector--heavily reported on the
news, & close to their area, the 2 drunk bikers had feelings. They
had recently lived right on the border of the riot zone. "The niggers,
the niggers, it's getting old. I'm sick of it." Their thin white arms
stuck out of bluejeaned vests, elbows on the bar and legs twined thru
the silver barstool rungs; they slid on red vinyl seats, heavy black
boots kicking into the side of the wooden bar, and snarls on their
faces, pissed because they had no money, and all this riot stuff.

Then Aretha Franklin came on the jukebox.

"Well one thing, they sure can sing."

"Speaking of which, here comes one of the little devils now. "Sez
Punk, evilly.

64

The jukebox pumped out song, in rhythm to red & blue blinking lights.

Saundra walks thru the bar **tap tap tap** on high heel boots, wind fills her coat, her face fresh from the cold air's blowing might.

Blue & red shadows cast over the floor, and bikers laugh and talk, or dance.

A lady, Saundra sits daintily on a barstool. Not noticing a short distance away the two, looks on their faces of total disgust.

Drunk, Jody staggers over to the brown woman, Punk is behind her. **"THIS SURE WAS A NICE CLUB BEFORE THEY STARTED LETTING NIGGERS IN HERE!"** Saundra turns around not believing what she's heard. Hillbilly hair mussed, jean jacket stained with beer Jody wavers in front of her, so drunk only her boots hold her upright. Couldn't control herself. -- After how they'd been disrespected in their new house, and all the hell they'd been thru in that neighborhood. Light colored eyes squint, vicious. Pounds one fist with, iron rings, into her open hand. Punk stands close behind.

"YOU PEOPLE ARE SLIME! YOU KNOW THAT DON'T YOU? *SLIME!* LOOK WHAT THEY DONE TO THE EAST SIDE! LOOK WHAT THEY DONE DOWN PAST THE FREEWAY!" And fixed the woman with a look, like she expected her to agree. "LOOK AT THE CHECKERS CLUB, IT WAS A NICE PLACE UNTIL THE COLORDS CAME! **THEY'RE BURNEN' UP THE CITY!"** Eyes heavy lidded, white face sweaty; so close the black woman smelled the alcohol on her breath, and Jody kept leaning closer. Suddenly a white fist shoots out and grabs the slender gold chain around Saundra's neck. "AND THAT **THING** YOU'RE WEAREN' AROUND YER' NECK! A FUCKING CROSS!   WE SHOULDN'T LET YOU WEAR THAT! NAW! I OUGHT TO RIP IT OFF YOU!" Saundra put her hands up to her throat, just as Jody gathered the chain around her wrist and with a yank broke it. The crucifix came off and scattered over the floor. "IT'S A TOOL MEN USED OVER FEMALES FOR CENTURIES! WE SHOULDN'T LET YOU IN HERE!   WE SHOULD PUT YOU OUT OF HERE AND TAKE OILS BACK LIKE THE ARYAN

AVENGERS DID LORD'S AND MAKE IT FOR WHITE DIKES
ONLY!" She shouted. Rage twisted her face. "I HATE MEN! I
HATE ALL THEY REPRESENT! I HATE THAT CROSS! I HATE
YOU! YOU PEOPLE RAN US OUT OF OUR HOUSE! WE
OUGHT TO RUN YOU AND THE REST OF YOU COONS OUT
OF HERE!" Jody screamed. Teeth gleamed as big corn kernels, blue
veins pulsed in her neck. **"LET ME TELL YUH SOMETHING!"**
Jody pushed the black woman, so hard she fell into the side of the bar;
& bottles rattled. She let out a scream.

White face, shocks of short brown hair inches from her twisting in
rage. **"TELL YOU WHAT! WHEN I WAS YOUNG I CAME
UP IN A ROUGH REDNECK TOWN, AND THESE GUYS
CAME AND KNOCKED ME DOWN, ABOUT 7 OF ' EM,
BOYS, AND I WASN'T' T BUT 12! I GOT A HABIT OF
GETTING RAPED---IT HAPPENED TWICE, BY GANGS !
AND I AIN' T GOIN' THRU IT AGAIN! --NOT WITH YOUR
PEOPLE! NOT WITH NO PEOPLE!"**

Bikers in the bar started to turn to see what the commotion was;
redlights streaked black walls like blood. Saundra saw the face in
front of her, suddenly it wasn't her enemy, but someone she had to
reach out to touch inside--because really they were on the same side,
in a very much deeper way.

Saundra found herself standing up straight, screaming, looking the
punk dead in her face;   *"WE DON'T HELP EACH OTHER! WE
NEVER HELP EACH OTHER!"* Screaming, as she looked into the
soul of the butch female in front of her.

Saundra's scream tore out of her heart, out of tears.

"So she slaps her, and me and Hawk & some other bikers, put her
out." Ebony finished the story a second time.

"She won't show her face in here for awhile." Sez Daddy George.
"Not without an *apology.*"

66

Black walls. Red, yellow lit. Bottles gleam. Ice tinkles. Conversation weaves. A few watched from their seats at the bar their biker president in black leather as she stood, scowling.

"I ain't done nothing to her." Saundra moaned.

"The club don't want us here." She said.

Ebony grimaced, and nods her head in agreement.

"They want you." Sez George.

An odd feeling rolled over her again--it was irritation. Like it had before, dozens of times a day. "We need you, and you need us." Heard herself say. "The more the merrier."

Words swallowed up in the din of jukebox music and noise of women just coming in the door, whooping & hollering, who didn't know what had happened.

George felt she was handing a baby pacifier to a kid-- and she was the pacifier. And damn it, that's what it seemed to take, this job of Leader. Damn it! A Dominant playing nursemaid. Being a slave of the group. And it pissed her off. But forced her coarse white face to wrinkle into a look of kindness and kept these darker thought to herself.

"These dikes, they play hard, you knew that when you joined us, didn't yuh?"

Saundra nods her head, full lips press tight, eyes brim with liquid tears.

"They don't mince words, they say what they feel, they don't hide and lie behind your back like a lot of people. Least you know what they're thinking."

"Yes." She shrugged her shoulders, and her stomach heaved under her worn sweater.

The Leader spoke in a base voice; "After what happened with her&. Punk--they had to move, leave their house and go live in some crummy room somewhere, and their pissed, so they come in here acting big, swaggering like they're too big for their bluejeans and try to take it out on you just cause of the color of your skin; 'cause its the same as them who harassed them; but yer' a lady, it ain't fair, so, what is fair around here anyways? George sez. "Just remember what the Warlords feel about you, .yer OK: or you wouldn't be here." George put a heavy hand to the brim of her cap. Pushed it up and scratched her head.

Ebony, the black biker leaned next to Saundra's shoulder and softly said she'd like to buy her a drink.

"NO!" Saundra kicks her small spike boot toe into the bar rail, young face squeezes tight; and turns to face George & Hawk.
"I come in here... I don't know what you people think of me! Or any of us black people! I think maybe that bitch Jody is the only one that's honest! At least she says what she thinks! Just like you said! Now I know what everybody else thinks! WAIT! Listen to me! I'm not a fool! I know how we don't always get invited to the private parties and places, and some people never speak to me... I think some of them hate us! But you'd never know it! Maybe I shouldn't come here anymore---if it's causing such a *goddamn* problem for everybody!"

And she cried all over again.

Daddy George held Saundra's orange Afro'd head gingerly between her huge hands, pressed it against her broad chest, and blood that was on the woman's face smeared the leather.

Ebony was belligerent. Her short hair was hot pressed into tiny curls glistening with oil. **"Shoulda smashed that bitch in the face."**

'Punk & Jody lost control. After what they heard about the rioting, I bet. Just lost their minds.' George thought, but kept this to herself and said, "If it had been me, I would have slugged Jody in the face, an' I would have said, "THE HELL WITH THAT SHIT! AFTER WHAT YOU DONE TO MY PEOPLE THE LAST 400 YEARS?!

You know," she winked at Saundra, nudged her with an elbow, "That Martin Luther King stuff?" Golden lights played down upon them. 'But,' George thought silently inside her mind; 'Saundra's a lady, what do you expect? They won't fight, all they do is turn on the tears.'

A white fem thick and short with frizzy blond hair came over; Lady Jane etched in a silver name tag on her motorcycle jacket, and told the brown woman, "Don't take it too hard, that bitch Jody pulled the same shit on me--a fight over nothing. The no good cocksucking bitch." And moved off.

Golden orb on the ceiling revolved spilling light down onto them. Empty glasses, napkins lay on the bar.

But Saundra wouldn't be pacified. She was going to go home. -- White bikers in the club might not have realized it, but the riots had been where she lived, it was grating fiercely on her too--and she was the same color the rioters were.

Got up to walk out, alone, with shaky steps of her stiletto spike boots.

The Leader Of the Pack knew Saundra had come in by bus & had to walk the 8 block difference. That she didn't own a car, and seldom had courage to ride on the back of a motorcycle.

Daddy George had a kind heart, and said she'd give her a ride home. Even as these words spill out of Georges mouth, she realizes; 'shit! The riot was probably right where Saundra lives! Another riot might break out! There's probably niggers with guns down there this minute aiming for the first white face they see! What have I done!'

So, she grabs Ebony to ride with her over to Saundra's house. 'She's probably in the middle of the ghetto--because she's so poor-- totally her kind and nobody, nobody of light skin not even Puerto Ricans or chinks, hmmmm.' And stalked off into the crowd, where she could be seen, head and shoulders above them conducting a

search, & returned shortly with still another black biker to take along.
--For extra blackness.

Went up to the bar a moment and asked Kelly for a six pack of beer
for the kid. "I got to be everybody's Guardian Angel." Sez George,
extending one powerful arm to pick up the pack of beer. Her silver
studs glistened on a leather chest. "First thing I come in a bikers got a
new job, wants me to cash her check, now this." The old he-she just
shakes her head and mumbles something, and wipes a rag down the
wet ringed place where their bottles & glasses have been. The
Warlord with the pink & green spike hair runs up, hands George the
keys to Rip's Cadillac as requested; they're gonna drive the pimp car.

They made a safari thru the club & out the door. Mammoth
George on one side towering over the small brown woman, Ebony on
the other, big shouldered like a football player, and the third biker
carrying the beer & Saundra's little pack of personal things brought up
the rear.

George walked tall, always. Leather cap sparkling with silver
medals.

Got Rips Cadillac ready to roll. Went over to her own van, and
emerged with the automatic rifle. "Now we're ready." And put it on
the seat beside her.

"I'm gonna send a car back 'round for you tomorrow night lady, to
bring you back." Saundra looked up at the coarse older face framed
by short mannish hair.

"Ok." She answered softly.

The two black dikes lumbered into the back seat. They pulled out,
tires screeched over cement. 'Why am I doing this?' George asks
herself privately.

Before they began their drive thru the cold city, she asked Saundra,
"Do you need anything at home? Everything ok?" The brown
woman just stared ahead and said nothing. She was poor, but didn't
want to put her problems onto anybody. "Baby don't need milk or

anything?" Sez George, big fists wrapped around the steering wheel, head turned, cap brim pointed down to look at Saundra. The lady didn't have kids, was just a lonely single lesbian trying to survive on minimum wage in a city without a heart. "Well… I guess I need some aspirin. My head hurts. And my arm hurts where she twisted it. I need some Ben Gay Liniment, I'm out. I'm always twisting my back at work. But it's ok, I can get it tomorrow." And is thinking inside, 'Shit, I'm coming home to that lonely room; I wish I had met somebody nice tonight, she could rub my arm, it hurts so bad!' And a tear glistened in the corner of her eye.

Saundra's words, with a faint hint of a southern accent faded in the stillness of the car. The two black bikers in back shifted their weight uneasily.

Knowing George she'd make a stop at a supermarket, pay for the aspirin & Ben Gay Ointment and throw in a thick juicy steak, some TV dinners and a quart of ice cream to brighten up the woman's evening a little.

One thing about George, she had a feeling for people.

Scanned the rearview mirror, contemplating. The long prow of the Cadillac pushed thru the street; sleek lines of a long fish nosing into uncharted waters. It was just one more on her list of worries, --racist tensions in the gang. Along with the fems simmering a revolt of some sort; problems with police, and always money troubles. Green cash money.

Chapter Ten

When George drove the Cadillac back off the Damn Road & went in the bar, Rip was there.

Pretty showgirl wife Debbie was not at her side, acting sexy, dancing, shaking her hips as usual, but gone.

Georgina sat by the bar, talking to Kelly, having a hot coffee topped with foaming whipped cream to give herself pep for the long night ahead.

Rip opened up a long leather coat, showed George a sawed off shotgun hanging by a strap at her side, and a pistol and ammo belt under her arm. Took back the keys to the Cadillac and hooked Them on her belt, dike style. Rip was prepared for riots, rival gangs of bikers, the mafia, and for the final world war.

Rip stood 6'5, taller then George, but weighed less, of a more slender build. The leather coat had a dull sleek shine. It proved she had money. Face white, pockmarked, that twisted easily into humor or hate; brown liquid eyes, and short black hair combed back behind her ears like a man. Rip had an animal magnetism.

Black leather boots rose up into leather pants & got lost under the coat; the hem of it hit her below the knees. A biker cap with the Eagle's spread wings.

George crunched one boot up on the bronze bar rail.

"Why doncha let her go to work at Valoria's on A Street? Then you won't have to sit here worrying about her, and sitten' up in straight bars watchen' her like a Hawk.

"You must be joking pal. I ain't given' that witch half of everything she makes."

Rip sold women. And did a few more illegalities.

Since her days as a juvenile serving time in the Log Cabin Reformatory, the butch dike had been in prison for assault, battery, theft, grand larceny, forgery, vagrancy, criminal trespass, armed robbery, car hijacking, burglary, arson, sales of narcotics, pimping and pandering.

George had been wanting to discuss the racial overtones at Oils, but found herself discussing Debbie's cunt instead.

Debbie was out on a date.

"Her pussy should be wore out by now." Sez George.

"She's still got some miles left in her." Rip sez; throws her feet, expensively shod, onto an empty barstool & they talked. The two had been pals 35 years.

"Yuh should have stayed with the Roller Derby Rip.

"They didn't want me back, after I got busted."

"Yeah, yeah. I never saw yuh so happy as then. When yuh was busy on the Roller Derby circuit. Yuh had responsibility, yuh had fame, yuh was busy all the time, and never an idle moment on yer hands. Jeez, those were the good ole days, huh?"

Debbie had turned 30. Been hooking for Rip since she was 22, and was off with a regular trick --$250 for a few hours.

About an hour later, while the party is sailing into full gear inside Oils, Debbie appears, full-length fur coat, tight silver torridor pants and a low cut blouse, high heels; long brown hair wet from the shower. Fresh. Smelled of perfume. Handed the $250 in green cash to Rip, who nonchalant counts it, and puts away it in a wallet inside her shirt.

"He wants a woman who looks like his step daughter to dress him up in her underwear and spank him. He feels guilty for lusting after his step daughter." Debbie confides, while Rip leafs thru the sheaf of greenbacks from the wallet--it's over $2,000.

Silver polished toenails flecked with gold peek from the open-toed shoes. Her tits are firm and big, nipples hard from the cold poke up under the blouse, expensive fur coat draped over her shoulders. Queen Georgina turned at the bar, acknowledged Debbie with a nod, secretly comparing the fur to her own ermine, which was slung over the counter.

73

In the off-light Rip's face looked ugly, compared to her fancy clothes. Debbie's blouse was tight, big boobs bobbed underneath. Very expensive lady; not yet a broke down whore. The Eagle of Death refracted light from the spinning bar lights off the silver metal on Rip's biker cap.

"She really don't look whorish." Daddy George confides; when Debbie dances off to play the jukebox.

"Being with me keeps her young." Rip replies. She was 52, same age as George.

"Debbie don't look like a whore at all, just a party girl. Or a show girl."

"Ten years we been together. And when we met, claimed she was straight & can't stand dikes."

In 1985, Rip averted disaster in her long criminal career. Sat up dejectedly in a motel room. Her last woman had left her. All the money was gone. Checked her gun in its holster, a.38 caliber Saturday Night Special. Examined the blueblack steel chamber & barrel, the burnished brown wood stock. Opened up the cylinder, revolved it, 5 copper tipped bullets. Didn't know if she'd be living in a motel or a jail cell within the next 12 hours, need was so eminent. Need that could cause murder. Need was as simple as hustling up motel rent for the night & a sack of greasy take-out food to eat--about $30 total. No political reason, no great ideal--just hunger.

She went out into the night.

She went into a restaurant.

Sat down at the counter, ordered coffee with the last dollar she had. To bask in the golden lights, get a caffeine & sugar high and be in the social environment of her fellow human beings before having to go out and hunt one down.

The waitress was pretty. So Rip sez, "Whatta' doin' tonight?"

"Nothing."

She looked down at Rip; waitress hat of stiff cardboard on her soft hair. "Nothing."

"Want to spend some time with me? I got $100, we can go to an allnight movie." Rip was lying. She was a professional liar.

"Well, **maybe...**" the waitress said. Looking Rip up and down. "Time is money, honey." She hinted. Rip looked like a very attractive man, in a silk shirt open at the collar, wool trousers and a long tan leather coat, & matching brown boots. On the other side of the counter, inside her mind, Rip knew the size of her wallet ---empty. But she was prepared to carry the lie still further. And the motel room was good until tomorrow at 11am.

Lamps blazed down upon the food, which the cook placed out on the ledge dividing the kitchen from the waitress area; filling orders; it was cozy. The waitress walked up and down at a fast clip casting looks over at Rip while she served customers. 'I better break it to her and make sure she knows I'm a she and not a he.' Rip was so masculine she could never tell if she was passing without meaning to.

By this time 45 minutes had elapsed, stirring the coffee, sipping gulping & getting the free refills; the waitress had got glimpses of Rip when she wasn't aware of it, the mannerisms, that certain something, and began to realize the truth, but wasn't sure.

Pockmarked face, smile that was more a sneer, Rip finally bends over the counter, says in a low tone; "Do you like women...?"

"I been in jail." Says the waitress, staring back into her eyes. "Yeah."

Oils had a crowd, despite the rain and trouble in the streets. Yelling and music & fun.

"Yeah! I had been in jail!" Debbie snaps gum. "I had never came down so low! I was earning $2,000 a week before I got busted. I'd had all kinds of furniture, clothes, leather clothes--like we have now, but I lost it when I went to jail. The girl who was suppose to help me put it in storage stole everything rented a van with my money and left town. I got out in three months and went to work as a waitress, it was lousy, the customers were a drag, and I was earning in one 8-hour shift what I could make in 1 hour--plus tips. So I figured I'd go with Rip and make $100 after I got off my shift, the big liar, I got up to her motel and she didn't have shit. But we had sex, and I got hooked--on her. Yeah I told her I hated women, & dikes but that was because of what there is in jail. Deadbeat dikes with no future. Dopefiend dikes. So we got together. And I got all the stuff replaced, better stuff. We have everything. Rip has been good to me, and kept me off drugs. I couldn't do it without her or drugs."

Debbie expected rough treatment; --they were rough people.

A slap in the face if she did something wrong.

A slap, then sex heavy in bed, doing everything Rip wanted to do until she was finished with her. And that made up for it.

Debbie worked the streets & out of sex ads, until she could build up a clientele. Gave cash to Rip, who handled their business.

In exchange she wanted for nothing. Had spending money, great food--restaurant meals. Minor dope such as marijuana, didn't have to get up to an alarm clock at any specific time, had a protector, and a trustworthy partner to bail her out of jail if necessary. And so it had been for a decade. Debbie had the respect of the club members & was a center of attraction--because of being a sexy lady, and because she was one of the Leaders women.

So, they'd stayed together--two desperate people finding an island of safety within each others arms.

"The sluts, they like sex. The more rough the better. They like it hard. They like to fist often. They like a lot of sex each day. --They go 2 sessions a day, morning and night. Or stay in bed all day and fuck. I got a small fist." Says the showgirl, "Dena lets me fistfuck her." Wiggles her fist in the air.

"Thanks for telling me." Say Daddy George caustically. Dena was her mistress.

The two mannish bulldikes leaned their elbows on the bar patiently, and watched as Debbie played with her fem friend. They flirted & kissed each other.

"THIS IS THE HAPPY CORNER RIGHT HERE! COME AN' JOIN THE HAPPY CORNER!" Yells Deb, grabbing more women into her circle as they arrived in the entrance. "THIS WOMAN'S GOT HUMOR IN HER *SOUL!* We can count on you for a good laugh can't we?"

Queen Georgina's black hair cascades ringlets down from the pompadour, over her shoulders as she whispers to Kelly at the bar; "Her and Rip are buying a house not far from Georgie and me. It's an exclusive area. They try to act normal, try to blend in, living in a *moral* area, but those hot pants she wears are pretty short to be passing herself off as normal. And they probably think Rip is a man."

Lady, Sleaze's wife, Crystal, Dena & Debbie are seated at the bar, & Frosty, the Indian's wife has come in; they dance with each other, a wild party of fems, feeling each other up, flirting boldly and acting silly.

Between dances they collapse on the bar stools exhausted, breathless & yelling; and have a femme gab fest.

"I was different names-- I can't remember them."

"You'll never make it as a dancer then. You have to use a whole bunch of names."

"I was Crystal, Alexandria, Sparkle, Starr."

"Everybody is Crystal."

"Well I was an *artist*." Georgina confides in Kelly. Looking at the younger women." I had one name--Lady Lenora."

"That's yer' real name ain't it sugar." Says the old greyhaired he-she.

Fat face wrinkles; "Shhhh !" Pointing at George. "That's a secret! *Georgina's* my name-past, present, and future!"

"Well sugar, everybody's got a past." Sez Kelly.

Georgina flounces her big bosom, straightening black ringlets of hair. "Well, yuh know, George *stopped* me from my career in dancing. After 3 years, because she finally found out what was happening. Georgie went down there to the nightclub one time, and she wasn't suppose to go, they hated gays there, and there was a lot of fine women down there like me. So then she got more worried about the other women stealing me away. She wasn't worried about the guys because she knew I didn't fuck around. It was the women. The other dancers who really bothered her, because some were attracted to me."

George & Rip discussed a topic in low tones. Their annual private X-mas party, which was for Warlords, their ladies and a few personal friends exclusively. George drummed her fingers on the bar, then ran them thru her coal black hair. Rip's big lean frame draped over the barstool. They were having it on Christmas day.

"Jews have a big thing about that, it's a problem for them, since they're the ones nailed that son-of-a-bitch to the cross."

"Yeah."

"Georgina's having a few fag friends & their little cute boys over."

"Let's have a nativity scene. They can put a big diaper on you and they can all lay you in the Manger." Rip snorts with laughter.

"Can It." George glares at her swiftly.

78

"It's gonna get out, that we're haven' a party without them, yuh know. What with you bringing that dike for your scene." Rip indicated the mob of Outlaws that filled the tavern.

"Too bad." George says.

"What a terrible, terrible shame." Rip agrees.

"What a shame." George, in bass, gurgled a gallows laugh.

She was at the end of her rope with problems anyway.

Debbie bought Rip good money. Cash from pussy. Over a million dollars in the ten years she'd been a working girl & the dike pimps bottom lady. They provided for each other well. Rip had been there, sober, to bail her out of jail, keep up payments on a home using good business sense, going with Debbie to hold her hand while she got penicillin shots at the VD clinic, and to comfort her at the abortionists.

Being a pimp & a prostitute, --and still be dikes—was hard to deal with in a lesbian society. All the tired old bullshit left over from the past. Its morality. Its judgments. Its shoulds and should nots. Deb should pay her bills, she should not hook. Rip should be a lesbian. She certainly should not be a visible butch dike. "If I was poor and had to be out in the cold again, I'd go hang myself." Was Debbie's final words on morality."

While a great many lesbians were going on to better status--to be a doctor, or professional, Deb didn't have the brains. So this was her only ticket to a high society.

They were both trash, both doing something unacceptable to most lesbians.

So they held each other.

Blue blue/green tattoo on Rip's muscled arm quivered.

79

Bar lights. Party nights. The driving force.

"I'd tongue yuh real good!" Pipes up a voice; the feminine women turn to see a fat dike who'd come up behind them with big boots and bluejeans & red suspenders, & a blue work shirt over very fat tits. Fat face earnestly peering at their beauty.

"Crazy Girl." Sez Debbie, tossing her long brown hair, which threw out a scent of perfume.

Debbie ' s legs are spread, she holds the fem Dena between them and is saying;   "Dena likes me to just fucking pound her and there'll be blood, but she don ' t care."

"I'm a crazy girl." Sez Stryker.

Debbie ignores Stryker, talking to Lady & Crystal, while Dena wiggles her hips and pops her fingers in time to the music.

"I like Angla women better. Their cunts are pink. They're cleaner and smell better. It's all Puerto Rican down at Checkers Club. All Puerto Rican women don't get along with each other, too many sparks fly. Too many clashes.   I'm only part. Only part. It's not part of my life." And tosses her long wavy hair.

Debbie was not a thoroughbred. Was white, or almost white, tho she was half Hispanic didn't look it much.

"Hi crazy girl." Dena blinked flirtatiously.

The short fat dike smiled back, her chubby face dimpled. Red suspenders stretched over her immense bust, clomped in motorcycle boots edging up to the bar. "I have a secret crush on Debbie." She announced.

Buried her face in Debbie's neck, who hurriedly jerked back, away from her. But scent of Eau De Lilac lingered on the fat dikes cheek as an inspiration.

"Buy us a drink." Sez Dena with a smile.

Stryker was so hot to make love. Was 4'11", a runt, heavy chested, big belly. No hips and a flat ass. Rode a bike and loved the motorcycle girl gang. Certainly didn't have muscles, but had moxie & had been training how to fight at Ronny's gym.

"I see you're back Stryker." Sez Frosty.

"I'm having trouble with my bike. I couldn't get out for a while. I push the button, get the compression kick. Johnny told me 'it's all in the knack.' Well, if yuh don't kick it right it'll kick yuh back and snap yer' leg in two. I ain't kicken' it right, and the carburetor is acting funny too."

Frosty introduced them. Debbie turned on her heel and looked away, whispering to Dena; "She wants me to sleep with her."

"Yeah, that's right. Ignore the creepy looking Jew." Sez Stryker. Fat lips scrunched shut, her eyes got big with a bit of hurt.

A fat hand reached into her wallet; Stryker bought the fems a round of drinks. That ate up a $20 bill. Kelly throws a few dollars change back on the bar. Suddenly the attractive hooker turns and focuses the limelight of her attention on the short fat dike. Ran a manicured hand up over her back and down across one thigh, and from there, into her crotch, for a second. "Thanks Stryker. That's sweet." Said she.

Quivering from the expert touch Stryker saw the love she'd been missing.

"I've been harboring a secret smoldering crush on Debbie." She announces to the group. They were all tall women, taller in high heels, super tall; they gazed down, sipping their drinks. "I came out in the '70's in the women's bars, and I was unpopular."

The bikers moved in a dance bathed in amber lights thru Oils bar, as Stryker told her story.

81

As a very young dike in gay bars, at 16, 17, she'd stood as a spectator while the others played--drank, sang and had women & pals, and fought and died--and lived life.

Yes, a few times she'd been chosen as she waited, a spectator. On the sidelines of the gay party. A pair of arms would reach out, enfold her, let her do her style of lovemaking & she'd join the dance of life. --Too few times.

Mostly, had been alone, left to herself, and so, to her fantasies.

Like most, she could look like she was having a good time--when she was dying inside.

Then Stryker had been accepted into the Outlaws clan. Obnoxious & crude, she fit in easily. She'd stand on top of the bar and yell out everything she liked to do in bed while the bikers clapped their hands in applause. **"I'M A VANILLA DIKE! ONE FINGER'LL DO IT FOR ME! I LIKE TO HUG AND KISS, BUT I CAN STRAP ON A DICK AND I CAN FIST!"** In a kind of rhymey sing-song voice.

Then she'd stomp around waving a dildo in the air, and give a triumphant cry.

The tiny dike had been given sex with sluts at big parties, in which everyone orgied--this was every several months. There was a lot of lonesome time in-between. She wanted more. In fact love was paramount.

That evening preparing go to the clubhouse, she put on a bluejean shirt, & pants with big cuffs.

Stryker felt things in her life were helpless; tho, in retrospect she had more then ever—(little of nothing by the worlds standards).

Remembered those days when she was hanging out in the gay bars & nobody even knew her name.

Times when she wanted to die, yet demanded to be loved. --And had the courage to keep on.

So she kept on, pushing her personality into peoples faces, hoping one day to connect & have a life, and be at peace.

Stryker wasn't use to having friends, nor being with people. -- Other then those long superficial associations in taverns, set in backalleys where straight society might not harass them as much, standing on the edge of the dancefloor without a sex partner, or, one booted foot on the bar rail; where she learned to make small talk and crack jokes and had rehearsed all the slang phrases at home in her mirror talking back to herself.

She appeared to be as one who'd been to a party that had a whole table full of good food--every kind of meat and pie, and she hadn't got to eat a bite. —For her whole life. But wasn't mean because of it.

Had years of training to be a non-person. By a world that hated her, and considered her the least. In which she didn't belong.

In a society that didn't celebrate her sexuality; didn't boast about how many broads she'd banged, in fact hated the idea of a woman having a woman as an object of love & lust.

Rejected. Not fitting in.

Stryker didn't need an umbrella--she'd been out in the rain so many times. Not just a simple while, but years of it. Years.

She wanted to be something when before she hadn't been nothing.

She was a train that had been running off course--off the track, running right along side the track all this time, running over a bumpy road valiantly on her fat little legs, while the ride for the others was smooth. They just seemed to glide thru life.

She was a being set apart.

Stryker lived 30 blocks away, downtown. Her motorcycle had not been running well; it needed parts changed, which she couldn't afford. She worked on the bike with Johnny at the garage, learning to do her own tuning and maintenance. A lot of biker dikes were pros, --doing their own tuning by sound; Stryker was just a novice. Tonight had had to take the bus.

Rode the long bus trip at night with 45 drunken men; just 3 females. --Her & the bus driver. And a mentally ill madwoman with possessions in garbage bags--they get raped also; -- and herself shivering in terror in the front seat of the bus. "I was saying prayers to the Virgin Mary." Amid the drunken violence; men howling and pounding their fists on the metal walls of the bus shouting obscenities. "I was saying prayers to the Virgin, Jesus, and to all the powerful gods I could think of, including my mother and deities I didn't know existed. The ride was safe, but I was shell-shocked, I'm going to take a taxicab home. I have been thru an urban battleground.

Is it worth it? I wonder is this my punishment for being crazy?"

Stryker was intelligent & literate. Back at home in her hotel room was a journal left open on a desk, one of the few pieces of battered furniture. She made this entry on it's pages:

Of all the terror between dusk until dawn, of unsafe streets; of not having money until my government check comes; still, the worst is the long rejection of myself by women. Because that just seems to go on and on. The betrayal by women, beginning with my mother. There is no place for me to turn. I can't go straight like some others because truly it's women I must have. What am I going to do?'
--Kislev 21, 5753/December 15, 1992.

Running down the street for my life. These girl gangs hate each other. The Avengers. PHOOEY! It's too bad they can't get along, then we'd be 300 strong. There is the constant threat of sexual abuse or being murdered by men, so why can't we females stand together like soldiers and guard the spark of peace? Aryan Avengers won't let me join, nor KT, nor Comancho, --because we are not WASPS. KT being black, Comancho being a Native Indian, and me, a Jew. When they burnt down our clubhouse storage room & killed Monique I went into shock. The worst thing was no only the physical brutality, which was over in minutes, but the fear. The fear has gone on and on. So far it has taken **months** of fear & trembling for their raid to submerge into my unconscious and descend in decibels of intensity so that I can tune the memory out, except in my nightmares --of the warlike

blond bikers attacking us with chains & bottles and me being caught in gun crossfire and having to lay down
in the streets behind our bikes to hide. I regained my spirit and go out into the world again with courage. I am still alive, but infuriated that women would do these things to each other. Still, these are isolated cases. Incidents between the Avengers and us Outlaws do seem to occur continuously, but weeks will pass, or months when there is a truce. Anyway, it remains that the long loneliness in my life for a female companion that is worse. Waiting between play with the girls at the bar, and the One Night Stands and the 2 Week Affairs, for the Serial Monogamous Marriage. Oh well, happiness is fat & gay & crazy.
--November 10, 1993.

Curly blond Crystal and Lady were having an argument about prostitution. "Would you let Lisa be one?" (Lisa was her daughter.)

"I'd knock her teeth out of her mouth!" Sez Lady. "That's different! She don't have to! I did! I was in the street! My folks kicked me out of the house when I was 14!"

And against the bar George & Rip reflect on how the city has changed. "I had to take the bus the other day down to Johnny's to pick up the Caddy, Debbie was out in the Porsche; it's my first time on the bus since 1977. Fare's gone up 75 cents. The bus is full of kids speaking Spanish and Chinese. --Not of a word of English did they speak the whole time."

Black walls of the huge bar are streaked with red fire from the lights. Women laugh. Tinkling ice cubes in glasses, & dancers marking time to rhythms on the jukebox.

"I been in this city 52 years," sez George. I'm a big fish in a small pond and I like it. There ought to be more clubs like ours, and more strong armed women. I like to see 'em kicking the bad guys asses on TV on the news."

Nights clock ticked on; the runt dike bought another round of liquor and soft drinks. Biker women are yelling over the music having fun. **"BIG CITY CYCLE, WING NUT CAPITOL OF THE WORLD!"** Screams a frizzy haired dike.

85

"At the union hiring hall, there's this old girl, she hates me yuh know, probably 'cause I won't give her a roll in the hay, 'cause I don't mess with straight women anymore; "EXCUSE ME SIR!" *Sir,* she sez. And I got tits bigger then hers, but she's a big dike herself, in a dress, and she won't give herself away. She won't give an inch."

"Naw, they won't. Them that's passing as straight."

They reminisced about the Great Wars, in which Oil's was founded, when they'd gone thru the neighborhoods on motorcycles in a pack kicking ass, establishing their turf. "There wasn't a thief or a hype left on the street around here when we finished. We kicked their butts, and who are they gonna complain to? The police? Because somebody's stopping them from mugging our women and breaking into our cars?"

"They try to bother one of our women, didn't realize she had a back up."

"We routed 'em!"

"It was a glorious sight!" Rip grins. "A glorious sight!"

Debbie balanced on one long leg, swinging the other, half seated on Frosty's lap. The showgirls had a party of their own going in a circle, with Stryker lumbering about in the middle like a delirious trained bear.

"When I first saw George, she's tall, she's big! I was in awe!"

Rip was taller then Daddy George, but not as heavy; they conferred at the bar together, two huge men-women. "One of them fancy places Debbie drug me into, where they tie your legs to the table so you can't leave unless you leave a $20 tip.".

"Georgina drags me into 'em. I hate 'em."

"Bunch of snots, looken' down their nose at us. We ought to build our own friggen' restaurant."

"Yeah, we was gonna, remember?"

It is the dream of many gays, as they idle away the hours in subterranean taverns--to build a city, with all the services straights have, restaurants, hotels, shops. Resorts where they as drag queens, and drag butches, and cross-gender persons can have fun & be at peace with their own kind.

"Well, at least we got Oils."

"I been here since I been born. There's more gay people around then ever before. Certain things in this city has gone wrong. Crime is worse, the city is bigger and meaner, and everybody's a stranger. Certain things has disintegrated 100%, other things has got better. It's better to be gay, but it's worse to be alive."

Slow sexy music. Angel came over to the party of femmes and took her girl Crystal by the hand, led her from their circle and began to romance her on the dance floor. The length of their bodies entwined; thigh to thigh. Leather to leather.

In the course of their conversation, George spoke of IT again; "I didn't think it would be like this! --to play nursemaid. I intended to Lead! To dress myself up in my best leathers and smile at everybody and tip my cap, make a mighty fist shake it in the air and yell something about dikes seizing power--and fire off my guns if necessary!" Her dominant role must hate this exhausting sugary sweet nurturing facet. To submit, ... to listen to the members gruesome problems--when they became no longer possible to avoid. And when she couldn't get some other Warlord to help. "It's nothing like the boy gang I had when we were kids... Nothing like it!"

"I bet."

George had a sexist view of the incident, which had occurred about two hours earlier. "Men are the ones suppose to stand up and take a stand! That's how you can tell they're a man! Them dikes should have come runnen' and pulled Jody off of Saundra when the fight first started!"

"Men are cowards." Sez Rip. "They travel in packs, 3 or more of them."

"A butch is suppose to rise to her feet to protect the lady, ain't that right!"

George was brave. She definitely wasn't a coward--mainly, was just a big strong woman very accustom to fighting, who lifted heavy weights year in and year out and knew and appreciated the strength of her body.

So many Outlaw ladies wanted to do a scene with Daddy George, & butches did too. George was a lion among lambs. Almost any female in the club would have layed down for her & consider it an honor.

So, it emerged over the 7 years of Outlaw history, that what their club did was have lots of sex, yes, and substance abuse if they chose; social life, which consisted of nights at Oils, parties in private homes, runs on their motorcycles; and motorcycle repair & shop talk. And, something else they dealt with was their interpersonal relations, group spirit and team effort.

So, it was not simple, it was beyond what a motorcycle club is expected to be.

"WING NUTS! EYEBOLTS! I DREAM ABOUT 'EM!" Bellowed the frizzy blond biker.

Rip sez about the world outside, the hustling fast life that runs along in the streets and gutters of the city; "Faces might change, times and dates, but the game's the same. Its the same old con, just new people playing it." She laced her brilliantly ringed fingers together; the expensive leather coat draped over her knees.

"BIG CITY CYCLE!" Howls the dike. **"WING NUT CAPITOL! THIS CITY'S SPINNING 90 MILES AN HOUR!"** -- Her ruined face smiles thru its missing teeth as a jack-o-lantern, in mirth.

Stryker had purchased another round. Feeble old Kelly tosses $2 change back on the bar. Then Debbie opens her arms, holding her drink in one hand, and Stryker stands up on the tips of her boots, puts her hands around that soft waist, presses into her bosom and their mouths meet. A long tongues mixing kiss; Debbie pinches the nipples of the dikes huge breasts with the tips of her fingers, then breaks off the kiss, taking a breath of air & flounces her long hair. **"WOW!"** Sez Stryker.

This scene caused Rip to turn, watch a moment thru languid eyes, then look away again like it didn't make any difference. Mentally she calculates; the night is passing and she hasn't paid for a drink-- they keep being set before her, fresh, cold with ice cubes & swizzle sticks, so she's gonna come out of the club with her money intact.

"FEEL ME SOME MORE WITH YER' FAT LITTLE FINGERS!" Comes a squeal from the femme circle.

"Nobody slapped me around when I was a child. Nobody abused me. I did what ever I wanted to do. I didn't have parents. I was raised by an aunt. She was old and she couldn't keep up with me. It was lucky. I ran all over the neighborhood. Climbed trees, wore pants--I've always wore pants, stayed out playing baseball in the alley--just as long as I was home at dusk, home for dinner. --I wouldn't miss dinner for the world!"

A bottle clattered to the barroom floor, then a glass. --It made a different sound as it shattered and pieces tinkled apart from the original whole.

"It's disgusting, that club." Says George. "About fifty females in the place, but the only one who spoke to me was a transsexual, male to female. She thought I was a guy. I sez, 'sorry to disappoint you, but...'"

"CYCLE CITY! IT GOES AROUND AND AROUND AT 90-DEGREE ANGLES, AND YER' STILL SPINNING!"

A dike with a shaved head howls.

A punk dike has got her first piercing--on her pussy lips. She struts around Oils & from time to time pulls her jeans down to show her flat young stomach tattooed in a solid blue arrow which points to her crotch; spreads her naked white thighs and lets the girls see the tiny gold ring in her cunt.

The crowd had piercings, shaved heads & tattoos. Some others were normal in appearance, but that they looked like a different sex.

Some bikers were so poor they couldn't afford bikes. Others, like Angel's woman Crystal steadfastly drove cars to many events thinking they were safer. Like Georges own Queen Georgina who would no longer get near a motorcycle on the runs--and would follow the gang on a timetable of her own, along with a little processional of cars and perhaps the blue bus, and catch up to the pack 45 minutes late.

Jobs were in short supply, as America weathered a long Depression. Some women worked in nude erotic theatres aimed at male customers. Some lived on the government dole. Others had good paying careers.

"Pimps are getten' to be a rarity out there." Sez Rip gesturing with a broad sweep of her leather coated arm at the Great Beyond outside the fortress of the clubhouse walls. "Most girls today, the driving force behind the extravagant amounts of money they hump for is drugs. Drugs pimp them harder then any humanbeing could. In fact, if it wasn't for me, Debbie would have chosen Crack Cocaine for a master. It's me who kept her off the stuff."

Beyond the present company, away to the rear of the tavern some fems clustered, talking angrily. These pretty women were in appearance different from the masculine denim jacket & trouser wearing dikes with thicksoled shoes, no make-up and short hair, who yelled and stomped and wrestled each other. They were lovely, their gestures soft and liquid, eyes painted in colors, clothing tight & sexy. "Sluts, I cant stand them. All these women running around calling themselves sluts! I don't like it!"

"Yes! And it's them calling themselves sluts, they wanna be, not the butches making them!"

"Well we need more for ourselves then! We need some butch sluts!"

"There already are honey, where have you been?" Sez one, whose fingernails match her lipstick, painted red, and a coiffed hairdo. "You know, the ones who slip around women's houses. Come over and service them after their butches have left for work."

"Yes, but not *official butch sluts*. At the slave parties there's all these women in panties and G strings for the butches."

"And for the fems who like fems."

"Yes, but what about us! Fems who like butches! ---Who aren't sluts, but want a slutty nasty butch at our service!"

The party kept up; empty coca-cola glasses, & bottles of beer pushed aside on the counter, old Kelly was getting tired, & soon would retire to sit at the bar herself & pay one of the biker bartenders to serve. Lady, Sleazy, woman is mellow & talking, weaving on high heels, tosses her shoulder length hair like the rest of the girls, dressed pretty in a cheep but attractive pants suit. "I been in the life, but no longer. I could go thru the hustling clubs and I'd be picken' 'em up. I'm a very pretty girl. When I do go to these bars I get picked up right away. I'll wear my hair back, I won't have a problem, especially if I go back to the dye and change my hair to blond again, and if Sleazy don't put a bullet in me for it, she don't want me worken' ever again. And Lisa don't want it. She's my kid. She's old before her time, we can't keep nothing from our kids."

Sleazy, a lanky butch in bluejeans slides her hand down Lady's slender thighs. "She always thinks about goin' back to hustling when she has a few drinks, 'n it's before payday 'n we're broke."

Debbie flounces her long hair, "Lady wants to go back to work for you." Says she, gazing at the skinny butch.

"She won't let me." Lady says. "The kids won't let me."

Debbie ignores this and says, "Rip's mad at me 'cause I'm drinken'. She's keeping an eye on me, see her! She told me to drink 7-Ups! But I'm being a bad girl! A bad bad girl!

Rip was good to me when we first met, so understanding. She still is. I was an alcoholic & a dopefiend. She let me drink, but she didn't let the alcohol go thru my system. She'd throw my head back & jam her fingers down my throat 'till I gagged, to make me throw up. I was a piece of trash."

"You still are." Sez Lady, with girl-to-girl humor.

Black walls of the tavern loomed into dusty space; body heat warmed them; their voices and music made a comfortable din. Some of the circle of fems sat on the bar down from George & Rip, others stood, tapping their toes or doing body movements in time to the music. "Rip lets me touch her. --She's a real woman too, under all that mannishness. She likes it, the greedy butch. She has a way of doing it so it still makes her feel like a man. Some don't even put a tampex in them-- they gotta get fully loaded on dope first to go to the doctors for a pelvic examination."

In a display of butch bonding two dikes jump up, fists balled **"PUT YER' DUKES UP!"** Circle each other, then leap on each other in a friendly attempt to wrestle the other one down to the napkin strewn floor.

They would fight as sisters, side by side, because they're tough, and mad at being messed-with. They like to fight.

"FIGHT FIGHT FIGHT FIGHT!" Yells one of the black bikers, and soon the club took up their chant: **"FIGHT! FIGHT! FIGHT! FIGHT! FIGHT! HIT 'EM WITH YER' LEFT HAND! HIT 'EM WITH THE RIGHT! KILL THE AVENGERS! KILL THE AVENGERS! KILL AVENGERS! KILL AVENGERS! KILLAVENGERS! KILLAVENGERS! KILLAVENGERS KILLAVENGERS KILLAVENGERSKILLAVENGERSKILL**

AVENGERSKILLAVENGERSKILLAVENGERS! Until their words slurred into one sea of howling rhythm.

And Debbie's answering a question poised by the lanky figure in scroungy bluejeans, her arm around Lady's waist; "I hate them, I think men are jerks, and stupid and self-centered and assholes, --but every time they hand me $250 I like them more. Yeah, I like them, and want to see them again."

And chubby cheeked Stryker was covered with red lipstick prints—as she paid for affection, ---kiss by kiss.

Then the dope dealer came in. An Outlaw member who sold the hard stuff, not the petty marijuana & pills a lot of bikers did, like the Indian sold before she got her job back at Technicolor. The dealer wore dark glasses because she used her product and even the subdued yellow bar lights hurt the retina of her eyes. The lights blazed with circles of radiance. She wore black cloth clothes, a cape furled around her angular shoulders. A car that belonged to her was parked across the street to get them, so as to never carry a huge quantity at once. If police came with a search and seizure on the building they'd have to get a separate warrant for the vehicle. She furled her classy cape. Women were around her almost immediately. When, if ever, she removed her dark glasses, it would unmask eyes wild and big and totally opposite from that laid-back, relaxed, cool character the rest of her portrayed. She stood, aloof amidst the throng of drug-using women, a smirk on her face. Someone planted a kiss of black lipstick on her cheek.

The dope dealer stalked into the toilet area--the Death Eagle spread it's wings; flunkies flooded forward.

"Cocaine, Heroin, Codeine, LSD, Mescaline." No amphetamine, for that was the territory of the Warlord Hawk, who was in growing disfavor with Daddy George. "Pills & powder. I got the powder baby...." Dope addicted women were tugging her cape, begging to be first to buy their hits.

"I got to get rid of that action." Daddy George tells Rip. "It ain't bad to use drugs, I use 'em when I need 'em. But why the hard stuff?

93

And night and day, night and day, they don't quit. Why can't they just pop a few pills, smoke some weed & party?"

"Cause that don't get it." Rip sez drolly. "It's their whole life."

"And Hawk is getting to be a problem, building her drug empire on the Outlaws backs. I told her, you want to make that $3,000 mortgage payment you got? Well go peddle your shit at Lords! Or one of them fancy dyke clubs! ---Yer' pushing it on my people too hard."

"Yuh put people in a box, they got to have an escape." Sez Rip.

"I know it." Sez George. "Why do you think I tolerate her selling 'em in here in the first place? I can't tell these people what to do with their lives. What am I gonna have them do? Go shoot up in the street down there in needle alley and find their naked dead bodies in the morgue-- victimized by the male pushers? I don't know what do about 'em, none of 'em wrote DOPEFIEND on their membership cards when they joined."

It was true. Through the club were now vacant stools, where women had abandon what they were doing before, put their conversations aside, left their partners on the dance floor, to make the long trek to the toilet to score. They'd come out with a bag of dope and a relived look on their faces.

On any given night, thru the sea of partying people there'd be the few, --the 15%, like puppets jerking like panicked puppets on strings until Hawk got to them; until her heavy duty crank injected into their veins set them in motion for hours and days, and then they'd come crashing down & drop into a profound 72-hour sleep. And with this dopeseller it was the same.

George felt the tingling of alarm. Saw Angel leave their group with her loping, confident stride, and make her way also to the toilet. A string of yellow lights beeped like signals across the bar. 'I don't believe this. Her? *Angel?*' The Leader tells herself, making a mental note to discuss this with Angel's mate Crystal. The Outlaw druggies hurried over to get their prescriptions refilled. --The dealer was a walking pharmacy. And Angel's broad back got lost in the shuffle.

Oils toilets were a filthy mess. Bloody kotex, toilet paper trompled into a piss-wet floor. Blood on the walls. The sinks were grimy and hair and crap stuck to them. One toilet was full up with paper & shit and overflowing onto the cement floor.

Beside the entrance a biker leaned against the wall, bluejeans and white jock strap down around her feet; bunched over her boots, her bare ass against the wall. A woman knelt before her, face in the pubic fur at her crotch giving her head. The dike receiving held a bottle by the neck, and between the rocking motions of her hips, which thrust her clit into her partners hot lips; paused, lifted the bottle to her mouth defiantly, and took a swig. It was a portrait glimpsed from a fantasy hell.

Angel walks by nonchalantly; she wasn't there to take a piss either.

Angel forced her way thru the throng. "Hi preacher." Comes a voice out of the drugdealer lips, which barely move when she speaks. People's faces are reflected back from the mirror-lenses of her dark glasses. Counts out single dollar bills in change to a woman. Suddenly someone is creating a commotion at her side. Crystal's fingers pry under the big blonde's arm. "No Angel! Don't!"

"I'll smoke it at the hotel." Sez--the blond butch. "I wanna get high. I don't feel good. My body hurts." It was the pain of old wounds--both physical, from her tragic accident those years before which had done permanent damage and gave her body a throbbing hurt at times--and pain of her soul; which over the years had become a private affair; that now, since she had Crystal, a mate, was slowly being forced to open up to the light of day.

"I'm sellen' it, so it must be the best." The dope dealer stopped to tell a dike, head sharply turned towards the woman so all they could see was her body language, a blank white face with out emotion; eyes invisible behind the shades.

Angel got what she wanted; cigarette shaped marijuana joint wrapped in white papers with both ends twisted closed. ---It was laced with heroin.

Pushed her way into the back of Oils by the new/old storage room to light it up. Fire from her matchbook, ironic streaked their forms flickering against the new plywood that had been nailed over the old charred beams where the disastrous-fire had been 3 months ago. Fingernails pried into her shirt, but she pushed Crystal away. "I gotta get high. I just gotta! It's been *weeks.* Don't get mad at me. There's things on my mind, I just want to let go and forget about stuff. And my body hurts."

Clouds of smoke filled the area, Angel coughed out smoke, sucked up another drag, held it in her lungs until her eyes watered then let it out slow. By now her curly blond fem was resigned. Leaned against her chest.

She only smoked half, then snuffed it out, and put the roach carefully away in one of the zipper pockets of her black leather jacket--as if it was gold. They went back to the bar.

About 15 minutes after smoking the joint angel found she had climbed inside the music. Was aware of it, within its rushing stream. Could feel each single note isolated, from the song. Actual time went by in it's own world above her. She was down IN herself riding on a new current, and Crystal, and everybody else was far away.

Was aware of her woman talking to Frosty, then George, and their heads turning to stare at her, but they were far away in time & space and she didn't care. 'By the time we leave this high will be gone, and I'll be straight enough to drive.' This was her last responsible thought, as she drifted off into a golden glow of fantasy.

"Frosty! Crystal! Dena! Lady! Stella! *Debbie!* I gottcha all to myself! I'm so lucky!" Stryker whirled, turning from one fem to the other.

"Awww... I think I better go back to my stupid act, it keeps me out of trouble." Sez Stryker after awhile.

"Gee... If I had two dollars, you'd see a drink setten' in front of me..."Coos Debbie in a soft little innocent voice.

Stryker hadn't grown even to 5'. Big bust --blimpy. The little dike bustled about within the circle of beautiful ladies. From time to time their butches would come by take their arms and lead them away to dance, and Crystal had left to stand behind Angel who sat on the barstool knees spread, head nodding, and encircle her with her arms.

"Yuh see, I mean business." Stryker sez. "I want one of you tonight." And all the women titter with uncomfortable laughter.

Georgina talks to a young biker about some domestic problem. The 70-year old Kelly's legs gave out. She'd been on the job 3 hours. Her hair was grey; high on top and slicked back behind her ears flattened to the sides of her head in an ancient butch style. Face wrinkled, but mirthful. ---He/she had survived lesbian life and lived to talk about it. She'd sent a young biker they'd trained to tend bar behind the counter, and then came out and sat next to Georgina.

Kelly was not a member of the Outlaws. Owned, and worked the bar, that was it. Kelly was more straightlaced then one would think considering the environment. Had her own circle of a few old friends she'd known since the 1940's, and other older dikes met more recently at conservative clubs. So didn't socialize with the bikers except at Oils. Not attending any of the private parties nor visiting their houses. George had been to Kelly's house only twice in the 7 years the Outlaws had been a club and that was on emergency business.

The fems had been together in a fem-fest long enough, --over 3 hours. And Comancho the Indian, a feather stuck in a red headband that held back her thick black butch hair, and Johnny, in greasy mechanics overalls, sauntered over for their wives. Rips long arm reached out and grabbed Debbie to her.

"Hello ladies." Sez Johnny as she walks into the circle, & takes her wife Stella Dallas by the hand.

"And gentlemen." Pipes up Stryker.

"Yer' no gentlemen Stryker. 'Course, yer' no lady either." They all laugh.

After a check-in with their ladies, and a few dances, the boys saunter back to the pooltable and their conversations, and once again the circle of fems converged. Debbie was getting drunk & talking girl talk to Crystal & Lady confidently. "Hell, I'd get up to go work, take a shower, and I'd have bruises. I'd have to cover them up with make up. Blue bruises all over me. She wanted to be rough so I let her. She's my man. When she wants it, she wants it right that second. Once I had to have a drink first, she slaps the drink right out of my hand. She throws me on the bed. I'm so use to it--been this way so long, 10 years."

"That's a long time." Crystal sez. "You're lucky you two have lasted that long. No matter if she does hit you sometimes. I never seen no broken bones."

"Times we're fucking, she'll grab my hair and throw my head back. I just don't know any other way." Debbie turns and looks down. Stryker has come up & with soft hands strokes her arm. "You're so tender." Deb tells her.

"I'm not rough enough." Sez Stryker.

"You're so big--short but big. Big hearted."

"And you're just the opposite. **Oops !** I mean you're tall!" Stryker blurts out, then covers her mouth. "CRAZY GIRL!" She yells, and slaps herself. Debbie looks down at her with patience bordering on irritation. Her lovely loose long brown hair hangs past her shoulders, tasteful make up, beautiful figure, big breasts and round hips poured into tight fitting blouse & pants. Ignoring the butch dike she turns back to the ladies.

"I lost all my clothes, my jewelry, I lost everything. Then I met Rip. After she beat me up, kept beating me, and beating me I told her, yes, I'll turn the tricks, I'll do anything.

She made me strong.

I just wanted to lay around our apartment and get high on dope & drink and watch TV and eat and I was getting fat."

"LET ME TAKE YOU AWAY FROM ALL THIS!" A voice explodes under her chin; the fat dike stares up, bleary eyes serious. Debbie pops a piece of pink gum. Looks down at her for a split second then continues.

"She pushes the hell out of me, that's why we got what we got.

One time when I was worken' out of this club downtown, I'm foolen' around with the other girls, chit chat, like we are now, and who walks in but Rip. I was drinken', and wasn't suppose to be. I heard a smack, it's my face. She threw me into the Cadillac and drove me home yelling at me--I was drunk. Knocked me around, gave me a bloody lip, raped me. --Probably raped me. So, 4 hours later she was so sorry for what she did."

Georgina's sitting at the bar not far away, and hears this heated conversation of the younger women. A fat hand pats black ringlets of her hair. Head bends to Kelly and confides, "these girls, what they go thru ! Me and Georgie never fight, not like that! One time I came out of a club where I was dancing and took a girl with me--I didn't want to be alone. I just wanted to be with someone, we had the whole evening to kill between shows, 2 hours off, then a 15-minute show, then 2 more hours off. We were going down the street to get something to eat and get away from the godawfull place, we're by the diner, and she had her arm around me, and here's George. --She spied on me alot. **'Ohmygod!'** I'm thinking, 'she's gonna kill me', but no. George is too levelheaded. She grabs me, throws me in her truck and drives me home. Shoves me in the bedroom & locks the door. I miss my show and get fired. I go to work somewhere else, she's hanging around there. She just gradually talked me out of my career that's all. Kept at me to get out of it. 'Dancing for all those damn men!' she said. 'I'll open a club and you can dance for women!' Well! Yuh see how often that is! -- Three times a year!"

99

"These dikes wouldn't know a good dance if they saw it." Sez the gray-haired bar owner, dryly.   "It ain't like it was in the old days, when they had really nice shows. All these gals want is smut. Smut and sex, and more sex."

"I use art in my shows." Says Georgina.

Debbie weaved on long legs, her arms entwined with Lady on her right side, and Dena at her left. "She does have rough sex, that's one thing I like. You're different. --I like you too." Debbie gazes down at Stryker, with pity.

"Rip and I are different people.   Different astrological signs, different ages, different sizes. And she's mean, I'm nice."

Debbie gave a little laugh, uneasy; then turned back to the girls to continue: "I don't miss her violence. To this day I get sick, from being shoved around so much. But it wasn't just Rip that done it. Girls in jail & men too. Rip calmed down after we were together a few years, after she grew to trust me; and because we both cut down on the drinking. I was so high and drunk, she might have done so much I don't remember. I'd black out.   Next morning I'd be in such pain, wonder what in the hell did she do to me this time?

I didn't mind if she raped me. If she shoved me around, hit me and punched me I didn't like that.   I was always drunk, then I didn't feel it. Not that I'm sober now, but she is stronger and much more wild-because we were both on drugs. Now I really regret it--that I got so fucked up on drugs, and I really resent her for that, treating me so raw. She body slammed me.

When I first saw George I hollered, **'WHAT A DIKE!'** I just stood there. She looked like the dike granddaddy of them all, she tipped the scales at 300 pounds.

Rip wanted me to meet George because they were best pals, for years, and her last woman had run out on her, and I was going to be her new filly. **'I BET SHE'S GOT A DICK! BET SHE DOES!'** I hollered, I was drunk. Rip pushed me across a table, and laid me out.

100

'LOOK WHAT I FOUND!' She says, and pulls open my blouse and pulls down my bra so my tits pop out and Daddy George got an eyeful."

"SAY SMART ASS! S H U T   U P! I CAN HEAR EVERYTHING!" Rip yells from her stool down the bar; her liquid eyes freeze into pinpoints, staring down Debbie. Her long trousered legs come untwined from the barstool rungs; shakes her shoulders loose under the leather coat like she's about to come over to them.

"WHOOPS DADDY! I'M NOT BEING BAD! I'M JUST HAVING FUN! I'M NOT BEING A BAD GIRL!"

"KEEP YER' MOUTH SHUT!" Rip hollers back, then turns her back on Debbie; facing towards the bar; George stares at the fancy women from under her biker cap a moment, then swivels back too.

Stryker says: "I been masturbating every night. I got to stop that; it drains me. I'm desirous. I got to do it every day." Stryker was a portrait of neglect, big pants cuffs whose ends were walked upon by her heels; turned-over boots, standing on the floor littered with cigarette butts.

"I'm always the last one sitting in the booth, waiting for some girl to come my way.

The hardest thing in the world is to be rejected by your own mother. I didn't have a father either."

Johnny was leaning against the bar with her wife Stella Dallas, on the outer edge of the femme-circle. She spoke; "I dunno about you good buddy, but I got a bitch tonight, a fine bitch in a leather skirt and high heels and a tiny halter top and chains instead of bracelets and wild teased hair, as you can see, standen' right here; she looks so fine; & she's willing. And she's mine. She does it for *free*. For *me!"* Giving the fat Stryker a dark look. "And I found her right here, in the Outlaws club. I'm gonna take her home, lay her down in my bed and ride her lesbian cunt with my slimy sex and open the doors to paradise. **F.U.C.K!"** And Johnny does a nasty dance, pumps her hips in & out.

"She don't know anything about me." Little Stryker tells the mechanic in greasy jeans; watching her pump her hips. "It's a relationship built on lies. She thinks I'm a jerk! She believes stuff people say about me behind my back." Stryker turns to the object of her interest, Debbie, and says; "Don't tell me about fisting, about the drugs, or the drinking, tell me about *you*." The tiny fat dike was hot under the collar and wanted to get to fuck that night, and felt if she didn't the need would back up like a clogged drain and cook her brains.

A young dike butch-fem couple in leather chaps & jackets, sexy, is talking to Georgina, one of them on each side. The fat Queen sat on her barstool throne listening and advising them on their new relationship. It carried weight to members of the Outlaws that their Leader and her wife had lived together 25 years--and were still sexually active together, and not merely roommates for financial security. The couple was identical but that one had very short hair & no lipstick, and the other had blue lipstick and teased hair dyed blue to match. By the end of the conversation, they were wrapped up within their leather arms, squeezing one another's tits; tongues down each others throats.

"Stryker, tell 'em about the time you got that date thru the sex ads." Asks a lady.

"I had a date with a nice square girl." Stryker complains. "I met her thru the sex ads in a gay newspaper. She's a WASP and works in the Financial District. Very middle class. She don't know nothing about life down here at Oils, and I want to keep it that way. 'This is my chance at happiness!' I thought. But she falls in love with some other dike--a professional who wears business suits & who is sane. She told me, 'If you really love me you won't stand in my way!' I went home, buried my face in my pillow and cried."

"How did you find out about our club?"

"I had a bisexual friend into all kinds of kinky stuff; an 80/20 dominate lady. We slept together in my bed, between my sheets. She had nice marks on her from whippings. Marks and Linen. Ha Ha.

Excuse the pun. She was 23. I met her at a pagan ritual. She was a member of the Outlaws and did biker stuff, then, once she gets me into it, she quits & runs off to live in the country with some guy with long hair and lovebeeds. Her philosophy was that all men are inferior. They should be submissive, and made to submit to women and ground under her high heels and those who wouldn't submit should be shot. She only lets lesbians whip her. She made me join the Outlaws because she said I needed to round out my education."

"Tell 'em about the times you went to Madame Valoria's house on A Street."

"All those men, I was the only dike."

Debbie tossed her head, stared at the crazy girl. "I feel sorry for women who pay for sex. They aren't getting what they're paying for. Because those whores really like men, they don't like women. Men don't actually get what they pay for either. The hookers hate the men they're with because the men are assholes, but when it comes right down to it they like men... The women that do come around me, I really do appreciate it, because I'm really sick of men. I had one wow, about a year back. She stuck a finger in me, fucked me."

"Did she come?"

"Yes."

Stryker nodded, solemn, looked up into Debbie's eyes.

"We used a dildo on each other. She brought it with her." Debbie tossed her brown hair, glanced down at Stryker. "Because I work the sex industry I see the other side. I see the shit those girls tell people. The shit they pull. I feel sorry for people like you, you're so fooled by it." Debbie was angry. Her mascara tinted eyes flashed. "Did those women at Valoria's ever compliment you on your lovemaking?"

"No..."

"How would they look at you?!" Debbie questioned the fat dike in a pissed tone.

"Like I was a weird freak."

"Did you always get off?"

"Yes!"

"Did some of the girls enjoy it?"

"Some of them like it Debbie!" Said Stryker, hopefully.

"Some probably do, because it's a change. It's a change from routine. It's hard to say, every girl's different. I've seen what's out there--it's some sorry shit. It ain't even worth it to talk about, -it's just bullshit. One thing about hookers," Debbie sez, her lipstick is faded pink; has worn off her mouth onto many glasses of alcohol. Lifts a painted finger to the sky; "Remember this Stryker! They're out for one thing---to get some money and they're trying to make it as short as possible. A working girl is just out to get your money! I'll tell you one thing about whores—they've been fucked so many times they don't get any pleasure out of it, it's a joke and the men think they really get off on them. And that's what they probably think about you!"

Then she added, curiously, "What made you cum the most?"

"Cunt to cunt."

"They're really from bad homes or they wouldn't be doing it from the beginning. They could be working minimum wage jobs, *anything!*" Crystal, the curly blond interjects. "So they're always in a bad mood, or high. I was a happy child, I don't have to do that kind of stuff. I'd rather *starve.*"

"When I was a kid I went in the 25-cent peep shows. In the nasty movie arcades. Now they got live private shows with a little booth, girl behind a glass cage; you look but can't touch." Says Johnny, the mechanic. Her stocky figure fills out under a uniform. Oil under her fingernails. "The problem is, guys really like to fuck. Straight women have all these guys after them, so they got their own

104

transaction going on between them. So, what does that leave a lesbian who really like to fuck? Zilch. Nada. Nothing." Johnny made a tiny circle with her oily hand. "In the first place the dike is broke, she's poor & trying to survive on practically nothing. In the second place she shouldn't have to pay another sister. No sister should be without sex, without companionship, without a roof over her head or food or fun times. We have to do our transactions different. We ain't got the money men got, or the power, so we gotta learn to build what we need together. To share & help each other. Now we got a club, we got our own women. A lot of girls like Deb who turn tricks, to others who don't even touch anybody, who just dance in those glass cages. They work those places for men for the money, & give their hearts & bodies to women exclusively. Just get an Outlaw girl, get her to put a show on for you. Get a sexy girl. Make love together. Make up all you missed in your past."

"When my butch Angel was a kid that's the kind of women she went for." Crystal said. "Cause there was no lesbians around, not visible. Just honky-tonk girls, was the only ones she could find. The good girls weren't coming out of their houses at night. So she didn't know who they were."

Johnny agrees. "A lot of butches get their education in love in the arms of women who ain't necessarily her sexual preference."

And then they were all talking about it. The lanky butch in bluejeans who worked as a janitor in a hospital, Sleazy, told the group; "I had a male friend in the past, he was always trying to help me get a woman, the best way he knew how---the way *he* got women. I got mad at the fact I had to go thru a man to get to a woman. That's the way the world was set up. Even the dike bars was run by men-- the Mafia, when I was a kid."

The Outlaws ran the gamut of bikers hooked on their Harleys, who liked to ride in the rain, in the hail, to sedate automobile drivers who wore their safety belts. Some experienced the unbelievable rumble between their legs; that power, the wind in their hair riding a motorcycle; others got to Oils club in a team of five, huddled together inside the Blue Bus.

Wither they owned bikes or not was negotiable. To make sure they had women. And to be a family. This was the main purpose of the Outlaws.

Females set up as sex symbols then locked behind glass walls, behind an invisible veil of Purdah. Or a state of sex slaves inside the walled harems of Arabia. --Except for dikes who sneaked into the harem, and went around lifting up their veils, searching for their own.

With the advent of the feminist movement, things began to change--for the better.

And all most lesbians wanted was to know their sisters, to find where they were, to make some opening in the straight imprisonment of the culture, which enveloped them and cut them off from each other.

"When I was 14;" Sez Crystal; "I wanted to know, 'who are these special women,' I wanted to know how to get them & what to do with one after I got her." And this fire for a woman burning in her sex, in her heart, in her mind, not yet expressed. That was the life of a teenager, trying to come out.

"My first woman stood up, put on her clothes and left. She didn't want me as a woman."

Debbie was angry. "I'm just completely disgusted by women who work the sex industry. --The dancers, the prosties, --it's all for men, and fucking men, and basically their straight.   I'm disgusted by it. Disgusted. It's an easy way to make money, but you should like men to do it, I'm beginning to hate it, and do it less and less; I try to do the kinky stuff to them, and let them jerk themselves off."

When Angel came out of the nod, the backdrop of the tavern surfaced back into her reality. Ordered a coke to satisfy a sudden craving for sweetness. Swiveled on the red vinyl barstool, wiped her bleary eyes on the back of her hand, to watch her friends. The 80-member club was partying strong.

About then Angel notices the fat short dike Stryker is setting everybody up, buying round after rounds of drinks. A young butch bartender barely 17 had replaced Kelly during the long absent mental no-zone in which she'd been in the nod; she poured jiggers of alcohol, and popped open the tops of bottles & set them on the counter in front of the partying femmes. 'Damn! Debbie's hustling her!' Debbie bent at the knee, tipped her head down once more to receive a wet tongue to tongue kiss and allowed her breasts to be felt by the dike, and opened her legs to let Stryker put her thigh in-between them and hump – for about ten seconds. The miserable scene revealed itself. 'That's what she's doing with her check!'

At the first of each month Stryker received a $660 SSI government check. Paid $260 for her room, the rest was for food, medicine, and expenses for the month. It was to keep her motorcycle running so she could get around town. But she was spending a big hunk of it tonight.

Party lights, red, & blue, & green. "You need a woman to take care of you." Ran one feminine hand expertly over Strykers shoulders, down her back, and around and down the fat front across her fly.

"YER GONNA GET THE POOR KID ALL HOT AND BOTHERED." Yells rip from the bar. Stryker shouts back; **"LET HER DO IT! LET HER DO IT! DON'T STOP HER! THIS IS LIFE OR DEATH TO ME! YUH JUST DON'T KNOW THIS MEANS THE WORLD TO ME!"**

Debbie pushed aside a patch of short hair over Strykers ear & whispered into it; "All they do at Valoria's is hustle men honey. You need a woman who knows how to service cunt." Ran red nailed fingers up the dikes shirtfront, over her big tits. "A lot of girls in here sleep around. Ones, who are single. Ones who are married, they still play." Stryker encircled the hustler's tiny waist--all that humping as a sex worker kept her thin---, felt Debs soft bosom, so full; as Deb continued; "A woman who *likes* a woman, who really *wants* a woman, like *I* do." At the bar George & Rip watch. The pimp eyes them with a languid expression, her knees open, leather on long legs; broad, flat chest in a shirt open at the collar; gold chains at her neck, man style, men's shoes on the rung of the stool, and leather coat trailing on the floor.

"Horny little dike." Debbie breathes into Strykers ear.

"How much do you charge?" Stryker breathes back into her perfumed ear.

"$250 for the first hour, the rest is negotiable."

"How much for dikes?" Comes the eager voice.

"………. I hadn't thought about it." Debbie replies.

Right next to them in the crowded space, Frosty and Crystal are nearly knocked off their high heel boots by the proposition they have just overheard. All their attention focuses on the runt biker.

"Uh.... *$200?* .... That's still a lot!" Stryker is saying. Wanting desperately to say yes, to agree with her price, but just amazed at the amount of money.

'Christ! I don't believe her!' The mechanic thinks, smacks the side of her head. On a barstool just down the way Angel sees it too. The begging dike, the glamorous showgirl. Blond hair flows to her shoulders & her skin, sweaty from the effects of dope, now worn off, has grown clammy. A frown on her face. Frosty & Crystal cast glances at each other, but say nothing for fear of offending their friend Deb, and Dena's watching, listening to it all with great interest. Finally Johnny breaks the ice. "Stryker there's sluts will fuck yuh! Just wait for the next party, or an orgy. If yuh just hang around Oils long enough you'll meet some gal in here!   Yuh ain't gonna spend yer last money like that –being a trick! --Yuh can't even get yer bike fixed!" Johnny gazes at Deb with thinly veiled anger; "This dike's bike is sitting in my garage this minute, broke. We're tearing it apart. It needs about $150 worth of parts, I ain't even chargen' her to work on it!   And yer gonna charge her fer' you to work on her? Fuck! Shit! Debbie! Tell her to go find a slut Deb! You ain't gonna charge your sister just for a piece of ass are yuh?"

Debbie blinks mascara eyes, gives no answer but a sickeningly sweet smile.

"NO!" Stryker tips back her head & yells, arms tight around Debbie's soft body. "NO! DON'T MAKE HER CHANGE HER MIND! I DON'T WANT TO WAIT AROUND FOR A SLUT! I WANT DEB! I WANT *CONTROL!* I'M SICK OF WAITING FOR SEX! AND MAYBE I'LL GET LUCKY, MAYBE I WON'T! EVEN SLUTS TELL ME *NO!* I WANT SEX! AND I WANT DEB, *AND I WANT HER NOW!"* Curly head Crystal gazes with venom at Debbie, expecting her to set things straight, woman to woman, sister to sister, but the pretty hooker replies only with the smile, not committing any opinion. And certainly not discouraging the runt biker whose drooling over her size 48-tits. The mechanic grabs Stryker under her arm with an oily hand. "Look chump, yer suppose to be Jewish, remember? Don't they count every penny? You got a bike sitten' in my garage I'm practically fixen' for free, and you been throwen' $20 bills around all night! I ain't asked you for $200 to fix your goddamn bike! Why should you pay a sister to fuck? There's women in here who free fuck! Don't be stupid! And how're yuh gonna get around town all this month if you can't buy parts for your bike?"

"I'M A JEWITCH! I'M JEWITCH! NOT JEWISH! I AIN'T THE JEWISH RELIGION! NOT NO MORE! I'M A *PAGAN!* PAGANS FUCK! IT'S PART OF OUR RELIGION! GODDESS WORSHIP! AND DEB'S MY GODDESS! *NO! NO! NO!"* Yells Stryker, furious, stomping her feet, as Johnny and Sleazy pry their hands under her fat arms, pull her off of Debbie and march her across the room for a man to man talk. Angel slides off the barstool and in a loping gait goes off to join them, grabbing the fat dike around her middle in a butch hug. There, the bluejean & leather crew confront Stryker:

"She's Rips woman!"

"SHE SLEEPS WITH EVERYBODY ELSE!"

"She sleeps with men for money!"

"Yeah! And she won 't sleep with dikes! .... Rip won't let her! Just Dena, or one of the party girls! Not another butch! Are you a party girl Stryker? Are you a pretty lady? That's all Rip lets her have! --So she can watch! She's a dirty old man!"

"SO AM I A DIRTY OLD DIKE! I'M DIRTY! I'M DIRTY! I WANNA HAVE FUN LIKE ALL YOUSE GUYS HAVE! *I WANT TO FUCK DEB!* RIP'LL LET HER SLEEP WITH WOMEN FOR MONEY!"

"NOT NO WOMEN IN THIS CLUB SHE WON'T!"

"YES SHE WILL! I BET SHE WILL! I'LL ASK HER! *RIP! RIP! HEY RIP!"*

Crystal reaches down and grabs the dikes shirtfront, mad; "YOU DON'T HAVE ANY MONEY! YOU GOT TO GET YOUR BIKE FIXED! YOU GOT TO EAT THE REST OF THIS MONTH! FORGET DEB! SHE'S HAPPY WITH RIP! YOU AREN'T GONNA SAVE HER AND HAVE HER FALL IN LOVE WITH YOU! SHE'S HAPPY! IT'S NOT AS BAD AT IT SEEMS!" Crystal sees deeper into Strykers need.

"RIP TREATS HER MEAN!" Stryker squinches her face up, and begs the crowd of dikes surrounding her to understand. **"I'D TREAT HER GOOD!"**

Debbie has danced back over to her pimp, there Rip informs her; "this is cutting into your money making time!"

Debbie jitters in open toed shoes, nervously.

"IT'S YOUR MONEY MAKING TIME!"

"Aw, give her a night off Rip." "Sez George.

Voices faint, carry from the side of the tavern against a redstreeked black wall. **"I WANT CONTROL OVER MY LIFE! IF I'M HORNY I WANNA FUCK! I'M SICK OF FUCKEN' MYSELF!**

110

I'M PISSED I GOTTA WAIT FOR SLUTS TO MAKE UP THEIR MINDS!"

'You didn't do any work!" Rip glares at Debbie from her barstool, where her once nonchalant figure hung lax & loose over the bar has now straightened up to full height; she's wearing a dead serious expression.

"I DID A LOT OF WORK! I DANCED ALL NIGHT! THAT'S MORE IMPORTANT!"

Rip glares at Debbie. "$250 for all night? I need $500! This is Saturday! Best working night of the week! Money's flowen' like water out there!" Gestures with a broad sweep of her ringed hand, moving folds of the long leather coat. **"Get into that phonebooth and call one of your regular johns!"**

"NO!" Debbie pouts. "I'm saving them for weekdays, when business is slower. I don't want to work tonight!   I want to have fun!" She points across the barroom floor: "That little dike there has got a wad of money, she's loaded. We're gonna come to an agreement ... *Daddy*. Now be nice to Debbie!" And twines her fingers thru Rips lapel, and blinks at her with a Little-Girl-Innocent Look.

"Shit."

Meantime Daddy George's big bulk has lumbered off the barstool. The black leather clad giant strides thru the crowd of partying female bikers on the dancefloor, to the group by the wall who are yelling at Stryker, holding her back, trying to talk sense to her; and she's yelling loud back at them, so the veins in her plump neck stand out; face tipped up to the ceiling: *"I L.O.V.E. HER!"*

It was near the end of the night.

Daddy George spoke with the inflection of one whose had a few drinks. **"Wait, wait! Just a minute, hold on! Let me talk!"** George raises her voice. "I'm gonna tell you this for yer own good, not mine! Because I know what those girls are gonna try to do to

111

you! Her and Dena both, they're tryen' to hustle you, that's what their fortunes built on. It's like a bad habit, they can't even help it themselves. Don't fault 'em for it! But they don't mean you no good. Yer gonna throw your government check away, and won't have no money for the rest of the month. Yer Outlaws club dues will go unpaid, we'll have to send somebody over there to bring you groceries--all on account of a piece of cunt. And after you do what you wanna do, and they got what they want from you, they're gonna forget you exist! They ain't gonna fall in love with you Stryker! And wait to see what Deb throws yer $200 away on! Some trivial shit that strikes her fancy-- A dress she's been thinkin' about buying but didn't have the time. She'll wear it once, & it'll wind up on the floor of her walk-in clothes closet with the rest of her crap. It's like a pig pen in Rip's house, they got so much stuff all because of suckers like you!"

"I WANNA FUCK! I WANT IT NOW! I WANT CONTROL OVER MY SEX LIFE I'M SICK OF BEING A MISERABLE RUNT WHOSE CUNT IS SLIMY AND WET AND AIN'T GOT NO WOMAN TO PLAY WITH HER!"

"HOLD ON! HOLD ON! Yer' goin' 90-miles-a-minute standin' still." George towers over the tiny dike.

"I LO.V.E. HER!" Stryker closes her eyes and screams from clenched teeth, veins bulging blue in a white neck.

Daddy George looks down at the fat dike without comment.

George, because of physical size, mannish demeanor and a commanding personality had got a fair share of women throughout her life. Once she took leadership of the club, females began to fall all over her, because of the position she held. Lack of women had never been a problem, not one single day of her life. George could go in straight bars, and charm barfly girls, who weren't quite sure what she/he was, and wind up in their beds the next morning. She didn't understand what it meant to be lonely, not with so many goddamn people in the world.

Daddy George had power. Lacked for nothing. Had attention and love of a life partner who knew her well. Had play partners for sex fantasy games on the side. With so many sex addicts attracted to their club, there was always a ready and willing labor pool of slaves who would play in any way and do anything demanded of them.

That air of superiority boys get when they become men, Daddy George had gotten it too.

Superior in size, power, she was always handed a greater respect, then as a woman. Dressed as a man, and passing much of her life, with a gruff manner to back it up, people went to lengths to either avoid her, or appease her. And she would fight, that was well known.

She was a sadist. Had enjoyed torturing weaker girls and boys in her neighborhood, as her boy's gang roamed far and wide. George had been a bully as a kid, and grown up to be a big sadist.

Maybe it was a kind of Devine Retribution, or Karma she now faced, with the weights of the world upon her shoulders, --those female problems and dike despondencies she had to minister to as Leader Of The Pack.

"Lesbians got to get things for ourselves." Somebody's saying.

"Yeah, but like this?" Somebody else replies.

The group relaxes their hold on the bantam dike, whose crying, big tears roll down her cheeks.

"Lesbians! I'm sick of the word!" Daddy George spat.

Like many strong men, Daddy George could make the remark, 'I've never been afraid to walk down the streets in my life. Night time, bad bars, downtown, or redneck town, nowhere. I never been afraid. I'm big, and I pack a gun. I'll kill anybody who gets near me.' The idea of fear was foreign to her. "Stryker," she said in a base voice; putting one meaty arm around the fat dyke; "I've never met anyone like you before. You just go out in the street, not even a dollar in your pocket, a bus token and nothing else. You don't give a damn if yuh fix yer bike or not. I got a van and a bike. Credit cards, cash, emergency tow card..."

"That's cause I'm crazy, Daddy." Sez Stryker.

She had wanted to kill herself, been afraid, --hungry, poor, and angry much of her life. And was amazed to think that this just wasn't a way of life for most Americans.

The two turned and walked, Daddy's big leather arm over Stryker's shoulders, left the others and went to lean against the bar further off, in privacy. "That's what the clubs all about." Sez Daddy George. "Taking care of each other. In fights. To back yer' sister up. To help dikes with their bikes… and with women."

"I want to fuck." Moans the small dike.

"I know." George pats her on the back with a big paw. "I understand. Hmmm. There's plenty women in here--all kinds. Some not so pretty. Some, Stryker, I know, have eyes for you, but, face it, not everybody's got the looks of Debbie, or Dena. There's all **kinds** of women. Ones that work legit jobs, even a few professional girls; -- we got an architect, one almost a doctor... You need a rough lady, a slut. --A nice polite girl is gonna give you earthly heartaches 'cause yuh can't keep her. She's gonna watch you eat one day at a fancy restaurant, see yer table manners, how yuh spill food down yer front, and she's gonna leave you right there. You know you ain't proper and correct, Debbie is proper and correct—that is she tries to be—'cause she's a poor girl whose turned rich. Yuh got to get a type who ain't got no manners to speak of. Now a lot of our girls, they don't care about that stuff and nonsense noways. You need a full time lady. 'Cause yer lonely. Get a full time partner. Then, concentrate on picking up quick lays on the side for fun. But have a real relationship like a lot of us do, so you won't be in so much in need. It won't be hard. There's older gals, and gals who ain't so pretty who could be interested in you. Once you get her, pound her in bed. Ladies like that, not just sluts. And you have a nice bike. -- Even if it is a Shovel Head throttle 'an yuh gotta take yer' hands off the handlebars to teach back to the throttle 'n give it gas, --Yuh got that. Yuh got a steady income, yuh can put a roof over her head. When you get her, pound her 'till she hollers Quit! I can go 45 minutes." Daddy George brags.

Late partyers drag out the door. Dikes gun up their bikes in front of Oils. Red streaked sections of floor are beginning to appear, void of people; as lights blink down onto crumpled napkins & litter.

Dena saunters by, casting a look over at George & Stryker. The Leader has her arm around the dike, one big boot propped up on the bar rail. Black leather & silver studs glimmer. Dena is Daddy Georges mistress, they have negotiations of their own to work out if she could spare a minute. Daddy glares back at her from dark eyes; knowing that Dena'd like to clip Stryker's wallet just as bad as Debbie, but she won't because of Outlaw rules.

"I gotta find a girl who likes big tits." Stryker sniffs. "Like mine. I once had a girl with fake tits."

"You had a lot of girls since you joined the Outlaws! You'll get more! Just don't go crazy and throw all yer'' money away! Then you'll loose yer' hotel room, and where're yuh gonna live? You won't have nowhere to bring her home to!"

"Rip ain't got no tits. Debbie can feel my tits." Stryker hooked her bootheels into the lower rung of a silver barstool, stood straight up, tall, thrust her huge bosom over the bar, and hammered an empty glass on it; **"BARTENDER!"** Hollering for more. All she could think about was the light touch of the woman's fingertips; how good it felt; and it was driving her wild. Then turned up the glass and gulped down her drink.

Some Outlaw women had come to maturity thru sickness, poverty and sexual abuse. They were attracted to the strength & hardness of the gang.

A particular sub-group, a lot of those dikes who called themselves sluts, who hung around the bikers as loose women, had been abused as girls. Might have been nine, or ten, weighing just 60 pounds; and had things done to her that shouldn't be done to an adult.

115

They had come from shadowy worlds of hardship and trauma. &
others from feast and plenty.

& everybody was looking for something.

Queen Georgina and Crystal let the hustlers do their shoptalk, and
had gone into a separate conversation: "To look pretty you can't bend
your face into just any kind of position. Wrinkles have more
character, yes, but in order to be beautiful you have to keep your face
in a certain position."

The motley crew disbanded for the night. Black leather, or for
those too poor to afford leather yet, bluejean vests & jeans, and
gymshoes. Dark interior walls painted black for the effect. Girl
dikes, and boy dikes, and kiki androg's look-alikes. Dressed in cute
pink outfits, or bad spike heels. What use did society have for them?
Most would never bare children. They kicked men's ass whenever
they could. They swore, smoked dope, and stole.

Stryker's still whining, to Johnny and Angel and their wives.
Daddy George has left. The butches help the fat dike on with her
jacket—a ragged vest with sleeves cut off, frayed white threads fuzzy
along the seams, non-existent buttonholes which were only gaps.
"She has everything handed to her on a platter because she's so
beautiful! She don't have to go thru the sex ads! She just walks in a
room, everybody *wants* her!"

"Yuh got yer sister Outlaws, yuh don't need the sex ads no more."

"But it's such a struggle! --It's not like being beautiful!"

"Yer beautiful! Yuh got a beautiful mind!"

I'm just a piece of meat! That's all!" Sobs Stryker. "My
government paycheck, that's all the girls want! That's all I'm good
for! She was gonna charge me **$200!** For just one hour!" Stryker
put her head down on the bar, folding her arms over it. "I was gonna
give her $200, if she'd come home with me right that minute."

"You need a wife." Sez Angel.

116

Chapter Eleven

Stryker was one of the Outlaws who lived downtown. They ran a gamut from luxury hotels which Deb, Dena and other Call Girl bikers of the club might rent to turn their high price tricks, to nice, fairly expensive room-plus-bath as Angel & Crystal; whose a shop girl in a Department store just a block away; to cheep rooming houses, and graffiti scarred transient cribs.

Hers was on the low end of the scale.

Making an impact when opening the door, were her paintings. They hung on each wall. Oils, most likenesses of friends who'd posed; or portraits from a landscape inside her mind. A mattress set up on a stand, with room to shove boxes of stuff under; crazy quilt over it. Radio, TV, a hot plate on a table alongside cooking supplies & canned foods. Homey. A cluttered space with an unusable bath; about 12 feet across by 15.

Here she subsisted on 'crazy money'-- Supplemental Social Security. For the insane. (SSI.)

Stryker was an artist.

Pictures of dikes hung all over her room. One, a woman with curly blond hair, cascading to shoulder length, in a blue evening gown reading a book, who looked suspiciously like Crystal; with an androgynous woman companion who arm was around her, and didn't look much like who she was suppose to be--Angel. The couple had been visiting her every so often. They had become friends.

Another, a crew cut dike in lipstick; tiny eyes set in a big head, army fatigues and a red striped tie, had been a recent lover.

These were Portraits From A Dike Planet.

So often Strykers spirit soared over the building tops into the sky, like a bird--out of imprisoning grim brick systems of the world; -- with raw ideas. With courage. Which is what it takes to be a dike. Get out of her body and sail off and be free.

The chubby dike returned from the group that night and entered her own private world of death.

In her solitary room opened a can of Spaghetti-O's, a prepared dinner; even tho it was 5am, and for some city workers this would be considered breakfast. Stryker didn't work, but was kept on the government dole.

She felt like she was trying to come out from under layers and layers of shit. 'Everybody's mad at me. I have offended strangers I barely know and hurt the ones I love. Plus I'm in debt.'

She ate.

Emotionally was in the deep end, floundering.

Indulged in some messy sex. Bloody, because she was on the rag. Put her fingers to her huge breasts, felt her nipples, squeezed them, then one hand searched between her legs rubbed her clit. 'I wish it was a massive Cum Together like they have at the club.' But this was not so. Moaning, felt-up herself strong & hard, and orgasmed; then curled into a little ball & began to fall asleep, a rag hastily shoved between her legs to catch the now-heavy flow of menstrual blood activated by her sexual release; her head on the pillow. 'Now I'm ready to commit suicide because of the horrible loneliness of doing sex alone. But, I'm not quite alone, and that thought's saving me. True, I couldn't get a girl, but I still have friends. It's the center in my life. The arms of friends, of a group, to fall back on.'

Dear Journal:
'Suicide is one of the most dangerous actions there is. It's the final statement to the Goddess. Unlike alcoholism, drugs and other escapes and protests of the human spirit--it is final. I have stood before the Goddess many times and threatened suicide, when my patience was gone. About two years ago I put a shotgun to my head and told The Goddess, *'If you don't send me an answer I'll blow my brains out'* In my heart I meant this. 2 weeks later I met

118

this Pagan Priestess, who is a Dominatrix. Also, mysteriously my shotgun turned up missing. It was this Pagan Priestess who first took me to Oils. She knew all about the Tarot, & Crystals, and knew nothing about motorcycles. I had been doing the I-Ching, it had informed me; **"SOMEBODY'S GETTING READY TO GET RICH! ---BUT IT AIN'T YOU! YOU HAVE TO LEARN TO BE POOR & LOVE IT!"** She did my Tarot, and I use it to this day, it's more full & gives more information. In Oil's I met so many biker dikes that I forgot my lonely hell, and started back on the journey of life with renewed passion. I did not try to kill myself. So my prayer worked.
--Av 12, 5752/August 11,1992

Now the tiny fat dike lay face up in bed, arms folded behind her head and mused aloud, to the four empty walls: 'I *know* Debbie probably is just playing me for a fool. But I'm getting more attention from them then I ever got from the square dikes in the good girls bars.'

Stryker's wallet sat on the dresser. Her overalls and shirt crumpled and wet with beer & sweat & pussyjuice & stains of blood which had leaked thru the cloth padding in her underpants were thrown into the single chair. $400 in green cash was in the wallet. She had spent $85 in Oils. **It's so *stupid*, Rip pimping her! I'd be *good* to her. She'd never have to go with a stranger.'**

The pretty showgirl Debbie had announced quite plainly to the bikers, "People try to take me away from hustling, and it's true, I hate it, but I love the money better, and wild horses can't drag me out of it, I wouldn't give up this life for nothing! I love having money and a nice house and nice things!" And Stryker had heard this along with the others, but it made no difference. She had a fixed mind, which was hard to change. Strykers conscious layers began to recede into layers of unconscious. She vaguely yearned again for a females touch; wished she had somebody--and could be like Angel, -- walk into the club and get the finest woman in it, in just a few weeks. **"OF COURSE SHE IS *BLOND* AND *THINNER* AND GOY AND BIG AND STRONG AND SANE! WELL!** AT LEAST I GOT TO SUCK CRYSTAL'S CUNT ONCE, AND SHE FINGERED ME A LITTLE ..... And at least we're all friends ..... Doing sex together makes women closer.... Uhhhhh ...... yeah...... aw....."

The rooms smelled of oil paint, and herb tea. Day was breaking outside in the huge amphitheatre of the sky, & people had begun to hustle along in the streets below.

Some people ran from the world, to the mountains, or to the sea. Her escape had been to take the inner city busline from the seedy residence hotel to the gay taverns, and sit and drink, and watch the pretty dikes, and hope, and go home alone, hope shattered night after night. --Until she met the gang.

Some people run from society to the water. Stryker'd been out to the water so many times before.

Angel has been to the water, so I know by this she is a sister traveler. We are souls who are ancient and alike. Only in her stint in the South where she was landlocked was she away from water, and couldn't wait to leave and head east to a city near a beach. The sea is a place a person can loose their life--jump into it's cold death womb, or, find catharsis. And come back to land with their load lifted. A change made, and at peace. Then came this event in my ordinarily bleak life, I found Oils. Now, when I am down near the waters edge it is in the company of 80 other biker dikes, not alone. I wandered in on the arms of a witch, and they welcomed me. Sluts sucked my clit and I sucked them. I buy them drinks they buy me drinks, and feed me at the big banquet parties. For all it's faults, the Outlaws is the best thing that ever happened to me.
--Cheshvan 7, 5753/November 3, 1992

A wonderful thing has happened. I have told my mother of this. Written her a letter--which could have been copied straight from you Dear Journal, but the language has been cleaned up. Mother is the type who puts 2 cigarettes in her mouth at the same time when she gets really excited and out-of-control. All her straight friends know that her daughter is a dike. I told her I belong to a band of girls, and that they ride motorcycles. I told her everything. And she is not happy with the news, believe me. She'd rather, I'm sure, me become an auxiliary to the Devils Disciples, and risk certain injury, disease, dishonor, or death, only because they are males, then me be in the loving embrace of my sisters--because they are dikes.—If she had only two choices. She hates the idea. Oh well. C'st l'vie.
 --Kislev 28, 5751/December 14,1990

I must write down these words, so I can remember them. Dear Journel, things have progressed since I last talked with you. I have publicly made my decission. This gang I have been seeing? I talked to them last night--in

120

a whirlwind of nights of Runs and parties and hanging out in their clubhouse; I told Hawk, a Warlord, and my friends, my intent of joining the membership. I said, *"I'M ALL DIKE! AND I'M ALL HEART! I'M GONNA RUN WITH YOUSE GUYS!"*
--Sh'Vat 8, 5751/January 23,1991

Chapter Twelve

Knees spread out at angles, bent into the wind; helmet first. RRRRRRRRRRRRRRRRMMMMMMMMMMMM!

Biker Mel, Crystals ex-lover redtail light in back; all you could see was her broad back with a woman's symbol painted on it, and the bubble shaped helmet.

Pig face, pert nose, turned down mouth; flat top hair in a crew cut barely visible behind the plastic visor; sweat pants, sweat shirt, hood over her head, and under her leather jacket; jeans. RRRRRRRRO OOOOOOOOMMMMMMM!

VVVVVVVVAAAAAAAAARRRRRRROOOOOMMMM! Here came Stryker on a bike borrowed from Johnny, a Harley naturally, --a Flathead that sat the lowest to the ground so she could feel every bump and dip in the road. Which the mechanic was going to sell but loaned to the fat dike for this special occasion; she having scorned a 450 Honda, open roadworthy, which was $3,000 brand new. Stryker was Hooked On Harleys. She wanted the real thing.

The babe on the back was a slut who'd probably give her some head when they got there & the little dike was exhilarated. A breath-taking Run into the country, & a sweet slut holding her tight--for dear life. Stryker envisioned how it would be; a sweet mouth on her cunt--orgasming into her face, and she in return, tenderly would suck off the slut, swallow her juices, feel her heart beat fast, thru her fingers as she stroked her tits; then slow after release. It was Dike Heaven. Arms clutched tight around her waist.

"Huh huh huh!" Cried the tramp, happily. A scabby wench; red lipsticked mouth. Roar of motorcycles speeding away; she was a speedster of a different sort--the drug. Methamphetamine. Lady Jane, who had been one of the Ladies in times gone by, but degenerated into a free-for-the-use-of-all slut over the years of drug abuse.

RRRRRRRRRRRRRRRRRRRRRRRRRRRRRR! Sleazy clutched her wife Lady's back. The Fem Top biker sped thru the crowd like a knight in armor; --of lace & leather; spikes of her high-heels on the bikes footpegs. Leather gloved fingers squeezed the throttle.

VVVVVAAAARRROOOOOOMMMMMMM! Rips knees stuck out at the sides of her big chopper. Complete with casings; a fulldresser that looked like suitcases on its sides. --Debbie in an exquisite leather motorcycle outfit clutched on behind, and wore a tiny helmet, to meet the legal requirement; which was more like a soldiers helmet on a half shell.

They were on a Run, in one of the last few days of early winter that were still warm enough to ride.

ZEEEEET ZEEEEET ZEEEEET! Highpitched sound of the rice burners. And the rumbling thunder of the Harleys coming.

Angel slowed a moment, then turned, threw the bike to an angle, leaned deep into the turn, went around the corner nearly horizontal to the pavement, then gunned up the motor and went forward down the street. Crystal was the Lady on the back, face coated with sunblock to protect her milk white complexion that turned red rather then tanning, even in the days of winter when the sun is a longer distance from earth.

Where was the Queen of the club? In the van. George rode the chopper, with her wild haired mistress on the back --Dena.

Georgina hated Runs, it was a chore. Never rode on the motorcycle, took their van and had to do a lot of fast driving to catch up to the bikers. She commanded the helm of the sleek grey/blue van. It had pale silver & blue lines across it from stem to stern, and was so long that there were 3 doors on each side. A tire in a silver case on the back, and a ladder also in back which went up to the roof.

Several other cars & a bus were in the procession, filled with dikes who didn't yet have bikes, in a carpool that tailgated immediately behind. With a mighty roar, tires spinning, the bikes thundered away.

As soon as they reached the outskirts of the city, the bikes would speed up, breaking the limit, and leave the vans and cars behind, to arrive at their midway stopping point in a time-lag of a half hour or so. The midway destination today was the Fairbrook Shopping Mall.

They drove over the Grand Concourse; the ocean opened up, appearing silver against the grey stone turns of the human-made cement sea bank. They followed the curves.

Street lamps arched overhead in mathematical sequence. Slick roads wet, kept them in it framework. Stoplights, uniform; red, then green. Birds flew in the sky.

The Grand Concourse opened up into a panoramic view.

White blue sky, tops of downtown buildings in the distance. Grey sky, heavy. Clouds and wind. Birds flapping, wheeling, and screeching.

It was a magnificent sight; 40 bikers roared around the turn of the Concourse five abreast, taking up two lanes of traffic. Eight deep in an intense pack of silver and black. Right behind was the cars, bus and van in which sat the determined Georgina, strands of black hair tumbling from a pompadour over her white shoulders; fat fingers glittering with jeweled rings gripping the wheel. Commanding the steering of the silver/blue van. George rode ahead by several lengths, leading the pack on her Harley Davidson motorcycle.

Inside various cars could be heard conversations; "Did that biker swerve? Is she loosing control?"

"No, she just missed a pothole."

"It's early. --Didn't you say there might be ice on the road in the morning?"

"'Till 10am."

They hit the freeway, gears grinding mechanical sounds of whirring inside. The van made strong power on the freeway. Bikes in tandem entered medium speed.

They rode in a formation of their own. A tension. Five Warlords; five bikes; eyes on the road: & the van in speed and space, with the other bikes behind, and then the cars.

Like invisible wires connected them. Five Warlords traveling synchronized at the same space. They had the feature that put their bikes on automatic drive.

Dear Journal, I will tell you a couple of interesting sexual things that have happened to me on a motorcycle. Uhmm, I have had a lot of partners. behind me that have put their hands around front and have really fondled the hell out of me when we were on a really long motorcycle ride, 'cause we were bored. And we didn't have anything to do so why not have a climax. It sure makes boredom a lot easier to deal with. So, I didn't really do anything to her, because I'm driving, but to have somebody playing with your boobs, and shouting sweet things in your ear--over the wind, licking your ears, and uh, fondling your clitoris while you're trying to operate left foot, left hand, right hand, right foot, two down, three up, and watch everything on the road. It is pretty funny. Challenging. I'd say that's a pretty common thing that happens, here with the Outlaws, that lovers and women do on their motorcycles. Because you're sitting so close together. You feel this huge, huge vibrator underneath you, and it's quite a sense of power and freedom. And you know there's a lot of trust. There's some good bonding that goes on, with 2 women when they ride a motorcycle. The passenger is putting all her trust in the driver. The driver at that point really learns to trust her judgment.'
--Cheshuvan 26, 5754/November 10, 1993

Their hair was full of oil from the bikes, and dirt from the road.

It was a small Run, not like the Memorial Day in summer, and half of the membership--50 or so showed.

124

It was no particular holiday, just a simple Saturday. Not a full moon. The idea just being to squeeze one last day of outdoor pleasure out of the failing old year.

The faster you get on the bike, the more revelations you get; the lighter the bike seems. The slightest smidgen of a difference in pavement can set off a complete overall vibration in the motorcycle; which can set you off balance completely and your ability to get out of a disastrous situation is the ability of what you can do in a millisecond without too much of a movement. In other words you can't move your handle bars left or right very quickly when you're going at high speeds. The slower you go the more maneuverability you have.

The Leader Of The Pack peeled away from the crowd, those who took the dare followed, 80, 90 then 100 mph, they zoomed down the familiar straight away, leaving behind the more tame bikers & of course the cars. Inside the van was food and supplies that had been bought and prepared prior to the Run. The cost was $5 per person-- RSVP. Which insured food and soft drinks & beer for everybody, in a grand feast, with stuff left over. It was to be FOOD FUN 'N GAMES! All each biker had to do was send in her fee along with the monthly membership dues, gas up first, and join the pack that morning, prompt at 9:30.

They'd do Harley Drag Races. It was awesome to see a dike biker go from zero to 80 miles per hour in 2.5 seconds. Had a Tire Drag contest, on which a biker is dragged on a tire behind a cycle; --she eats a lot of dirt. A Slow Driving Contest—to see who can go the slowest. A Weenie Bite; -- lines with hotdogs hung from them; the cycles race by underneath and the bitch in back stands up on the foot pegs and takes a bite out of the weenie as she flies by. Whoever bites the furthest wins.

They'd win trophies for all events. There was trophies for the oldest member of the club. Who had been in the club the longest. The fattest biker & the skinniest.

The gang roared down the country freeway. They went by an army truck with a stack of bombs. The warheads were 8 feet long, 2 feet in diameter. And painted olive green. Cylinders that rapidly narrowed into a tip, a nipple; around which a blue circle was painted.

"Hope we don't see much more of that." Sez the occupants of one vehicle.

"If we go to war you will soon."

"It's scary."

"They look like rockets."

"No police entourage or nothing. The Avengers or Disciples or some gang could hijack 'em and use 'em to blow us up."

They left the slow moving flatbed down the freeway, it was going about 20 mph.

"BOMBS! GIGANTIC HUMUNGOUS BOMBS!"

A long truck, 5 layers high, 5-wide and full of five bombs per layer laying in length to nose cone to rocket base.

"We really are at war."

"Yeah! And nobody in the White House is telling us! Funny the shit you see out here in the country where nobody's around!"

Rain had cleared and a huge rainbow arced thru the stratosphere. Red, yellow, orange, green/blue, & purple. Its perimeters fading into a blue sky, disappearing into the foothills.

And they all felt free. Dikes. Their bodies bound by heavy weights, and chains of flesh, released by the twist of a wrist at the ignition. The tap of a boot toe on gears, the squeeze of a hand on the throttle. The unbelievable rumble between their legs, that power; the wind in their hair. All within the capability of strength in the grip of

fingers, arms and shoulders, upper body mastering the handlebars &
the wheels over the road.

A while, further down the road, the pack sees the Leader swerve in
distance, so they slow. Within minutes they see the problem-- a door
made of wood with a doorknob sticking out of it lies in the middle of
the highway, fallen out of somebody's vehicle. A car with difficulty
could ride over this, but it could kill a motorcyclist. From a raven-
black crow flapping its wings can see the odd design of a pack of 30
bikes swerving around a section of road, followed by the cars &
trucks, which do the same.

Bikers. What they really worry about is finding a place to piss. In
the city areas the dikes spent much time worrying about a place to
pee. A restaurant with toilets. If you're a motorcyclist, it's ok. But if
they think you're bikers, it ain't. Waitresses won't let them into their
restrooms.

It was for this reason, and to regroup, and refresh, that 40 miles
into the Run, they stopped at a suburb shopping mall.

FAIRBROOK Letters etched in stone planted inside a miniature
lake with ducks diving and paddling around it.

The bikers dikes roared into the main entrance of the Mall, and
turned off into a parking lot dotted with pricey cars and new station
wagons; not yet full for it was early in the day.

The wounded returned into Amerikas heartland, with venom.

The Mall was dry--totally dry as a bone. Water had receded down
thru the pavement, and air dried it like it had never rained at all.

The 2-tier cement structure stretched three city blocks by five. It
contained department stores, restaurants, coffee shops, grocery
outlets, theatres, small boutiques, jewelry & clothing and shoe stores,
& banks. A city within itself. The normal appearing suburbanites,
teens, middle age housewives and retired senior citizens were going
about the routines of their luxurious lives.

The housewives came with their hair in curlers. Others arrived only after having spent 2 hours doing their hair fancy. They came with 3 strand lengths of pearls adorning their necks. Others wore old sweatshirts. They were prepared & others unprepared to face their worse nightmare---for a lot of people they knew to see them without makeup. Instead, as they walked across the parking lot of the Mall, they saw the bikers.

In pairs, and groups, the dikes dismounted. New arrivals poured thru the mouth of the Mall, skid in a hail of sparks to a stop.

The biker women had nothing to worry about but the warriors themselves. They never wanted for money or dope food, or a roof over their heads.

Walked the streets fearlessly in their colors. Knew that nobody male nor female dared mess with them because of the power backing them up--the dangerous girl gang.

They could do pretty much what they wanted to all day.

Soon 50 biker dikes in black leather strutted around, attracting a lot of attention. Local teens made nasty remarks, and gossiping housewives gave rude stares. "They don't know any better. They're like animals." Comes a voice out of the crowd.

"We came out to the country to get away from all that." Sez a biker. --Referring to the hostility of the locals.

A fiery biker yells back; "WE'RE NOT HURTING NOBODY! WE'RE SHOPPING!"

"YEAH! AND PISSING!" Another dike takes up the cry.

And at that point, fed up with wandering about to find one restaurant with a toilet where they could all buy a cups of hot coffee and piss, a couple of dikes just climb into the decorative foliage beside the blue waterfall, hike down their pants, squat and urinate among the ferns.

128

Housewives squeal, men yell, somebody throws a softdrink can at the leather crowd. In retaliation, a biker wearing a teeshirt which reads; "I MAY NOT GO DOWN IN HISTORY, BUT I'LL GO DOWN ON YOUR LITTLE SISTER." In a macha display picks up a chunk of fake rock from the waterfall and heaves-it back into the crowd of suburbanites.

Two leather women begin a long sexual kiss, bodies entwined, rocking in motion. More and more shoppers stop to gawk as more and more dikes wheel up to the area, climb off their cycles & strut over to join the rest of the black leather clad crew. A more enlightened person in the crowd whispers; "They're not normal gay's, they're wild!"

"They're rabid!" Replies another.

A shoving match occurs on the fringe of the crowd of suburban shoppers where it intermeshes with the gang.

Back at the parking lot their bikes gleam like crowned kings, all silver-- rear view mirrors, handle bars, machinery, exhaust tubes, spokes, forks & wheel rims.

Now the first car turns into the Mall, then the van; & they park, just to have a harried biker race up on foot and yell at them in a breathless tone thru their windows, what's gone wrong. **Damn It.** Georgina sez. **"The kids didn't give me time to powder my nose & use the little gals room!"** Her eyes took in the lavish Mall in a glance. They were all the same to her. She'd worked as a hairdresser in plenty. Georgina fit in quite well, a pink muumuu, leather coat—full-length--- adorned with a fake fur collar; and black lace up boots. The van was a suburbanites dream; long & sleek. But parked in a sea around it were the handlebars of a herd of bikes arched up like horns of wild animals.

"Well, I guess we better drive back out of here and hit the road before somebody calls security." The Queen informed the biker this, then waved her plump arms out the window at the other cars just driving into the lot with their loads of bikers & supplies, grabbed the wheel with white knuckled fists, made a U Turn and slowly proceeded up the driveway where she'd stop and wait, ready to drive off when she saw Georgie and the rest gun up their cycles and race out of the exit.

Like Huns come down from the North, sweeping over what remains of civilization, they had come; not gang raping, murdering and robbing, no, the Outlaws were overturning garbage recepitcles, pissing in the bushes and making public displays of their lesbian sexuality. –Kisses, deep-throat; and pulling up their tops and wiggling their tits at the straight people. **"WE SET CHILDREN ON FIRE! WE KILLED A MAN DOWN AT THAT SHOPPING MALL ACROSS THE BRIDGE AND WHEN WE GET A HOLD OF A TEENAGE GIRL WE DON'T LET HER GO FOR HOURS!"** Screams a smartass biker.

Pretty soon chaos rules. The bikers spin out of their pack and stomp inside shops overturning clothes racks and snatching garments which they wave in victory, like flags. Others run in formation thru the crowd of normals, pushing and spitting on these squares who hate them so. The shoppers back up shrieking, clutching each other at every incursion of the bikers.

A biker dike sees a pretty woman go past, who is unaware of the events. Wheeling her motorcycle thru the crowded lanes of the mall, "A BITCHEN' WOMAN! WOW SHE'S FINE!" She yells. The woman wears a bluejean tank top, short dress, pretty cloth coat, has tan skin, bleach blond hair with brown roots growing in. Dainty feet in sandals, despite the chill weather. She's pushing a baby carriage.

"BITCHEN'!"

"GO GET HER!" Screams her buddy.

The biker rides her cycle around the woman. "DON'T BE SCARED LADY! WE DON'T BITE! WE WON'T HURT YOU— 'CAUSE TODAY'S MOTHERS DAY!" Seeing fear in her eyes, the bikers ride off, --up onto the sidewalk and deeper into the Mall. Passerby's shriek and jump against the plate glass display windows of the shops. The bikers whoop, yell and with a roar ride back to join the rest, who are in a mad confrontation with the pushy pack of rabid suburbanites.

"I Thought They Were Motorcyclists From Hell." One lady would say later when interviewed on the 10 o'clock news. As TV cameras surveyed the damage.

What possessed Angel to suddenly grab Crystal, kiss her hard on the lips, then stick her leather gloved hand into her crotch groping her in the suburban mall?

Saundra, the black biker had a big white butch with her today. Long hair, wild; broken teeth in front from old battles. Her biker grabbed Saundra and slammed her in an embrace so hard it rattled the chains--draped over her right shoulder. Their leather legs entwined. Orange, African hair/straight, greasy butch biker hair combined. Bad enough they were an interracial couple, but dikes yet! And **leather** dikes on top of it! The biker butch, grinding her hips into Saundra's in a long sensuous movement; their bodies pulsed. –To the frozen horror of the shoppers.

"GO BACK TO HELL WHERE YOU CAME FROM DEVILS!" A woman screamed out of the primarily white, middle-income crowd.

"DEVILS! DEMONS!" Screamed another.

The sight of two fem bikers dressed in full regalia; shiny black leather, silver spikes & chains, smearing each others lipstick in a long kiss, as they held each others faces with naked fingers, nails painted black, which protruded out of the end of their leather gloves, whose tips had been cut off.

Angel; blond, a clerics collar at her neck, wore a fiery expression. Knew well she was no demon. She was shaped by the world. Given birth by a mother who had deserted her in infancy, and raised by a father who loved her.

She was flesh and blood. And she felt the pain. And definitely hadn't lived well as demons are suppose to do.

The religious citizens of the mall screamed at them. A gang of teens jerked like puppets on a string, hollered profanities, yet afraid to fight, there were too many of the lesbian bikers.

George sat in the saddle of her Harley; apart from the fray. 'Let 'em go on and have fun.' George thought. 'They can't get enough security out here to stop us, not for awhile.' Before they sped away on their cycles, leaving the mall in shambles.

An industrious biker had procured a gallon of mustard from a fancy hot dog stand and threw it down an aisle, where suburbanites began to slip & slide in yellow goo.

Another had prepared herself with cans of spraypaint and had sprayed **DIKES FUCK BABES!** In giant crooked letters on a shop wall. A small presence of security police had arrived. Three blue uniformed men who carried no guns. They stood together, watching and talking on a two-way radio.

CODE 45, SECURITY! CODE 45, SECURITY! Had finally begun to boom out of the Malls loudspeakers.

Two of the black bikers, KT, and Ebony stomped around shaking their fists at the suburbanites calling them everything from racists to senile old dogs who collect welfare--their social security pensions.

George had gone back to the lot, got her motorcycle and rode it back into the fray. Peered at the members under her motorcycle cap brim. 'God loves a good show.' She thought from her bike, towering in the background, gloved hands clutching the handlebars; cap with the Death Eagle spread in silver wing tips.

"YOU ARE ALL GOING TO HELL!" Screamed a hysterical woman trying to drag her young children away from the scene. The kids were obviously enjoying this sight of corruption immensely.

"NOT SO SURE THIS AIN'T HELL!" Screams George back. A woman in dyed purple hair—a conservative style-- veins standing out on her neck from outrage just stares at George in disbelief, she's so big.

The bikers went wild. *C.R.A.S.H* ! Went a metal advertisement sign thru a plate glass window. The aisles were strewn with dirt & plants from overturned flower bins.

A black lady, one of a very tiny percent of colored minorities in this lily-white town was moaning; **"I like people! I like everybody! God made us all! God just made some of us *FUNNY* that's all! Oh Lord help us!"** And threw her hands up in the air. **"OH LORD HELP US!   When we get up there to heaven everybody will be there! Even these ladies here on their motorscooters! GOD SAID I GOT A PLACE IN HEAVEN FOR *EVERYBODY!* Oh Lord! Oh Lord!"**

Angel was too intelligent to engage in brawling. And didn't have a scarred face from the belligerent world. --Her marks were inside. Most she wanted to do on this sunny, but cold day at the Mall was insist about her sexuality; to open peoples eyes—to blow their minds; so she flaunted it, sticking her pink tongue down Crystals throat, lapping at Crystals face, then crouches down on her knees, pushes Crystals leather skirt up around her waist & sucks her clit, face mashed into her fragrant pussy, while Crystal grabs her blond head and humps, driving her pussy into the butches mouth. The suburban women shriek. One points out Angel in her clerics collar & leather drag; **"YOU HAVE YOUR NERVE!"** Screams one Christian believer. **"WHAT ARE YOU? WHAT ARE YOU SUPPOSE TO BE?! YOU'RE NOT A MINISTER!   WHO ARE YOU TRYING TO FOOL!"**

Stryker was one of the smallest of the pack, but was a plucky little dike. 200 pounds on her 4'11" frame, black leather, bluejeans & gloves with their fingertips cut away; handcuffs, and boots decorated with chains. Immediately, upon hearing the Christian woman's complaint, flung herself down on the ground, and squeezed her head between Angels thighs as she knelt giving Crystal head—sucking her bare pussy with wet lips--- & yanked down the blond butches zipper, and began to roughly lick her clit with slobbering strokes, -- in a ruckus three-way. The on lookers screamed, violated. Not to be outdone, The Slut who'd ridden on the back of Stykers bike went around and began humping Crystal's rear end; with each lusty thrust hollering unintelligible curses.

Next thing they knew, the Outlaws flew out of there.

Squeal of tires, the smell of burning rubber away up over the hill.

The last of the pack, all the cars & van spun out of the Mall, and soon they were gone.

Outlaws had drunk some drinks, and pissed--in the bushes of the Mall. Shouted at their enemies, did sex in living color to shock the hetros, now they continued to ride out to their destination in the country.

"YAHOO! Yelled a biker. It was Saundra. This usually mild mannered Saundra fem waved a bra by a strap in the air--with the price tag still on it, --lifted by some of her sister dikes in quantity and distributed to the gang.

Comancho the Indian, war whooped. Her wife Frosty tightly hugged her waist as their Harley ate up the road, and they curved in and out between the other bikers to catch up to the Leader Of The Pack, George, who raced ahead, having given the signal to disperse and vacate the Mall, just a few minutes past.

The suburbs were expanding. Older ones turned into cities. They had to drive further and further to get away from civilization.

Hills are foggy. A big blanket of fog everywhere.

They couldn't wait to get to the National Park, far from the jeers of straight people.

Looked foreword with anticipation to get into the wilderness, kick their boots off, and go barefoot, even if just for a few minutes, in the cold.

By the time they got to the wilderness preserve, Angel's mouth was full of bugs.

It had warmed up considerably when they got there. Blazing sun beams would keep them warm for a few hours before the shortness of winter days shut down the light in its distance from sun to planet earth, and it would turn freezing cold. So they still wore their jackets.

The group spread out over the park in a camping clearing. Trees stood every 15-feet between their little groups & pairs, each industriously engaged in having fun; and so it was not as apparent what a large group they were.

They were glad they'd got there early. --Had the campsite to themselves. Motorcycles parked nearby.

Moved over their territory thru the trees in little groups of 2's, 3's and more.

Others were in the park also besides the club. Straight families camping out overnight, with BBQ grills. Tho they had gone to the most deserted place they could find.

Wine, beer and pussy juice flowed.

Lay in the green grass having a nice time. A biker picked up a blade of yellow-white grass, dying from winter approaching, put it to her lips, cupped her hands around the blade blew on it, and made it whistle.

"Ain't that nice, we got a watchdog." Lady and Sleazy admired it. --A little skinny dike Bottom in an undershirt and no bra, a tooth missing in front, a big 10-gallon cowboy hat on her head, and her woman—the Top-- holding the end of a chain attached to the dog collar around her neck. The butch would sit faithfully at her side, a slave for the days festivities.

The bikers piled food and drink out of Georgina's van, and Comancho's blue bus. They came in handy for hauling stuff--and to carry back any broken bikes that might fall causality on a Run.

The four-wheel vehicles arrived at the pre-designated area of the Wilderness Park, about half hour after the bikers, since they weren't breaking the speed limit.

All a dike could carry in her saddlebag was a few sandwiches & a six-pack, or thermos. More if she had big casings on her bike sides. But the cars & trucks held cartons of roast chickens, slabs of cheeses, loaves of bread, racks of hotdogs, case upon case of soft drinks, cases of bottled sparkling water, pies, cakes, roast beefs & baked hams.

A biker with a great gold cycle with parcels & compartments like a traveling motor home carried a stash of marijuana rolled into a hundred joints; soon the pleasant aroma of the herb floated thru the trees, mixing with nature.

Star, a novice member sailed in on her chopper, wind in her hair. And here came one of the biker's wives--on foot. --Not a good sign. Walking in sox, now wet, thru the damp grass, holding her heavy motorcycle boots with thick soles by the laces in one hand, & dragging her jacket thru the grass in the other so she's wearing just a tank top, shoulders bare, lush breasts bouncing. **"I'm riding back with somebody else!"** She protests. "My man is acting too crazy! She tried to kill us back there on the road! Remember that door? **She was gonna drive right over it!"**

"Ride in the van." Sez Georgina, not bothering to look at the woman, as she hauls out cartons of their prepared feast, she's driven hundreds of lady bikers home from countless runs.

Now, one bikers old lady was getting close--breathing hard. "OH!" She moans, tossing her head of greasy long blond hair.

Her mans hand is inside her, the other hand having unfastened the metal snaps on her cut-away-bluejean vest, once a jacket, and was

136

squeezing her tits firmly, and pulling her nipples. Her lady lay back against a tree, heaved, humped, and came, making a drunken bellow.

"How many is having sex right as we speak? Half the club! I bet $5." Sez a biker. And takes several $5 bets.

A novice was appointed to go around and count the couples under blankets.

She came back with 40.

"40? There's only 50 of us here! And 20 of us is right here with the food!"

"I meant couples. No, I meant women... Uh... oh... I forgot... I counted wrong."

Music's strident beat pounded out of an amplifiers system. A black female singer's lush voice rising and falling in emotion.

But they didn't need a beat to match their tempo; fingers thrusting in and out of her hole; raising her hips off the blanket on the ground in orgasm, while her paintednail fingers clawed the blue denim jacket on her lovers back.

Beautiful brunette hair, smooth skin, a beauty. Not a mark on her. "She's a better bitch, it's true." Commented an observer to her friend, as the young biker wiggled her ass, humped her hips thrusting up into the air, and all the way down to smack the ground, yielding her hot pink pussy to her lovers hand.

Sleazy's loving her Lady, when a couple of bikers swagger by drinking beer tossing a coin to determine who would be first to fuck the available woman in their party. They stop to stare at Sleazy & Lady. "Yep, she's a veteran. She's worked the trenches. GOSH! Guess what guys! She's still got milk in her tits!" The butch hollers. "MILK HER GOOD SLEAZ'!"

"SAVE SOME FOR ME!" Yells the other, goodnatured.

"YAHOO!" Hollers Sleazy.

A pair of legs stuck out of the van, someone was kissing its toes. Georgina was long gone to the picnic site. A biker knelt at the side of the van sucking a lady's toes, soon had half a foot in her mouth, sucking it, then the whole foot disappeared into it, toes wiggling down her throat.

--In the meantime the woman made cries of rapture. A second biker was on top of her inside the cavern of the van, fucking. The van bounced up and down as the biker screwed her lady--with a little help from her friend, who squatted outside in the dirt, with mouth engulfing her foot; who was too busy sucking & choking to notice.

Stryker lumbered about with a drink in her hand. Had had a slug of Vat 500 whiskey & mixed it with a beer—against the advice of her physician. –The pills she had to take to make her body chemistry sane. Could hear it sloshing in her belly. Whiskey combining with beer as she walked, SLOSH, SLOSH. Little Stryker, big breasted and heavy shouldered like a clumsy bear not accustom to be up on it's hind legs, nor to dance either.

Stryker was glad they had got to the park early, she loved to play.

In one area the games had begun near the picnic site. There was plenty of activities for a dike to do.

More dykes had music playing. Stryker drifted from camp to camp. The closeness of women. She loved it. Mellow rhythm & love filled the air with chirping of birds.

Stryker was getting her fill of women for a change. Instead of a dull boring life she'd lived before.

So she'd got up and danced like a dancing bear. Alone. Danced, whirling about in blue denims, big boots clomping, tits bouncing under a teeshirt & a bottle of drink raised to the sky. Across the meadow somebody saw Stryker. "She's lonely." They said.

Now the fat dike didn't realize she was alone. Felt so good to have friends. Lesbian friends. To have something to do on a Sunday instead of be so blue. Tho today she didn't have a particular girlfriend, Lady Jane having drifted away as sluts were apt to do; it didn't worry her. The cause of feminism was out this morning--from lovers who stroked fingers in their lovers wet cunts marking time to the music, to swirling figures in a dance circle by the campfire.

The companion of the pretty brunette had finished stroking her to orgasm, now got on top between the wenches thighs--legs up in the air, to get off herself. The more graphic love acts the biker club members enjoyed was embarrassing to Stryker, because of her middle—class upbringing, for she'd noticed others--straight people with families-- also shared the park space, tho at distance. "Lets invite her over to join us." A voice drifted over the meadow; **"HEY STRYKER! YUH LOOK LONELY!"**

"Me?" Amazed because she was having a great time.

"Hell, here, use my lady awhile. —She'll let yuh."

The butch got up, pulled a shirt over her tanned belly, zipped up her shorts, still wore motorcycle boots, and was soaking wet where her lady's fingers had been playing in her crotch. Her own orgasm had burst between her legs moments ago. She smiled, and pointed to the blanket.

Stryker choked, looked down at the earth, embarrassed.

Her companion was a hard tanned woman, hair in ringlets; teeth missing in front, but still a fine bitch.   Lay on her back, grinned up & her arms opened to Stryker.

This was just one of many many times a couple had offered to let a single stranger have sex with one of them.

Shy, Stryker kept her clothes on. Their thighs fell into place. It had been so long, without the intimate caring sex of a real partner that Stryker felt starved; so much so, that the movement of the woman

139

under her, thigh between her thighs made her come right away, thru her clothes. The woman held her tight a long time. So, she had her orgasm with love, tho she didn't know the woman's name.

Later the three of them sat on their blanket and talked. The woman who she'd fucked said; "We thank you're special Stryker. Everybody accepts you, just like you are, don't feel so shy.   This ain't a club like the square girls have, it's not about impressing people with how much money you have, or how you dress; how successful you are, or that crap. You can always come back to me and my honey here in the future if you got any problems and need advice, or a shoulder to lean on, or hugs or love, or if you need stuff to share, or food."

"Thanks." Stryker said. Her big eyes rolled unsteady in her head. "Thanks youse guys." It was just another in a series of many small initiations of love, into the gang.

A while later Johnny throws a blanket over the figure of a fat biker & her wife Stella Dallas, and with lounging steps walks away. "Hey! Guess whose making it with my old lady?" The mechanic strutted around, holding a soda bottle by the neck and a grilled sausage sandwich, in the other.

"Who?"

"Well, whose missing?"   Sez Johnny, munching.

All heads at the campfire turned around. "Stryker?"

"Stryker!"

They looked back at the rustling blanket, then one tossed a cowboy hat into the air. Soon all the dikes were whooping it up, throwing their hats and helmets in the air and dancing like a pack of dancing bears, just like Stryker had done.

So the fat dikewitch had made ready friendships with the whole gang.

140

Trees; spaced apart. A river ran along one side of the campground.

The dikes were banging their broads in the park on a sunny winters day.

One banged her fist into her little broads cunt at an easy rhythm, one of the fems feet waved up in the air, the other braced against the side of a tree. --On all fours, the movement of the butches shoulders was visible as she pounded her fist into her lovers cunt. Further on, thru the woods, toes twitched, and sounds emit from under a blanket. "UH OH UH AH!"

Stryker pulled up her bluejeans over her fat belly and stumbled out of that group, towards the next party. --She wanted to hug--hard. Dived onto a blanket so the fat on her stomach rippled and rolled. Eyes wide & uncertain. The couple was Mel & her lady. Bluejean jacket hung on a handlebar of her motorcycle, also a black vest and a big bubble helmet. Mel & her lady engulf Stryker in a huge group hug. Suddenly, from nowhere comes the slut Lady Jane who the fat dike had brought on the back of her bike. Drunk, bleary eyed, she pulls Stryker out of the couples arms, and back into her own, planting wet kisses down her chubby neck, like she's gonna love her any way she can.

The first couples of dikes to arrive had been caught up in passion; in the wild wild open green spaces of the park, and later, the others were inflamed by the sight of all that humping, so they started humping too.

In short, the whole gang either ate & played the games, or fucked. They lay on blankets unrolled from the van, pleasuring their ladies, and being pleasured, when somebody thought they heard a scream. A woman's scream.

Hawk & her pack of punks are laughing and telling tall tales. While they share a slut between them, taking turns standing above the woman whose on her knees; hot mouth sucking them off. The green & pink spiked hairdo'd Hawk cuts her initials into a tree trunk with her knife point; stops, looks & listens.

141

Outlaw dikes, banging their broads in a lazy sunny day.

It hadn't meant to turn into a sex party, but it was...

Dike pussy scent from sawed-off jean shorts & rich dike aroma from sweaty underarms in cutaway teeshirts. Energetic motion of tanned limbs.

Extra clothes flung off and hung on bike handlebars like scarecrows.

Some had finished their acts of sex and were just laying there, eyes closed, aware of someone walking near. Others had just begun, feeling juices flow out of their cunts from the stimulation. All those women, & semi naked bodies.

When a young man and his girlfriend stumbled on to their scene. Horrified they holler at the first dike couple they see.

The man and the woman run off hand in hand over the meadow, the man jerking the woman along fast, as if in terror; only to return minutes later with a group of other men. By then the bikers on the fringe hoot and jeer to greet the straights coming back with giant strides over the green grass. Hawk has climbed into the saddle of her motorcycle and tears over the meadow like a madwoman.

By the time Hawk arrives over the long-span distance of the clearing the group of men had backed off a hundred paces, and were turning around and walking back to the woods on the other side.

"I TOLD HIM I'D KNOW IM DOWN & KICK HIS TEETH DOWN HIS THROAT! THEY WERE SO AFRAID THEY DIDN'T EVEN TRY TO FIGHT, YUH SEE THEM BACKING OFF! — AFTER THEY SAW THERE WAS MORE OF US QUEER CREEPS IN THE PARK!"

We'll keep a watch guys." Hawk exclaims. "In case they get some more assholes and try to come back."

**"I'LL SHOW YOU WHAT A REAL DIKE CAN DO
HONEY!"** Mimics a biker. She'd been singled out for rape in the
past, because some men knew she was gay and now she hated them.
Fighting hard would undo the hurt of the past. Now the biker dike
would never be unprepared, carried a knife or a stun gun.

Somebody laughed in agreement with the dikes; and in scorn of
the cowardly bullies, whose tall figures had shrunk into dwarves as
they disappeared into the distant woods. And the couples went back
to their fun. Back at the main campfires the games had continued
without interruption. The dikes there had barely been affected by the
shockwaves the incident generated. The bikers on the front line held
their ground. Hitched their thumbs in their belts, strutted and joked.
One laughed; "My old lady does a better job with 3 fingers then that
asshole can do with his dick. She puts them in the right place for a
vaginal orgasm. I come all over myself." And another demonstrated
with uncanny timing. Pushed a hand held cock over her partners clit,
which was swollen up in heat, so as to contact there by the angle of
thrust as well as going in and out of her vagina, as she wreathed and
strained in the final moments before a corkscrew orgasm spiraled thru
her body, carrying her up on wings of release.

The dikes on the frontline relaxed, but with a wary eye trained to
the line of thick trees across the meadow. They were to shout for help
at the sight of trouble from any straights who might head their way.

One by one they forgot about the incident. One put a finger in her
lovers hole & rolled it around & around, pulled her tits awhile, and
then wanted her to give her a blow job bad.

So the dikes were really getting down to the fun. Sun rose in the
sky, it was 2pm.

Johnny & Stella Dallas were off a ways down from the campfire,
romancing. Two beings fucking in peace. A slow easy fuck on the
sun warm grass. Johnny was on top of Stella under a blanket. It was
very obvious what was happening. Motion of her rump rising and
pushing in, pushing her cunt around in Stella's cunt; whose knees
stuck up making little dents in the blanket, their heads, hair mixing
together stuck out one end. Sounds, "OH, OH! **OH!**"

"STRYKER! COME OVER HERE MY OLD LADY WANTS TO SUCK YOU OFF!"

"All these women!"

A biker is sucking milk out of Lady's tit, Sleazy sucks the other tit. Left over milk from the couples last baby. "Gotta milk her, or she'll be sore. The baby's so big he's eaten' out of a plate now."

Right by the campfire a dike is fucking her buddy dike with a huge cock. Someone marvels, "Your woman takes all of that?"

"Practice and Discipline." She replies. Entering her asshole from behind.

"She's not putting it all the way in is she?" Asks an observer.

"KEEP THEM IN ORDER!" Bellows Georgina, flipping a row of hamburgers on the grill, Angel's helping.

"How big is it?" Queries a biker whose joined the crowd watching the couple.

George and Hawk & Rip confer beside a tree, watching the horizon. They have made their weapons ready, in case the straight people decide to band together and come back to fight. The campfire rises flashing streaks of light over their warlike faces, contorted in anger, with peeks of flames.

They dined on a lovely meal of hamburgers and home made French fries, tossed salad with blue cheese dressing and few dozen home made apple & cherry pies which the ladies had prepared.
They were barbarians; ate with their hands, tore into the roast chickens like King Henry VIII, waving drumsticks and guzzling bottled water.

Seeing the blond butch flip hamburgers, a black handkerchief tied around her head to catch the sweat as she labored over the grill made a biker think of the place she'd just worked, and she was recounting a story about it. **".... So they fired my motherfucking ass."** Sez the biker, finishing.

"I hate to see you have days like this, don't cry on my shoulders! It's all that liquor you drink on the job! And everywhere else!" Yells her companion. "Aw, don't mind her!" She yells to Angel & Crystal, and the others beside the cookout. She's been fired from the donut shop that the bikers frequent, the one where Crystal wants Angel to get a job. "That's how alkies get when they get old, they sound like frogs." The woman complains. And curly blond Crystal is politely asking them did anyone replace her at the donut shop, because Angel needs a job bad, or she'll be in trouble with the police, because of the place she works now.

"YER'" ALL IN TROUBLE WITH THE POLICE!" Bellows the drunk. **"IT'S THESE CYCLES! RIDING THESE GODDAMN MOTORCYCLES DOES SOMETHING TO YUH!"**

"SHE GOES CRAZY OVER ANYTHING IN A UNIFORM HONEY!" Somebody's voice shouts in mirth over the music and there's the rising sound of wind.

Just out in the park to hear some mellow sounds.

Little islands of dikes between the trees and over the rolling meadow.

Stolen bras hung from some treebranches; trees and handlebars sported teeshirts, sox, and the gay flag fluttered; red, yellow, orange, blue & green.

The campfire roared, and food was free. The gang had tried to be as disciplined as they could, ---finding a spot well away from the other heterosexual campers--before they went wild.

Like monkeys, soon they were swinging in the trees.

Stryker took in the sight of the other women. It inspired her. Glad she was still alive and hadn't committed suicide, even tho she was still crazy & in pain in her soul, she was managing to enjoy life. Glad

145

she was outdoors, felt she'd been neglecting her life, holed up in a room-and-a-half oil painting & writing poetry & talking to no body but her journal. Life was so rich! So much fun romping with the dikes!

All day long, the long ride had vibrated the bike between her legs; Angel had envisioned Crystal who clutched tight to her back, riding in the saddle behind, hot crotch pressed to her ass. Couldn't wait to strip off her pants and get to her mates hot pussy, especially after the hot lather they'd worked up performing in front of the crowd of straight suburbanites in the Mall. The day was so relaxed, she thought; 'I'll do it here. Why not?'

Trees, foliage. Day was chill, but the sun kept them warm enough. Without asking the big blond butch merely reached over to Crystals fly, pulled down the zipper, and yanked down her girls femmy pants; then pushed her thighs open. Soon her fingers worked in her cunt. This is how bikers code stated it was suppose to be. A biker wouldn't have a woman who didn't obey her. Or have sex when, and how she requested. After her fem got good and wet, Angel stripped down her own leathers too, unzipping the legs first so they'd come off over her boots, & she could keep wearing them; and removed her jockey shorts too, the same way. So she lay on a blanket in the grass, ass naked, but boots and heavy jacket clanking chains; motorcycle cap still on. With a firm grip held Crystals head between her thighs as her woman's hot mouth pressed down on her cunt, sucking, tongue licking. It wasn't shocking. Many of the other dikes were making the same sweet drama on their blankets, under the trees. Blue sky overhead.

Saundra was getting raw dike love. Dressed in her best short black leather skirt--its hem barely reached to the tuffs of brown kinky pubic hair at her crotch, a stretch of naked legs met by high top boots rising from the toes of her feet. The brown biker Saundra leaned against a tree, legs apart in a defiant stance, her fine arched highheeled boots planted in the wet earth & was being fucked by her hefty white butch, who was really pumping hard. From a distance Angel watched for a moment as she went to climb aboard Crystal and finish, with an orgasm done cunt to cunt. She thought, 'I shouldn't be so polite. I

146

should have brought my dick out here and strap it on and fuck Crystal with that too.'

Saundra and her big biker lay, finally, wrapped in each others arms, on their blanket, exhausted. The dike was glad she had a femmes hole to use. Her thick fingers smelled of pussyjuice. Saundra was glad she had a butchwoman beside her. She lay, pleasantly fulfilled, stomach fed, warm, face up on the blanket viewing the overhead view of the sky & treetops of the park.

Dikes Day Out. Sounds of gay women's laughter. Dancing. Drinking. Stolen pink bras fluttered from the handlebars of their choppers parked here & there thru the trees. A campfire roared in the clearing. Smell of grilling hot dogs. Gigantic bowls of potato salad.

"STUPID CUNT LAPPING BITCHES!" A scream tore thru the trees. Fifteen men had returned to their campsite, baseball bats and an ax in their hands. Already the Outlaw Warriors were racing down across the meadow on bike and by foot to fight them. The first man leaped at the dikes swinging a baseball bat; ducking, a woman narrowly missed having her skull bashed; she retaliated, kicking him in the knee. The line of men charged at the women, but they had risen up drawing their knives, with eight to ten inch blades flashing as sabers slashing and cutting the hands that held the baseball bats, as they kicked and blocked and took the blows on fleshy parts of their shoulders, while protecting their skulls. **"FUCKIN' QUEERS!"** A man screamed, holding his bat in a limp hand streaming blood from a severed vein. Then a shot ran out and one of the men fell, struck in the groin. The women on the front line had trained to fight & were prepared with protection. Johnny was the first to arrive at the scene violently transpiring on the outskirts of their camp. Carrying a five foot length of heavy chain she swung it clanking up and around in a circle striking the enemy men, one after another. **"OUR KIDS CAN SEE YOU OUT HERE YOU NASTY LESBIAN SLIME!"**

W H A M! The heavy-linked section of chain slapped one man across the face, breaking teeth, & blood and saliva gushed out of his mouth. **"SO GO HOME & SIT ON HIS FACE AND LEAVE US THE FUCK ALONE!"** Spits Johnny to one man, referring to his

147

friend, staring at them in rage and makes the fuck sign, fist raised up in the air.

"GET A REAL MAN AND SEE WHAT IT FEELS LIKE!"
Yells one youth, 6' tall, hairy faced, he & his friends are tossing over the dikes picnic baskets, and the less aggressive women scream. Men are striking dikes with baseball bats. Johnny swings the chain back with two strong arms, brings it down, **CRASH!** in the center of the men, and it connects; several of them holler; one of them clutches his elbow.

Rip crashes thru the bushes and bursts into the clearing on foot; pointed silver toes on her black boots kicked the first man she saw, while simultaneously swung her fist in a powerslam punch, connecting with a whiskered jaw. Another man swung a bat at her, missing when she sidestepped. Another jumped on her. Four more men broke thru the little line of dikes swinging bats and trapped some women on the blanket who screamed and huddled together. Meanwhile four more men had raced across the meadow running towards the scene to help their buddies.

Hawk, with a spike-haired punk on the back of her cycle dismounted and ran to the fray screaming curses, brandishing a length of pipe; her pink & green spike hair quivering like the quills of a porcupine as she rammed the pipe into the balls of one man. He screamed in agony griping his crotch in his hands & sinking to his knees. **CRASH!** A baseball bat came down, glancing off her shoulder as she swiveled away to avoid it, but not quite enough. One of her punks leapt on the bat with both arms, trying to wrestle it away, and the wounded Hawk mustered enough energy despite searing pain to twist the pipe back and then forward to **SMACK** the man on his skull with a dull spongy thud. It was a royal battle. 19 men vs. 7 warlike dikes--and dikes were pouring thru the trees from campsites everywhere towards the meadow. More dikes, came running. Two bikers had one man down; had wrestled his own baseball bat away, and began knocking the shit out of him with it. Blood squirted into the air. 400 feet across the meadow at the line of trees bunches of family campers watched, horrified. A dike grabbed a man by a fistful of hair and kicked him between the legs. Dikes & men were swinging, fist to fist; but slowly the men were beginning to see their

19-strong army being overwhelmed by a greater number of females. A woman was down, blood shot from her nose, two men kicked her, one after the other, but an enraged Warrior leaped on both of them at once howling with vengeance. Ugly men just moments ago laughing, evil and full of the energy of hate, found themselves outnumbered, surrounded by a gang of smaller dike bikers. They were prepared; using weapons; as always armed with pipes & chains and other items that could be carried anywhere & used as weapons, but in appearance not obviously illegal like a gun or a butcher knife. —As for the high caliber weapons, those were hidden away. And they had plenty. Because guns are easier to get then some of the things people really need.

George rode into the fray, her huge figure bouncing on the chopper over bumps in the dirt & rolled to a stop, motorcycle boots skidded on the ground, balancing the bike upright. A rifle, reconfigured to full automatic fire on her lap. The huge biker kept watch, coolly, thru darkglasses. Alternately surveying the hetros way off by the line of trees, ready to spray the meadow with bullets to hold them back if they decided to charge; and keenly watching the few men still fighting, to make sure none of them might make a sudden desperate reach for a concealed gun, as it was apparent they were loosing the battle badly. At any sign of firepower she was prepared to shoot her weapon --to kill.

The gang of women had grown to 30. Two of the men lay face down in the grass unconscious. Another wreathed in agony, bleeding from a bullet wound. Three of the men had stopped fighting. Shirts torn, flesh bloody, big freckled hillbilly faces simmering violently, twisting, ugly; they said nothing. Stood surrounded by the pack of warlike bikers. They looked at the enemy facing them. A circle of dikes yelling at them, hurling insults, hammering the baseball bats they'd taken from the men against the earth in warning.

An inner core of men still fought on, one swinging a deadly ax was held at bay by three dikes; two held baseball bats and a third the branch of a tree; which was being splintered by the swings of the ax. Another carefully singled out shot fired by a dike brought him down gasping for air, his leg shot out from under his heavy weight; where

149

he was converged upon by the three, kicking & stomping dikes wielding their sticks.

A dike ran out of the fray **stomp stomp** thru the grass, swinging a length of chain she kept on her cycle, ready for the purpose of battle.

Fleeing ahead of her across the field, ran a man 6'5" large, in leisure sports wear, ran, deserting the battle, retreating back towards the line of trees where the straight people were camped. Two other dikes ran at a trot behind them, waving confiscated baseball bats.

"LESBIAN BITCH! YEAH! THAT'S WHAT WE ARE YUH REDNECK SON OF A BITCH!" Snarled the first dike, whipping the chain in a circle; and they hadn't been doing nothing but taking a peaceful fuck in the grass.

Ten men fought on viciously, outnumbered 3 to 1 by fighting women.

A biker came running straight into the crowd of males wielding a lead pipe taking the opportunity to attack as one turned to slug another woman; she struck him in the forehead; hearing the **CRACK** against his skull. A scream gurgled in his throat, he tottered toward her, outweighed her by 100 pounds, **BAM!** In terror her foot met his stomach in a karate kick; but he kept coming--falling in momentum, flat on his face into the earth.

Two men, their pale faces contorted like white sheets of anger swung their fists and bats, screamed obscenities at the dikes, but had backed up to each other in a circle of defense and looked around. Wondering 'what in hell's going on?' --They hadn't seen the rows and rows of parked motorcycles behind the trees before the attacked; and hadn't known how many biker women there were.

A Warrior rode over on her cycle, skidded in the wet mud & grass. Threw down the kickstand and leapt into the fray. **Crunch crunch crunch** of her motorcycle boots, fast, fast as she could run. The dike with the lead pipe swung out, crazed, an insane look in her eyes, got thru the men's defenses and hit another of the powerful masculine giants on the side of his head, a glancing blow, but enough to send

150

him down to his knees. **BANG!** A baseball bat clipped her on the neck, the pipe spun out of her hand. A furious male wielding a bat back and forth, knocking dikes from one side to the other. Hawk leapt thru the space between his arms, punching with both fists, slamming into the man's face, while jamming her knee into his crotch in a 3 prong attack, and he went down. The next dike leapt on his fallen body kicking with her boots **crack crack** into his ribs.

Suddenly rapid gunfire fills the air. **KBLAM! BLAM BLAM BLAM BLAM BLAM BLAM!** A line of bullets whips along the mud 200 feet from where they're brawling along the meadow; and in distance, a group of men who had headed in from the line of straights by the trees, now returned across the meadow back to safety. And they hear the cry; **"CALL THE RANGERS! CALL THE PARK RANGERS!"**

Two dikes held a man in restraint. Arm lock while another clutched his leg, her teeth biting into the meat of his thigh. He was fighting back, vicious punches of powerful arms, when the teeth sank into his flesh, he screamed, fists clenching into claws that ripped the air.

At 6'8" a giant compared to the women he wreathed on the ground in Bermuda shorts, & a flowered shirt, lapsing into a coma from the blows rained upon him by the squad of smaller dikes. Blood oozed under his clothes; face up still moving & moaning, his heart pounding blood, which rapidly spread in a pool under him.

The dikes kicked some last hot licks. Sound of cycles as more dikes flooded into the area, squealed to a stop; then gunned up their motors, spun their tires, revving in place yelling warwhops, or, raced around the battleground in a circle. The men had all but stopped fighting. Angry dikes surrounded them, some nursing injuries, violence in the their faces, hate; screaming for greater revenge then the toll their dike fists & feet had already taken.

Six men fought on feebly swinging their bats with twenty women kicking them, punching them, slapping them with chains and prodding them with pipes on any unprotected arm or leg they could catch. It was a victory for dikes. Three men who had stopped

151

fighting minutes ago broke thru the crowd of dikes, running panic struck back across the meadow in full retreat. At a run, at the sight of them turning tail the bikers yelled **"YAHOO! FUCKEN' ASSHOLES! RUN BACK HOME TO YER' MOMMAS!"**

It was over in 5 minutes. One man half dead, another bully, maimed. 4 more running at a fast clip in retreat back to the line of thick forest that separated them from the other, hetero, campers.

Johnny and Hawk, the first bikers to jump into battle were covered with blood, and seeing stars from blows they'd received. The mechanic's oily hands were streaked with blood. The feminine women and a puny butch dike of the group who'd first been attacked were huddled together, nursing bruises from the blows that the men had rained on them; and had watched the lesbian avengers with awe. Faintly across the meadow at the line of the trees could be heard curses screamed at the bikers from the square campers, but they kept their distance.

The last bullies had been reduced to cowards. They were trying to run off, but some dikes swung their own weapons at them, herding them back into an imprisoning circle. One man got pushed down and several dikes stomped the shit out of him. A big Amazon in black leather and blue denims stomps up and down on a man, while waving his flowered shirt ---leisure redneck men's ware—overhead in victory. Another man tries to crawl away, out of the circle, but he's being kicked by female feet & beaten by their weapons, so he must turn and scamper, a quivering mass of fear-filled jelly, back with the rest of the captive men; And more bikers are pouring in from all sides nearly the total gang surrounds their prisoners.

BAM! One of the interloping men inside the captives circle receives a mouthful of blood. Their bats having been wrestled out of their fist are instruments turned against them. Now the fun begins. Two other big muscular men are singled out for attack; are beaten with no mercy by the raining fury of pipes and bats down to the ground, where they lie, unconscious. The lesbian bikers vent their rage on the four remaining men, who now stand terror struck, clothes ripped, hair wild, sticky with their own blood. The dikes keep harassing them, with glee.

When the last man is down on his knees, begging for his life with dike bikers ready to smash his skull like they hit a baseball with the bats, it's over.

George gave the bikers orders they should let their prisoners go-- before somebody died.

The bikers withdrew a few paces, and the men still able, ran off, leaving the other fallen goons face down in the grass.

Whipped.

They had repulsed the attack. But the park was no longer a peaceful place.

The words of hate lingered in the air in a blue poison. Rage, vented thru their fists, had left an empty space within their hearts; and in their bodies, a state of exhaustion.

One runt weasel biker squatted down by a man rummaging thru his pockets and came out with a wad of cash, rings and wallet.

Some of the dikes followed suit, falling on the defeated enemy and stripping them of anything they could use; while others, satisfied to be champions would not stoop so low, but merely strode over the disabled male bodies & went back to the blankets & sites where they had lounged before duty called them to do battle.

The word went round to assemble.

The bikers moved their outpost, each individual group & person packing up their blankets, bedrolls & music, and trekked back to the mother camp by the cooking food and campfire, to join the safety of numbers. The Leader rode her Harley down thru the meadow, weaving thru the trees, marking a silent line between her gang and the crowd of straight campers in the distance; while calling up any stray dikes, to make sure everyone had heard they were leaving. Then she came back to the bloody battleground. Hawk stood, a booted foot up on a rock, spike hair bristling green, & pink, slowly examining her knuckles. Her fingers flexed, sore; her cutaway leather gloves from which the pink fingers protruded were ripped. Under her jacket her shoulder bruised purple and was swelling. **"The cowardly punks! We kicked their ass good!'**

"Yeah." Answers a biker, standing, boots in blood-wet soil.

"I had my foot into one guys ass, up to the hilt." Brags another.

"Uh huh. Uh huh." Sez a dike, as she gingerly felt her lips swollen to the size of a balloon.

Nearby, another biker was on her knees, heaving up her guts, after being struck in the stomach. Two dikes stood beside her, ministering to her; holding her & mopping vomit off her face.

"I jumped on 'em and forced one of the motherfuckers down. Then somebody whips him with a chain." Drifts a voice thru the day.

"When they saw how bad they was outnumbered, they ran, but they couldn't run fast enough."

"SHOULD HAVE KILLED 'EM!"

"YUH RAN 'EM OFF, IT'S GOOD ENOUGH!" Bellows Daddy George.

"Yeah, and now *we* got to go home! Shit! Dikes are always settling for less!" A biker complains; gazing sullenly at the bodies of the unconscious men laying scattered in the grass. And others gazed longingly at the once-peaceful meadow where they'd wanted to play.

"YUH' MET 'EM TOE TO TOE! IT AIN'T WORTH GOIN' TO JAIL OVER MURDER!"

"THEY'RE BIGGER THEN WE ARE! WE GOTTA MURDER 'EM!"

"Always somebody getting in our way, stopping us from doing what we want to do!"

"BE GLAD YUH FOUGHT 'EM TOE TO TOE AND WHIPPED THE SHIT OUT OF 'EM!"

All the old timers privately agreed. It had been a successful battle. A lot of times they'd had to run, when they were in small groups and of few numbers, and wait, then return to the scene and do something sneaky to get revenge back at the enemy, --for their own self satisfaction --because they had not been big & strong enough to go toe to toe in a fight from the beginning.

Now, the idea was, to clear out of the park and disappear. Before a Ranger could be located see the bodies of beaten men bleeding & broken lying in the meadow and start asking questions and writing down names & drivers licenses.

"THEY LOOK AT WOMEN AS POWERLESS, BUT WE GOT POWER!" Daddy George made a fist. The bikers cheered. The black leather clad giant leaned to Hawk, who had mounted her chopper, still nursing a swollen hand. Hawk tipped her pink & green spiked head up to listen to George. "If it's any one thing I want to say I taught them as President of the Outlaws Motorcycle Club, it's to stand up and fight for yourselves as women & as dikes!"

"Yeah. We did it!" The smaller Warlord snarled, unceremoniously; **"We shoved their fucking dicks down their throats."**

The sky spread out in cinemascope end to end, with nothing to block the view of its magnificence. Ridge of black mountains, clouds as smoke on top, lit by the startling sun.

The gang rode home in silence.

Chapter Thirteen

Stryker was a Jew. She was a biker dike. A lezzy. A queer of kiki capacity; an androg, more on the butch side who was 25 years old, who wrote poetry & was an artist & was judged insane by the

155

authorities of the world. So, a check was deposited into her bank account at the first of every month. SSI. $660, and she could write & paint and lesbianate to her hearts content, possessing enviable free time.

Usually referred to this Supplemental Social Security Income as her SS money, accompanying it by impersonating a Nazi Officer & giving a HEIL HITLER salute.

Her drab room looked out on the world from the 8th floor--at pigeons on nearby roofs & clouds on a magnificent horizon.

"The system we have is crumbling." Styrker tells her visitors. "It works for the people on top, and the upper middle class. The middle class is constantly striving to keep from falling, and to the lower class it is a death sentence. Every dike I know is struggling to keep a toehold in the system, ---or doing time."

Clouds floated by outside the window. Scent of oil paints, turpentine & linseed oil hung heavily in the room. Crystal sat on the bed, looking pretty, listening to the short earnest dike deliver her tirade. **"I'M A JEWITCH! I'M JEWITCH!"**

After she's done, Angel stares at her with a sense of marvel. "Stryker, yer' one of the smartest dikes in the Outlaws."

Stryker wore monster glasses, triple lenses. She had grown up watching TV thru a telescope for being nearsighted. The fat dike was hysterical. **"I'M CRAZY! A CRAZY LADY!"** She grabbed Angels lapel in fat fingers & eyes gazed up frantically from her short stature into Angels. **"LISTEN TO ME PLEASE! JUST LISTEN! I RESPECT YOU! I WON'T STAND HERE AND TELL YOU ALL MY PROBLEMS! I KNOW THAT'S A BAD THING I DO! I PROMISE! BUT YOU *HAVE TO KNOW THIS*! I HAVE A PSYCHIATRIC DISORDER! --IT'S KNOWN AS MANIC DEPRESSIVE FOR WHICH I'M PROVIDED THE DRUG LITHIUM, AT A DOSAGE OF 500 MILLIGRAMS! BIG CAPSULES, WHICH I MUST TAKE TWICE DAILY! *SEE!* ON MY SHELF, A BOTTLE WITH A PHARMACEUTICAL PRESCRIPTION!**

IT IS NOT MY INTENTION TO OFFEND!"

"I know! Calm down!" The big blond admonishes, as she sees the woman go mad before her eyes.

"Well! I'm agitated, but I took a pill before you guys got here, it'll calm me down." Stryker replies. Already feeling herself subdued. "I'm not suppose to drink when I take 'em."

"THEY HAD ME IN 4 POINT RESTRAINTS!" Stryker shouted once more, but her hysteria was loosing the battle against the drugs.

"My baby quit her job, she's gone legit." Crystal says after a few minutes. And squeezed Angel's hand. "It's a relief, every day I'm expecting to hear she's been carted off to jail."

"I ain't totally quit, it's just part time." Sez Angel in a quiet voice.

"Now, if I could just get her drive my car, it's so much safer. Instead of riding a motorcycle everywhere.   Their dangerous! She almost got **killed** on one!"

Stryker looked at Crystal a moment from her big wobbly eyes behind thick glasses. "The only thing I'm afraid of about my bike is when I'm riding thru a bad neighborhood somebody might try to snatch me off of it."

The artists room had originally come with a bath.   Narrow, 4 feet wide, it ran the length of her room --twelve feet. It was cold, in winter she always kept the door closed so to keep the main room hotter, and used this side room for storage. The toilet had been disconnected years back, & its seat riveted shut. Oil paintings were stacked on its enamel lid, and leaned against the bathroom walls. The sink worked, cold water only; and was stained with green, red, yellow, and black smears of oils. The smell inside was of cold linseed oil & turpentine. Brushes sat in a jar of solvent disengaging colors from their bristles. Paintings were everywhere, stacked, hanging, leaning. Approximately 50 of them, big to small. A window at the end of the narrow storage room overlooked the downtown city.

The young blond couple seated on Strykers bed nestled close together. "Yer' the only artist I know." Angel sez.

"You're special Stryker." Adds Crystal.

Solemnly the fat dike watched her friends. Her room was about the size of their own, but Stryker had lived in hers a lot longer--5 years. Her & Angel had dwelled side by side, but blocks apart, not knowing each other, until the club had brought them together.

Now, she showed Angel some paintings, & explained what they meant. "This one, this *person*, she works over in the Green Light District. She's a male transvestite sex worker."

Angel bent down and studied the figures created of thickly applied oil to canvass, and asked; "*Green* Light District?"

"Yeah. They're Martian sex workers."

"From Mars?"

"Yeah."

"Aw! No shit!"

Stryker wasn't as much of a fool as people thought, --just a crazy lady.

"Debbie's still wearing that leather mini-skirt. —She wears a mini skirt no matter how cold it gets..." Stryker mused. "But I don't care, I got a slut. She took care of all my needs... I had that slut on the Run too, yuh know." The fat dike boasted, she was back, seated on the foot of the bed with her guests. Angel & Crystal leaned against the headboard, feet outstretched onto of the covers, wrapped in each others arms. "She stayed with me all thru the Run. Then, I had this other slut come to visit me here in my room. We bumped pussy's all night and I'm still sore. I rode her and she rode me. It was a regular riding academy--complete with the riding crop."

"Oh yeah?" Said Crystal, happy for her. Reached to the nightstand and took the cup of herb tea Stryker had prepared for them, and sipped it.

"Glad yer' not up here all alone pal." Sez Angel.

"What slut? Cookie?"

"Naw."

"Lady Jane?"

"Naw, I took Lady Jane on the run; naw, a pretty slut. Real pretty. I dunnoe her name. She didn't say, I didn't ask."

"What's she look like?" Asks Crystal.

"Beautiful wild black hair, sultry. Tall. Skinny."

Crystal looked puzzled.

"Well, she left, I'm alone. The slut had to go out *slutting*. But that's ok." Stryker said with false enthusiasm, as tho it wasn't important, yet it was very important.

"Black hair?"

"Yeah."

"DINA!" Crystal gasps, throw a pink fingernailed hand over her mouth. **"You slept with *Dena! Daddy Georges Mistress!"*** Crystal jumped across the bed and grabbed the chubby butch by her lapels.

"Say man! Yuh fucked one of George's ladies! Congratulations!" Angle laid back against the headboard, blond butch hair to her shoulders, cracks a smile across her broad face.

159

"Dena? Yeah, that name does sound familiar."

"Oh God!" Crystal shrieks, excited.

"Yeah, and she clipped me for $100."

"WHAT!" Both Outlaws screamed together. Angel jolts up from her leaning position.

"It was worth it." Sez Stryker. "Even tho I didn't offer it, she just took it. Out of my wallet on the dresser when I was asleep."

Stryker made so many mistakes she felt she was living in a world of her own.

"It's ok, I don't care about Dena or my $100. I'm falling in love."

"Who?"

"Don't tell."

"We won't."

"Promise!"

"We won't! Who!"

"Debbie."

The two looked at each other.

Stryker wasn't crazy, but often lived in a fantasy.

"I was in Seventh Heaven. I dreamt I had sexual communion with Debbie. It's like a Holy Sacrament. It's a spiritual experience. She does it and don't even do nothing but be herself. Her hair is so pretty. She doesn't have to wear any special clothes. But I am in Seventh Heaven. She is so loving. It's the way she touches you, and her pussy is so sweet... She is so good…. **POOF! POOF!"**

160

Non-stop talk, again, Stryker was getting wound up.

"Yer talking to yourself again buddy." Angel reminds the dike. "Yuh got company, you don't need to do that."

"POOF! POOF!"

Her medication was kicking in to her system, and Stryker drew closer back to earth, like a wounded kite. Fairly soon she might fall asleep in the iron, relentless grip of powerful anti-psychotic drugs. "Guys... uh... yuh know what they call me at the clubhouse? They say, 'Oh no! That runt butch!' I'm a runt... I don't deserve a pretty girl."

Stryker had struggled to try and improve herself, to be successful, and to win a mate, to champion & carry home a lover in her Amazon arms.

"I looked up some books on Bulimia, but all they tell is how to cure it, not how to *do* it. --For my diet." Sez Stryker.

"That's when you throw up after you eat? To make yourself thin?"

"Yeah. The Romans did it. They had vomitoriums. They'd go there between courses at the banquets. It was right next to the ladies lounge."

"Ugh."

"I gotta get thin. I gotta be *loved!"*

Stryker said, "I wouldn't want to live in ancient Rome, or even ancient Greece with Sappho. I want to be in a country where the women are free. Not a country where even one woman is a slave to men, and has to wear a veil or stay locked up in the house."

Afterawhile, her social concentration wore thin, and Stryker launched into a steady stream of annoying babble. The two blond lovers faded further from her, and began a conversation of their own, as they prepared to leave.

"I'm so self-amusing I can just sit here in my room and talk to myself. I'm so interesting..." Stryker's voice trails off, in mid air.

One other time when they were visiting Angel glimpsed the envelope to a letter, it was addressed to Shelia Libowitz.

There was a document hung in a glass picture frame on the wall written entirely in Hebrew script.

These were the substances of Stryker's life.

Over the tiny fat dikes dresser was a photo-montage of bikers. Blond, blue eyed Amazons. Angel noticed this one day and stood there examining it with interest. All their motorcycles were top-notch, expensive Harleys, Screamin' Eagles with turbo jet carburetors, full dressers; Harley hogs fat as Cadillac's—with big seats; Goldwings; and curiously Angel didn't recognize any of the bikers in the photos. Handsome Nordic women a lot like herself who looked like powerlifters who work out with weights at the gym daily. Gazing closer, Angels blue eyes squinting to examine the assembly of photos composing the montage she noticed several bikers sported **WHITE POWER!** teeshirts, flexing their muscles on Styker's mirror. A handsome blond biker's photo was pasted in the middle of them. She had a blond moustache, a bikers cap on her head. MY SECRET HEARTTHROB was written in red pen underneath. All the pictures had been cut out from other photographs and pasted with care into this one whole portrait. Angel stood, admiring the bikes when Stryker stomps back in, from the bathroom down the hall.

Angel looks up. "I don' t recognize a single woman in these photos! Who are they?"

"The 'Vengers." Says Stryker, peacefully. And sits down in the armchair, folding her pudgy fingers over her belly.

Their rival gang. A motorcycle club whose headquarters was out-of town.

"My God!"

162

"I got 'em from some dizzy dike who use to ride with 'em. She came over and joined us Outlaws, and gave away all her old Avenger stuff. It's a great joke, don't you think? *My* photo montage?" Pretty funny, considering: they don't allow Jews to join their gang."

Angel & Crystal's was a higher grade of hotel. Theirs had a private bath that worked.   "I get zits on my ass sitten' on that toilet seat." Sez Stryker, with a wave of her hand indicating the throne room down the hall.

At that point in time, Stryker didn't seem like she was going up the ladder of prosperity, nor down. Just holding on. While Crystal & Angel were making plans to move into an apartment somewhere away from downtown altogether. The fat dike with her problems seemed destined to live out the remainder of her life in the soot dirtied shabby transient hotel where hardly anybody knew if she was alive or dead.

"I'm writing a poem to Daddy George. Wanna hear it?"

"Yes!" Said Crystal in a motherly fashion. She gave her attention.

"Well," Stryker's eyes squinted behind their triple paned glass lenses; "it's about pain, & how she rides a big Harley motorcycle and all. And I just put the fight in; that we had on our Run.   I ain't finished it.----

Daddy George was the Leader
Of The Pack.
She rode a Harley,
 and she wore black.

We went on a Run to a mall
 out of town.
How many of us did it take
 to bring them down?
1 to 3. Women to men.
We need strength, we need muscle.
 We have our gang.
 They seen us coming
 and away they ran.

Like I said, I ain't finished it. I'm writing a Christmas poem too.

I use to be a Christian did I tell you guys? I use to be a regular attendee at a group who wuz feminists and celebrated the Christian Eucharist. But I discovered after a year of attendance I hadn't made a single friend there. I kept going back, back, back. **Back, back! BACK!** *BACK!!!!!* every Sunday." Said Stryker duefully, bristling with annoyance like feathers on a mad hen; she went across the room and came back with a sheaf of papers entitled **XMAS POEM**, and plunked her wide ass down on the bed. "They'd come up and shake my hand and say hello and ask me how I was, when I walked in the door--but that was the limit of it. My new friends in the club are closer to me. They're always drag racing by on their cycles, waking me up in the middle of the night to party with them, or to tell me their troubles. --Their old lady won't speak to them, that kind of troubles. Their old man-dike kicked them out of the house. They ain't got no money. Their old ladies want them to get a real job--like you guys yuh know. And some of the ladies are trying to help me dress right and clean up my room so I can get a real lady and not just sluts. I had a date with a professional Jewish girl. Did I ever tell you? A JAP?"

"She was Japanese?"

"No. A Jewish American Princess. She was great. She was hot stuff. She dumped me for another professional. They worked in the banking industry. It broke my heart. Here's the poem, I gotta have it ready for the holidays, to read in front of the club!"

> **'Twas the night before Xmas,**
> **and all thru the club**
> **dikes was fucking & fisting**
> **and their whips drawing blood.**
>
> **Spike heels was hung on the**
> **backs of their chairs,**
> **off comes their stockings,**
> **and soon they'd be bare.**
>
> **Dike children were sleeping**

at home in their beds.
While down in the club, mommas and daddies
on their knees giving head.

ON DOMINANT MASTER, ON SLAVE, SLUT
AND VIXEN!
ON UNDERGROUND SOLDIERS!
FUCK TRIXIE AND NIXON!

THEN TO MY EYES AROSE SUCH A CLATTER
MERRY XMAS TO DIKES
AND THE REST IT DON'T MATTER!

Angel & Crystal chuckled. They told her to try to finish it.

"It's hard to concentrate when I'm on medication. I need *help*. I can't remember all the original lines.

"There's some bit about a sugar plum fairy…"Offers the curly blond.

Stryker folded the poem, and put the papers away. "Have you heard? I'm gonna do a scene at a Christmas party with Daddy George." Stryker sez, proud. "& it's a surprise."

Crystal clapped her hands enthusiastic. "For the club's party!"

"No!" The fat dike closed her eyes. "It's suppose to be a secret. For a private party at her *home*. Just her and the Warlords."

Chapter Fourteen

The Nazi's had their Luftwaffa; the Church it's Popes. All groups have their licensed cliques, their secret cabals. And the Outlaws had their inner circle, the Warlords.

Each year Daddy George attended 3 Christmas parties. The first was for her and Queen Georgina--a private group of their sissy friends, mostly rich older fags, and the four other Warlords, plus a minor selection of favored members from the club. It was held at her private home.

The second was a novelty party, this year it would have SM demonstrations, a Slave Pit, and was to be held at a rented site--a boy's dungeon in the warehouse district. Members Only.

The last one, by far the biggest; who which all were invited, members, friends & anybody; was the Grand Christmas Party at Oils.

Daddy George and the other Warlords held mammoth biker parties at their luxury homes from time to time, but it was at the smaller private parties that the food tasted most delicious, --fancy feasts to whet the pallet of the most blasé connoisseur. Finest caviar, both red & black, from Russia. Mineral waters imported from France, Germany & California. Pate, pheasant, foi-de-grais, fruit juices, and liqueurs. Catered buffets. With the most mellow marijuana. It was these private parties of the Warlords and their friends that the common bikers seldom saw.

Tonight Daddy George wore full regalia. Black leather, eagle sparkling silver on her cap. Wore her tool under her leather pants, --- a 9" cock, fully simulated with a dickhead & veins.

During the day one could see rainbows of red, yellow, orange, blue, green reflected in the crystal candle holders, and on the great table's burnished wood of golden brown, created by refracted light thru prisms from a floor length window, from which the drapes had been drawn back. At night, the drapes were closed; but the same rainbows appeared on the table caused by candle light emanating thru their crystal holders.

This banquet table was place-set; 12 settings on either side, with George at the head, and Georgina at the foot commanding it's regal expanse, & the 24 guests.

For the evening they'd hired a live band.

Some baby dikes, 14 & 15 year olds had been paid $5 an hour to put up a ceiling-high Christmas tree & fully decked it with lights, bulbs, silver tinsel, & red/white stripped peppermint candy canes.

George wasn't the personification of the Anti-Christ, she just didn't believe in a male God with beard and flowing robes who hated gays, scorned females & couldn't see past the old testament into the gay unisexual beyond of the lives of Angel and Johnny, and Rip and Ronny and herself.

She/he celebrated Xmas, not Christmas.

The rooms of their lavish home carried the sweet smell of Frankincense & Myrrh.

Whenever the couple prepared to go out--especially to a party, or to Oils, donning their fancy dress, the Queen seated at her vanity mirror might yell, **"GEORGE!"** When the bulldike came running, she might gaze at him-her with beautiful deep dark eyes and query, "Do my eyes look crooked?"

"NAW! THEY'RE FINE! NOW COME ON! WE'LL BE LATE!"

Voluptuous, seated at her dressing table facing her image in 3 panels of mirrors, bulbs blazing light, a stars wardrobe, she'd turn her face from side to side. "I've got green eye shadow on. I haven't had on any colors for a while. Do I look made up?"

"Yes!"

"Do you like the green?"

"Yes!"

"… Or are you just *saying* that!"

"YES! YES! YES!"

Tonight for the gala' event at their mansion Georgina had been preparing for hours.

Some people who came over to their house, their hetro neighbors, could never tell what sexual orientation they were. Outside, to those who weren't visitors, the house was austere, sterile and magnificent like all the other places on the block--except for a urinating water fountain statue placed in front to one side of the entrance, a suggestion from one of her fag friends, that Georgina had followed up on in one of her madder moments, and a big eight by ten foot gay flag hanging on the flagpole, red, orange, yellow, green, blue & purple.

Inside came the true revelation of what kind of home it was. All kinds of lesbian dirty books-both by lesbian pornographers, and by the hetro world. Lesbian music selections in a rack covering one wall. And black sadomasochistic traipsing.

Georgina greeted her guests at the door.

Rip & Debbie were elegant. Debbie tall, and high heels made her taller. Still, next to Rip she was smaller, Rip towering at 6'6" in thick-soled boots, and resplendent in an ermine pimps coat. Deb wore a luxurious white satin diamond decked jumpsuit (zip front for quick removal) and a fine fur--all earned out of her cunt, and by Rips expert management of their affairs.

Georgina's eyes swiftly traveled the length of Rips body in a glance, took in the leather tuxedo with leather tails and a red leather tie. Georgina's eyes traveled down the length of Rips lean frame to stop a moment and dwell on the imprint of her dick.

The dick she was wearing--to the left side--Georgina marveled at the size of it, then, a little miffed, looked away. 'Gawd! It's bigger then Georgies. Damn! Now it's too late for her to go strap on The Colossus!'

They exchanged hugs, as cool winter winds blew a draft thru the entranceway. The big woman pressed slender Debbie's attractive models body against her bosom, and thinks privately, 'She's skin and bones!'

Dena arrived with an older dike in her middle 40's. The butch probably earned quite a bit of money in a profession of some sort, which was the type Dena liked. She wore a tuxedo made of cloth, and a grin on her face, her arm linked under Dena's. Having no idea whatsoever that the younger woman was George's mistress.

Next to come thru the door was a tall stately fag in his late 50's, grey hair oiled; delicate; quite swish, dressed in a mans suit, but a flowered tie and a cape lined with velvet, taller then George; with aquiline features, hands dripping with diamonds and bracelets of diamonds, and a diamond necklace upon his thin chest; escorted by his life mate Spencer. A very straight looking short pudgy man, who was bald and wore a business suit.

"SELBY!"

Georgina and her dear old friend embraced, stepped back to gaze at each other's outfit, clasped back together in a hug again. "Oh! It's good to see you! You look *Mahvalous!"*

Eighteen more guests, fags and dikes and a few freeks arrived. Including Stryker.

Daddy George didn't mind fags prancing thru her house; having run a boy gang when young and spending decades in redneck men's bars, passing as a man at work, and spending her middleage in fag bars, she was practically a man herself. George tho, had never been as intimately close to as many people as when she'd got the dike gang. So many dikes, so many feelings. In a way it was a relief to get away from it all.

During the course of the evening the fag Selby would graciously excuse himself to go up to the powder room with a swish of his hips rise out of a stately mahogany chair, furling his velvet cape, he was gone up the staircase, twirling diamonds on a bracelet of one hand.

Selby would wander thru the halls as she/he would one day wander thru heaven with God-Our-Mother, and step inside the bathroom— lock the door for good measure. He hated to admit it, by letting

169

others see him do this--at least not in this early stage-- taking a jeweled medicine compact studded with rubies & diamonds, opened it. Inside were 4 pills--for emergencies, on evenings he might not be able to get home; taken from a bottle of Retorovir Capsules. (Zidovoire). Each capsule contained 100mgs of the drug commonly known as AZT. The anti-AIDS distributed by drug a major pharmaceutical house. It was proven to help sustain life in those patients facing certain death from the disease. These small bottles cost a fortune, but he was a wealthy gay man. With proper diet, exercise, rest, he might live 7, even 10 years with the illness. A cure might be found within that time, who could say. Selby was fighting for his life. Something his oldest and dearest friend, Georgina suspected, but neither was willing to deal with yet.

Daddy George and her Warlords dressed up in full regalia. The shiny patin leather visors of their caps bore the club insignia in full color miniatures. And larger, in living color, they wore it on their backs. The mansion seemed full of tall leather dike giants in black boots laughing deep belly laughs & joking. Striding on thick boots. Jackets, vests, and leather chaps adorned with the appropriate loops of chain on the left side, handcuffs, keys, and fine black silk handkerchiefs in the left hand rear pocket.

The Warlord Hawk escorted a beautiful model she'd rented from an escort service --$1,000 for the night, who reaped hateful, envious & cutting glares from femme dikes & fags alike. This beautiful female's sale price was not expensive to the 35-year old Warlord; paid for from her dealings in illegal drugs. She was by far the prettiest of the women there.

Stryker had elected not to fix her bike, but wait 'till the New Year and use her money instead to spend in Oils on ladies & pals, hoisting soft drinks or brewskis, elbows on the bar; and to take cabs as needed. To have more fun with her last $150. This particular evening she had been picked up at her hotel and driven to Georges by limousine.

The fat bosomy dike bustled about, carrying a huge satchel on her back, which contained a change of clothes for after the show, of which she was the bottom part.

Stared across the vast sweeping living room at the fireplace a moment, as she stood beside the grand tree, while the band tuned up their instruments. "Is it warm?" Stryker asked, about the fireplace. George had tired of hauling longs & chopping wood long ago. --The double size house had two such fireplaces, and this one had been converted to gas. An iron pipe with 6 gas jet flame burners. Stryker gazed down at it. "It looks like a Post Apocyopital Menorah." She comments. **"And it's on fire!"**

George looked at her blankly.

Sticks came down on the base drum, **C R A S H!** Signaling the beginning of the party.

It made such a loud sound, because of the amplifying system, that Queen Georgina sat bolt upright in her Throne chair shrieking; **"OHMUHGAWD! THE CAT'S KNOCKED SOMETHING OVER!"** Clutching George with her delicate white fingers bedecked with rings; then wringing her chubby hands in dismay.

One of the favored parts of any party was discussing Times Past.

Georgina and her fairy friends were up to their perfumed armpits in gossip. One of the he-shes had wore a blue gown, floor length, rolled up & hidden under her coat, and put her wig on after she-he arrived.

Stryker strutted around in her best chaps, & bluejeans with red suspenders over her huge belly & majestically large tits. She sauntered over to the fags and told them the tale of the bikers Halloween Party, and how Daddy G went as Dracula. "A problem arose." Said the fat biker. "A lot of women in the Outlaws wanted to be Dracula's bride."

"Oh yes they did Georgie." Chimes in Georgina. "I remember that year! It was a ghastly affair Selby!" Cried the Queen, thumping the other queen on his hand. "Of course I was the Première Bride."

"Yeah! Dracula! It's a comedy-horror film, --kind of like my life…"Muses Stryker.

171

Down the living room, cuddled in a large-stuffed upholstered sofa beside her professional dyke, Dena the Showgirl blushed; red expanding from rouge cheeks to redden her entire body. She knew her position well-- Bride Number #2. Fat Stryker rears back her head, sticks her thumbs under her red suspenders. Her cheep black imitation leather chaps glisten in the refracted light of the Christmas tree, turning her into a multi-color harlequin; her boots are polished, a fine black shirt over her large bosom. **"So for 3 weeks before Halloween, at the clubhouse, one by one, all these women go up and beg Daddy George if they can be her bride! They crawled 'n they begged! A *parade* of women!"**

"Uh *yes*. And Georgie gets too much liquor in her and forgets who she says 'yes' to."

"So, here, a week before the 31st, is all this talk going around Oils; 'I'M GOING TO BE THE BRIDE OF DRACULA' --Daddy George's bride! *'NO! I'M SUPPOSE TO BE HER BRIDE!'* Stuff like that. One comes up, 'Well I heard so-and-so is going to be her bride.' 'We we *both* are!' 'No! So-and-so is!' 'We *all* are!' And in all Daddy George had 17-brides!" The fags burst out laughing.

"Not so! Georgina snorts. It was ten, if that! --Counting myself!"

"Well, you know Dracula had more then one bride." Sez Selby. Patting her hand comfortingly.

"Yeah." Stryker nods. **"Remember that movie where the brides came in the castle and got that *man*, and they kept *pouncing* on him? Remember?"**

"Oh my dear." Sez Selby, tossing his head, he felt a little faint.

"Well," Stryker continues. **As a prerequisite, each lady, in order to be a bride--she had to be fisted."** At this the distinguished grey haired sissy knew he felt sick, but his curiosity got the better of him, and regaining his composure he continued to sit by the fireplace next to Georgina and listened to the story. **"So Daddy George is**

fisting the brides, --they're lined up in a row on the floor of the
clubhouse, 'n each is jumping over the other trying to get to be
next. So Daddy George got to the 5th one, and she's *exhausted.*"
The giant George had quietly walked over to stand beside Georgina's
Throne, and listened in amusement. She too recalled the fateful
episode. Some of her brides had required much vigorous pounding--
the others, just a gentle insertion. The next 2 in line had already got
down on the floor, legs spread clamoring for their share. George had
used hygienic latex gloves, and globs and globs of lube. **"Well as
fast as she'd peel off a glove some biker with a secret crush on
that girl who'd just been fisted would run away with the used
glove, *gosh*, it was a madhouse. Well, when it comes to the 5th or
6th girl, Daddy George is worn out. 'I hate to disappoint you.'
She says, 'however, the Spirit is willing but the Flesh is weak!'"**
The chubby biker droned on. Georgina took a swat at her giant
husbands leather clad butt. A fag put a perfumed handkerchief to his
mouth and held it there with a limpwristed hand.

"Well Dears, it was a madhouse that year, but, several years before
that, --this is before you joined us, *Stryker,* -- when Daddy and Rip
had that terrible fight, --Rip was mad that Daddy had stolen her idea
(so she thought), it was the year the club got 2 *Dracula's,* was a time
in infamy. They looked so handsome in their red & black capes and
fangs, and their hair slicked down with grease like patin leather so
their heads shone, or was it the year youse two wore them black
wigs?"

By the time Stryker had told every tale she knew of biker lore,
George was mildly sick at hearing the sound of her voice. She and
Rip excused themselves, and slipped away from the party for a few
minutes. **"Jack Shit! She thinks she knows everything! She don't
know the half of what we done!"**

"Well keep her around, I'm sure she'll find out. Soon she'll be a
regular fixture of the club."

"Yeah, *stuffed*, and hanging on the wall in my den." Replies
George in a base voice.

The party was in full swing. They eaten, and danced. Half-a-dozen fag friends, bikers, George's mistresses, and sexpartners. Lady Dena briefly acknowledged the presence of Stryker--who she'd clipped for the $100.

Stryker looked her best. Chubby body in black & blue; a bikers cap with the death eagle on its visor, bustled around with an air of authority. --Tonight she was somebody. It was only the second time she'd been invited to Daddy Georges private home.

When the 350-pound Leader sat, one could feel a great pressure on the sofa; & when she left, the absence of her heavy weight all but tilted her vacant end up in the air.

George strode out of the room, leading the guests down the back staircase, into the basement dungeon.

The show was about to begin.

Chapter Fifteen

"ACHTUNG!"

Shadowy candles in the dungeon lit, flickered fire in streaks up the walls, and licked out over the floor.

George's chamber of horrors, lit by row after row of candles. A rack center stage built of huge beams, cross-shape, to which eye-bolts were attached, thru which chains or handcuffs were strung to secure the prisoner.

Doing a scene with Stryker; at first the idea did not seem appealing-- The Master, a big butch, and another basic butch for a slave--fat, definitely not femmy and yielding; a loudmouth, and a firebrand; but also, definitely, compliant. It was to be a different sort of erotica. The 4'11" Stryker had informed Daddy George she wasn't to be whipped too severely if you please; just a taste of the cat-o-nine-tails, a precious few cuts from the bullwhip, but she did need desperately to be humiliated.

174

George strode with thunderous boot steps to the backdrop behind the empty rack waiting for its victim; yanked a cord, which pulled back a curtain. There behind it was the Nazi flag. Huge, from floor to ceiling. Black swastika in a white circle upon red. George disappeared into a side room; when she returned she wore a brown uniform--black boots & belt, gun holster with an official's Luger automatic pistol & a nazi emblem on her armband. Uniform of the dreaded SS. Hitler's elite fighting force of fascist Germany.

A great gasp; "AHHHHH!" Issued from the audience.

A naked Styker, head bowed, was led on stage by an assistant, she was wearing just a harness of black leather & chains across her chest and back.

She knelt before the Master.

"HITLER SHOULD HAVE FINISHED THE JOB JEWGIRL!"

"Yes Master."

"LIBOWITTZ!" Bellowed the behemoth. **'THAT'S A GOOD NAME FOR A JEWESS!"**

"Thank you Master."

"HOW MANY FACTORIES DID YOUR FAMILY OWN-- BEFORE WE CONFISCATED THEM JEWGIRL! YOU DON'T DESERVE TO HAVE FACTORIES! YOU DON'T DESERVE TO HAVE BUSINESSES! BECAUSE YER' SLIME! YER' ANIMALS!"

"Yes Master!"

"YES WHAT JEW GIRL!"

"Yes, I am slime Master. --Thank you Master."

175

The giant biker then handcuffed Strikers thin wrists to the cross; naked white flesh, trembling, she stood, her back to the audience, preparing to receive her punishment.

The banter kept up awhile longer; the audience twitched & moved in awe in the theatre seats installed facing the stage.

It was pretty easy, the humiliation. George had never liked Jews much, so she just thought up all the ugly stuff she'd felt about them from the past. She'd never known any as humanbeings, --until Stryker. George had grown up in a poor white working class neighborhood. Hebrews owned a lot of companies and stores where she worked or shopped. They had owned the steel mill where she labored & they pulled cheep tricks on their employees to save money. As the whip lingered in space, then came cracking down, to cut into the flesh of her sister dike, time seemed to stand still. Just a few years back Stryker had joined the gang, hollering her rabid political views, same as the intensity with which she hollered this evening, **"YES MASTER! GIVE ME MORE THANK YOU!** *PLEASE* **ONE MORE LASH OF YOUR WHIP MASTER PLEASE!"**

The crack of the bullwhip broke the sound barrier, making a tiny sonic boom.

CRACK!

The dungeon was damp. Subterranean. Flickering fire of the candles, cast wavering shadows. The humanbeing chained to the rack trembled. Nude pale flesh criss-cross with bullwhip marks turning blood red. Two-dozen pairs of eyes followed the arc of the Masters powerful arm.

CRACK!

"LOOK AT YUH NOW YUH KIKE CUNT! BEGGING FOR MY WHIP!"

"Please Master! One more lash! Please!"

176

"YUH CAN'T TAKE ONE MORE LASH YUH KIKE!

"Yes I can Master! Please Master! One more lash!"

Next morning, Georgette, the cat stalked over the bed. Daddy George lay asleep, short black hair tousled, wet from sleepsweat. A huge arm flung over the covers. Big Georgina cuddled to her side. He jumped off the bed to the floor and sniffed her jacket, experiencing some of what its occupant had done the night before. Knew instinctively the leather animus of the animal who had occupied that skin previously. Sniffed the human blood from where she'd played. It was interesting to a cat. Along with the usual odor of sweat, dope & other people's cigarette smoke, which lingered in the fabric.

In the mail would be Thank-You's from fag friends. In a few days notes on babyblue stationary would arrive. Georgina loved it. To be formal. Elegant. And looked forward to the flood of flowery handwritten letters from the fags after her events. Of course the dikes never wrote.

"Christmas has been fine! The gourmet cooking you do, all of your dinners were excellent! The cake was tastier the 2nd time around; you really must be very tired; you did lots and lots of cooking! We surely enjoyed the two blazing fireplaces, Swan Lake, and your live band playing The Nutcracker Suite! *Fine* choice! The DeWars Scotch and L'Air DuTemps Rose Geranium Spa Soap, Gourmet Magazines, the bacon or'deourves, chocolates, nuts and all else we enjoyed at your place for the long weekend & the live band! Oh La La! Words cannot describe my dear! How fortunate we were!

We hate to leave your place, you have such a lovely and grand beautiful home, your Christmas tree and table decorations are the greatest, and the crystal Christmas trees along side of the table are *very* festive!

The Poinsettias *AND* pink Tulips! --Very attractive and colorful! We took in everything and loved it! What a pleasure it was to see them!

Your new Chandelier prisms are excellently facetted, and the more Spencer and I thought about them, the more beautiful they became! You have it hung in the *perfect* place; it's worked out fine. The brilliance, once the prisms were cleaned, is magnificent! It really is a beauty!

The whipping scene was *delicious.* We must remember to use some of your lines at our own play parties. I must commend George, she hung her slave up so efficiently! And how clever of her to find a Jewish person who really enjoys this! --And to do it for *Christmas!* I'm sure it might have been a problem to the slave to explain to others of her race, just as it is a problem for all of us to try to explain, to those who don't play the games & do the scenes of SM!

As usual, dear, dear Georgina, your invite for the holidays has brought us joy! Many thanks for all the cooking and other hard work, such fine fires in the fireplaces--excellent food, beautiful Christmas trees; and for inviting Leslie & Marlin, and all our old friends--and also cooking for them. --Felt so much at home with you, such grand hospitality!

> Yours, Dear Friend,
>   Love,
> Selby

Chapter Sixteen

Dena was in a hurry to get to Oils. Wrapped herself up in a coat to walk past some loitering Puerto Ricans so as to show her tits less and be modest, rather then walk down the avenue brazenly in front of them; and run the risk of being hooted & howled at.

Johnny got off the job & came in an old black leather jacket that was cracked and worn.

A novice arrived riding a motorscooter.

Cookie came, **roar, roar, roar** as a lion roaring up to a stoplight in an all leather outfit, gas tank of the cycle painted zebra stripes black/white.

Daddy Georges van was parked outside. All the club members knew it. Big, shiny, blue & silver. A car phone inside. Huge aerial to pick up CB radio bands, a TV & liquor/soda bar in back. He & Queen Georgina were inside.

Screech of bike tires over pavement. A bike waved from side to side, a lesbian biker planted her gymshoed feet on the ground as it stops.

So many cycles pulled up to the entrance that a thick smell of gasoline hung in the air.

The next in the series of biker parties was held at their Clubhouse --given the humble name of Oils, after the lubricant in their bikes.

There was a lot of bottles broken everywhere where some dike had had a bottle smashing fit. Bottoms of brown beer bottles, triangular pieces & jagged shards.

Inside, some dikes employed there were setting up; it was the beginning of the evening. Four clean plastic trashcans of 48 gallon capacity each were being filled with icecubes from the ice making machine.   At the end of the evening they'd be used up--at 3 cubes per glass, and remnants melted into water lining the bottom inches of the plastic bins.

Georgina watched as the girls came in the door, laughing, expectant. She saw young women out in the night alone, the worry on their faces turning to happiness as they entered the protective yellow arc of light cast thru the barroom door. Her black hair cascaded from a pompadour, in ringlets down her bare white shoulders, liquid eyes bore a look of understanding. Georgina thought of her own secure position in life, --to have money in the bank, a house built like a fortress, to be big boned, strong herself, to have a mate who could pass for a man, prepared with guns, and to travel as they did, usually in a group of dike bikers, who were more like a family.

Hungry, poor, cold & unsafe, some of the women came into Oils just to live a few hours in the limelight, and cast off their worries.

Sweet smell of marijuana floated thru the ventilating system.

179

During the regular nights kids came to Oils so hungry, they ate out of the bar service trey-a silver divided bin of goodies pre-chopped by the bartender, intended to go into mixed drinks. Picking their miserable little fingers into lemons, limes, cherries, onions, and olives. Enjoying a poor dikes repast which left a salty sweet taste in their mouths; then washed it down with a glass of free water.

Tonight, however, sections of the bar, plus tables covered with tablecloths were lavishly furnished with food. Slabs of roast beef, baked hams ringed in pineapple slices, chickens, turkeys & all that went along. Dressing, gravy, cranberry sauce, yams & marshmallows, corn dripping in butter, greens, salads, macaroni & cheese; the list went on & on.

Women in body harnesses--nude but for the black leather stripes studded silver; oiled bodies & biker caps prepared for the SM show.

As the Nazi Reichstag. of da Fuhrer, Stryker & her Master George sat at the bar of Oils over a beer discussing their scene. Da Fuhrer & the butch Jewess had traveled in time.--More then 43 years had elapsed from 1941 World War Two, until the present day, 1993. 43 years since their scene set in Fascist Nazi Germany-- or so they would have it.

"The guests liked it."

"You came quite well, and so did I."

George uttered a base laugh.

"You did come huh?" Queried Stryker, her eyes rolling behind triple thick glasses.

"Yes."

"WOW!"

"Yuh had yer' mouth in the right place Jewgirl." Daddy George's eyes twinkled, & she gave Stryker a nudge in the ribs with her elbow.

"The whipping made me high." Styker says.

As they had got together before their scene and talked over what they were going to do, setting those limits neither wanted to go beyond, establishing safe words--one that would stop the scene and draw them back to reality if it got too hard for the submissive bottom to bare; so now they analyzed it afterwards.

"I come from an abusing, dysfunctional family." The fat dike informs George. "I'm truly from the intelligentsia. If you think I'm crazy you should have seen *them!*

By doing these scenes, it's good for me; *I'm* in control.--I've chosen to do it, and I can stop the scene at any time, by using my safeword. It was not the case the way I was raised at home. Also, it works thru a lot of stuff about me being Jewish. Not many of us in the club are, and even fewer who talk about it. About being hated and persecuted in the outside world. They keep silent. That's about as bad as being tortured. The scene set me free. It gives me power."

George nods, in sympathy. If she had a cigarette, would have lit it and smoked it right about now, even tho having given up the nasty habit years past. George couldn't understand why some people liked what they did, nor their need to unburden their souls talking about it. George didn't need reasons or explanations. --She loved being a sadist, and thank God for the players in the game, whatever their motives were. "Yeah, yeah." Sez George. Lacing her thick white fingers together contemplatively. "Yep. One child grows up and gets a soft touch to show her the right path. And another gets a fist in her face to keep her subdued. That's life."

"You understand!'" Sez Stryker, gazing at her adoringly.

Yellow, blue, party lights. Dikes yell. Music blares. Beat thumping thru the floorboards & vibrates down the bar. Privately the Leader Of The Pack thought; 'things happen fast.--This club has grown beyond my control. It's not just the bunch of personal buddies & a few ladies like when it began. Now we got Jews. And Orientals.--5 of them. They're catching up to the blacks. That's about ... 9 now. Half the gang's gonna be kikes & coloreds, just like the

Avengers accuse us!' George could hear their taunting cries echoing down the dim corridors of her mind, remembered the fire, and the murderous raid, just months ago. Yet another score to be settled in the future.

A sight brought George back to reality. Stryker, on bended knee, in new bluejeans, and inch thick soled boots, sweaty workshirt tight over her big bosom and fat stomach, solemn eyes gazing up at her from the bowed position of a subservient. "It's to *you* Daddy George, & all us Outlaws!" A biker came by and stopped, staring. Soon a crowd gathered around them. The runt biker hollers; "I'M WRITING HER A POEM!—DADDY GEORGE & US! IT'S CALLED *THE LEADER OF THE PACK!*

OH THE HANDCUFFS AND THE CHAINS!
OH THE PLEASURES AND THE P A I N!"

Stryker rambled on for verses, some of which made little sense, stretching the rhyme scheme into unbelievably.

Finally it was done. "Very good." George said, condescending. – "Show me when yuh have a whole poem."

"OK!" The dike answered, brightly.

Hawk stomped over to where the Leader sat. Angry. Narrowed eyes gazing up at the stage area where an SM bottom was giving a demonstration. The sides of Hawks shaved skull glistened with sweat, its row of pink & green spikes bobbed down the middle like a Porcupine quills. "She's high! Somebody ought to snatch her down off of the stage, look at her wobbling around, she's gonna give the club a bad name."

"She knows better. She knows. I've talked to her before."

"I sell drugs, we know that, everybody knows that, but I don't tell 'em to be fools about it! And in case you wanna know, it ain't my drugs she's high on." And gazes sideways at George, nostrils with a silver pair of tusks protruding, wide in anger; her guilty conscious pushing her into this unnecessary confession.

182

"Yeah, I know Hawk. and not from eavesdropping either. My co-top brought it to my attention. Then I talked to Royal, and she said the same thing. She's high off the junk supplied by that drug dealen' bitch who comes in here. That druggie bitch is pushen' my people too hard. I know whose drugs it is. But until I figure out what to do I'm tellen' everybody she can't see." George pointed a fat ringed finger to the player on the stage. "It ain't drugs, she's trippin' 'cause her eyesight is bad. Her eyesight is bad, she needs glasses. Look at her knocking stuff over."

"The lighting *is* bad." Sez Hawk. Let me go adjust those spot beams."

Predators have eyes set in the front of their heads. So they can focus on their prey. Prey have eyes on the side, so as to be ever watchful of attack.

George felt more like a Tarantula, or some species with a thousand eyes—all going at the same time. When George came in Oils that evening she felt the tug of many problems of many people & many messed up situations. Hawk left her sitting there, forehead wrinkled in thought, expression slightly bewildered.—Portrait of a human mind dealing with big concepts; sweaty, palms of her giant hands left prints on the bar, eyes squinting as she thought; trying to figure out right from wrong, or at least better from worse.

It was an electrifying night in club Oils. Music pounded. Dancers swirled. Leatherdikes & regular dikes.--Those who walked the edge, and those who partied with them. The clubhouse was open to all that night; and about 300 females were in attendance.

Cookie, the slut came up to Stryker.   I can ' t function all morning--because you fucked me good. I need a donut for some energy. --Come on! Take me to the donut shop, I've got my bike!" Times like this the fat biker felt she was 10 feet tall, and not 4'11". Big bold & bad.

They left Oils and tore out into the night. Stryker driving the sluts motorcycle & Cookie clutching her from behind. When they got to the donut shop the slut insisted on going to the counter to pay with the $10 Stryker handed her, --and never gave back any change for two 40-cent donuts. Then, a few minutes later, while they're munching she says, "I gotta have $10. I need some makeup." Stryker hands a second ten dollar bill to her, sheepishly out of her wallet. "Thanks." Sez Cookie, frantically shoving it into her bra between pink firm round flesh of her cleavage exposed in an open faded blue workshirt. The fat dike studied her companion across the plastic tablet; eyes occasionally shifted back and forth in her head from effects of the medication she took. 'Cookies just hustlen' me. But I ain't got time to take her home & get my money's worth, 'cause I gotta get back to the club.' They gobbled up the last crumbs of donut off sheets of waxed paper.

"There's cake at the party yuh know Cookie." Sez the dike butch, solemnly.

"Yeah," the slut replied; lipstick was smeared over her lipline, and the green cash showed between her tits in the low-cut shirt. "Yeah, but I'd rather be here alone with you."

"Gosh. Yuh really know how to turn a butch on. Yuh got me all hot & fuzzy feeling.

"Yeah, I oughta know, I been doin' it for *years*."

"Yeah, so I've heard, well, you do a good *job*. Wanna come home with me tonight, after the party ?"

"Maybe."

"I figured you'd say maybe. Don't you guys ever say *yes?*"

"I'm not a guy. Guys, butches that is, say yes or no. We girls say *maybe.*"

Stryker took Cookie by the elbow and escorted her out of the donut shop, head held high in the air, proud.—They were the center of attention of the mundane straight customers; a short fat dike in red suspenders & jeans, and a glamorous biker showgirl. Soon cement

184

sped under their bike as they raced back to Oils. Stryker $20 poorer, but a lot happier. She felt needed, which she was.

Oils kept a low profile outdoors, brick & wood front. Sound barely permeating its thick walls. But inside the club was gaily decorated. Red, yellow, green party streamers. And their Club Colors proudly displayed on a banner hanging on a spot-lit wall.

Some times the married couple looked suspiciously as if they were on their way to a costume party. George in full leather, biker cap, SM chains clanking from the left epaulet & left bootheel; asparkle with silver studs.--And Georgina in a full length ballroom gown, and matching high heel pumps. Diamond necklace with pendulant diamond earrings that matched.--Hair in a high pompadour, its coalblack tinted just a hint of purple, made up like she was going to the Inaugural Ball.

Ross was an older butch; mannish, kinky hair hot combed, relaxed, slicked up away from her smooth brown forehead, and back behind her ears & cut short. Grey at the temples. Wore men's shoes & no makeup. Ross was an old man-woman just like Kelly. Had been a patron of the original bar decades past before it was a bikers club. The two had been friends since.

Ross's ancestors had come from the Sudan region of Africa, a tribal heritage of thousands of years. Kelly, of a European lineage. Two ancient souls, they sat, one on either side of the bar, discussing past times--The Good Old Days. Advertisement lights blinked, blue, red & green.

"It's a natural party in here every night. Every night is Christmas in here."

"Oh the kids know how to have fun."

"We had some fun too, back in the old club." A wry smile her dark face.

"Sure we did. Sure we did." Kelly agrees. The pretty Georgina sits beside Ross, smiles too. "Where's your lady friend ?" Kelly has asked.

"Aw! That yella gal? Aw! She packed her things and left. Been gone months... 'There 's nothing to do in this city,' she tells me. She'd just moved up, you know. She tells me, 'Oh, it's so much better down South, they have mixed clubs, with the gay boys and such, where they have drag shows and there's nothing like it here."

"Cute little gal."

"Ah, Kelly, I tell you..." Ross launches on to one of those familiar Lesbian Tales; "Ah, they come over to our life, the straight girls; 'Oh I thought lesbians had these lavish nightclubs and secret bars! --Underground clubs of only women where everyone dresses in tuxedos, and evening gowns, and all these luxurious places that only women know about!   I was so disappointed! There's nothing to do! No where to wear all my fine clothes my husband bought me when we were married!"

Kelly and Ross & 'Gina tipped back their heads and laughed.

"Underground clubs! HA! That's rich !"

"Ah, if they only knew!"

Georgina joined their conversation with an observation of her own. "Such horrible music these days. Not one good tune all night long."

"Aw, they had good music when I was a teenager and first came out. We had houseparties then for the gays. Nobody had clubs in this city. ---Now, lets see, that's the year the Fox Trot was new..." Kelly mused.

The three women too were from different eras. Every so often Kelly would begin, "Remember that old dance, The Charleston... aw shucks, that was before your time." Georgina and Ross both being twenty years her junior.

So, the long bittersweet night at Oils progresses, with all it's drama.

The slut was fisting herself on stage.

Music pounded, biker dikes cheered under the stage, clapped their hands and whistled. Her bare legs spread open, down on her knees on the dirty plywood, her right hand in a latex glove pushed into herself 'till only the edge of latex on her wrist could be seen surrounded by pubic hair at the rim of her hole. Her sphincter muscles contracted as her cunt swallowed up the hand. Meanwhile, her torso, bare, undulated, shoulders swayed, wreathing in time to the beat. And she embraced herself with her free arm.

"I'd like something with more *art.*" Georgina comments, dryly. "Like a nice burlesque show."

"It's been years since you done burlesque 'Gina." The bulldike Daddy sez, leaning over, resting her huge head in its biker cap on her wife's bare diamond draped shoulder a moment.

"Yes, since you came in the club one night and found out what I was doing." Ross & Kelly laugh.

"Sex is overrated I think." The old owner sez.

"Especially in a relationship." Ross agrees. "When your with someone, sex is the last thing there's time for. You have a household to care for, maybe kids, animals, bills, a job, it's endless. I'm glad I'm single again."

Having a conservative nature, Queen Georgina still thought the girls up on stage were tacky. "Why can't you just have a nice drag, or striptease?"

"We need these scenes !" Sez Daddy George gruffly. "Don't underestimate the power of them !"

Two nasty sex kittens came on next in the list of entertainment, and they were good. Two femmes making love together. The applause was wild.

"Well, *that's* more normal then the whipping." Kelly whispers to Ross.

Georgina confides in Ross: "Ah, they told me when I was young, "ah, don't become a dancer, those strip joints are terrible places to work. You'll become an alcoholic. All the girls that do that kind of dancing are alcoholics. Well, I made tons of money. And Georgie and me was sitting up, freezing sick in our house, we couldn't afford heat, it was horrible. So I got a job dancing, and she's carrying steel at the steel yard, and we bought our house. And I didn't become an alcoholic or a drug addict or didn't nothing come out of it, it was just a job to me."

Next the bikers were having a bosom measuring contest. All females, with large boobs could apply. Some butches clung to the walls, big jacket hiding their tits--of which they were ashamed, but Stryker proudly boasted about hers. Women walked around with a tape measure and a slate, checking off names & numbers. The fat dike thought she might win and recoup some of the money she'd been spending like water all thru the holidays, but there were bigger tits then hers at Oils, she only placed 3rd, and won back $10.

"IT AIN'T NUTHIN' BUT A PARTY!" Yelled a black biker.

The aroma of dike sweat, incense and marijuana.

Black jacket, leather chaps, naked ass, spike hair pink/green; a muscular ex-marine, Hawk cut quite a figure, awed many femme --& butch hearts at the Clubhouse.

Under the tutelage of Hawk & Daddy George, many mastered the whip.--The green/pink hairdo'd punk gave the next demonstration on the program of entertainment. "DON'T STRIKE IN THE AREA BELOW THE LOWER RIBS AND RIGHT ABOVE THE BUTT. YOU MIGHT DAMAGE THE BOTTOMS INTERNAL ORGANS. THE BEST PART IS HER BUTT, --IT'S PADDED."

"Wanna see my marks ?" Stryker asked a group of pals assembled by a battered sofa & some armchairs against the wall. Comancho the Indian wearing jeans, feathers and beads; Angel, Johnny, Sleazy, KT; plates of food balanced on one of their knees, and their lovely showgirl wives perched on the other; spike heels and sequined fem boots tapping time to the rhythm. ---Frosty, Stella Dallas, Crystal, Lady, and Gerri; arms draped over their lovers shoulders. The short, heavy butch turns her back to them & pulls down her jeans, then with a chubby hand yanks her underpants up tight so they become a string that disappears between the huge white moons of her butt. Her ass had dark bruises and cuts, more on the right cheek, Daddy George was right handed; then pulled up her shirt. Crosscuts on her naked back, of welts already healing.--From the Masters expert flogging.

That evening Stryker Showed Her Ass in Oils for the hundredth time--in the vernacular of the black biker KT, tho this time graphically, as well as figuratively.

Women who have had no success at life, and who never can get what they want-- the houses they want to live in, the clothes, the cars, the places of entertainment to go, the respect. The way to fuck that they want; trapped within an unfree lesbian population--at the low end of the economic scale; they found a vent in Oils. A lesbian with stirrings in her heart for more then just one sexual partner had access to more, without condemnation.

Angel was happy with her new mate Crystal. As far as she was concerned, it was the beginning of a life marriage. Yet from the beginning she told her curly blond companion, that she must be able to have sex outside their relationship sometimes. That she had grown past the formal two-person monogamy she's labored under with her first wife Pam for 5 years, and that the stirrings of a new way were in her heart and must be spoken to. And that it would not, must not interfere with their love, their home or their commitment. Great thing about the Club, women were able to do this, women who wanted, & needed the same thing as herself, ---a walk on the wild side. To lift up women in their ready arms.

Angel sat, arms entwined with Crystal; both wore matching blackleather jackets with identical silver belts & zippers; while

Angels chains were worn looped thru the epaulet on the left side, her lovers on the right. As they embraced, staring out of the warmth and sanctity of their partnership they could see the sadness in other women's faces. Those lonely and unsatisfied. But tonight, even this sadness was postponed for a few hours contentment as all women rocked within the large numbers of their sisters.

Since the Outlaws was a large club, over 80 members & growing, it was possible to move thru the clubhouse seeing people but never getting to know them.

Later, Angel & KT wandered among the crowd together to see the festivities. Motorcycle boots clomping on napkins, empty plates & pieces of spilled food; and they ran into a friend of the black biker who Angel had talked to in the past, but had forgotten her name. KT reintroduced them; the pretty woman smiled. Her orange lipstick blended into the brown of her skin. They shook hands. 'Is this diplomatic?': Angel thought --about the handshake. 'Or would she let me get between her legs and get my cunt on hers?'

As Angel moved away, she felt a pair of eyes lingering on her; with that too familiar hint of longing--of the single woman.

A while later the two walked past a large ebony colored biker dressed in full leather regalia; with elaborate stitching on them, costume-like. She & KT nodded curtly at each other, & went on by. Angel had noticed everytime she saw Gerri & KT they stayed well apart from this biker. Finally, curious, Angel asks did they know each other?

"KNOW HER?, HOW CAN I HELP BUT KNOW HER? THERE AIN'T BUT 7 OF US BLACKS IN THE CLUB!" KT fairly bristled with rage, so upset she unconsciously yanked out a twenty-prong silver tip afro-comb which was stuck in the pockets of her bus drivers uniform and jammed it into her thick shock of hair. "'Course I know her, I know who she *is*... She don't even have a bike. She has to borrow a bike." KT scoffed. "She's all show. Just goes on the Run, and rides in the Gay Day Parade on a bike. She's chicken. She's scared to ride. --And she got no class." And turned her back in the butches direction, to shut out the sight.

Many of the dikes bore marks of the battle they'd had in the park. One had fresh black scars with red swelling around it, of a mans heel print in her face. They bragged about the battle; "I tole him, YUH MUST NEED TO GET YER' ASS KICKED, YUH'VE COME BACK FOR MORE! But I was sure scared. You know you can't win every fight. I seen him, so big & muscular, I sez to myself, 'uh oh, he'll kick yer' ass.' So, my partner gets him first, a quick blow to his kneecaps, I didn't count on help, so that made the difference. I ran in, picked him up by the shirt & slammed him down on the ground and jumped on him with my boots, BOOM! BOOM! BOOM! **'WHO DO YOU THINK YOU ARE YOU SON-OF-A-BITCH! TRYEN' TO MESS UP OUR HAPPY PICNIC!'** BOOM! BOOM! BOOM! I stomped him! I was stronger then I thought, --it's from being around Oils here, breaken' up fights and shit!"

And, they talked about God.

Back at the bar some other dikes were having a discussion of wither God was a cocksucker or not. "THOSE PEOPLE IN LONG FLOWING BEARDS ARE ALWAYS COCK SUCKERS! THEIR THE WORST ONES!" Screams Debbie, waving her dainty fist in the air, bootheels hooked into rungs of a barstool, elevating her into the air so she towered over the rest of the women. "I'VE TURNED TRICKS WITH ENOUGH OF 'EM! I OUGHT TO KNOW! I'LL TELL YUH ABOUT GOD! I'll TELL YUH ABOUT TRICKS! I'll TELLYUH ABOUT PREVERTS IN LONG FLOWING ROBES!" Then who should come down the bar but Kelly, managing her barcrew; the old dike was a Catholic, so that ended that.

At the end of the evening, the pretty fems. Dena & Debbie were wrapped in each others arms, their big tits under sweaty sweaters, strands of long hair falling in their hot faces. "I was gonna go over to Hawks house and get some Crank, but I decided I won't show up. I'm gonna sleep all day long tomorrow. I'm not gonna work. Yer' lucky yuh got Rip, I'm gonna be all alone. I'm just gonna sleep. I don't dare go buy Crank. It's a very easy thing for me to do. To shoot Crank, but it's a dangerous path."

191

"Come sleep over with me & Rip honey." Debbie cooed; her bluepainted eyelids drooped, she was drunk and tired.

"You can't help me all the time! It ' s up to me, and it ' s a battle all the time."

"Too bad Georgina's such a meanie, you could go home and be with her and George."

"That's part of my problem. I'm suppose to be The Leaders woman, but I can't see her when I want to, just when she can get away from her *wife*. I love her and she loves me, but she ain't rally *mine*. I feel I need to make some changes. I need to feel good about myself… So maybe I *will* go get loaded."

"What happened to that dike you were seeing ? The business woman, the one with all the money ?"

"I'm too lowclass for her."

"She said that ?"

"She put it different... Let's see, uh, how did she say it, hummmm, oh, yeah, 'You're not of a professional class.   I want a professional woman like myself.'"

"The big shit!   She's *mean!*"

"I'm on my diet again, I thought I'd go get Crank.   I thought about it all night long-- so watch out!   I might do it!   I never know what's going to happen to me now! I'm having real problems. Low self esteem."

"She did it!   The bitch! The professional woman!   She made you loose your self esteem!" Cried Debbie, shaking Dena,-- so hard their hair flounced. The two attractive women, slender as reeds, with round tits & asses, clattered their high heel boots on the littered floor; as they slipped, then hugged, trying to gain balance in each others embrace. "Then I thought, gee, I've had such a nice time at the party tonight, maybe I should just go home and rest, like normal people

192

do.... Or, I could shoot drugs all day long and go to the movies and watch 'em four times. If I don't get drugs from Hawk I'll buy 'em on the street. If I feel this way now, the minute I'm away from the Clubhouse and all my friends I'll really be depressed. I'll get into dope. I'll drown in it. I don't need to hear nothing about drugs, or getting high or partying. I'm weak."

"Well, just eat some more food, we'll get some plates & wrap 'em up and come home with me & Rip."

"I can't! I can't break my diet and get fat! And I can't go home with you because Rip is gonna start buggen' me about going to work for her!"

"She's *mean!*" Debbie agreed sympathetically. Red lipstick had blurred to pink over the long night. Her diamonds flashed, cold, stern—as the final rule,--- but she drooped tiredly.

Dena was weary--felt hunted, like many a single girl. She was use to being trapped or tricked by men & dikes; and thought up a good alibi to tell her friend, and told it. When Debbie asked; "I didn't know Rip is still trying to get you to work for us!"

"Yes." Dena lied.

Now there was no way Rip was going to get Daddy Georges mistress to go to work for her, but in a paranoid need to escape, to feel free, Debbie must keep her options open. Nobody, nobody could pin her down. Not as a friend-- Debbie, to be trapped, in finale inside someone's drug-free home, not by the idiotic Stryker with her clammy hands pawing Dena, and whispers of love & marriage; not by Georgina—who would accept Dena into her home on the condition that she be a virtual salve at her own beck & hall, to be a house cleaner, waitress & cook—as well as Daddy Georges bed partner. Not nobody. Dena, lean, buxom and wild. She was a boxer battling demons. --The foul today, --and the rag tag spin-offs of things past.

Dena had begun this evening at Oils wrapped up in an expensive coat. Had since thrown it off & wanted to climb out of her skin as well. Some members felt stronger when they were protected by guns.

Dena wanted to feel safe and powerful --and couldn't get it from within her own psyche. "I'm always running after something or somebody." She moaned.

A young dike felt Daddy Georges hard muscles—built from pushing iron at her weight bench. New bikers with young cheerful faces, scrubbed, clean crew cut hair, in sweat shirts and bluejeans. Baby butches with rosy cheeks mimicking her attitudes, and following Daddy George around like dikelets, --her being the mother dike.

"Men live less physically harassed." Sez one small-stature dike.

"Hell naw!" The bulldike claims. "Other men hate them too! --Not just you dikes!"

"They're safer!"

"Yeah, safer, except when they're beat up and knocked down." Sez Daddy George. "And I'm gonna show yuh how to do it, next week at Sleazy's gym. So be there!"

"Remember that big dike who came stomping in that time & claims she could whup me wrestling or boxing?" Sez Daddy George as she went back to join Georgina & friends. "Well one of the members works with her, and she's passen' herself off as heterosexual! I just heard about it. Imagine! The big dike! She's as butch as I am! The liar!"

George had grown big very early. She hadn't been kicked around much, not even as a child. Few dikes challenged her, nor men. Because of this physical advantage which had evolved also into a mental edge, George had more overview of situations. And was steadfastly trying to impart this idea of power balances to smaller women, who were more cowardly.

She had been able to get well paying men's jobs as a passing woman, and later when they found out she was a female--after she relaxed more in life & let her tits hang out, and didn't strain to lower.

194

her voice, or control her mannerisms--it was already engrained. --
The idea of being accustom to male privilege.

Bar lights blazed, tinkling notes spilled thru the sound system. The
place was wreck, the party food was gone. Ice had melted in the
trashbins. George had one last word for the trail of dikeletts who'd
followed her thru the club that night: "You understand what men feel.
That's one of the biggest attractions for myself and other female
motorcyclists is in doing a lot of things men do. Now I see it in you
women, I see it in yer' eyes. Now you know why men go out and act
wild, because it's exhilarating. Because its fun. There's a natural
adrenalin addiction. If you know many motorcyclists who have not
been motorcyclists for very long, generally they either they like their
cycles all the way, or they hate them all the way. If they've ever had
a bad experience, a spill or something, they want to get off of their
bikes altogether. Never ride again, and that's fine. Then again you
have your diehards that need that adrenalin fix. It happens to me in
the middle of the night. sometimes. There's only 2 things that can
settle me down, that's either a lot of sex, or a late night motorcycle
ride. Because there's just that adrenaline flowing through. The
endomorphs have got to have something to do. That's natures way of
getting us up and down and letting us have a fun time. When the
endomorphs aren't excited, then we are depressed."

"THANK YOU DADDY GEORGE." Cried the novices.

"Daddy George wants me to finish writing my poem. She likes it."
Stryker said. " I got the first stanza and the last-- I need a middle."

At the end of the evening the fat dike approached Crystal, laid her
sweaty head on the fems chest and blurted out; "I was in the toilet &
I heard Dena talk about me! She sez I'm the one who carries her dick
around all over town but never gets to use it on nobody but sluts who
ain't even lesbians but who like men or *anything*. 'Pathetically
carrying her dildo.' That's what I heard her say!"

"Women are cruel." Crystal says. "You just have to know that.
I'm a fem, I know what they say, and how they are... Fems can be
really mean, --when they're pretty and everybody wants them, then
they're the meanest."

195

"Yeah." Angel agrees.   Long blond hair to her sturdy shoulders, the butch gazed pensively at their buddy, face nestled between Crystals warm breasts, while she stroked Stryker's wet hair, comforting.

"I'm a fem. I know. But I was never mean." Crystal muses. "Well... yes I was. I was mean. And I said *no* a lot Stryker. --I really did.   I told a lot of women no, when I could have said yes."

Georgina had retired to sit on a sofa by the wall with her friends, & watched the young people who were left rage on deliriously, with their energy.   "I can't wait 'till tomorrow noon--breakfast, then I can have my steak." Sez Georgina. "It's part of my diet. I'm starving. I hope I don't go crazy tomorrow since I haven't eaten since this morning, & being surrounded by all this food."

"I can't wait 'till I get to the Hereafter; and all my problems will be over." Sez Kelly.

Grey at the, temples, -distinguished; Ross nods in agreement.

"I'm 70 years old. A lesbian since 15. Gay all my life. That's 55 years of gayness--now if I made love with one woman per year-- average, all my life, just one woman, that's still 55 different women. Now 18 years I was with Maggie--so, subtract, say, 20, that leaves 35 women. Well, get my point. These kids think they invented sex, well I've had my share of sex, and plenty of it!"   It was scenes of running across roof tops and fleeing down back stairways in the middle of the night as a minor dike, escaping with her underage lover from their parents who hated gays & had called the police on them. Fleeing from police years Before Stonewall. It was some of the drama that life in the Secret Society was all about. "--So you might say, I'm ready to meet the Hereafter, because I've *lived.*"

"Well your luck was better then that! Come on now! Confess! One woman a year! You had hot dates & a lot of relationships before & after Maggie!"

196

The hour was late, they could not talk falsely now... The old butch began discussing her funereal arrangements. "Give me pallbearers in tuxedos. Butches--or some of these gals here in black lipstick. . .. Time's runnen' out. I see they buried Audrey Hepburn. I read the obituaries every day. I wouldn't miss it. That's my favorite column."

Many young dikes looked to Daddy George for guidance & leadership. Finally tho, they must turn from her shining sun, and look into their own murky lives, taking the lessons they'd learned. Many women that night would get lucky and connect with another single female, and they'd lay in bed together peacefully getting two fingers; and examine each other's bodies within the wonder of love & kisses.

Georgina felt the weight of George as she lowered herself down onto the sofa. As usual, by instinct the huge arm went around her shoulders jarring her diamond necklace.

Rip sat askance in an armchair pulled up to the sofa, her feet kicked out on a wooden chair, with Debbie on her lap. Pounding rhythm of musical notes; they were surrounded by a sea of bikers still dancing, or going to the exit, bodies glittering the jewelry of chains and silver studs and buckles of their motorcycle jackets.

"WHERE'S MY COAT!" Howls a dike.

"Back there in the back with the rest!"

"GO GET IT FOR ME!"

"Ok. What does it look like?"

"BLACK LEATHER."

"But *everybody* in here is wearing black leather!"

"Boy, we've come a long way." George told Rip.

Chapter Seventeen

The mechanic went over the bike with a flashlight & precision tools, trouble-shooting. Blue uniform with dark stains of grease. Seams of its back pockets were blackened from oil. Work jacket. Oil under her fingernails. The worse problem was the cold.

They got pummeling rain; torrents of water that could turn to snow in a temperature drop.

Wind blew, then it was a driving rain.

Comancho and Stryker stood outside Johnny's garage, right under the roof; boot wraps of oil-soiled denim handkerchiefs; hands jammed in their pockets, when they weren't holding tools & going numb in the cold wind, working in the open doorway.

Comancho started a fire in the steel drum using pieces of wood from broken pallets and some newspaper.

Wind whipped their hair and collars of their shirt and pants. Everything blew.

Motorcycles sat, leaning on their kickstands. Everything was wet. The road had been slick as a mirror coming over. Soon a fire roared in the drum.

Most Outlaws worked honest, for days pay.

About ten percent of the bikers in the Motorcycle Club were honest and did no crime. Earned their money on the square and indulged in little offense other then partying with other bikers who did.

They worked hard, paid taxes, got mildly high on liquor or weed or pills on occasion only & were the good girls of the bad girl set.

Not all of them possessed criminal minds.

As a lesbian biker came in the garage, a mixture of oil, gasoline, dike sweat, and acrid burning wood smoke from the steel drum would flood into her nostrils; while tales of terror assailed her senses.

"Everybody has accidents. But never like that one. Five of 'em wiped out at once. Hells Angels people. A logging truck came to a turn going too fast, spun out and wiped 'em out all together. They died instantly."

"Aw hell, I'm liven' too fast. Liven' on the edge. It's crash & burn. I seen death already. I've had friend die! I don't want it to happen to me!"

"Aw, the novice riders are the worst,--the young ones. They all expect to live to be 100 years old; they think they're indestructible."

They talked about death. And death on bikes. They talked about mechanical stuff & parts for their choppers.

"On my Goldwing alone, the two front forks was $150 apiece, new shocks, that was $350." The cycle was parked on its center stand, wheel up in air.

Fire raged in the steel drum stocked with wood the Indian had chopped up with an ax.

"She traded a bike to me, it was a beautiful bike!" Johnny sez, with an expression of bliss on her face, as her oil covered hands moved in air describing a visible resemblance. "When me & Stella rode in the Gay Day Parade, --it was back in '89, the Avengers turned nauseous green shades of puke and envy." When the mechanic laughed her belly shook, fat from a lot of red rare steaks prepared by her wife.

"Avengers! Ought to see 'em run! --They've got enough legs!-- The creeps! **HAW ! HAW HAW!"** Yelled Sleazy over the noise of the cutting wind.

Stryker's bike wasn't running right. It needed carburetor work, an air filter and forks. And was all but resigned to sitting in storage for the winter months ahead with forecasts of snow when it was perilous to ride it anyway; or until she could save enough money for the parts then she & Johnny could make the repairs. Having spent her money at the tavern. Parts on a motorcycle are expensive, more so then cars, because it's considered a luxury.

"I'M GONNA WHIP HER ASS!" Stryker howled over the wind. **"I NEED SOME NEW YEARS NOOKIE! NOOKIE! NOOKIE!** *NOOKIE!"*

"SHUT UP!"

"I had a dream." The fat dike said wistfully. "I was in a brand new camper shell full of beer. Cases & cases. But no truck, just the camper shell. So I couldn't go nowhere."

"Yer' nose has been runnin';" Sez a dike staring down at the chubby biker; "been able to catch it? HAW! HAW!"

"HERE."

BLAM! Something wizzed by her shoulder and hit the cement beside her feet. A package of marijuana.

"AW! THANKS YOU GUYS!" It was a loan, she'd pay them back for this stash out of her Govenrment check the first of January. 2 weeks left to go.

Her piece of machinery was parked, a tarp thrown over it like a baby in a blanket.

A red car was parked outside Johnny's garage, being fixed for cash to keep her family fed. It had a mysterious electrical problem which they hadn't yet been able to diagnose. They'd tinkered with the car for days and the tail lights still wouldn't work. "BLOW TORCH IT MAN! BLOW TORCH IT!" The owner finally screamed in frustration, slamming the hood shut with a metallic clunk.

Inside, were shelves up to the roof. Which had bottles, cans of solvent, tools, electrical cords.

Johnny's talking to a novice; "You always look for inconsistencies in a road, where there may be uneven pavement. For instance one time, this is a good one, my lover Stella and me were riding down some street here in the city...."

They'd work on their bikes & not be riding much over the winter. Chew the fat, exchange tips on motorcycling.

"If yuh come to a stop and leave your key in it, you might run your battery down. At that point you don't have a kick start. Jump on it a few times and turn the piston over, that gets the compression going and that will turn it over for you. Johnny told the new biker. "I've got to kick my bitch to start her, and if she won't start, just go on without me. What the hell."

And somebody's telling another of countless long winter biker tales: "So there I was, out in the country, nobody around for miles. I blew a fuse. So, I got some aluminum foil from my gum wrapper -- it's a conduit of electricity, something to bridge your wiring with, and started it."

"Have you heard? Crystal's got Angel a job flippen' burgers at the Donut Shop."

"Yeah Angel?"

"Yeah. I'm a cook. 2 days a week is all, at that hamburger joint we all go to."

"Angel's got an honest job! No Shit!"

"Man, yuh cook good! You flip a mean hamburger! Yuh always help Georginia at the Runs."

"Quit that phone room ?"

"New." Angel sez, inspecting her fingernails with a nonchalant shrug. "Naw. Money's too good to quit. Just cut down my hours."

Chapter Eighteen

Lady was having a Tea, her kids would be there, & other biker kids. Somebody had offered to pick up Stryker. The butches & anybody else who slowed up who wasn't exactly a lady was to practice karate in Sleaze's basement gym after indulging themselves in teacakes.

Sleazy & Lady had worked a long time, both hustling & conning & had been on the square since 1986, five years, and were finally buying a house near Oils on the edge of a neighborhood with increasing property values. They fought to make the payments each month. Had a lot of cats in the yard which they fed, and a dog.

Mothers & Ladies sat, drank tea and gossiped. While downstairs the Dads & Butches rolled around on top of each other grunting & sweating on gym mats & hit the punching bag with their fists and practiced power strikes with bare knuckles on the Makawazi board. It was a regular do jo; where they did kick fighting & blocks with padded shin & arm guards. Horrible "UGHS!" and THUDS!" echoed upstairs.

They had started wearing chest protectors & helmets when they worked out, so they could do some serious sparing.

"Yuh know who don't wear a chest protector? Rip don't wear one, and Rocky, and Alicia; and Jody."

"George makes us wear helmets when we work out."

"Angel wears a helmet, and Johnny wears one."

"HIT HER HARD! I'LL TEACH YUH HOW TO PUNCH AND KICK!" Yells a coach.

A group of fighters clustered on the sidelines in bare feet, just outside the mats.

"I didn't believe in wearing a mouthpiece until Star hit me so hard, I was spitting up blood."

"Hawk is fierce. She comes at you, she really hits hard. She hits you straight on and hits you straight on up. I didn't think she'd hit so hard."

"Now Stryker, she's afraid to block. She's too feminine. She's afraid to block. She sees yuh coming, she runs. I tell her, all you got to do is step aside, then whirl and kick and punch. But she turns and runs."

"Jody got hit in the leg at the fight, the one at the Run with them stupid rednecker fucks. They stomped on her leg. That's why she ain't been walking right. She ain't been walking right for weeks."

"BLOCK! THEN RETURN YOUR PUNCH! *HIT HER!* MAKE CONTACT! *H I T H E R!* SHE AIN'T GONNA BREAK! SHE'S GOT ON HER PADS! HIT HER! YEAH! THAT'S RIGHT!" Instructs Royal; who works as a weight trainer in her private life.

"WOW! Lookit that! She busted her! She busted her good!"

Sleazy had long stringy hair and a skinny body. Teeth stuck out in front, bucked; and a ready smile. & hillbilly hospitality to any bikers who came to their place. She was a happy butch, had, Lady, their 3 kids, and a decent job as a janitor. Friends guaranteed thru the club. Her house full up on Sundays. They weren't alone.

The middle kid was 2. Ricky. He wore a cute navyblue jumpsuit. His tiny feet in white & blue gymshoes. The kid would run up to a biker, she'd pick him up & hug him, then set him down on his feet to toddle around. His cheeks were rosy in fair skin & hair jet black.

Company gathered in the living room by the fireplace. Tongues of fire licked over logs. There sat a cart with a large silver hot water dispenser—containing 40 cups, plus boxes of teabags, cups, saucers, spoons and plates of teacakes & cookies furnished by the guests.

A Christmas-tree of green evergreen needles stood in the corner, bedecked with yellow & red & blue bulbs, lights & tinsel. A golden star sat on top.

Lisa was a little hostess, serving the leatherdikes slices of cake, and pouring hot water from the spigot on the silver pot into their china cups.

Lisa, age ten was their oldest child. A trick baby. Conceived when Lady had been hustling johns for a living in the beginning of their relationship, and an accident with birthcontrol had given them a beloved child. Two other kids followed--by artificial insemination. A baby who slept in her crib next to the parents bed, and the two year old toddler.

Other children had been brought by their parents, five at last count, and the adults took turns watching them in Lisa's room, where they played with her toys.

The femmes & a few butches laughed and talked around the cozy fireplace, sipping tea. One began a story; "We went to a lecture, it was called Emergence To Consciousness. That was our first date." Sez a biker, who was single; she wore a disgusted expression. "She wants to be a feminist, even tho she's dirt poor and ain't shit, like me; so she's reading books and taking lessons. And has no sex."

"Huh?"

"Yeah, that's right. They have no sex."

Now to most bikers what they did when they laid down in bed with their women was a lot of what mattered in life. Sleazy'd come home, tired, sweaty, and dirty, and liked nothing better then to get into a hot bath prepared for her by Lady, and after, lay down in bed & fall into her sweet arms & make love.

Sleazy sat in a chair, thin legs crossed, in bluejeans, lanky arms in a blue workshirt, a teacup balanced on her knee, watching the bikers with a quiet, but merry expression, like an owl.

"She became a feminist, and stopped having sex. Her fingernails grew long,--all ten. Her dildo hung in it's harness in the closet gathering dust. "It's a tool of the Patriarchy!" she cried everytime I

204

inquired about it. We couldn't make love, hardly at all and then only side by side, & not in the Missionary Position, and nothing kinky, no no, nothing like that!"

"I saw an SM workshop advertised in the gay newspaper." Interjects Sleazy, with a story of her own.

"Was it good ?"

"Good ? It cost $35 ! To teach me to tie a broad up? Forget it! I can buy food for the five of us for 3 days for $35!"

"Using hamburger helper."

"That's right." Sez Sleazy.

Lisa came to rest, falling into her mothers embrace, after racing around breathlessly at top speed. Lady was a femme Top, pretty, strong & tough; a bitchen' biker lady. She straightened the pink bow on top of her daughters head, and tugged her frilly pink dress back into shape & told her to go back in the kids room with her friends, so Momma could talk adult stuff.

"I've *heard* it already." Lisa said. She was ten years old, going on twenty.

"There was this woman, a feminist who was going with one of the bikers, who came around with her kid for awhile. She was trying to keep her daughter out of sexist clothes--as she called it. And the kid is wearing all these frilly clothes, like Lisa & me, anyway. She found these clothes for herself, despite her mother. The lacier the better. "What have I done wrong?" Says the feminist mother. "I just don't understand why she'd want to wear these sexist clothes! The frillier and lacier they are the better she likes it! I don't understand it!" The mother says, "you can't *play* in these clothes! Don't you want some nice jeans?" **"NO!"** Says the daughter. **"I WANT SOME FRILLY CLOTHES!"**

The dog stretched its front legs, then it's back. **AGGGGRRRU-- UUUUUUFFFF!** Fire roars in the hearth. The living room is plain, comfortable; rugs on hardwood floors and stuffed chairs and a sofa full of biker ladies & a few gents.

The dog rolled to one side, and barked a tiny **YIP!** Then rolled to the other side and barked on that side, **YIP!** Then leapt up in the air and barked **RUFF! RUFF! RUFF, RUFF, RUFF!** Somebody was coming up the walk.

"STRYKER! YOUR NOSE IS RUNNING! STOP PICKING YOUR NOSE! Get her a napkin somebody!" Lady says, leading the chubby biker inside. Her bluejean vest & pants were cold & wet.

"Wipe your mouth Stryker!" Says Frosty, in a motherly tone. "You have grease all over your mouth! Let me see your teeth!" Obediently, the fat butch stops, clicks her bootheels together, stands at attention and opens her mouth. **"HA!** Just as I thought! You have food all over your teeth! Just don't smile!"

"STRYKER! YOU'RE DROOLING!"

"I did that on purpose! I like youse women to nag me! I'm sick of being jealous when you nag your butch husbands! I want to be nagged!" Stryker pulled up a chair by the fire, wringing her pudgy reddened hands, happy to be with company.

Angel and her pretty wife Crystal sat hugging in a loveseat. The blond butch balanced a cup & saucer on one knee; was postponing the horrible moment when she'd have to leave the animated circle of femmes and walk down those basement steps to join the other butches & daddies who were grunting as they wrestled, punched & kicked each other, and squatted and did pushups until they were sweaty & their muscles got sore, in the Martial Arts class.

Two year old Ricky toddled over to the couple. Angel stood up, all 5' 8", her stocky form in leather and bent down to hug the healthy kid. He giggled & smiled. She squeezed his shoulders then picked him up and held him up in air at the length of her arms. An ivy plant hanging from the ceiling was in front of his face. He giggled and swatted at the green vine & leaves with a chubby fist. Angel put him on her back, his little gymshoed feet against her chest, and walked around the room. He grabbed fists full of her hair with his little fingers.

Now the butch held the kid on her lap, pressed to her zippered front. The little boy was merry, his eyes twinkled. His pudgy hands grasped onto her leathers. Biker kids were well loved. All the biker dikes there held Ricky or played with him sometime during the teaparty.—He was a sunny child. A round, healthy soul in thick gymshoes.

Most biker children were poor, but well dressed in bluejeans or little sip-front jumpsuits; fancy pants & sweater outfits & gymshoes. Some wore biker skirts and boots, others baseball caps. Soon it was Crystals turn to hold to tot in her arms. She straightened out his mussed teeshirt and placed a toy in his chubby hands.

Lady & Sleazy had invited all the mom & pop bikers she knew who had kids of their own. The kids had fun playing with each other. Of the 80 or so lesbians in the club, about 14 of them had kids or were co-parents of the Outlaws total of 23 children ranging from infants to 18 years.

Rick took turns sitting on leather knees; so a stranger who came to this gang event couldn't tell who he belonged to at first. It was that the child had a big loving family of many relatives.

Finally, the baby rested in bliss on Poppa Sleazy's lap, a baby bottle of milk tipped up in his mouth.

"Such cute kids. kids. Such sweet kids." Crystal whispered to Angel, as she leaned her curly head against the butches zip-leathered front. Saying this with a special meaning; because the two females had discussed before the idea of having babies together.

Stryker overheard them. Somber face; the fat dike in bluejeans & red suspenders, offered her opinion; "Yeah, they are sweet kids. Being hugged by one person after another for 2 hours, no wonder."

"NO MOMMA! I WANT TO TAKE A NAP! NO! I WANT TO GO HOME!" A kid stomped her feet. **"I HATE IT! I DON'T WANT TO DO THE PRACTICE FIGHT! I WANT TO GO SWIMMING IN THE PLASTIC POOL! JENNIFER IS LUCKY! SHE'S LUCKY! SHE DON'T HAVE TO DO HOMEWORK! SHE DON'T HAVE TO TAKE A NAP! SHE DON' T HAVE TO PRACTICE FIGHT! SHE'S JUST HERE 3 MINUTES THEN SHE GETS TO GO PLAY!** *I'M GONNA GO KILL MYSELF!"*

"My, you certainly are in a bad mood today! What can we do to get you out of that bad mood?"

"I DON'T WANT TO DO THE BOXING! I HATE IT!"

Down a curving wood stairway of pie-sliced steps was a cement basement with a low ceiling which stretched the length of the house. One half was covered with gym mats, grey padded canvass, on which two opposing lines of combatants faced each other. Some wore Karate Gi's --white canvass uniforms for the beginners, black for the advanced; others, plain sweatshirts & jeans. They were barefoot. The right line attacked, the left parried the punches & kicks with blocks & retaliated with kicks and punches in sequence of five strikes. -- Overkill. Hawk stood in green camouflage shirt & trousers, barking commands, a red sweatband around her forehead, dripping glistening beads of sweat; pink/green spikes of hair drooping from moisture. She'd learned the fighting arts in the military.

Daddy George stood head and shoulders above any dike there. She and Star, the novice butch, conferred on how to make a striking fist for maximum impact. Patiently George curled Stars big fist in her huge one, fingers tucked in, rolling inward—"Jest like yuh do when yuh fist yer' lady, only the thumbs on the outside. HAW! HAW!" They taught the Outlaws to defend their civil rights as they walked the land. The whole basement was a dojo, complete with striking boards, fighting sticks, & floor length mirrors to observe themselves in action to check their form.

Cement walls painted white, electrical cords with blazing lights strung over the low ceiling.

Angel could feel herself strike.   It was the best feeling in the
world. To extend her fist out at length, pushed from the shoulder,
powered by a twist of her hips, forced from the heart of her body out
into someone's face, and let out all her anger into them.   To let out
the rage. All the pent-up stuff held back. From the times she'd wanted
to stand up and fight when she was being insulted or she & her
woman were meek, afraid of being hurt.   To stand up and kick ass.
Blond hair shoulder length. Solemn, blue eyes stared out of her broad
face. Determination grew in her spirit.

 Stryker ran thru the gym a blimp in a bluejean shirt with rings of
sweat under the armpits; and a size too big trousers, pounding her
chest like Tarzan.

Any young bikers who did their lessons rigorously--fighting for her
survival--could be seen in bandaids. Her toes tied together as a brace
for each other. A knee bound up for support. A finger in a splint.
Many bikers had scrapes of reddened skin, bruises & black eyes from
the fight some weeks past. So they took the fight-training seriously.

The Outlaws were given fierce karate lessons.   Their fists hit the
makawazi board until their knuckles swole up permanently, with a
cartilage build up from repeated punches.   Their index and 3rd finger
knuckles,-- which was the striking point--got huge, the remaing
knuckles much smaller at their normal size. Muscles grew big from
lifting weights, and iron hard thighs from the deep-knee-bend squats.
They became robust warrior women.

And their children.   They too trained.   To make the girls strong.
Boys also. In the children's class. Later, the parents gathered around a
makeshift ring, & let the kids slug each other, dressed in masks &
protective gear.

"FIGHT! FIGHT! FIGHT! FIGHT! HIT HIM WITH YOUR
LEFT HAND HIT HIM WITH YOUR RIGHT!"

**"MOMMY! MOMMY! NO! NO! MOMMY NO!   NO!
MOMMY! NO! NO! NO!"**

209

"DADDY! NO! NO! DADDY! DADDY! NO! NO! NO! NO! NO DADDY! NO DADDY!"

It was strong medicine.

Chapter Nineteen

For the Club Christmas party, George and the other Warlords had rented space in a boys dungeon--a few days after the actual date of December 25th. The dungeon was in the warehouse section not far from Oils. A less affluent area with lofts & studios of musicians playing techno-industrial rock music; and disfranchised singles eking out the ends of their lives in small rooming houses & hotels.

Guests had to buzz the bell & be let in.

Lou, the poorest of the Warlords got out of a beaten up old car, rang the bell, then went around the side of the building, hollered up from the street to the second floor apartment at the owner, a fag. He buzzed her in, turned over the keys to his dungeon which was situated on the first floor; and soon after the Warlords & helpers began to arrive, to set the place up for the party.

The boys used the dungeon 7 days a week--kept it full of paying male customers, even on blue Monday. Weekends were especially crowded, so the women had to rent the space on a weekday. The place was a converted flat of originally 8 large rooms, now containing catacombs of sex booths, a carpeted slave pit, an SM room with racks, chains, slings & hoists; a kitchen with 3 refrigerators stocked full of cases of soda, mineral water, beer & hotdogs, relish & buns; and a stove on which to cook the stocks of goodies to keep the partying/ screwing people fed; a video room with sofas & chairs which faced a large screen TV on which lesbian sex videos played continuously, 1 bathroom, and including a tub in a separate cubical used for golden showers, and a large carpeted room for orgies. Boxes of safe sex supplies were distributed freely-- latex gloves, dental dams, nonoxydal 9 lubrication, regular lube; and a huge, dispenser vat of Crisco--which girls shouldn't use in their cunts.

The party was by invitation only --for all 80 members of the Club and 1 guest apiece only.

Twas the night after Christmas, and they would throw their problems away, at the party. Assemble together. Talk loud. Laugh long. Forget the world and the bills & the collection agencies & the ever pressing poverty many of them felt in their lives. Men coming to the door to repossess their furniture, stuff like that.

The sex workers in the slave pit were to be, primarily, sluts.

The Sluts were a powerful contingency among the Outlaws. Not simply passive cunts to be fucked, they had power as well as voracious sexual capacity and had plots and designs of their own. With eyeshadow and makeup craftily applied, like spies they discussed plans. Not just ladies, but sluts too had been known to make or break a warrior.

Some of them were bi's--80/20, who wanted to lez around before they settled down and went straight. Some grew old in their role as vestigial sluts, and partied till they died. Some were hot ho sluts. Others worked in offices of the downtown financial distruct, with key positions in corporations.

The wives of bikers were the Ladies. They had prestige. No stray biker better mess with them. It was best to know who was who before you tried to pull a female off a barstool at Oils & carry her away on the back of your bike. Sluts would strip off their clothes, lay down and engage in sex when others would not. Sluts were part of the free-for-all. They were the backbone of orgies. With them, anything goes.

Sluts were always getting in trouble. Drunk. Men picking them off as they wandered off alone, separated from the group, and hurting them. At the suggestion of George, and other mad-raging dikes, on quite a few occasions a group of bikers had had to get revenge--find

211

some man and kick the shit out of him either for hurting a slut, or being the lowlife type who would hurt any woman if he could. Many sluts came into the Outlaws with brains burnt out on drugs, crazy, and had attached themselves to the group, giving sex to anyone--in return for being cared for. They could be a constant liability.

A typical slut costume was modeled by Cookie--day in and day out, the same. This some-time wife of the Warlord Lou was running amok all over the dungeon in a tiny shiny mini skirt--very fancy black satin-with nylon stockings on and no panties; her large boobs stuffed into a tight blouse with a plunging neckline, showing as much skin as possible.

Sluts pranced around near-nude, reminding onlookers of our animal nature, instead of the covered dress of socialized wear.

It was Lou who'd pulled Cookie into the Outlaws. Poor, the lowest income by far of the Warlords--due to her inability to either hold an honest job, or pursue criminal scams. Lou drifted from welfare check to minimum wage jobs, thru a series of low income hotel rooms. A hefty bull dike stocky & trim, muscular from hard work & lifting iron weights; who stood midway between the shortest Warlord, Hawk, and George; at 5'10', dressed usually in a bluejean outfit and a pair of scuffed orange construction boots. Her share of Outlaw dues money--which came to around $200 per month-- was the only advantage that separated her from abject poverty.

Lou hadn't held a job for years prior to meeting Cookie. Outlaw business took up a portion of her day, but it still left a lot of time on her hands. Lou was semi-illiterate so that eliminated reading books or newspapers in the public library. She hated TV because of never seeing bulldikes like herself upon it's silver screen. She had come from poor people. A father who wore rough clothes just like hers were today, and a mother trying to be decent, face perpetually fixed in a look of fear, holding onto her children. They were hillbillies crossed over from the mountains of the Midwest. The family thought they should give-up and go back to the clean open air of the piney woods, but stayed on, hoping for opportunities; father knocking on doors which seldom opened for poor white trash—as such they were considered to be,-- and the city was better for Lou, when she grew into a teenager, to be a lesbian.   Theirs had been a bad neighborhood--just like Lou lived in now.--The cycle of poverty being unbroken. The family had had to tolerate liquor and drugs & hookers right outside on their front steps. Many fights & knife cuttings, screaming, and gunshots kept them terrified. As she grew, Lou learned to fight and cut. As she came into adulthood many of her women had been prostitutes, so she neither had a low opinion of them, nor shame to be with one as a lover.   One day she was walking the streets, mad, kicking anything in her path with a worn boots; hands shoved deep into her jeans pockets, half wishing somebody would start an argument because she was mad enough to kill.   Frustration of being poor was the cause. When she saw Cookie.

Cookie had been an unwanted child. Like many juvenile delinquents she grew up into a crime state, drawing nourishment from the criminal life which surrounded her. A runaway over & over, a street kid panhandling & stealing, a drug sales girl who'd had her teeth knocked in.   Both Lou & Cookie were like mirror images reflecting on the state of their mothers.   These mothers--their powerlessness and anger, transmitted to their kids. Women forced to bare circumstances beyond their control. The lack of control over their jobs, over childbirth, over their destiny. And these two daughters saw this, feared it --and had gone out into the world seeking power in their lives.

Each had become a free woman, not hooked to a man, nor to the patriarchal society but by the few thin life lines by which it was necessary to survive..

Cookie sat at a busstop in front of the foodstamp office when she saw the bluejeaned Lou--an unmistakable dike striding along in a crooked line beside the curb. Lou was looking at her. Their eyes met, and so Lou said a gruff 'Hello'. And Cookie sez to herself, 'why not? What the hell ?' She'd done blowjobs on women in jail & they'd done her.   It wasn't so bad. Maybe this butchdike could do more for her then all the men had done.

So that's how a lot of sluts came into the Outlaws. --It was a gang of women who were Doing Something. They tolerated females in the Fast Life without giving Attitude, and these women, in turn, kept away the 1onliness that the bikers would have experienced, if they were single –which they would have been if they were more straightlaced and picky.

"Have yuh heard! The fems are gonna revolt!"

"Revolt?"

"Yeah! The fems! They're planning something--they're gonna start protesting. They want equal rights with us butches. They want stuff. They want a fem Warlord. They want sex slaves just for them in the pit. In fact, they're gonna have a butch sex slave in the pit tonight! They're gonna do a lot of stuff they say! There's gonna be changes in the Outlaws!"

By the time the first members & their companions began to drift in, the word had circulated thru the dungeon--be prepared--the fems are gonna stir up some shit.

The slave pit was a carpeted room with a large hole cut out in the middle--where the floor was dropped by a person height, into which were crammed women, nude, oiled bodies, in chains.

A beefy biker at the entry door gave out tickets at the price of $25 apiece, entitling the buyer to the services of the slave of her choice for 1 hour.

After this came the checkpoint in which the biker was handed a trick towel and a sack of safesex stuff. Condoms for dildos which might b inserted into the ass of a slave, then into her vagina, thus needing a fresh condom as a protection from bacteria, as well as using the dildo on different women. Latex gloves for penetration, including finger fucking & fisting. Latex dams for licking & sucking cunt. & sheets of saran wrap (a clear plastic wrap, cheap which unrolled off a tube), for cunt on cunt screwing. Lube. Both non-oxidal 9 germicidal variety and plain. There, at the second checkpoint, another slave wiped off the boots of the bikers with a towel before she walked onto the lush carpet surrounding the pit filled with screaming, nude female flesh. Later, when the biker & her purchase reached their cubical, the slave would humble herself by removing her dike masters boots-a sign of submission.

The slaves waited in the pits; they were there for their own pleasure--the chains were for thrills, they weren't really captive. They had a common key--which was consent. They were slaves because they wanted to be & could get loose any time they chose.

A biker butch--or another fem-- could choose a slave, lead her up the carpeted steps, and out of the main room thru the maize of catacombs; tiny booths with no doors, barely big enough to contain a person lying down; choose a booth, go inside & make love.

Up to this point in the history of the club, the slaves had been femmes. But a strange turnabout was to become apparent this evening.

Two attendants were on duty in back, amid the catacombs. In the beginning they were standing around, in black leather chaps, nude asses showing, naked torsos, oiled shoulders & breasts decked in harnesses of leather straps & chains; and black motorcycle caps on their heads; projecting stern expressions. But when the action grew heavy, even 2 of them wasn't enough. In addition to their other duties, they had to go in the cubicles once they were vacated and clean out any used supplies-cunt wet gloves, dams, and change the sheet on the mat, & throw in some spare towels.

A second visit to the pit or an extra hours stay was only $20, and a third, if a dike could go that long, was $15. This was not for profit. The club raked it $1,600 in monthly dues for that. But to add to the clubs emergency fund; to pay the attendants and girls a little for their work, to furnish sex supplies and to provide the lavish amount of food and drink available in the outer rooms.

A biker had but to go down over to the edge of the pit, look down at the nude women and see what each had to offer until one stirred them to desire.—By the size of her breasts, her slender legs, thighs, inviting. The way she styled her hair, her face, how pretty she was. Some slaves acted the part of total sluts. They spread their pussys with their painted fingers to show the customers & clamored for

215

attention. At the end of the party the slut who turned in the most tickets-who had served the most clients—would receive a $100 prize, plus, equally important to most of them, a gold trophy engraved: **DUNGEON SLAVE SLUT NUMBER VII.—1993.** Some bikers wanted nasty girls, other appreciated the manner of attentiveness a slave might show her as well as her endowments. It was a treat. To buy the sweet meat of another woman, her bosomy tits, her round hips. A way to spoil dikes, so many of who were living a hard life. ---To give them some fun. To provide release, both physical & spiritual. For then a dike had power. Had simply to point to a slave, then take her by the chain and walk her up the carpeted steps out of the pit, to follow, obediently, barefoot, respectfully behind.

It was later in the evening & a line of jostling bikers snaked thru the entry waiting to visit the slave pit; about 25 slaves were in & out of the pit, some returning from a session wet from the shower, and here & there bikers tucking in their shirts, straightening their clothes as they exited the room, having spent their lust with one of the women. Suddenly 4 fems charged into the line of predominantly butch bikers. Four Top fems--behind them, on a chain they paraded a butch, naked, oiled, tall, excellently built --a powerlifter with a sturdy, wet, glistening sinews muscled body. It was Star. The novice butch.

Star was tall, elegant, strong. A magnetic butch vibration resonated in her piercing gaze. The femmes paraded their butch slave around the edge of the pit clanking in her chains, to a growing wild applause. In leather mini skirts, halter tops & long hair the seductive femmes looked more like they should be slaves in the pit, but this was not to be so. They were buyers, seeking their pleasure. Bent on getting their needs met. Not vehicles for some other persons pleasure. Two femmes went off into the catacombs leading their giant butch slave by her chain. The other femmes selected femme slaves out of the pit, and off they went, to a roaring applause.

"This demand for butch sluts is gonna grow, believe me." Whispered a biker; masculine, in denims, boots & sporting a crew cut .

Later Angel watched as her wife Crystal walked daintily around the edge of the slave pit in spike heeled boots and choose the giant butch with the nude oiled body and long hair to her waist-- a perfect body. The butch smiled up at Crystal and mounted the carpeted stairs, came up out of the pit of flesh, encircled her Mistresses waist, then, Crystal walking ahead determinedly, they disappeared into the catacombs.

Inside was dank. 3 close walls. The 4th side was open, providing a view of the narrow hall down which stumbled jeaned, booted bikers & their naked slaves. Cries of female orgasm and moans from here & there thru the sea of party sounds.

Crystal stripped off her clothes in a hurry; her butch slaves big hands helping unfasten her bra and pull her lace panties down over her slender milk white legs. Just beyond the slaves huge well oiled muscular shoulders was the black painted wall of the cubical, the air was close; woman-scented. Music piped in thru loudspeakers above the area. Crystal lay back. Star watched, a bemused grin on her masculine lips. The femme wiggled her ass excitedly. "Make love to me! Kiss me all over my body!"

"Yes Mistress." Replied the big butch; who leaned over her and began to kiss her breasts. Pink tongue darting over her firm nipples. Crystal felt a thrill run from her chest down to her vagina.

Two fingers touched her pearl-clit, wet by spit from her slaves mouth, rubbed gently up & down while Star kissed her tits, neck, chest, arms, and licked smooth strokes over her stomach, then finally her head hovered over Crystals thighs, her powerful hands pushed them open, and her tongue probed the hard pearl, licking with rapid strokes the orgasmic spot her fingers had made hot & ready.

Crystal moaned, eyes closed, body wreathed; hips slowly lifted up off the mat pushing her pussy deep into Stars face. Big hands were squeezing her tits; Stars tongue was probing deep into her pussy. "Oh! Fuck me! Fuck me now!"

"Yes Mistress." Replied the captive butch. Sunk her index & middle fingers in, pushing in & out of the blond femmes pussy like a piston, as her mouth hungrily sucked Crystals nipples, greedily demanding more from her breasts. Deeper pushed the fingers, three, then four, as the palm of her hand slammed into Crystals clit, rocketing her from a plateau of bursting horniness towards out-of-control release. Crystal clutched Stars bronzed thick back raking her fingertips over that muscular flesh, as she panted and sobbed, while Star took more and more of her cunt, fucking harder, faster.

By 30 minutes time her hips thrust in orgasm with wild abandon, under the handsome naked oiled butch Star.

Back in the main area it was a lively party. Howls, screams, laughs. A crowd of bikers jostling at the door. OHHHHH'S, and AHHHHHHH'S!

Another long haired femme in leather boots up to her thighs, a tight spandex miniskirt, came to the pit and chose a slave--another femme like herself. Some sluts were pleased with feminine attention, it brought out the freak in them. Others preferred butches, for they felt very weird, and disappointed when a total femme—with long hair and makeup approached them. In this case, they might ignore the attentions of the would-be customer. If they wanted her, which was much more often, they made that known by response; letting their eyes linger on her, & stopping their milling-around with the other girls in the pit to stand in front of the would-be-buyer and demonstrate with acrobatics what sexual favors she might do for her.

Tonight was a surprise. It had happened infrequently before-a fem buying a slave, it was rare. But tonight a lot of them had come down to the pit as if by a common decision. And one of the femmes had recruited Star for the job. It hadn't been any of the Warlords who had selected the list of slaves before the party.

Angel, handsome in full leathers, decked in glittering rings, could be seen sauntering down to view the pit,--which she could do, without having to buy. Crystal her woman served her well enough. And, if for erotic reasons she wanted a new sex partner to play with she'd probably choose her from the supply of single ladies, not sluts. The blond butch looked over the edge into the pit of oiled female flesh. flesh. Arms and legs, tits & hips, of different flesh tones, alabaster to ebony, & every shade inbetween. Long hair, lipstick, rouge, mascared eyes, bracelets, rings & chains. Blue tattoos. Nose rings accommodated silver ball shape ornaments. Labia piercings, earrings, rings thru their tongues, rings thru their nipples.

Later as the evening wore into a frenzy Daddy George came in to have a peek. The bulldike stared hard at the biggest slave in the pit. The woman was not difficult to identify even without her usual leathers; anyone could see by her Amazon height and broad shoulders--it was Star. "A butch slave." Sez Daddy, dryly.

"Star is a slut?" Asks somebody.

"The girls are demanding butch slaves, and she volunteered." Sez Daddy George.

Daddy George was a true master. A dominant, and basically disliked dominant fems. But, another genius of her leadership was to be able to tolerate different preferences. To rub elbows side by side with all. And to include almost anybody in the gang, as she fought like hell, to roll with the punches.

The pit of slaves remained steady at about ten women, between commings and goings; naked but for their provocative clothes--garter belts, lace panties, push up bras and nothing else, --strings of clothes that showed as much flesh as possible.

Butch Stryker was choosing a slave now. The fat dyke had a solemn face, big boots crushed over the carpet as she led her slave up the stairs out of the pit down the carpeted hall to one of the 20 small cubicles furnished with its mat & towels.

It was for sex.

It was for Outlaws.

The slaves must love this work, because it was voluntary. Little money exchanged hands. They got half --$12 per hour. $25 was the maximum most poor dikes could afford. Rich dykes weren't members of the club as a rule. Like the rest of their organization it ran on both cash and exchange. A biker would be well take care of.— Have a garage to fix her chopper, free karate lessons, a carton of cans of food when work was slim. A slave, after serving in the pit might call George up one day crying the blues; "My car needs a tune-up & I'm broke." And the Leader would give an address of a mechanic who'd give free labor, just the cost of parts. Or a woman in pain needs to see a dentist, it's an emergency; teeth rotting out; George would take money out of the club funds to pay the bill. They tried to help each other. That was the clubs main purpose.

The slave obediently followed Stryker, who strode in her big boots making indentations on the carpet.

Each cubical was small, 4 feet wide. ---- Big enough to spread eagle so that both a woman's feet would touch the sides of the black painted wall, and 7 feet deep, enough to hold the biggest biker horizontally.

A mat of a few inches thickness filled the space in some, others had just bare carpet. A ledge to one side midway up the wall held a single red candle in a white dish, which provided the only dusky light.

A second shelf below the first was for safe sex supplies; alcohol tissues for wiping toys, condoms for their dildos, latex dams to go over pussys when they rode each other, or to lick; for those who chose to play safe, and halt the spread of communicable disease.

The entrances were for the most, uncovered, no doors, but the better cubicles had a velvet curtain hung to the side so that those who wished privacy could order the slave to; **"close it wench!"** Often, bikers might walk thru the maize looking into various compartments at various couplings of many positions to titillate themselves, voyeuristically, before they selected a room for their own conjunction. In addition, there were two large rooms up in the front of the dungeon which could accommodate up to 7 people for those who preferred orgies with more then one slave, or friends & their slaves.

A slave could refuse to do anything she didn't want to do. Of course if she refused too many times, and it got back to the Warlords, they might rip off her chain and tell her to leave the pit--permanently. Most slut slaves were game for many things, but no one was forced against her will. It was consensual.

Slaves liked it--slaves chose it.   It was fun, being a prisoner to be sexually used by a biker with the price in her hand, but too it was a game which either could stop at any time.

Stryker went into the cubical with her slave, a not very attractive girl, much older then her own age of 25.   The slave helped her off with her heavy jacket, rattling its chains & zippers & studs; sliding her hands up over her fat shoulders and back.   They sat down on the mat together. "What do you want to do?" The girl asked in a musical tone.

"Oh I dunnoe." Stryker sez. "Uh… Can yuh spread yer legs and let me lick you *there*, and then you lick me--at the same time?"

"Yes." The slave smiled.

"Then later, I'll fuck you with fingers.. and maybe my toys…uh my strap on.... And... and... tell me you want to be fucked by me."

"I want to be fucked by you honey. *Yes.*" Answered the slave.

The walls of the room were barely more then a shoulders breadth apart.   Stryker's jacket lay at the end, glints of candle fire twinkling in its silver studs. She sat in bluejean shirt, bulging fat, and her x-tra large jeans. Gazed at her slave, chubby hands touched the slaves face. "Yer the most beautiful woman I saw in the pit. Yer so pretty. Yer hair. Yer face." Stryker caressed her slave. "Yer like a Madonna. A real Madonna. I feel... so privileged just to hold you in my arms. It's almost enough. I won't ask you to do much, just lick me, you don't even have to do the dildo stuff--'cause I bet all the dikes are gonna want to do it and it'll wear yuh out. I'm more then satisfied to have you lying here naked. To hide you in my arms from the others out there, and to kiss your body." Cookie smiled to herself. With caresses and touches and pulls of her hands she soon had the fat dikes shirt and jeans on the floor in a little pile with her jacket, and began to kiss the soft fat white folds of flesh, while solemnly Stryker stared down at her with those ever-shifting eyes. After what had been done to her by life, Cookie didn't care about herself much any longer; but here Stryker was, treating her like a Saint.

"MY FLAVORFUL FLOWER! MY TREASURE! MY SWEET CANDY COATED COOKIE!"

The walls of the tiny cubical were rough. Brush marks frozen in plaster, painted a dull black, which had lightened to grey in part where the wall had had to be washed down from blood & other bodily fluids. The red candle flickered, casting its fire; sounds of the bikers howling and laughing, and music were a constant backdrop from the arena around them. And it was punctuated by the staccato of female orgasm. In continuum, every few minutes a rising moan, deep from the soul and guts of a female humanbeing growing into a powerful yell & its crescendo, a vocal scream cleansing every ounce of inhibition out of her body as she humped & quivered in a wild abandon. The action was non-stop.

Cunt smells. Touch. Each woman saw herself in the interior mirror of her mind--and each was no longer the same person. Cookie turning the corner at 43 would soon be a hag, her teeth had been knocked out, or rotted; and never fixed so her jaw was loosing it's shape.   Hard living had dulled her eyes, and quenched the spirit of an ever-renewing psyche that some people keep alive for a century. But tonight she was made to feel like a beauty, by a fat butch who took the time. And Stryker, who had begun to get hysterical from lack of love, over the long weeks had now gained tenderness. And cum in Cookies arms, so willingly.   Each slave was responsible to gauge the time, rough 1 hour, but for her $25 Cookie gave Stryker two.

Late that evening, Cookie got off work and met the fat bluejeaned butch again, and bikers could tell upon inspection that the two were a couple. They walked thru the crowd arm and arm, got plates of food together, danced and sat together in one armchair. Over the months prior to the SM party the two had got closer and this night, a friendship bloomed. What a wonder love was ! Often the short top-heavy runt Stryker had yearned in her loins for a beautiful woman such as Debbie, or Dena, but with the personal attention Cookie gave she felt like a King. Her friends could see it.--The happiness that shone in her fat face when Stryker was in command. When she was provided for, sexually, and given attention. And tho her income was marginal here she was, living like a King! The best food! Music, pals, a woman on her lap; & only for paying the dues!

The gay boys dungeon rocks like a boat from stem to stern, as dike bikers make love with their ladies & butches. Music rolls over them in waves. Rhythm pounds in invisible tides. They cuddle in an armchair. Cookie sucks the fat flesh of Strykers neck, on which would appear blue bruises by morning. "Yuh can show yet friends yer hickeys babe, so they'll know yuh been loved.---By the *best*. Me."

"I don't have to prove nothing, they can see us right now !" Stryker boasts, proud of herself.

The line of leatherdikes waiting to go to the slave pit was without end. A new shift of women had come on duty to service the horny bikers, who stood, jackets off, in sweaty teeshirts. Biker caps pulled low over their eyes, nervous grins on their faces. Their cunts were hot in the crotches of their bluejeans, dripping with discharge even before they fucked, they were so sexually aroused by all the hot action. The live sex shows, SM scenes of dominance & submission; and private couples on display.

Having sex in a sex club was like going into battle. They needed knee pads to fuck on the rough rug. Latex sheaths to combat the spread of the AIDS virus.

Heavily armed warriors who wanted sex went there, carried whips & handcuffs & restraints in their tote bags--because many women demanded discipline in exchange for the privilege of being held in their muscular arms and being fucked. A long sadio-sexual scene filled with verbal humiliation was often an exchange for fucking--to the SM players.

True to their commitment--of being primary lovers, but having a relationship open to other sex partners, Angel played openly in an orgy room with a slut. The carpeting was green, worn & burnt black spots here & there from the lit ends of marijuana sticks; the front windows painted black so no one could see inside from the street and view with horror the goings-on. Several couples and a threesome lay

223

nearby on stuffed pillows. Long blond hair splayed over the collar of Angles black leather jacket which was still on—having removed all the rest of her clothes, including teeshirt & outer shirt,--and was now nude but for the jacket with its official epaulets & chains. Her firm white breasts with hard pink nipples, stomach, arms & legs downed with blond wisps and blond pubic hair glistened as a nubile statue in the flickering candlelight. She mounted the slut doggie style, her strap-on dick pushed into the sluts butthole & drove it in up to the hilt. Drew her cock out so its simulated cockhead played around the rim of her asshole, then shoved it in, buried it deep in the sluts ass. Meanwhile her arm snaked around the sluts waist, fingers thrust into her wet pubic fur & jacked the sluts clit up & down vigorously. Slam, slam, Angel drove her hips, blam, blam, thighs slapping against the sluts rear, driving cock, her own clit rising to a temperature hotter & hotter that would end in a climax. They rutted like two dogs.

Angel fucked fast. Her toes dug into the carpet, her knees were raw. Her clit rode against the dildo and both she & the slut panted breathlessly & hollered with animal enjoyment.

Ronny was at the SM party, she was in a bad mood, because she/he felt uncomfortable about her body. He talked to the Indian, Comancho who, with her wife Frosty rented trailer space in the yard of Ronny's house, about her new house mates--who lived indoors. They all sat in the main party room amid the food & drink. "It's bad enough all 7 of us sharing one lousey bathroom. But they're pigs. They leave their enema bags dripping over the tub They leave their dildos & harnesses everywhere; in the sink, on the towel racks, they don't care. Shit. I'd put in a second bathroom, but I gotta save money for my sex change."

Ronny is single, but always has a girl. A real girl, not just a slut. He has worked hard most of his life,-- earning just woman's pay. & acquired this house in the gay/ghetto lunatic fringe of the metropolitan district near Oils. Ronny is 35, stocky from a lot of muscle building workouts plus injections of male hormones. Short, at 5'4".

"Ronny, if you get a sex change you won't be one of us no more."
Says the lady on his arm, touching with her fingertips his fly front
right over his cunt.

"Yeah, so I been told." Ron tells the lady. "Maybe I'll go out to
California after, where nobody knows nothing about me. Just take
me for a man, period. My beard is growing in from the hormones, but
my friends still call me 'she'. Once people know you use to be a she,
they don't forget it. They find out and they start calling you 'her'.
Yeah, I'll just leave the Club, sell my house and move out to
California. Ain't no snow there in winter. I can ride my bike all
year round."

   Ron & his/her lady drifted away thru the cacophony of women
dancing, partying, drinking & eating and having sex. The two were
linked arm and arm. Privately Ron thought, 'it's happening again. It
always happens. I pull a woman out of the crowd, we talk, she likes
me, wants to be with me, enjoys masculine... butches... But don't like
men. Don't want me as a man.... Fuck... it's so confusing... I need a
woman, so bad. What would it be but hell, to be without one... A
lesbian won't have me.' And doubts about the straight women. One
operation will leave him flatchested; the shots give him body hair, a
male build in musculature & a deeper voice; but is without a dick.
Like a man who'd been wounded in war. The operation will remove
his female sex organs; and for a great price operation can build him
testicles & a non-functioning cock. Such was the state of the art in
Female To Male sex changes in the year of our Lord The Mother,
1993.

   As the couple stroll away, arms entwined, behind them, seated on
the carpet, backs against the wall, Comancho muses to Frosty. As a
renter on Ron's property they knew the situation too well. "Ron's
having trouble with his woman I bet. He gets high and lets her make
love to him as a woman, and gets mad about it the next day. He feels
angry, and ashamed because he let himself be made love to—using
his cunt. I'm glad I don't got that problem, huh honey. You make
love to me a lot, huh honey. Yeah. And when he wakes up the next
morning he's even more determined to have the sex change, and it's
all we're gonna hear about for a couple of *weeks.* "

Ron and his girl came to rest in a large room, in which was to be a demonstration by the Queen of the Club. A sling was being prepared; it hung from the ceiling by a chain of thick links. The woman in Ron's arms hugged tight around his still female body. "I want another woman honey, a strong man/woman like you are now. I don't want a man. That's why I'm with you..... I love a masculine woman. I want that… strength. But I want a woman too...."

Ron tipped his head back, eyes find a field of vision in the murky haze somewhere at the far corner of the place. Stuffed his tears frustration and emptiness back inside somewhere in his sol & slammed the closet door on it. it wasn't going to work… again… He wanted to be wanted as a man... not just a lesbian having women. 'I need somebody to build me up, not tear me down. I don't want her reminding me I still have a females sex organs. But I got to be wise. If I have the change, I can't go back. I won't have a dick that looks much like a real one; and don't get erect with out a stiffening rod yuh gotta put in it. I might not be able to have an orgasm, like I can now. I might not ever get women to sleep with fast like I can now, and wind up alone. And some sex changes develop liver problems from the heavy doses of hormones we have to take, and have to quit them. Then their bodies go back to being female. I got to think this thing out, but it's driving me crazy.' The soft voice cooed, head against his chest which still had tits, bound down tight by wearing 3 teeshirts; "I don't want a man, I want a woman. Women are so much better. So much gentler."

"I thought you said you like it hard." Sez Ron.

"You can fuck me as hard as you want to Ron. I love the way you fucked me...."

"If I had a dick to fuck you it would be even better."

"No it wouldn't... Ron, your women, do they like the way you fuck?"

"Yes."

"Do you fuck them, just as you are now--still female?"

226

"Yes."

"Do they stay fucked, afterwards? They're satisfied?"

"Yeah."

"Well then! You're as good as a man, you're good as ten men !
You ' re great, even if you don't have a dick. Better! You get right
into a woman. A lot of women here want you Ron, you can have your
hearts desire!   And that was good cunt to cunt. You made me cum
with your cunt. My man! My woman! My butch woman/man! Do
you want me to lick your ass to prove it? Get on all 4's then! I'll lick
your ass right up on that stage there!"

A spotlight played around the stage before them, and a crowd was
assembling.

The woman buried her head in Ron's embrace.   "I like you butch.
You're more man then a man--because you have a cunt. You're
strong; a powerful, aggressive lesbian butch, and the world needs to
recognize you as such."

Queen Georgina's Demonstration drew 3/4 of the crowd.   It was
on Anal Fisting. Dikes squatted on the floor, sat in chairs and stood
on tiptoes, peering over the heads of those in front of them.

The mammoth woman stood on a stage built of plywood which
raised her several feet above the crowd. A spotlight illuminated it.
She pulled on a latex glove.

A contraption called a sling hung from the ceiling on a chain with 4
points of leather like the straps of a beach chair in which a person lay
or sat, suspended.

A woman climbed up onto the stage, nude, but for stocking &
boots, went to the sling and with the aid of two helpers got in. Lay
back, her legs spread open.

The sling slowly revolved as a helper turned it, for the view of the large audience of biker dikes sweating in their leather chaps & bluejean vests. "It's best to fist in this position." Georgina was saying. The dikes had often seen vaginal fisting in a sling, but not much of a fist up the butt hole. It was instructional.

"Everybody thinks Queen 'Gina is so square." Sez Debbie from the audience. "But she has to be kinky, or she couldn't have kept George all these years." She should know, as the wife of Warlord Rip she'd witnessed scenes at The Leaders home too many times to count.

Queen Georgina was a total lesbian, always had been and always would be. But had done assplay with gay boys sometimes while they did each others hair. In fact, Georgina had been playing this way in the fag community for years.

Quickly the whispering began, racing thru the crowd like wildfire behind hands, in confidentiality. The Club members wonder, "how can Queen Georgina be a lesbian and stick her fist up a faggots ass?"

"Well that's where she learned it, she just said so! Didn't yuh hear her? Aren't you paying attention?!"

"Yeah, it's what she does for old friends--it's non-sexual to her. Her cunt is totally lesbian."

"It's her freakish side." Says somebody.

"I thought she never *did* SM!" Moans someone else.

The spotlight shone down on the immense woman. Wearing an emerald studded satin dress, black boots with spike heels, and black ringlet hair cascading down past her shoulders. She continued; "Yes. I learned everything I know about assplay from faggots--the masters of the trade." As her delicate toned, but booming voice filled the room, one by one side conversations died, until a hush came over the crowd, all faces glued to Georgina's impressive figure upon the stage, the echo of light from the spotlights overhead lit their faces so they glowed like angels; and the woman swayed in the sling hanging from its chain which disappeared into the ceiling.

"In ancient times, when an enemy was conquered, all the males were made to line up, nude, and bend over; a special man was appointed who would walk down the lines and pound the men's asses with a stick, to get them to open up so the soldiers could sodomize them. That's how they use to rape the male missionaries in Arabia; pound their ass and their assholes open right up. I've met some fags who are surprised to know that." Sez Georgina; and with one latex gloved finger reaches into a jar of Crisco bringing out a gob & begins to gently massage the rim of the woman's asshole, her butt & thighs surrounding.

Georgina had 2 Co-Tops, to help her with her scene.

"We'll be more gentle. I'm gonna let her open up with a lot of attention & stroking & just let her asshole suck me right in."

The Queen pointed to her side in the front, on her satin gown with a latexed finger dripping a gob of lube. "You can fist with an arm this far up a mans butthole, it's actually to the Transverse Intestine. That's about this far up the ribs--from the front view. There's an old saying in the male SM community,---'You can have my heart --if you can reach it.'

My hands are small and perfect."

"Lovely hands." Murmurs the woman in the sling.

"She's got no problem finding playmates 'cause she has real little hands." Sez one helper. This Co-Top, a leather dike is stroking one outstretched leg of the Bottom in the sling, while the other Co-Top who stands on the other side massages her shoulder.

Georgina probes the woman's asshole with her index finger.

Suddenly a cry of horror floods space. **"AGGGH! Y U C K! THIS IS DISGUSTING! YOU ARE ALL PERVERTS! AND THAT SLAVE PIT IS LIKE DANTE'S INFERNO! LET ME**

OUT OF HERE! WHERE'S THE DOOR!" ---Screams a novice to the Club, who gets up, stomping in her big boots crashing thru the seated figures, clawing her way towards the exit. --- But most of the women could deal with it. Some eagerly took notes, others were blasé. They'd seen these Demonstrations before.

"It's important to clean the shit out of yourself first. Rinse out your ass. The fags don't even know about this one. --- Yuh bend over on all fours, shoot the water up inside to the first sphincter, then tense and contract yer butt. Tense and contract. It rinses it out. In fact it rinses around in yer ass like a washing machine."

A voice from the sling speaks; the Bottom sez; "it's easier to get inside with intense clit stimulation." Her voice is higher then 'Gina's booming operatic tone. The Queen has continued to play with her butthole non stop. Going an & out with the tip of her shiny latex finger. One helper now runs a thumb over her clit. The helpers stand to the side, caressing her, making her comfortable. One presses a hand against the Bottom's bottom, whispers into her ear. Then kisses her foot in it's boot & blue stocking. The other Top strokes her clit, until she utters a low moan.

"I won't push her, it's not a macho thing about forcing your will on her. Just put my hand here, and start with a finger, then two fingers, and let her swallow me up, and then comes the fist. Just stand here and let me do all the work, her ass will swallow me in."

"My ass wants attention, then my clit wants attention. It defuses. My ass need does. It's not as fierce." Intones the Bottom from the sling.

The Co-Top stroked her pussy.

Her name was Liz. Naked body doubled in folds of flesh into the sling, except for her feet in the pair of blue stockings, black boots, and a piercing. A gold ring on her pussy lips. A Co-Top handed her water in a sealed container. Her butt forced air in and out. "I'll try a bigger butt plug." Georgina sez. Liz's clit was demanding attention. A Co-Top stroked it. Crisco was thick. It was as if they were baking a big cake between her legs.

The three women worked, played with Liz. "Don't press her clit too hard."

"I need some tension too." So the helper kept her hand, in a latex glove, on her clit.

"It's gonna be E-Z honey." Said the Co-Top. "She's gonna get her fist in your asshole."

"Yeah, I got almost my whole hand in there now." Sez the Queen.

Queen Georgina withdrew, reached to the stand on which was the jar of Crisco, a package of latex gloves, and various toys made of rubber, or plastic. Picked one up, and showed it to the audience. "This dildo has been around the fag community. I got it from a male friend. I prepared it by washing it in alcohol, but it won't hurt to put a condom on it, just for safety. The Co-Tops touched the woman in the sling, caressed her legs and buttocks.

"MY LEGS GOT A CRAMP Oh I hate that!" The Co-Tops stretched up her leg, so the blue stockinged, black booted toe pointed at the ceiling, and rubbed & stretched, working out the kink.

"In this position, the only bad thing, it's harder to fly, my middle's bent up." A deep strong moan came out of her midst as gently Georgina placed the dildo into her ass, which was by now filled with Crisco. The Co-Top massaged her toe.

"That's what I hate about assplay, my clit goes crazy." Liz breathed in, WHOOSH! Great WHOOSHES of air. A Co-Top slapped her thigh.

The immense woman pulled out the dildo, and wiped Liz's butt with a towel, the lube came out pink from traces of bleeding internally.

Georgina wiped her hands on the towel, then pushed a ringlet of black hair from off her sweating brow. The spotlights beat down. The silent crowd sat, transfixed at the scene. It might seem hard to

231

believe, to some in the audience that the three weren't torturing Liz, but giving her pleasure.

As one's arm brushed the Sling, moved slowly with its weight from the ceiling on the silver chain. The other lights in the room were dim.

Georgina wiped the woman's butt with the towel, more pink. It was blood, mixing with the Crisco.

Liz puckered up her mouth and kissed one of the helpers. Now all 3 were working her over. Another low moan. Caressing, probing. "There's a little bit of blood." Georgina explains. "The rectum is lined with blood vessels, and it's thin, it's very easy to rupture. But it's not serious, it's not a lot of blood." And went in with her fist, and came right back out because it was too intense for the woman in the sling. More pink lube came out with her hand. Blood.

Georgina went back to four fingers, while a Co-Top dropped a steel egg--a sex toy into a condom and pressed it against Liz's pussy lips, and slowly it sank inside.

"It's just a membrane between the cunt and the ass. I can feel the egg in her cunt with my fingers inside her asshole."

The sling was a net; weaves of leather. It forced the Bottom's ass tight; cheeks pushed together. But it worked. And that way the assembly of 80 or more dikes could observe the scene.

Georgina's hand was in, curled her fingers into a fist, began shoving in and out of the Bottom's asshole, gentle but firm.

The helper Tops caressed Liz's head, gently.

Liz began to hump rhythmically to the fisting, made low animalistic cries. Then a shriek. The chains of the sling want **clank, clank, clank.** The 3 women paid her attention. Rubbed her clit, the Bottom humped, Georgina thrusted; **CLANK! CLANK! CLANK!**

"THOSE IN THE FRONT ROW, I BETTER WARN YOU, LIZ IS KNOWN TO SQUIRT WHEN SHE CUMS."

"Just not in my hat." Sez Rip, who sits in a chair, long legs & arms akimbo, viewing the scene.

"She's been known to shoot 4 to 6 feet. I don't want to scare you girls!" **CLANK! CLANK! CLANK!** The chain rattles as the Bottom humps, and the Top's stroke, and Georgina's fist pounds hard, fast; it's all going faster, then an arc of clear fluid, like water gushes out at 5 feet and hits dikes in the front row. The sweet sticky fluid of female ejaculate.

Liz's thighs are greasy and wet. The Top pulls the condom out, with the egg out of her cunt. And Georgina removes her fist from her ass. More blood. "She's bleeding. It's the mucus membranes, the capillaries--small blood vessels."

"Don't stop, it's ok, it's ok!" Liz pants.

Georgina uses the smaller object for the last go round. Holds the dildo by the base & sticks it into her asshole.

"The boys always have permission to jack themselves off." Sez Liz, taking her hand and pushing her fingers on her clit, pushing deeper, deeper. Georgina thrust's the dildo, Liz works her clit with her fingers, humping hard, her butt round & white at the edge of the sling making the sling rock by her vigor. **CLANK! CLANK! CLANK! CLANK! CLANK!** The sling's shaking harder, harder, Liz rubs her own clit, faster, and **B O O M!** She cums. Ejaculates a 2nd time; Georgina takes her cue from Liz, and keeps right on thrusting the dildo in her ass, Liz works her clit, franticly and climaxes a third and final time; an arc of water shot out in a fountain.

"I'm drippen', I'm drippen." Sez a Top. "She shot all over me."

"It poured out."

"Did I get you?" Asks Liz.

"You're a mess."

Chains clank, as the Bottom begins to climb down. Somebody gets a chair for her to step on.

"Thank you Liz."

Georgina has a clean towel and pats it over the Bottom's ass. "Yer soaked."

"You didn't use Elvira!"

"Elvira is this two headed Dildo, I presume." Sez Georgina staring down at Liz thru purple painted eyes. "This is Elvira." Liz produces the 12 inch long two ended cock, black, made of satiny latex.

"I love to play with pushy Bottoms. I'm perfect for them. They have permission to be as pushy as they want with me." Sez Queen Georgina, fixing Liz with an gaze of both ice and sugar simultaneously. A bit miffed at being admonished for not using the two-headed toy. The audience talks and laughs around them, having lost their hushed awe. "How do you feel?" Georgina asks in a motherly tone, as she mops up the lube from her hands, and the table.

Liz replies; "I feel like I just Bottomed."

The final event of the evening was a mock prisoner scene.--Set back in Nazi Germany.

Comancho sat clustered with her wife & buddies a third row back. A feather stuck out of a red headband around her thick black Indian hair. Drops of sweat glistened on the brown skin of her forehead dampening the red denim band. The dikes were packed close together, shoulder to shoulder, butt to butt. Angel had her jacket off, plus shirt, and sat in her undershirt showing tuffs of blond hair from her armpits, one arm slung around her mate Crystal.

As they unfolded the flag, of red, white & its black Nazi insignia, Comancho whispers, "See, we do it for play. The Avengers, they mean that stuff. They take the Fascist stuff serious.--If they found out one of them was a Jew, or one of their own parents was a Jew,

234

they'd probably slit her throat and dump her bleeden' corpse in Lake Montezuma."

. "They got swastikas all over their clubhouse. Crystal's been there."

"They *mean* their Nazi Swastikas. Ours are just for play." Sez Comancho again.

After the scenes of the evening were done, Angel felt aroused and sexually charged.

It's what a lot of leatherfolk felt.

Sometimes the blond butch felt a lonesomeness inside when she was right in the middle of her friends the Outlaws. Or, even when she was with Crystal. A fierce lonesomeness, like a hunger. A needing, beneath the veneer of her personality, rooted in a deeper, darker place of her soul. A need, as vital as breath. It was of the same reason that George needed her mistresses.

'I've learned a lot about life, since Pam. I wanted a lover so hard since my teenage years, then, God sends me a wife, a loving wife, but there's still something missing. I need other women to relate to,-- and a group of women, a community. That's why I told Crystal from the beginning, I'd never promise anybody to be monogamous again. Tho I might love her, really love her, 'till the day I die.'

For a lot of questions there are no answers.

She was out here alone, fumbling around. Not knowing why she did what she did.

Not knowing the demons which pursued her.

The rooms of the dungeon were breaking up with couples leaving, groups shouting in horseplay. Workers packed up the tables of leftover food. Slowly the blonds Crystal & Angel in their matching black leather outfits walked to the exit within their group of friends,

235

inside the greater swirl of Outlaws; like a planetary system in a nebulae, held within a dance of gravities & attractions.

'I got down on my knees and preyed to God Almighty to take this feeling away from me, this hunger, this want. --Now I have a new wife. And her pussy's sweet, and she's built just right for me to cum easy with my clit in her pussy. Crystal wraps her arms around me and gives me all the love she's got.--What kind of drive is this that makes me want something more? Not a month will pass, and I'm looken' at other women.'

Fun for some was happiness, picnics, drama. And sex, a topic to be avoided. Sex always stirred up some uncomfortable feelings.

Angel. Like most good Tops, she'd been Down. Served as a Bottom for years.--But not, however under the studied art of SM, but within a more unconscious role of a woman. The gender role of a woman in the world. –Under economic domination. Being a police-chased criminal, at the illegal jobs she did to earn cash—big cash like men earn. Being harassed for her queerness. So, the blond butch had as few others do, a view from the bottom. And when she emerged as a Top, after a climb up the long ladder of life, it had made her harder, better.

At thirty-three, she'd been a slave in handcuffs.--Literally been put in handcuffs by the police departments of several metropolitan cities; been shackled by the inability to get what she needed from the world too long, while, it seemed, everybody else was helping themselves; she'd still been on the outside looking in. Before she'd learned to master women. To master money. To master the streets. And mainly to find out how to get the desires of her heart. And make dreams transpire into tangible reality.

So what were these feelings that coursed there now, in that dark channel?

Like many lesbians, she'd lived in a subterranean city, but come out, moving into the light. Straddling, one foot in the old world oppression of cops with Billy clubs breaking heads of queers in nighttime raids, and B-girl bars with red lipsticked, fishnet stocking hustling ladies, and lonely streets and empty hours--moving out of this into a new world of lesbians holding hands in public, shopping in deppartment stores & buying houses on the avenues. Of gay people as a political force, now seen in media & TV. Gay weddings in cathedrals. Of accepting families, and friends in a gay community united.

Crystal stood a few inches shorter then Angel, blond hair in curls. Before the butch had come into her life, when she'd first joined the club, and become for a brief time the Warlord Hawks woman, she'd been whipped, branded, shamed & humiliated. Angel had been her white knight in shining armor. And Angel had been alone a long lonely time, so much so her fire had frozen to ice. Arm & arm they turned to survey the dungeon before they left; napkin strewn wall to wall carpet, rising into spectator stands at one side—3 tier high; open cartons spilling their contents of safe sex supplies, empty plates of food & overturned waste cans;-- as the workers cleaned up the remains of the party & the show.

Once, they'd talked about a deep subject. Angel'd talked & Crystal analyzed. "Your mother left you and your dad when you were very young. For her to be so cold, she probably wasn't very loving to you in your earlier years either. It must have gone on a long time, maybe since you were born.

"Dad loved me. I had that. And I really loved him. He stayed with me and didn't abandon me, but he had to get my grandmother to watch me, because he was at work all day. And she was cold. And violent. I didn't have peace. And I wasn't safe. And tho my dad was a good father, it was a mothers love I missed. It made me so sad."

The first times I was with women, it wasn't so hot either. The very first ones were straight--my highschool chums. Then, in my teens, 15, 16, after I dropped out of school, I began sneaking in B girl bars that had some gays in them as well. It was an underworld dive. All about hustling & fast money & crime. I got drunk, which was easy for me then, just a couple of shots or hard liquor; and the place would be a blur; I'd stagger back to the room where I was staying, without getting what I wanted, which was to be with a fancy woman. A pretty woman in a silk dress & her hair done gorgeous & makeup on her beautiful face. Feminine. Finally one night I got a chance to be with this women working in the club. She was pretty, lots older, so I thought, but now looking back I realize she wasn't much older, so I thought, but now, looking back I realize she wasn't much older then me, --maybe 4 years, but experienced. She wanted to look at my money. It was about maybe $30, I can't remember. I had a newspaper route back in the old neighborhood, and I worked for an old lady cleaning & helping run errands. It was all there was left to live on for that week. I was nervous. Opened my wallet and showed her a glimpse of the cash. The woman got off the barstool, took me by the hand & I didn't know where we were going, maybe to a room in a hotel, that's what I figured; but she just led me back thru the hall to the toilets, right around the corner where the hall turns, so we were out of sight and we lean up against the wall. She took my money there, and then she jerks down my fly. It was rough, & it was so fast; she puts her fingers in my cunt--on the outside & finds my clit and begins jacking my clit up and down and around so quick and hard it makes me breathless; & I'm wet, and I got my hands on her tits— fumbling trying to get under the satin dress and her face is inches from me, I'm trying to kiss her, but she's turns her head away, impatient, and her fingers keep circling in my cuntlips fast, & hard and before I know what is happening I melt in her arms, but already she is shoving me away. I was relieved, but disappointed. The crotch of my pants was wet. I'm clutching onto her, it's such a thrill, she's so exciting, the smell of her perfume, the female animal magnetism she has; I'm squeezing her, I run my hands over her tight dress & pull her to me, feel her, touch her breasts & hips. Then she's pushing me away hard, and breaks loose and I can't figure out what's wrong, she took me to her one minute, now she's pushing me away; 'did I do something wrong ?', I'm thinking. And I was disappointed we hadn't gone to a bed, and got her nude and touched her sex. And took the time and did all the things I'd dreamed about for so long.

But in the next few weeks I went back. Found same woman again, & she knew me too. I showed her my money and we went back down the hall, which I expected. We stopped by the toilets. I told her to let me touch her breasts first & let me put my mouth on her pussy. She said OK, but hurry. Then I pushed up her satin dress, and she didn't have any panties on underneath. I knelt in the hall, down in the litter and dirt there and licked her hole. Her female smell drove me wild.

I got up, wiped pubic hair off of my face, my mouth; my cheeks were wet with her pussy juice; and asked her would she do that to me? "Nobody here in this club's gonna do that to you!" She said it harsh. "Now come on!" And jerks me back against the wall. Saying, in effect that I better let her do me like she had before, the easiest way for her, with fingers, or I wouldn't get anything. And she had already taken my money. My money was gone; shoved it down the cleavage between her big breasts. And she used her hand on me again, jerking me off, her face twisted in a grimace, like she was disgusted. And that's the last time I went in there for months. There was no gay bar in my town for a long while, just freak bars, and I'd been wanting a woman since I was 13 and could formulate my feelings about females into realizing I was gay. Wanted sex, & wanted love, and this lady was only one of a precious few I'd been able to get, and since before I could remember I'd been fantasizing about it.

But as far as tonight, a seasoned veteran, the blond butch couldn't wait to get home and push her clit into her wife's warm cunt, pump up and down in it and cum.

That night, hungrily she went to Crystals arms for love.

A few days after the SM party, after thinking about the subject, Angel told Crystal. "I'm glad we went to the Slave Pit & you had sex with Star. You know I want to have another woman to play with. I want us both to be free in that way. I really need it--I don't understand why. To have a second woman, sometimes, it takes the pressure off of what I feel. Baby, I'll never leave you. I just need somebody different. I won't go off and do it and leave you lonely. You can be with us, you can watch, or participate."

"Anybody you have in mind?"

"Sort of." Angel sez.

Chapter Twenty

239

Daddy George spoke; "I'll send somebody 'round to pick you up." Indeed, the desildike ordered a biker to drive downtown on her motorcycle & meet Stryker at the hotel.

It was strange how fate intervened with human lives that night. The biker had bike problems & family upsets. Water got in the distributor cap & her bike was disabled for a period of time until it dried out. Plus, one spark plug wasn't firing right; and, when she'd finished fooling with that, had marital problems with her woman, which made it later still.

Meanwhile, Stryker waited by the window listening for her bell, looking out thru a dusty pane down at the downtown street, & alternately going down to the lobby--with the frantic impatience for which she was noted--to wait for the biker to arrive there, in case she forgot the number of her bell.

Stryker's eyes were deep wells reflecting black. Magnified thru triple lense glasses; fish eyes lit full of emotion, confusion, a thin wisp of humor about the situation. Electric light bulbs reflected from the ceiling against her glasses, blinding, as she blinked, issuing out a single tear.

'They've forgotten about me.' The fat dike thought, morosely. It was Saturday Night. Their signals got crossed. Stryker waited by the window of her 8th story room, watching the street below, people ant-small, and cars no bigger then toys. The enthusiasm of the evening wore off as minutes ticked by on the clock, and a hollow feeling replaced it. And when it got late, impulsively she decided to go down into the street in front of the seedy hotel, where she anxiously paced in the icy winter chill, thus missing several phonecalls the biker placed.

As the club had grown so large, invitations now must be printed out, where before they traveled by word of mouth. But as confidentiality was necessary, an address was not printed on a flyer in case it fell into a strangers hand and harassment followed.—An Avenger, or an enemy of the anti-gay Right Wing.

240

All Styrker had was the name, date and what kind of party it was, that it had food, and what kind of kinky activities to expect—but no location. The phone number on the flyer had been for prior RSVSP's, and no one was answering it at this late date. Stryker didn't know the exact address of the party. Her own bike was dead. In storage inside the basement locker with the mice and damp, deep, deep underground beneath the hotel. She didn't have the biker's phone number either. And when she finally called Angel, then Johnny, & then Comancho & Frosty-- everyone had already left.

By the time the biker got her life in order, and phoned a final time and got no answer, she figured; 'well, it's so late. Stryker has gone ahead and left by herself.' Without realizing how serious the little biker took being left behind. –She took it to heart.

By then the party was in full swing at a members house, and Stryker was left out in the cold.

That feeling of fullness, happy expectation when the sky had been grey-- twilight as she waited eagerly by the window for friends to come, 2 hours later, emptiness overtook her--inside.

Stryker was near-hysterical. Ran from the window to the elevator, down to the street where she paced like a madwoman, then came back up stairs to watch, frantically, as time's last sand grains fled from the hourglass.

Evening turned into night. By 8pm--3 hours late, Stryker still waited. Nobody ever did arrive.

A sane person, or, one more reasonable would have stopped dwelling on negative thoughts and found something else to do. But the dikes mind was fixed; it was part of what made her crazy.

The unfortunate mix-up confirmed what she already knew-that she was a worthless piece of shit. That she would be unhappy forever.

By that night of a full moon, her life was ruined, and she was obsessed... Jotted down some suicidal poetry; made an entry in her journal and headed out the door to Oils, by taxicab. More disappointment awaited her there. ---Frequently Oils closed on a whim of Kelly. Knowing of the party that night, and that few bikers would drop by, the old owner had simply not come downstairs to open the tavern, and when Stryker pulled up inside the taxicab nobody was there. The street deserted. --No motorcycles. A chain & steel padlock on the doors locking them shut. Confused, from Oils the dike returned home alone in the taxicab having wasted $15. Now thoroughly depressed, and desired only to go out of herself into the night and get lost.

Life was not easy for a kike dike who was nuts, and walking the edge.

All her poor mind could do was obsess about the club off somewhere having a wonderful event & she couldn't participate--it couldn't untangle itself.

The fat dike collapsed in her stuffed armchair; trousered butt filled it well; ran her chubby hands thru her hair until it was wild; her face streaked with tears, her booted feet stomped the thin worn hotel carpet.

For a week she hadn't seen Cookie. This depressed Stryker.--That she couldn't even keep a slut. Which was a mistake; that's why Cookie was a slut. With front teeth knocked in. Because she floated from pillar to post on waves of whims, an aging butterfly. It was a mistake for anyone to try to pin her down. But Stryker wasn't using reason. Thinking only with her heart, & her clit.

'I really use to love Debbie. But now I hate her! Debbie is a Food Nazi. She's so thin. She conducts a diet of fascist self-improvement regime. I can't be the lover of a Food Nazi,--- not someone who puts duct tape over their refrigerator door after 6pm, to lock it, so they can't sneak snacks; and who sticks their finger down their throat & gags themselves to vomit & takes enema's so as not to have any food inside of them to turn to fat. And Cookie, well that's a joke. She tells me she loves me, & then I catch her with Lou, whispering the same thing. I think her mind is so burnt out from liquor & pills she can't remember who she loves from day to day.' The hotel room was small. A few strides in any direction met with a wall. Covered with

242

gay paintings of sunburst color that few other human eyes had seen, and for which few had given her credit... The little dike was confused. Night after night two years she'd made a beeline for Oils. Biker events had been her destination. Suddenly she saw how dependant on them she was.—Literally didn't know where else to go for fun that evening. She wore her best black pants, blackshirt & a buckskin jacket with fringe on the sleeves, & black boots. A scent of men's aftershave. Now in the mirror against a drab wall she winced to see herself all dressed up with nowhere to go. Against another wall, was a shelf she'd built of salvaged boards & plastic milk crates. She went over to it and thumbed thru some papers until she came to a flyer on a lavender colored sheet. It was an advertisement for a lesbian bar across town. ---A place she'd never been before. 'They forget to pick up Styrker. She's just a crazy kike anyhow. I looked out my window an' looked and nobody came. I'm sick of the Outlaws. Dena stole my money. Deb is a Food Nazi, and Cookie is a three-ringed circus. They can't even send somebody to pick me up! I guess they think I'm fat and nuts, and not worth it! Well, it's Saturday Night--that's the High Holidays of Dikedom, and I ain't staying home in this room, or I'll kill myself! It's time I found a new club. And try to meet some new women.' Stryker had been hanging by a thread emotionally, anyway, and now the bottom fell out. So, with a dwindling supply of cash, she went outdoors, hailed a cab in the downtown street and went off into a new territory, where nobody knew her face.

Many gay people are separated from their families due to the problem their homosexuality causes. She had little else, but to try to be with friends, and to seek a lover.

Stryker kept going out--in search of her own sexuality.

When the fat butchlette got to the club, instantly she could see it was a mistake. Tho her mind was whirling in it's daze, and her thinking had begun to bend thru the liquor she consumed, she could definitely see these square gay girls were repulsed by her. Her too big boobs, crew cut, and being fat.---They were trim, sophisticated and professional. They wore business suits, and talked in sedate tones. **'AHGGG!** It's been so long I been to a straight dykes bar I forgot what they're like! **UGH!'**

The club was in a strange part of town, she wasn't familiar with. Crumpled up the lavender advertisement in one chubby fist and dropped it on the floor. No one would talk to her, and even the bartender was cold.

A little voice inside told Stryker to take her last crumpled dollars and catch a cab back home. If she'd been in Oils there'd be friends to take care of her. Somebody. ---Even strangers who didn't know her would have felt responsibility to a sister biker. Here, she was a stranger, alone. Plus, she was an outcast among them. Women gave her dirty looks and moved away or turned their heads when she tried to be friendly & talk with them. But she was stubborn. As if glued to the bar. Sat back in a fancy wooden chair with a carved back & arms, like King on a throne. She ordered another drink.

She felt like burying her face in her hands and crying, it was so cold, blue & lonely in the dyke bar, but it was easier to order the bartender to open a bottle of beer. After a few drinks sorrow turned to relief, ---the temporary sort. Golden liquor hit her bloodstream producing a dizzying high. Boosted her ego until she felt like a humanbeing again; like king of the world. In this state, a smile on her fat lips she climbed down from the bar chair and as she swaggered up to women and tried to talk to them she found how unpopular she was. Gradually the smile turned into a pout. Stryker made several more forays thru the club. --Got down off the bar chair again and again, to trot after women and ask them to dance, but when it was apparent she was getting nowhere, she finally just sat there & started to drink heavy duty, non stop. Toss them glass after glass, & retreat into private thoughts of a make-believe fantasy, incorporating the women around her into it, like a stage play which could be controlled and sat; with a black cloud of gloom hanging over her head & drank herself silly.

Lesbians in pants suits, & austere dress were quite different from the nose-ringed, bald & tattooed dikes who hollered and stomped the night away.

The first half of the evening then, Stryker felt she was getting somewhere. --Liquor's golden glow fueled her delusions. 'I'm free of

244

Oils, I'm in a new club with new dykes. This music's great, I ain't heard none of it over & over like in Oils, Ugh. This tavern is very pretty.' The pumping music fueled adrenalin to her fantasies. It was Saturday Night, and on one lone bar chair one miserable dike in her best clothes had a party all her own. A hollow party.

The last hour, at 3AM. in a frenzy, Stryker went wild, danced by herself. Still had had no success. Met no one. 'I'm too wild for them. I'm too strong, and they're too tame. I'm so lonely. It's killing me to death.' The red and yellow party lights revolved. Gentle tinkle of melodic voices of the older sophisticated professional women provided the backdrop of the evening. Drunk, she worried; 'Aw, if I was just thinner. Maybe I'll dye my hair blond… Aw, I don't mind being alone. It's better to think that way. I want to be alone. **I Want to be alone!** Aw, it was a mistake to come here. Aww… Shit.'

Then she wanted to get away from the judgment which she saw radiating out of the eyes of people... The hate… Wanted to go away and hide.

Stryker had taken a taxi to the club; but was so drunk when she was ready to go, that she staggered out the front door & up and down the street to look for her bike--it wasn't there.

Cold icy blocks of 4 story apartment buildings stretched away to the east and west. A frozen sky hung above. Black night. A few blocks away from the dim red & blue neon lights of the club she remembered she needed a cab, but forgot where the tavern was, so she couldn't go back & call one to come pick her up. She blacked out of memory, and when she awoke she was still walking.

Big boots shuffled thru the slush of an ice-filled street. Pants cuffs were wet. A fog haze of snow filled the atmosphere.

Smell of burning wood in fireplaces hung in the air. **Drip drop drip** of a rainy snow settled off tree boughs and roofs of buildings.

Noise of icy slush running in the gutter below the city. Night was windswept, slick ice, wet. She traveled by a parking lot made of cement covered by a light film of snow; iron fence, and cars inside, their grills like teeth grimacing, as they sat parked for the night.

All was still.

Cement steps of a church were lit, but its heavy oak door locked. A passageway led further into the deserted church courtyard. Grounds between official cleric buildings. The fat figure staggered on in a crooked path. Stryker did not realize that the club grew further and further away, and that she had left the populated area. A few apartment buildings had their lights on to ward against burglars, but there were no people. Then another mammoth building of the church, then a school. Deserted. And next to it a park-sized lot. Sounds of her foot falls, wavering, uncertain.

Neon street lamps every 100 feet. Windows were closed with no eyes to see.

A police car maneuvered thru the snowy streets like a shark.

Stryker saw it, and managed to carry herself upright, so as not attract attention. The police slowed at a corner. The dike was angry. Cussed at it under her breath. **'Fuck! Goddamn cops!'** But they were only keepers of the peace this night and not there to harass her. As a last hope the police squad car disappeared around the corner, red lights thru the snowy fog.

The last building in the ecumenical cluster, a Covent, towered 7 stories into the falling snow sky. It is the story of nuns, who weep and wail and chant and pray, cloistered in their churches of this earth. Having the hurt of somebody who is born into this earth, into flesh, who wants to become spirit. Sometimes, inside, as Stryker'd suffered, she felt like that.

An awesome sight. The turreted castlelike building, snow and the moon. It protected the nuns. They were in bed by 9pm besides St. Mary's Cathedral. Safe women. A sign 4 feet by 10 hung on the grey stone fortress; its large black letters stated:

BINGO

EVERY SATURDAY NIGHT
PAYS $250.

There was no sanctuary to run too; the scene focused down to locked grey stone buildings. Cement walls echo her footsteps, and don't see her. Nor the nuns, can they see her, hiding their faces from the world. As they turn from being women who bare the sorrows of childbirth, and child death; abuse, rape, powerlessness. Who see life die, and loved ones go. To become virgins. Welded in Spirit to Christ.

Great walls of the convent above her small figure loomed in stone.

Not 15 blocks down from this quiet neighborhood was a very poor sector of the city.--A barrio. Drunken Puerto Ricans and other Hispanics milled in the street terrifying the decent citizens of their own nationalities. Men, a lot stumbling drunk. Carloads of these no-goods drove up and down the main drag that ran about 30 blocks, and was a slum from one end to the other. Poverty stricken immigrants who had fled their country of birth because they were in a hopeless condition, down on the bottom of the barrel there, to try their luck in the USA. Too many of them remained in the dregs of the class barrel here.

Gangs of them stood out in the street, huddled in doorways of shops closed for the night, drinking liquor in the cold. More and more of them could be seen as the economic depression of America widened, & the slums grew. Seldom were there Latina women in the street when it got late, and none in gangs like the men, and the few women who must be out, returning from late night employment were afraid. These low-acting men milling around, drunk, gazing at the women with lust, staring at other men with hate, or fighting, acting crazy, loud music blaring were a potpourri of trouble.

5 police cars, a fire engine and an ambulance wailed down the 30 block stretch, there'd been a shooting.

The men fought all night long. **"I'M GONNA KILL YOU CUNT!"** --Saying this to each other, in their low opinion of women. Struggling for dominance violently among themselves.

247

The later it got, the drunker they got. Drunk men do foolish things.

A van, old and rusted, had come up from the strip; strayed out of it's territory, weaving thru this night filled with gangs of loitering men, left the poor section of town, and traveled into the better section of the sleeping city.

The vehicle was beaten into dents from many accidents. Inside were 5 drunken men.

Street lamps blurred in pools of slush snow water. Cement echoed the dikes lonely footfalls staggering down the street. Not aware she'd picked up a trailer. Alcohol roared in her ears; so she couldn't hear external noises. Narrowed eyes in alcohol-red faces in the front seat of the van had seen her. Spotted a lone female, disabled, who walked crookedly over the sidewalk; not somebody who could put up a fight.

Stryker came to an intersection. As the one before it, it was deserted. 'Where's my bike?', A slow drunken thought passed thru her mind. She blinked. Thought she saw a van, yellow headlights baring down at her.

At the corner she turned. They turned.

Why didn't she have the right to get drunk & stagger thru the streets that a man would? To pass out in the gutter, and awake when webs of alcohol moved off her mind, and the worst thing that would have happened would have been to be robbed of her wallet & it's meager coins; & maybe her shoes and jacket.

Why? Because of being female. Genetics made her smaller, weight less, more slight of build. Hormones making her less vicious & them more so.

The word rape, meaning something bad done to women, and hardly ever done to men, comes to mind. That they would want her for that body that encased her soul & mind,--& not just something she carried in a purse.

Alarmed, she walked faster, the van sped up--as if a decision had been made inside its ragged interior. Snow billowed in the sky where stood the spires of the Cathedral, towering like primeval turrets. Black and white night sky.

Tires swish thru slush, gears grind over asphalt in pursuit. The van bounced over bumps in the road, ate up space between them in seconds. It drove right up beside her as close as it could get, then hit the brakes & jolted to a stop, its front end shaking. The rear door jerked open, banged a dull metallic clank against the side, and two swarthy men reeking of alcohol stumbled out, half falling in the snow.

Bigger men then she was, they were looking at her, with frowns & leers as they cut across her path. Then the hate in their faces mingled with sick grins. Sex was on their minds. A third climbed out, a sleepy look on his face. Alone, he would do nothing, but being with evil companions brought out the pack mentality. The meanest one was in the front seat, too drunk to fuck or fight, but it was he who'd seen her first, it was his idea. They began to laugh as they surrounded her talking Spanish, in drunken slurs among themselves as they closed in like a pack of mad dogs. They had been unable to find a woman and get her to have sex with them. There were no prostitutes because they had no money. They'd driven around and around spending their last coins on bottles of beer; drinking, looking for somebody to rob, looking for women. Looking. It was a crime of opportunity, and not planned.

Maybe one man alone would have stayed back on the strip & got into a fight; another might have found something to steal from an unlocked car. But in the pack, the suggestion of evil ignited them into this ugly purpose. Hairy hands grabbed her. Stryker screams, flails her hands, tries to run, to escape. Men are all around her, and inside the van she sees two more; brown faces, white teeth laughing in the dark. **BLAM!** A blow struck her on the top of her head, a spongy give to her skull. **BLAM!** Again, with a piece of wood, now bloodied. A dull pain ebbs out of the would as blood drips into her face. She feels her legs buckle, flairs her arms, discordinate, trys to put up a fight, frankly she isn't much of a fighter. One put an arm around her head, **"I GOTTA GUN ! I GOTTA GUN !"** One man yells in broken English, his eyes wild, revolve in his skull, pushing her towards the van. Another pulls her by the jacket, they're forcing her over the steel floor of the van, dragging her inside. **"I GONNA BLOW YOU BRAINS OUT BITCH!"** Thru foggy alcohol part of her waited to hear the gun that might go off at any time. There was no gun, just threats & brute force. **"AI! SENORITA! AI SENORITA!"** Coos a drunk inside. Another is screaming at her to get in, to stop yelling or they're going to shoot her, and she's drunk & petrified, not knowing what's happening, and its all happening so fast, in seconds, a nightmare. Hands yank at her, the cold metal of the van under her body. Men scream at her like they're enraged at her & they've never seen her before. Angry because they don't have women. Angry because they don't have money. Angry because they can't speak English, or read or write. Angry as blind, deaf, dumb, powerless babies.

They drag her inside. One throws the bloodied piece of wood out into the snow. She hears the steel doors slam shut. Inside now, the world has drastically shrunk into a stinking 8 by 10 foot space that reeks of liquor, stale clothes, male stench, & marijuana smoke. The first one to force himself on her has a hard on, and is taking his pants down. Another laughs, holding her torso down with much greater weight then her own, as she tried to fight. They rip her clothes off. And she knew what she's in for.

After Stryker has been pulled inside, the van keeps driving a ways. When it comes to a stop she'd already been raped by the first man. This is nothing erotic. It is torture. Not a fantasy. The fear for her life, the physical pain and terror. Another drop of acid against the human cause. Of women's fear and men's hatred. Men's self-isolation & male inability to get what they want out of the world so they turn to weakness and rage to attack other living beings.

"FUCK IN HER ASS! FUCK YOU DOG BITCH!"

Hands pawed her. Searing hot flashes of pain in her sex.

Whitish faces in neon, flushed red, black curly hair & moustaches. Angry, leering, stinking of liquor. Only 3 of the 5 were able to sexually assault her, the others were too drunk. It would be just one

250

nightmare that would remain with them as long as they existed in the drunken hell of their lives.

It was torture. Hell. Way back in Stryker's mind, like a frightened child, part of her waited for a way to escape. Hoped she'd escape alive. This was not a sex fantasy. It was without her consent.

Human beings can take a lot of abuse. The body is rugged. Cunts stretch. She was pounded. Beaten. Face & head bloodied. Then, it was over. They pushed her out the door into the slush of the street, dazed, dizzy. She vomited, struggled not to pass out. Feebly pulled her torn clothes around her. The van sped away weaving drunkenly, red taillights in the dark.

Stryker did not know where she was. The grimy snow-filled streets were silent.

Time had stopped.

The van of horror was long gone, fleeted into time. Her money was gone. Wallet missing. To be tossed out of the window somewhere into the snow. The cowards had robbed her as well, of what little she had left. But Stryker was practical in some ways. There was a few dollars stuffed into the instep of one boot.

Bleeding, sick, she made her way back home.

Chapter Twenty One

Comancho flew back to the house. Skidded up the driveway and banged on the metal door of the trailer.

Ronny looked out the window across his property where they all lived, past the motorcycles in the car port to see who it was. Inside the trailer Frosty barely had time to wipe the sleep out of her eyes; "What's wrong?" It was different from the Indians usual slow pace up the driveway, stopping to holler **"HELLO!"** to the dogs. Thru the window, at a distance Ronny heard her;

251

"STRYKER'S BEEN ATTACKED! I JUST HEARD IT! SHE GOT RAPED BY 5 SPICKS!"

Ronny comes out of the big house & runs over to the trailer. "Stryker? What happened?"

"YEAH! THE FAT DIKE WHO LIVES DOWNTOWN BY ANGEL & CRYSTAL! IT HAPPENED OVER ON THE OTHER SIDE OF TOWN, BY SOME GAY CLUB SHE WENT TO! NOT OILS! SOME OTHER PLACE! SHE HAD TOO MUCH TO DRINK AND LEFT THE CLUB, AND SHE AIN'T GOT HER BIKE, AND WAS WALKIN', LOST, WHEN THEY GOT HER!"

When they heard about it thru the grapevine, bit by bit of information pieced together into the true story, the gang was furious.

Chapter Twenty Two

Rape threatens the victims sense of safety and personal power. The five men had pounded all the humor out of her. Her poetry was gone. And a dead frightened soul remained, staring up from hollow eyes.

Stryker woke again as she had for three consecutive days; head pounding. 'I can't take no more abuse.' She'd been slugged and dragged around in the assault that night; pain throbbed thru her cranium, her vaginal cavity she was injured and her bladder had become week. 'I can't take it. Suppose it happens again? The world is full of rapists, men out there waiting for some woman to make a mistake, to not look behind her when she walks down the street at night. To stand on a deserted corner waiting for a bus. I can't take it.' She felt powerless.

Stryker had got a gun from one of the members and slept with it under her pillow, and put a chair against the door.

Wouldn't go anywhere alone, --to buy food, to get her mail from the lobby, --unless an Outlaw went with her; it was complicating her already precarious life.

The fat dike had heard rumors that the club was going to do something about it, but didn't know what & it didn't make much difference.

After the attackers had run, red lights in distance, it left her to clean up the mess because she was the woman. It was her body which had been violated. She had to get a pregnancy test, an abortion if necessary, VD tests, & worse a waiting period of 6 months to take the AIDS test which was the deadly sexually transmitted diseases incubation period. That was what it meant to live with a nightmare.

"They hit me in the face, knocked me down & dragged me inside that *place*. I was full of blood." Stryker mumbles, without feeling, numbed in shock at what had happened to her body, out of her control.

"I'd gladly stomp his fucken' teeth in, but right now we're gonna take you to the clinic and get a VD test, and see if yer ok."

Angel, Crystal, Comancho, Frosty, Johnny, Stella, Ron, her girl had gathered around Stryker bunched up in her blankets, holed up in her hotel room. The blond biker butch gazed down at Styker huddled under her bedclothes, it was late in the day –4PM, & she still hadn't got up. Her wobbly eyes rapidly shifted back and forth from the effects of the medication she had to take from craziness.

"I took a triple dose. If I drink a beer I hope it don't kill me." Angel watched those brown eyes flit back and forth and back. Thought, privately that she'd never seen Strykers eyes move so fast.

"I'm bleeden'."

Angel groped under the covers and got Strykers chubby hand, and held it. "We got to get you to a doctor, a Gynecologist. To see what's wrong."

253

"I ain't goin'. Not after how I felt in the emergency room. No."

"We'll take you to our doctor. A lady doctor."

"How much is it?"

"It's $110 for a visit, but we've got the money, the club has all chipped in to help you with anything you need."

"We love you and we'll take care of you." Crystal cooed, gazing down at her. Stryker felt, thru her dulled sensations; the kindness coming from the women.

"Maybe I'll go..." Her voice trailed off.

Bikers big & small shifted around her bedside. Boots & jeans & the smell of perfume & men's aftershave. They crowded the place up. She felt safe. Surrounded by a battalion of fighting women.

After they'd gone she lay alone. The appointment was set for early next morning. Several couples had urged Stryker to spend the night with them so she wouldn't be alone. It was as it always was--they were in couples and she was the lonely one. The brutalization at the heavy hands of the violent males was a spark which had ignited the whole inflammable residue of her life. Those long months of running with the gang, but still no lover. No woman to call her own. Upon whose chest to lay her head at night, to be held and cooed to. Since childhood she'd always been the odd girl out. Love had been but a few instances--so few that Stryker could remember all the nice things any person had ever done for her in her 25 years.

The pudgy dike had been outside in the street when they found her. Ringing Crystal & Angels bell over & over until they came down to the lobby; horrified, as they saw her thru the snowy window, bleeding, clothes torn.

"I GOT TO LEAVE TOWN!" Was the first thing Stryker had exclaimed. It had been her reason to keep living, to make her way across town with a purpose, by bus & on foot, and now just lay down and die where they'd dumped her body.

**"NO YOU DON'T HAVE TO LEAVE! YOU'RE NOT
GOING TO LEAVE US!"** Crystal had shouted back. Ire had
glinted in her blue eyes, and a righteous woman's rage fired her mind.
**"RAPE HAPPENS TO A LOT OF WOMEN! *N O!* YOU'RE
NOT STUPID! *N O!* IT'S NOT YOUR FAULT! 1 OUT OF 3
AMERICAN WOMEN HAS BEEN SEXUALLY ABUSED!"**

They'd taken her to the emergency room of the public hospital.
Filed a police report. Cared for her. Somebody gave her a .38
caliber gun for protection.

But life was dramatically altered as she'd known it. There was
terror, moving in with it's baggage, pushing, heaving & crowding out
her art, her oil paintings, the poems. --Terror became her focus.
There was room for little else. –Just a great depression. The blues.
Stryker saw how precarious life was. She was a week female,
essentially alone, little money, no family. Blood relatives who
condemned her for her sexual preference and gave no support. And
living alone in a seedy hotel with a flimsy door, and long cold
unguarded passageways. Now she didn't even feel safe to go down
the hall to the washroom.

The next day, the little dike hadn't been awake more then twenty
minutes, when the negative poison of events began to drip into her
mind. She reached under the pillow and felt the cold black steel
muzzle of the gun –from which could spit fire & death. And held its
wood stock. The 10' by 12' room was ice cold. Sky outside the
window with pigeons flapping their wings. Fear was everywhere
outside the radius of her small arms reach holding the gun. The room
was too silent. Alone again. --Everybody else had a job they must go
to, to survive. Maybe her problem all along was living on the
government dole & having too much free time on her hands… Angel
& Johnny were due to come over to take her to the Gynecologist and
hold her hand while she went thru still another pelvic exam. They
were self-employed and could take off a few hours. Crystal couldn't
be there, having to put in an 8 hour shift at the department store. Life
seemed to be going on by without the fat dike; and to herself she
seemed worthless.

Stryker woke up that morning with a sense of loss, of rage, and of regret, that she had gone off from the gang that fateful night, by herself to a strange tavern in an unfamiliar part of town. 'It's my fault, 'cause I'm crazy. If I'd been in Oils they'd have taken care of me, not like those cold dykes in that upper class straight dykes bar. If I'd just used better judgment.' Stryker blamed herself on every count, when the real blame lay directly on the ugly men who had violated her civil rights. Some Outlaws words came back to her thru the foggy soup of her medicated brain. 'If you'd been at the party with us, you'd have never had to go home by yourself. Some of us would have drove yuh. Or yuh could have passed out on the rug with the other dikes who can't hold their liquor. Why didja yuh wanna run off to somebody else's clubhouse? --A straight dikes joint ?'

'Because everybody already knows I'm a slob at Oils.' She'd told them. 'I thought I'd meet a girl who don't know me.'

The actual rape & attack had lasted 25 minutes, but when the story had been told thru the clubhouse it became 4 hours. The blacks claimed it had lasted longer then a motherfucker. The feminists declared that an man who looks at a woman with that idea in mind should be castrated. Some ladies cruelly suggested that Stryker had had a vaginal orgasm while being raped, --and the humiliation had driven her insane. Others claimed that now she had gone straight because she felt the ordeal was a punishment for being gay, and enjoying her life as a dike and it was sinful for any female to have that much fun as an independent, total, fulfilled person. Still other dikes strutted around, bragged, claiming they were invulnerable to rape-- they'd fight to the death first. And flexed bulging biceps under rolled up denim shirts, sweaty from pumping iron, or workouts practice fighting in Sleazy's basement gym. A pack of stories from a hundred dikes. Tongues wagging, lips chattering, but somehow, inside, in each woman, that's not how they felt at all.

"THEY KEPT ME THERE IN THAT METAL BOX, IT SEEMED LIKE HOURS. THEY MADE ME DO ALL THIS AWFUL STUFF TO THEM." Stryker had been sodomized as part of the deal. "THEY RIPPED ME."

"Rip use to do that to me all the time." Debbie adds her 2-cents worth opinion to the whole matter. "They ripped her 'cause she wasn't ready for it. Rip use to do that all the time, with her fist."

Stryker was very busy that morning. Dressed in bluejeans & worn red suspenders, shirt & boots, she moved in the small circumference of activity around the cold black steel revolver—within ready reach—on top of a table, for protection. Had thrown the nice new clothes she'd worn the night of her attack in the trash. Frightened of them. As if they had brought her bad luck. She arranged things around her small room, leaving notes.

Dear Crystal, I have also left my collection of Aryan Avenger photos for you, because I know you rode with their gang awhile & know some of them. --And for you Angel, specifically you can have Rock & Roll Fatima's G String which was over her pussy. Her actual pussy. All this is payment for you being my pals. Please don't hate me! I already miss you guys!

The fat dike walked around her bed, making it up. Her chubby legs unsteady. Efficiently fluffing out the pillow and drawing the cover across. Then, walked to the table & picked up the gun. Went to the window. Looked out--snowy clouds floated in the sky. Down, eight stories, past cement ledges which were walkways for pigeons that stuck out of the old hotel, at ground level, people small as ants scuttled about on their lives. Stryker brought the cold steel pistol up in front of her, stared at it long and .hard, and then pointed it to her head.

Stryker's fist turned from pink to white, as it gripped the wood stock of the sinister black object. She raised the cold steel pistol up in front of her, stared at it long and hard, as her chest in bleu denim rose & fell for several breaths. Sweat dripped under her armpits, tho the room was freezing. And then pointed the muzzle to her head.

The round bore pressed against hair and flesh of her scalp. Her heart beat on steadily, outside clouds floated in the sky.

"G O D D A M N   I T!" She shouted, loud. A moments jarring thought broke her mood of misery in which she felt so low. *"I DIDN'T FINISH THE GODDAMN POEM FOR DADDY*

257

GEORGE!" The weapon dangles in her hand. **'How could I have forgot that? I arranged for all my stuff but that!'**

Oil paints scented the cold air of the room. Colors, so bright upon dusty drab white walls. The chair was gone from in front of the door, and it had been unlocked. On the mirror was clipped a handwritten note to the club.

Dear Outlaws:
I'm sorry, to all my sisters but I have to get out of this. I'm leaving everything in my room that's not specified to somebody, to the club, you can sell it at the fleamarket. There is the remainder of this months rent on the room, so somebody can use it to crash for free. Sell my stuff and keep the money. This is the only way I can say I'm sorry, but I have to do this.

Part of the three torturous days since her ordeal the room had been in shambles. When anger had burst forth, Stryker had kicked walls, smashed her fist thru paintings, ripped canvas, their frames broken into splinters of wood. & destroyed many of her things. Armchair thrown on its side, and the narrow side room full of paintings had been torn asunder; like the bath of a hurricane had blown thru her place. But now it was clear.

For a few years in this room, life had been tolerable; had given her space to create colorful portraits with paint. Poems, & a journal. But now the fat dike had to get out in a hurry.

Styker aimed the gun at her head; finger slowly squeezed the black metal trigger. Her flesh pushed tight against the ridged half-inch wide metal piece. Didn't have the guts. Put it down. There it hung, in her hand at her side a moment. Then, finally, in a desperate burst of energy, jerked the gun up, pointed it at her midsection, and squeezed the trigger.

The force of the bullet drove her against the wall.

She slumped in a streak of blood onto the floor, heart pumping crimson red blood out into a pool that spread into the carpet around her body.

Chapter Twenty Three

"THE MEETING WILL BE CALLED TO ORDER!"

Bikes roared over the damn road to Oils.

As if a rattle snake had bitten her in the side and injected a lethal dose of poison, and somehow she'd acclimated to it, Hawk raced down the road on her cycle, spike hair of green/pink bristling like an angry porcupine. A punk held tight to her midsection--a butch, dressed in a black leather vest & chaps, head shaved bald & a black bikers cap sitting on it. Another punk drove a foreign made bike in tandem beside them. Life was not wine and roses. It was mean & nasty, and the spirit of vengeance rode along. They rode their motorcycles to Oils on a supernatural power of hate. The rattle snake had bit her long ago. She'd pulled it out of her by the tail, fangs dripping venom, & wielded it as a weapon ever since.

Like a rattlesnake ready to bite, that's how Hawk'd felt when she found out about Stryker, after coming down from a weekend binge of narcotics. --Phone messages on the answering machine totaled 22.

The large building clanked with hollow echoes of noise.

Over 80 bikers shifted uneasily in Oils.

40 friends of the club stood along side. Menacing looks on their faces; shoulders square inside big jackets; facing the podium waiting to hear what was happening.

Folding chairs had turned the place into a meeting hall. Already funds were being accumulated. $3 for the bikers. Non-members had paid $5 to attend, because they were mad.

A biker dike slapped her waist, "I carry a knife on this side, another knife on this side." She wore a dark shirt and pants. "A 9" knife down here under my trouser cuff, another small knife here," she patted the sides of her body. "And my brass knucks in my pocket!"

George strode across the stage; plywood groaned under her weight, went up to the podium where a microphone was set up. Jet black hair slick behind her ears, swept up off her forehead. Bulky stature in smooth expensive leather head to toe. With narrowed black eyes the diesel dike glared down at the surrounding sea of lesbians. George was cold and cruel. Her sadistic side had found them amusing in the past. Innocents to toy with & pass the time. She also had a great sense of loyalty. Of family. And, George was female enough to be enraged at the traditional stepped-on position forced on women.

Tonight she felt like God-The-Mother must feel, Who, after all, had created George in Her image, as well as all the other dikelettes of the metropolitan city; how She gets in a rage--a quiet rage. Holds Her peace, and then returns in the cool of the evening with a Vengeance. George already had mapped out a series of strategies for revenge. But was not quite prepared to talk about it, not in such a large & public meeting.

The room hushed. Leatherdikes in black sat, or squatted or stood, eyes trained on the Leader.

"WE OUGHTA BE SICK OF THESE ANIMALS USING WOMEN'S BODIES TO JACK OFF IN! WE OUGHTA BE FUCKING MAD! WE OUGHTA *DO SOMETHING!*"

By the date of the Outlaws meeting, 4 days had gone passed. The grapevine buzzed with outrageous news. With information & misinformation.

"DO SOMETHING! DO SOMETHING!" The cry went out of the microphone swept thru the room and bounced off the rear walls of the huge tavern. It echoed thru their ears into their unconscious collective soul. Bikers turned and looked at each other as if for conformation; in disbelief, or in rage, as the story unfolded. Some still not sure exactly what had happened & who it happened to.

"IF IT HAPPENS TO ONE OF US IT HAPPENS TO ALL OF US!"

As females they took so much abuse before. Since they were girls. And now, more, as gays. Hemmed in by the framework of society, which made it a crime to go after and avenge those who would hurt them, or, someone you love, and take an eye for an eye, a tooth for a tooth.--So long solitary, so long afraid--now, en mass, they had the power to Do something!

Bikers still were coming in. It was apparent anybody even remotely connected to the Club had come out. Former girlfriends of bikers, their friends. Ex members. Rumor was that an action of some sort was being planned, and the women wanted to know more.

Members filed in past a biker at the door who nodded in greeting, busy, brim of her cap pointed down, checking a list. Their grubby hands fished in wallets produced their Outlaws Membership card, as the biker went thru an alphabetical columns on the list and put a check mark after each members name. The others dug out $5.--To help The Cause. The Outlaw at the door was young; crew cut hair, dressed in black leather and bluejeans; tough from head to toe. The Death Eagle on her cap. Thick soled boots. Her mouth pursed into a thin line as she checked off a name. Shocks of brown hair under her cap, wet with sweat. 'I never seen such a big meeting.' She thought.

The house lights were turned up full--like they were when the club closed down for the evening--and you could see everything. The black walls, dusty, appeared more grey in the light. Brushstrokes and splotches visible. It was no longer a dim den in which to relax, it had been transformed into a meeting hall.

Their colors, --an 8 foot by 5 flag with the inscription; OUTLAWS MOTORCYCLE CLUB FOUNDED 1985, hung against the back wall behind a plywood & board stage.

It was the same simply constructed stage they used for shows and demonstrations; and for their regular monthly meetings. 2 feet high, and increased to its maximum size by the addition of extra panels, to 16 by 32-feet wide; which was the length of four pieces of plywood sections nailed onto boards, that would later be folded up and put in the storage room. A microphone and a barstool completed the setting.

Hawk was fierce; a gold earring in her nose like a wild beast, spine of green/pink hair down the center of her otherwise bald head; stocky in leathers--and a gun in a holster openly strapped around her waist. Ten minutes ago she had shouted; **'THE MEETING WILL BE CALLED TO ORDER!"** Then the Leader Of The Pack had taken the stand, microphone in one beefy hand, while Hawk stood to the side, bristling in rage.

Silence had fallen over the crowd as they listened. 85 members and the rest. Some recognized dikes in the crowd who didn't want it made public knowledge but they rode with Avengers and Outlaws, alike, depending on the event, having not yet made a choice of clubs. Everybody in the motorcycle & leather community. Gold lights droned. One biker who'd been out of town and had heard nothing was surprised, she'd never seen such a big turnout for what she'd assumed was an ordinary meeting.

"I'M GLAD YER HERE! YUH COULD BE SETTEN' HOME WITH YER TV SETS, UNCONSCIOUS! GORGING YERSELVES ON CANDY OR HIGH! I'LL GIVE YUH THE FACTS, SINCE BY NOW MOST OF YOU HEARD IT THRU THE GRAPEVINE AND A LOT OF YOUSE GOT IT WRONG. FIRST STRYKER AIN'T DEAD, BUT SHE'S IN THE HOSPITAL. SHE WAS ATTACKED LAST SATURDAY NIGHT BY 5 MEN, WE TOOK HER TO THE EMERGENCY HOSPITAL, SHE WAS RELEASED AND ON TUESDAY SHE ATTEMPTED TO TAKE HER OWN LIFE. SHE'S ALIVE, IN COUNTY HOSPITAL AND MEMBERS OF THE CLUB ARE TAKING TURNS STAYING BY HER BED." Daddy Georges voice bellowed thru the microphone, giving facts; the severity of the wounds, how long she'd be confined; the voice spilled into all corners of the bar, where dikes couldn't even see her, just hear. A wave of response ripped thru the crowd after each statement.

"That runt butch? The crazy-acting one? Fat? Shit!"

Voices began as a murmur thru the crowd. Everybody was angry.

"ANGEL WILL GIVE YUH THE RUNDOWN, 'CAUSE ANGEL & CRYSTAL'S BEEN WITH HER EVERY DAY!"

The well-lit Oils was a shimmering sea of women in black leather skins like a school of fish. Up in front an iron bar had been jammed across the door, with a doordike stationed nearby to open it for latecomers. They could take this information home digest the news into the wee hours of morning, and fantasize about doing it to women themselves--- gang rape, or, even more secret, of having it done to them--in play only, not the brutality. Not the death. All were against these males. And a rumor within a rumor was circulating. Something about a posse of sorts, a selected group of bikers to go out and find & destroy the enemy. No one on the stage speaking now was specific, nor would the Leader commit herself over the microphone. Too many strangers were in attendance. They sat, or stood. Some looked like men, others pretty, and fem. Each must ask herself, did she want to join the struggle for vengeance. There was going to be a line, single file those who wanted to would come forward to volunteer, and a special group would be chosen out of that.....

George walked to the stage once more. Climbed up the step to the platform which sagged under her 350 pound bulk. Her boots shook the plywood as she strode to the microphone. "THEY'RE PICKEN' OFF OUR WOMEN ONE BY ONE!

WHY DOES ANY WOMAN HAVE TO WORRY BEFORE SHE GOES OUT IN THE STREET AT NIGHT!—WORRY ABOUT MEN, ABOUT HATE, ABOUT FEAR!

WHY DOES ANY GAY PERSON WHO LOOKS QUEER HAVE TO WORRY ABOUT IT!

THEY MAKE A SOCIETY WITH RULES! THEY TELL US TO OBEY THE RULES! --BUT THEY CAN'T PROTECT US, THEY CAN DO LITTLE FOR US! SO IT'S UP TO *US!* WE GOTTA DO SOMETHING FOR *US!*

WE GOT A RIGHT TO BE OUT IN THE WORLD AS FEMALES, AS QUEERS! TO WALK ALL OVER THE PLACE AS MEN DO WITHOUT A THOUGHT ABOUT IT!

AND THAT BRINGS ME TO ANOTHER SUBJECT! --IF
STRYKER HAD BEEN WITH US THAT NIGHT NOTHING
WOULD HAVE HAPPENED! SHE WAS OUT HERE ALONE
AMONGST US AND GOT REJECTED!

SHE WAS LOST OUT THERE WANDERING THE STREET
DRUNK 'CAUSE SHE'S CRAZY AND NONE OF YOUSE
WOMEN WOULD TAKE HER IN THEIR ARMS! SO SHE LEFT
OILS AND WENT OFF TO SOME SQUARE GAYBAR OUT OF
TOWN WHERE SHE DON'T KNOW NOBODY!

WE ARE ALL AGAINST THE SONS-OF-BITCHES WHAT
DONE THIS! WE GOT TO FIGHT! THE WAYS WE'RE GONNA
USE WILL BE KEPT SECRET IN GROUPS WITHIN THE
GROUP. YUH KNOW SADLY ENOUGH THERE COULD BE
SPIES HERE RIGHT NOW, FROM THE AVENGERS, OR THE
POLICE DEPARTMENT. BUT IN SMALL GROUPS YOU KNOW
EVERYBODY. --WE ARE GONNA ORGANIZE! JUST LIKE WE
DONE BEFORE! WE AIN'T GONNA LET THIS GO BY LIKE
WATER UNDER THE BRIDGE! NOT WITHOUT A FIGHT!
NOT WITHOUT A STRUGGLE!

When Hawk took the microphone again she wasn't as subtle. **"WE
PUNISHED EM' BEFORE, WE'LL PUNISH EM' AGAIN!
WE'LLWHUP 'EM! AND STOMP 'EM! AND HUMILIATE
'EM! WE'LL CRUSH 'EM! WE'LL NEVER FIND THEM
SAME GUYS! YOU ALL KNOW ITS DREAMSVILLE TO
THINK WE'LL EVER FIND THEM SAME GUYS! BUT WE
CAN FIND SOME OTHER CREEPS WHO DESERVE IT JUST
AS BAD!**   Hawk pounded a gloved fist into her gloved hand. **POW!
POW! POW!** Emphasizing each statement. **"SOME SCUM
HANGING OUT IN THE ALLEY! SOME MACHO MEN!
YOU KNOW THE TYPE! WE'LL DO IT TO THEM! WHAT
THEY DO TO US! AN EYE FOR AN EYE! –REMEMBER!"**
Hawk's spiny pink/green hair shivered. She raised a black gloved
finger up to the ceiling; eyes bright. **"DO THIS FOR THE SAKE
OF OUR WOMEN! FOR THE SAKE OF ALL WOMEN!"**

Blond butch Angel stomped up on the stage; black leather. Steel-
toe boots, the kind best used for kicking ass in a fight. And her cleric

collar. With a pale hand grabbed the microphone, put it to her lips and yelled out a wild prayer. "GODDAMN IT, GOD HELP US! GIVE US THE STRENGTH! MOTHER GOD! GOD WHO WINS BATTLES! HELP US! WE'RE GOING INTO BATTLE IN A FEW NIGHTS! WE NEED GOOD LUCK! WE DON'T WANT TO GET CAUGHT! WE NEED YOU WATCHING OVER US FROM ABOVE! GOD OUR MOTHER! GOD OUR LADY! NOSTRA DAMAS! HELP US! WE GOTTA FIGHT! FIGHT!   FIGHT! FIGHT!   FIGHT! WE'RE GONNA FIGHT! FIGHT! FIGHT! FIGHT! FIGHT! FIGHT! **FIGHT!   FIGHT!   FIGHT! FIGHT! FIGHT!   FIGHT!   FIGHT!**" The clubhouse roared with her. It howled as a single animal, shocked down to the bottom of it's foundation. Soon every biker was lifting ringed & big knuckled fists to the skies inside Oils. To do something.   To express their anger & their fear.

   "KILL THEM! KILL THEM! KILL THEM! KILL THEM!" The spike hair Warlord rushed over & suddenly she and Angel were fighting over something real—as Hawk grabbed the microphone, and the blond butch gladly let her do it; Hawk screamed, *"KILL THEM! KILL THEM! KILL THEM! KILL THEM!"* Daddy George looked on, electrified. The chant went up. **"KILL THEM! KILL THEM!"** Beer bottles swinging arcs in midair caught glints of the overhead lights. Black motorcycle jackets on hundreds of thrashing arms of a single animal. **"KILL THEM! KILL THEM! KILL THEM! KILL THEM!   KILLTHEM! KILL THEM! KILL THEM! KILL THEM!   KILL THEM! KILL THEM! KILL THEM! KILL THEM!   KILL THEM! KILL THEM! KILL THEM! KILL THEM!   KILL THEM! KILL THEM! KILL THEM! KILL THEM!   KILL THEM! KILL THEM! KILL THEM! KILL THEM!   KILL THEM! KILLTHEM! KILLTHEM! KILLTHEM! KILLTHEM! KILLTHEM! KILLTHEM! KILLTHEM! KILLTHEM KILLTHEMKILL! KILLTHEMKILL! KILLTHEMKILL! KILLHEMKILL! KILLTHEMKILLTHEM KILLTHEM KILLTHEM KILLTHEM KILLTHEMKILLTHEM KILLHEM KILLTHEMKILLTHEMKILLTHEM KILLTHEM KILLTHEMK I LLTHEM K I LLTHEMK I LLTHEM KILLTHEMKILLTHEM KILLTHEMKILLTHEM**

K I LLTHEMK ILLTH EMK I LLTHEMK I LLTHEMK ILL THEMK I LLTHEMK I LLTHEMKILLKILLKILLKILL KILLKILLKILLKILLKILLKILLKILL!!!!!!!!!!!!!!!!!!!!

Beside the podium, George was sweating. Eyes bright with an inner fever. Later, when the excitement died down, they organized. The crowd buzzed with talk and motion around them, as George whispered privately to Lou.-- "if Stryker had just tried to get help when it got too bad for her. Found somebody to talk to, and waited it out.

"I jes' feel shitty 'cause it was my Cookie she wuz seein'. I could have told Stryker Cookie ain't nobody to put faith in. She'll leave yuh each an' every time. I stopped worrying about it when she left me years ago. I just look forward to being with her when she decides to *come back*. That's the kind of lady she is. Nobody's lady."

"If she'd just have waited it out Lou… Waited… And her hormones would have kicked in and she'd have cried & screamed and beat the pillow & vowed to kill the next man she saw, and just got it out of her system; enough of it to make it thru to the next day… Enough to keep on living… I knew a girl once, she wanted to kill herself bad. Real bad. She went to friends and spilled the story of what had happened to her out of her secret guts. She cried and cried and had a couple of periods pass by in which she cried and cried some more and got some of the poison out of her system. Then she was ok. Wiser, but ok."

Angel and Comancho talked, mad; as they sat in the audience watching the tables. The Indian said; "Why bother having a civilization? Civilization is based on the idea that you call for help and get it. They can't give us protection, but they expect us to play by the rules anyway."

"FIGHT! FIGHT! FIGHT! FIGHT! FIGHT! FIGHT! FIGHT!" The chant was taken up in distant parts of the bar. And a line was forming, snaking forward towards the stage, composed of bikers who'd leapt up off their barstools upon hearing the call. And the last Warlords were sitting down, taking their places behind the tables. George whispered to Rip behind a beefy ringed hand; "We gotta handle this matter ourselves. Stryker don't want the police nowhere near her anyway. She's afraid they'll put her back in the mental hospital. And we ain't gonna use guns this time. You do big time in jail for guns. Just carry a few firearms in case their armed or too strong fer' us and things get out of hand. A few guns for emergency's, as an equalizer. But we ain't goin' in guns blazin' like we did last time.

Hawk leaned over from George's other side. Her narrow lips snarled open showing stained teeth. "We should go in groups of, maybe 8." This youngest Warlord's face furrowed. These three leaders huddled together, discussing the plan in earnest. Royal & Lou sat at either end. Hawk spoke, hissing vehemently in a loud whisper; Naw, groups of five. Whatever fits into a car."

"Yeah. A driver, 4 fighters."

Lou pulled up closer to the huddle from the end of the table on her folding metal chair. Cheap faded jeans, and a faded blue jacket over her strong build. "We gotta choose the ones who'll do what they're expected to do. They can't run in a panic. They can't die if they see the police. They gotta be cool. They got to be tough. We don't need a bunch of kids, but if they're too old they're useless. And none of 'em should carry guns. Each of us should pack the arms."

"Yeah, and drive the car."

"Yeah. If there's a problem the fighters can't handle we take out the guns and end the problem."

"It's gonna be hell looken' 'em all over." Sez George, her eyes lifting from her small close group of Warriors to gaze over the long angry line of bikers who shifted with pent-up energy on their black booted feet. "But that's a good idea. If we just send 5 per car, and there's only 5 of us Warlords, then that's just 25 fighters. That's what we need. Just 25. Get the rest to do something else useful. Like help raise funds to bail us out of jail.—If anybody gets caught."

Roy was the secretary. She said: "There's 241 in here tonight."

267

"Tell the rest, the ones we don't choose to go home and wait and get ready. Get ready for some fund raisers we're gonna have. For bail, and for Stryker. The first one is the weekend after next. $10 per person, pay in advance. $12 at the door. Anything they can do for entertainment, or services they can sell we can raffle off. They got 8 days to sign up to volunteer, and cook & do everything we need."

The line of bikers jolted forward. The selection began. Some the Warlords knew personally were chosen without a word--to work for the benefit party, or, for the secret mission which was to occur the following night. Even tho some were little in stature, they would not back down like fearful sheep but would fight. You could tell by the fire in their eyes. Most of the room of biker women went forward to volunteer. One by one George & the Warriors had to turn them away. The big dike woman bent over the table, fixing them with coal black eyes. A white scar across her chin, hair mussed; the intense mask of her face was startling; she asked; "Physical violence is called for, & that means breaking the law--in a major way. Are you ready for that? Can you afford to be in jail, go to court, maybe even do time, and loose your job? Have you got kids? You might get hurt. Whose gonna take care of your family? Stuff like that. Think about it. Maybe yuh ought to help with the party instead."

The Warlords sat like apostles of the Last Supper in a Rembrandt masterpiece painting—in black & silver; along two tables before the gang; slouched, gangling legs & arms akimbo, or hunched over the table ferociously, faces studiously appraising each biker. George, Hawk, Rip, Lou, and Royal. One by one the bikers stepped up; listened as one of the Warriors repeated the statement and questions – which they would do over & over until they turned blue-- and the bikers made their choice. Wither they themselves thought they were capabible to do it or not. And after a brief conference of the Warriors, were either chosen or told to go home and wait.

KT, a black biker swaggered up; dressed in her trademark fashion, brown leather from boot to cap, including brown gloves; unusual in the club. She dismissed the statement with a wave of one gloved hand. **"SHIT! DON'T GIVE ME NO MESS! HELL! LAST FIGHT WE HAD I COME OUT FOOTS FLYING, SHIT KICKEN' AND FISTS POPPEN'!** *BANG BANG BABY!* YOU

KNOW ME, AND I KNOW YOU! I WON'T LET YOU ALL
DOWN! I NEVER HAVE! I'M IN THE FRONT LINE! YEAH,
I'M SCARED! SHIT YEAH! WHO AIN'T! BUT I AIN'T
GONNA LET IT STOP ME!   **HELL NO!** AND I GOT A GOOD
JOB DRIVING BUS, I GOT LOTS & LOTS OF SICK LEAVE
LEFT! AIN'T GOT KIDS, NOT YET! AND I GOT ME A GOOD
LADY, GERRI, TO WATCH OUR HOUSE IF WE GET
INCARCERATED. SO, WATCH OUT! I'M READY LIKE
FREDDY!" And she pounded one fist into her hand for emphasis.

Behind the table rip snarled a smile of approval. "Where's
Freddy?" Sez Rip with cynical humor; "We need her too! Bring her
along will yuh?"

"Yer' ok KT!" Sez George. With a motion indicated to the biker
who stood in front of her tan full dress leathers what direction she
should go--to join the small but increasing group of dikes who waited
behind the stage.

Bikers continued to come up. One hundred more sat and drank
soft drinks or beer in the front of the tavern, milled around in small
circles of discussion.

A new young biker Mel, just 18, built like a bull, holding a huge
motorcycle helmet with a bubble top and black visor in one hand
stepped forward. She was chosen.

Sleazy came next. Two Warlords stood up and yelled at her to go
home as they saw the skinny runt-faced biker, jeans slung low over
her narrow haunches cross the plywood boards with her familiar,
loping gait. **"NAW! SLEAZE! YUH GOT 3 KIDS! YER'
HANGING BY A THREAD NOW! YER' BROKE! YUH
CAN'T AFFORD TO GET HURT AND BE OUT OF WORK!
LADY'LL BE KICKED OUT IN THE STREET!"**

"GO HOME! *GET LOST!* --WE LOVE YUH!"

Saundra, the brown skin Nurses Aid with orange tinted African
hair walked across the stage; her spike heel boots made a sharp
staccato on plywood as she came up before the Warriors, who were

269

flabbergasted to see her, a fem. One so sensitive she'd cry if a person even said anything mean. But there was fire in her eyes. Saundra was a lady, tho she wore a cheep imitation leather jacket and a second-hand mini skirt which was all she could afford. Saundra stood in front of them, in the miniskirt which barely came to mid-thigh, but also wearing tights modestly covering her legs. Scarred faces of the brutish Warriors reflected amazement as they watched. Saundra's eyes were bright. She moved in jerky abrupt motions. Pulled a pair of nurses scissors out of her pocket and shook them in air. She balled her fists up angrily. **"I HATE THOSE MEN! I *HATE* THEM! I HATE WHAT THEY DID TO OUR STRYKER! I GOT MY SCISSORS THAT I CARRY TO WORK! I'LL STAB 'EM! I'LL STAB 'EM! YES I WILL! I STABBED A MAN ONCE WITH 'EM WHEN HE BOTHERED ME WHILE I WAS WAITING AT THE BUS STOP!"** Saundra shook the tiny little scissors in rage. **"YOU CAN REALLY HURT SOMEBODY WITH THIS! 'N THEY DON'T SEE IT COMING! JUST STICK 'EM WITH THESE SCISSORS AND WATCH 'EM RUN!"** Hawk slid off her chair, came around from behind the table and grabbed the young woman in her muscular arms, enfolding her in a bear hug; and walked her off stage. "Yer' a lady! Go home! We need you for other stuff! Lady's don't need to fight. They got other important jobs. For one, us butches can't live without you." The brown skinned lady began to shake & cry in Hawks tattooed arms. Hawk reassured her; "Just go home, get ready to start cooken' for the Benefit Party. All the gals are gonna cook. --At my house & George's."

The pink/green spikehair Warrior was correct. Frosty & Georgina and Lady were already coordinating a telephone tree to call all the femmes and planning what supplies they would need. 50-cakes must be baked. To eat & to raffle off to raise money. 10-roast beefs. 19-hams. 40-chickens. Numerous salads. The party would be open, and advertised throughout the Gay Community at large. A 300 person turnout--at $10 per head could be expected; minus costs, a $2,800 profit. It was a worthy cause.

The Warlords continued their interview. They weren't telling publicly, but not all the projected proceeds from the fundraiser, nor the extra money--$975—they'd got at the door that night were going to Stryker, not directly. First they must have emergency funds for bail & lawyers if they were stopped by the police. What was left would pay for the hurt dikes medical help; and to set her up in a better living situation when she got out of the hospital.

Finally, it was 3am. The chosen sat in a semicircle at the foot of the stage. The Warlords sat on it's edge. And the rest had gone home, to sleep fitfully, and to plan the next line of struggle.

"NOW, YUH DON'T KNOW IT, BUT WE GOT A HOMELESS BIKER TO OCCUPY STRYKER'S ROOM. RIGHT NOW AT THIS MINUTE ALL HER STUFF, HER OIL PAINTINGS & CLOTHES IS BEING PACKED UP AND SENT TO MY HOUSE FOR STORAGE. FOR WHEN SHE GETS BETTER AND THE DOCTORS LET HER GO HOME. SHE'S GONNA LIVE WITH SOMEBODY IN A STABLE HOME, MAYBE EVEN WITH ME & QUEEN GEORGINA, UNTIL SHE GETS HER LEGS BACK UNDER HER, AND HER HEAD ON STRAIGHT. THEN SHE CAN GO BACK TO THAT MISERABLE HOTEL ROOM BY HERSELF IF SHE WANTS, OR, WE'RE GONNA GET HER A PERMANENT SITUATION LIVING WITH SOME OTHER DIKES. TO SHARE, IN A *COMMUNE.* YOU KNOW WHAT THAT IS! IT'S A BUNCH OF DIKES LIVING TOGETHER LIKE A FAMILY, LIKE PEOPLE DID BACK IN THE OLD FASHION DAYS! THE CLUB IS GONNA RAISE THE FRONT MONEY FOR RENT DEPOSIT ON A HOUSE. THERE'S SEVERAL MEMBERS HURTING WHO DESERVE A BETTER PLACE TO LIVE THEN WHAT THEY GOT. RIGHT NOW STRYKER'S IN BAD SHAPE. SHE'S BEEN SEWED TOGETHER & CLAMPED UP & SHOT FULL OF ANTIBIOTICS FROM THE GUNSHOT WOUND SHE DID TO HERSELF. SHE'S SERIOUSLY WOUNDED, BUT SHE'S GONNA LIVE. WHEN SHE GETS OUT WE WANT TO GIVE HER THIS SPECIAL NEWS, THAT WE GOT A NICE PLACE FOR HER & THERE'S GONNA BE SOMETHING BETTER IN HER LIFE WORTH LIVING FOR. A CHANGE FOR THE BETTER. NOT THE SAME OLD BUSINESS AS USUAL. WE WANT TO DO SOME DAMAGE TO THE PAIN!"

Bright lights blazed down on the small group of bikers in the back bar. 20 dikes. Fighters. Knuckles swollen hard as rocks. scars, and the set of their jaws showed that spirit within them. It was cold in Oils. The meeting had been called so hastily the old owner hadn't come down, the heat had never been turned on, and now that the crowd had dwindled to a fraction of it's original size, the blowing wind outside, and ice temperatures made them cold. The Leader Of The Pack got up with a grunt, her huge thighs tensed as she unfolded from a squatting seated position; she stepped back up on the stage and began to pace its distance along the edge in front of them. Long strides. A scowl for an expression. "I told the rest to go home, 'cause they can't do what you can do. You can do battle. With this!" Raised her arm in the air. At the extension of it was a black steel object clenched in her fingers. "ALL IT TAKES IS ONE WOMAN WITH A GUN." And the group exhaled thru their teeth in a collective hiss of appreciation. George said, "SHE CAN BE 4' TALL LIKE STRYKER AND STILL PULL A TRIGGER. SHE CAN BE 70 YEARS OLD LIKE KELLY AND FIRE OFF SOME ROUNDS IN SELF DEFENSE. SHE CAN BE IN A WHEELCHAIR LIKE SOME OF OUR MEMBERS YOU SEE. ALL IT TAKES IS ONE WOMAN WITH A GUN! WE CAN'T STOP FIGHTING 'CAUSE THEY WON'T LEAVE US ALONE. IF IT HAD BEEN A MAN OUT DRUNK LOST IN THE NIGHT HE WOULDN'T HAVE GOT RAPED WOULD HE! AND THEY ROBBED HER TOO!"

"Yes! My civil rights are violated everytime I walk down the street past some males." Spoke a voice from the group. The beautiful butch Star. She too had been chosen.

"WE'LL NEVER CATCH THOSE GUYS, BUT WE'LL FIND SOMEBODY JUST AS BAD AND NAIL 'EM."

The dark walls of Oils were streaked by shadow. The clubhouse temperature had descended lower into cold regions in the absence of body heat. The 30-odd females seemed dwarfed in the huge vault of ceilings and sweep of space, as they clustered by the stage.

"We're breaking into groups of 5." Came Rips low voice, low but strong. "Each group has a Warlord who will drive. She'll be carrying automatic firepower. You will not. You will carry chains, pipes, clubs, anything that can do damage. To function together we have to trust each other. We have to be **loyal**, because we gotta protect each other. Protect each other from what? Those creeps and rats, these guys who are bigger then us-- who we are gonna drag out of their alleys in the middle of the night and beat the shit out of. We gotta have obedience. If yer' leader sez do something, *do it*. If yuh don't obey the command, yer a traitor. We gotta back each other up! We're out here on our own! Fight together, --then we're strong. If we have to use gunfire we all might serve time in the penitentiary for murder."

The raid was to begin at 12 midnight that Friday. –One week after the assault. The idea was to go out on a series of raids.

"No men with women or children of course. No fags. No men in uniforms--like garage mechanics or hospital orderlies, or cooks in some crummy restaurant--unless he's part of a gang. No tiny men, no handicapped. No men in a group over four, or we might have to shoot 'em and kill. We got the element of surprise. We got weapons ready."

They left Oils much later, the plans were made. **"MEETEN' ADJOURNED !"** Hawk bellows. They stand up, stretch. Lanky legs in bluejeans, fists raised to the ceiling in a salute. Each face etched with lines of seriousness. They move thru the littered Clubhouse. **"NOW PICK UP THEM FOLDING CHAIRS & GO HOME! BE AT GEORGE'S HOUSE BY 11PM FRIDAY. WE'LL GO OVER STUFF AGAIN! YOU KNOW WHAT TO BRING!"**

When Daddy George got home it was 6am. Fingers of dusk began to touch the heavens. And there was time. Time for the Leader Of The Pack to sleep, eat & plan to have a little scene--real soon. A very special scene with one she trusted.

Chapter Twenty Four

Rip got to Daddy Georges house early. A rainy snow poured down so thick the bulldike couldn't see nothing further then her headlights thru the black night thru the black night. But it soon would clear.

It was no surprise to see a different Daddy George; they'd been told what to wear. But heads turned nonetheless to see their Leader wearing no leather. A size XXXtra large bluejean shirt, men's dark trousers, and workboots. The car she'd drive was plain, unmarked. They kept it just to attach a trailer too & haul junk to the dumps.

The two tallest bulldikes conferred privately in the den of George's mansion. "Yer' chicken! Yuh lost yer' drive! Yuh waited so long! ---It's been 5 days!"

"I AIN'T LOST MY DRIVE! I AIN'T FORGOT! I'M AS READY NOW AS I WAS THE MINUTE I SAW HER BLOODY FACE 'N HER BROKEN BODY!" The Leader yelled. Bound books of many eras, surrounded them; the Classics, stacked on tiers to the ceiling. One theme ran constant thru them all, --the overold story of war & peace. Leather chairs pushed together over the tapestry rug held the two middle-aged dikes; a yellow reading lamp made the room cozy, but tension cut thru that; for they were busy writing their own history that evening. Involved in war of their own. "WE WANT REVENGE AND WE'RE GONNA GET SOME! I CAN'T JUST GET A FULL MEETIN' TOGETHER THAT QUICK! I HAD TO DELIBERATE ON *PLANS*. IT'S JUST IF I'M GONNA DO IT, I GOTTA BE READY TO *DIE*, THAT TAKE'S SOME GETTIN' READY." The Leader growled. She was cleaning her gun with a wire brush.

Rip stretched out in the luxurious chair. The he/she wore dark trousers & jacket. Plain boots. An anonymous appearance. Sighed, eyes not looking at George anymore, but boring into the tapestry rug in which raced busy designs, a lot like the worry in her mind. "Faces might change and dates. But the game's still the same." --Rip indicates with a ring decked hand. "The tough guys, those hypes & pimps & con artists and teenage punks... The game they're playing out there in the streets, it's the same rules. It's the same evil. The same woman-hating. The same macho. It's just more violent. If

274

we're gonna step in and change the game & upset the rules we gotta step in and change the game & upset the rules, we gotta face the consequences.---I must be hearing from God—Think before we act! What we do we're gonna have to live with."

"It ain't no doubt in my mind." Sez Daddy George. "It ain't no doubt at all."

"We gotta do this. Yet, if we do what we say we're gonna do, and there's a slip up, somebody gets killed, we'll have to live with the consequences. We got away with that before, we been lucky."

George cast rip a dark look. The barrel of the gun was oiled; it glistened blueblack. "That's why I made the rule, no guns but the driver. So that responsibility's on the Warlords. Just whip the shit out of 'em, we don't want a murder case. It's gonna cost us. Girls is gonna get hurt. They can't go up against men without getting injured, but their gonna wreak havoc on the bastards as well.---Without a shot fired. That's what I'm counting on."

The yellow lamp buzzed down a warm light. Rip was lost in the tapestry. A million threads of red, beige, blue, creating flowers & trees & arbors. Scenes within scenes, all swirling in one circular tableau,--with an urgent purpose. The he/she mused; "Whatever we do, we gotta live with it. Face the music & dance.—So think before yuh act. I learned that sittin' a long cold time in jail, my ass on a cement bench."

"Well, are yuh with us or not!"

"Been with yuh all these years!" The lanky diesel dike snapped.

As the appointed time of 12 midnight grew near, 14 motorcycles were parked along George's driveway. Some members had rode together; rider on the back.

Two Outlaw Ladies wee riding with the pack tonight. Powerhouse femmes trained in karate, & with the desire to fight and to win. Storm roared into the driveway on a cycle with her lover Alicia hugging her waist. Their thunder echoed down the hill. They wore plainclothes, flat shoes. Stripped of their spike heels and chains & jewelry. Disguised as boys, blending in with the rest.

The sky had cleared. Clouds drifted. The moon peeked out. Night beat down with ferocious tension.

The two Latina sisters strode into the house, a biker showed them to rooms where every one was meeting. "I KNOW THE KIND OF GUYS THOSE WERE." Pretty dark eyed Alicia took off her cap and shook her thick black hair. "I GREW UP IN THE BARRIO. THEY DESERVE WHATEVER THEY GET. WE'RE GONNA GIVE 'EM *HELL!"*

Her companion cursed in Spanish. "WE JUST WAITED SO LONG. WE SHOULDA DONE THIS FROM THE BEGINNING." Her face was stark, teeth clenched.

A rumbling vocal agreement rose from the bikers. They milled around in the living room. It was 11pm. "MEN!" The Hispanic sister spoke, vehement. "THEY HAVE NO LIFE OF THEIR OWN INSIDE.—THOSE CREEPS THAT HANG OUT IN THE STREET. BECAUSE THEY'RE ILLITERATE, THEY CAN'T GET THRILLS DOING ANYTHING CONSTRUCTIVE. SO THEY LOOK TO THE OUTSIDE WORLD FOR AN ADRENALINE RUSH. IT MEANS ATTACK AND FIGHT. CRASH AND BURN. THEY STAND AROUND WITH MEAN LOOK, GLARING AT ME & STORM. THEY WANT US TO START SOMETHING, SAY SOMETHING, STARE BACK, ANYTHING: SO THEY CAN START TROUBLE. THEY LIVE FOR IT, BECAUSE THEY HAVE NO OTHER LIFE. THEY ARE A PROBLEM LOOKING FOR TROUBLE."

"Those are the type we're gonna hit." Said another.

By 11:30 all 20 bikers had arrived. By cycle & car. They assembled in the living room of Daddy Georges Mansion, the Chosen Ones. The avengers. The Avengers. A 25 member army. They were told which Warlord would lead them, and soon they would split up into their designated groups.

It was well organized.

As instructed, each woman brought a sack containing a change of clothes & underwear, with their name printed on it in big letters; and left this with Queen Georgina.

The dikes assembled ranged from two femmes, --total ladies, to androg's, to butch. Mel, a husky dike, shorter at 5'6" but a huge frame, well muscled, built like a brick shithouse on wheels--her bike, & Star, over 6', statuesque, a beautiful butch more like a tame pussycat, but a fierce lion too--a tooth & claw fighter; were among the newest bikers.

The gang was unrecognizable. No one wore leather. No motorcycle boots. No bald heads. The absence of nose rings or wildly colored hair was striking. They wore black knit caps pulled low over their heads. Trousers & jackets, dark, zipfront. Plain dark boots. Like an army of small men.

They brought chains and lead pipes and they were prepared to break skulls.

"They'll be in a different state of unconscious--when we finish with 'em. We'll cripple 'em. I want to see 'em limping around the next 5 years."

"You know the type we want. Not just anybody out on the street. Not some poor flunky waiting at the bus stop--he might be on his way to his mothers house. You know the ones."

"YEAH!" Spat Alicia. "THE TYPE WHO TRY TO GOOSE YOUR GIRLFRIEND WHEN YOU WALK DOWN THE STREET!"

They milled around in the yellow lit house, undistinguishable from each other in dark clothes. Conversed in low voices. One by one the Warlords assembled their groups. "Lets just try to hit men who look like criminals. I mean, well, one could be my father if he was alive. Or Sleazy's son, if he was grown."

"Their ain't no good men." Yells back an angry biker, with teeth missing in front.

"YEAH! KILL 'EM ALL! RIP 'EM APART LIKE THEY DONE US!" Two fighters held up their fists in unison. Then three. Then the room came alive with women shaking their fists.

Each Warlord gave instructions to her small group. "HIT 'EM WITH YER' WEAPON FIRST. STUN 'EM BEFORE THEY SEE YUH COMING. USE THE PIPES, THE CHAINS, THE BATS. THEN BRING 'EM DOWN WITH KICKS & PUNCHES. WE DON'T WANT TO KILL 'EM. THAT'S PREMEDITATED MURDER, THE ELECTRIC CHAIR OR LIFE IN PRISON! STUN 'EM SO THEY CAN'T SEE NOTHING BUT STARS, SO THEY CAN'T FIGHT. AND BEAT THE SHIT OUT OF 'EM AND LEAVE 'EM IN THE STREET. USE THE ELEMENT OF SURPRISE TO OUR ADVANTAGE.'

A short distance across the thick rich rug, Warlord Lou crouched in dark pants, sweater & heavy boots. She held an automatic rifle in her coarse pale hands. Four fighters sat crosslegged on the rug around her. Lou drawled with a hillbilly twang, speaking slow and serious. "If the cocksucker pulls out a gun, I'm gonna shoot him & kill him. Don't be afraid. I'm gonna be in that car watchen' every move. If he pulls out a knife, hit him with the chain, or a bat, two of you on him, or three, if yuh ain't busy with the other ones. If its just you alone& he pulls a knife, back off. If he goes after yuh, well, --this rifle fires off 20 rounds in under 5 seconds. I'm covering you."

Royal was the businesswoman of the gang. She looked nondescript. In glasses, and a mans suit, a dark fabric, like the rest, and no tie. Her hands were rawboned, fleshy. Teeth crooked in front & stained, that showed her years as an older dike. Her gang formed a semicircle around her against the wall. "When we finish a sweep of a location,--we don't want a man left standing. Want them down. Down on the ground. In pain." And she flattened her hand down into the carpet as she cussed out the words. From inside her suitcoat Roy produced a 9mm pistol reworked to fire automatic rounds. 15 at a clip. "This will be on the seat beside me when we ride. The idea is to overpower them in hand to hand combat; if we get caught by the police & I've used this gun its a higher felony offense. But if a bastard fights back & starts to win, I'm gonna blast his asshole to hell and back."

The Warlords went to confer one last time. To coordinate their schedules & territories. And the small groups flowed back together as one, milling around, talking in low tones which belied the anxiety they felt growing. The time was getting near. Somber dikes. No joy flickered within them tonight. Dark jackets & trousers & moods to match. They knew their strategy. They had a purpose. One fighter spoke to her teammate in a low whisper;" You punch & kick him. I'll go around and hit him from behind with the pipe."

"Slap him with the chain, I'll kick his knees."

KT showed an icepick to her crew. "Put it right here," she pointed to her back, on the side, "1 hour later he's dead. I been in the US Army, I been trained to kill quick. Hit him here, **BANG!** Here, **BANG!** Here, **BANG!**" Sez KT.

They had decided to use cars, so not to be as visible as riding motorcycles. The first place the police would investigate would be Oils, a well known lezzy biker club, if dozens of incidents were reported involving assailants on cycles. Plain cars, not fancy Cadillac's or customized vans. And not to be seen in leather. So they'd be less recognizable.

The cars they had chosen were dark in color. A prerequisite, they had 4 doors so the team could get in and out fast. 2 would ride in front, driver & fighter. 3 in back. Each vehicle had been overhauled by several mechanics who had labored all day. Rip had underworld Mafia connections and had outfitted each with new license plates, & registrations, in case they were stopped by the police. The line of cars sat in George's driveway--all gassed up.

"Yer gonna make 5 hits, for each group. That's 5 separate men or groups of men. That can be 25 to 75 men down. It took 5 of the cowards to attack Stryker, so we're gonna raise the ante."

They went outdoors. Night had pushed the temperature lower. Stars wild in heaven cast silver light from millions of miles away in space.

The Warlords stepped into their cars, each behind a steering wheel. George first. Then Rip. Hawk. Lou. & Royal.

The fighters spoke over the low wind. Shoulders hunched, jittering nerves. "Where's Sleaze? Didn't she get chose?" Asked a dike as they walked towards their respective vehicles.

"Sleazy ain't here because she & Lady got 3 kids, and if she gets injured she'll loose her job. She's a janitor, she gotta use her body. Sleazy begged to go, but everybody talked her out of it."

The air had warmed due to the snowy rain. Stars swirled in the sky, and there was a full moon drifting, peeking among the clouds. Inside car number #1 commanded by the grim Leader, George, was the big biker with her flat top crewcut, --now hidden under a wool knit cap, Mel. As she leaned back in her seat, thought; 'I wonder if I'll live to graduate from College.' Beside her sat Comancho, and a punker. Both wore caps also; one to hide her bald head. And Johnny the mechanic rode in the front seat beside George.

At first, Angel had wondered, in the solemn privacy of her thoughts; full lips pressed tight together, why she hadn't been chosen to ride with Daddy George, but as if knowing the blond butches doubts, without being asked, the Leader confided in Angel; "It's cause I trust you. 'Yer strong, 'an I seen yuh fight 'n I know what you can do. So we need you more in another car to help them."

Rips car rolled down the long driveway second. It held the black biker KT, Angel, Ronny and a strong armed hillbilly who lifted weights who worked out regular in Sleazy's basement gym.

Hawk had two of her best fighting pals in the car she drove; their punk hairdo's also hidden by caps, and gold nose rings removed, plus the two fem bikers Storm & Alicia who worked as a teem.

Roy and Lou had some of the toughest fighters, including the pretty butch Star, they were all weight lifters and karate trained.

Each cars driver was responsible to begin & end the action; to remain behind the steering wheel, gun aimed out the window, foot on the accelerator & call in the fighters when it was time to go.

Anger rode with Angel.

And anger rode with them all.

Cars roared down the driveway.

In the rear seat, snugged in between two other tough fighters, Angel rested her head back on the upholstery. Looked thru the cool pane of glass window at stars whirling up in space. Then she turned to see the processional of cars behind. For a moment caught a glimpse of the grim face of Hawk visible over the wheel in the car directly behind them; the pink/green Mohawk spikes of her hair hidden under a black knit cap. Thought back about the fight she'd had with the 37-year old Warlord--in her struggle to take the woman Crystal from her. Grappling in the dirt, their flesh interlocked-- sweating muscle to muscle. She knew Hawks weakness, --the failing power of a fighter past her prime. Had tested the faltering power of a woman weakened by drug abuse. Knew her venerable points. Angel wished now that she have strength. For battle against the sheer night's street terror they all faced together. As she leaned back against the upholstery of one of Rip's extra cars, inside her heart, Angel made her peace with that long simmering feud with Hawk.

They would drive out into the inner city, in the netherworld below the freeway; and there divide & head off in 5 separate directions; staying within the parameter of a map each Warlord had photographed in her mind.

Red taillights flashed on the first car; bumper dipped when it took a sharp curve, rear tires spiting gravel. Stern, behind the wheel The Leader sat strong & big, with a nonchalant grip maneuvered the road at a breakneck pace with a clam demeanor. George's eyes fixed on the road ahead. She had thrown her fate to the wind. Ideas carefully rehearsed in the machinery of her mind, now to be executed. Worry and fear were blotted out in the powerful blazing light of righteous purpose. Inside, George surrendered to it. It was a relief that things were underway. Her big chest heaved a sigh. Relief.—That she'd given guidelines who was a target and who wasn't. That the bastards would get what they were due. The women were full of rage, more then expected; it was surprising. They'd endured so much harassment by lowlife males that they were kegs of dynamite waiting for their fuse to be lit. 'Their gonna do some damage tonight. --It needs to be some creeps who deserves it.' George saw the seriousness of her cerebral plan begin to unfold into the material plane, --there it was, 4 pairs of headlights, bold, blazing brilliantly thru the night, following snakelike down the hill behind her.

Cars ripped along the streets. Blocks flew by. Anyone who was in their path was in danger this night, they weren't going to stop for nothing.

Yellow light, neon bright, blinking.

Snow had stopped. A wet slush on the ground spat backwards by spinning tires, and the temperature was warmer.

Friday night. City of Light.

The caravan rode around the glassy human-made lake of the Grand Concourse. Neon lights reflected in it as blurry doubles.

There in the park a Warlord saw a Viet Nam vet, ruined by the war and fallen to poverty, in an old army camouflage jacket of green & pale yellow, muttering to himself, a bottle of wine in his hand. He suddenly turned and screamed at a passerby an unintelligible curse under the moon.

No matter what his circumstance, nor what fate had made him fall, this was one of the types of men of whom women are afraid.

Before the night would be done, men like him would lay sprawled in blood on the urban battleground.

Rip roared thru the streets, swerved so as not to hit a mongrel dog nosing garbage in the gutter, tail between its legs. In profile, masculine, she half turned to the fighter beside her, then tilted her chin up to glance a moment in the rearview mirror and spoke in a deep voice, "We're about to split off & go into our territory. We're gonna see opportunity! We're gonna stop, get the job done, yer' back in the car, 30 seconds flat, a minute at most. Don't get chickenhearted; show no mercy. --Think what they did to Stryker, think about her bleeden' body and what they did to her mind; and how she feels about herself & what she went and did to herself after---then do it! Strike! Punch, kick, drive 'em down, when they're down keep striking! Until they don't move. Do it! Do it! For all women!"

The freeway twisted like a snake, suddenly it went up 7 stories tall, 150 feet high, so they looked down at a sleeping city beneath, overpassing two other layers of freeway. The cars sped over the black strip of asphalt of four traffic lanes ahead. The cars gunned down the freeway. Black night punctuated by neon city lights; and domestic yellow bulbs from apartment buildings.

Spilled out of the mouth of the freeway exit, and drove down the streets, taking the curves, wheels held the road; until time came, the 5 car caravan row of twenty five black clad women split off into their solemn routes. Returning to the area near where the crime had been committed.

Soon, each drove thru the city streets wet slush at a reduced rate; scoping doorways of cheep eateries, mouths of taverns, the red & blue lit shops closed for the work hours, where loitering men took refuge to be among each other & howl, drink & scream in the dark.

To look thru the antisocial males of the landscape & select those to be punished.

In a residential street full of two and 3 story walkup apartments was a liquor store. Its windows dusty, cluttered with samples of merchandise & ads. Protective security bars still open, and liquor signs blinking off/on. From a distance of half the block the Warlord slowed, scoped the entrance. There emerged a drunk. A white alkie, empty-handed cursing the shopkeeper, "**AW YUH RICH MEN**

283

GOT WHAT YOU WANT!" His evil face twisting in violent frustration that he could not beg nor borrow more liquor, and had been caught stealing. He staggered in front of the store taking away space from everybody else, king of the walk for a brief life time. The Warlord saw him. "He looks like a hellraising rednecker." The car skids to a stop, slushy snow parting in its wake, and the four fighters jump out, racing thru the space of the gutter & curb chains flying, **CRACK!** A chain crashes down on him leaving a trail of crimson red. A kick, from another fighter. A series of punches from the third. The man is engulfed immediately and crumples down onto the pavement. Four angry women stare at him not sure what to do.

"**COME IN! COME IN!**" Howls the command from inside the car, they race back, feet leap over the bum who twists in his own blood, dazed, looking into a rapidly darkening tunnel of unconscious.

The fighter from the front seat leaps into thru the open door & slams it. Three black-clad dikes slide into the back seat; one slams the back door, even as the car jolts off, a heavy foot on the accelerator. "I HAD MY GUN TRAINED ON HIM, BUT YUH DIDN'T NEED IT. JUST TO MAKE SURE YUH ALL GOT BACK SAFE. **THAT'S ONE DOWN! FOUR MORE HITS TO GO!**" Breathless, the bikers puff for air inside the cold interior of the Warlords car. "We can't just hit drunks & crazy men, we got to go for some gangs members; some young male dogs." Next block down was a cheep hotel, another liquor store, and a well-lit café. About 20 people hung out in front, mostly drunks some dopers, including women. Among them was a snarling trio of young men raising hell, drinking & appearing so threatening by their actions to innocent passerby's who must negotiate the night streets to get home from work; that they have to make a wide detour around them. By the time she sees the trio, the Warlord has over shot the mark by half a block. Tires skid. Her thirst for blood made her bold. Shifts the car into reverse, wheels ground in the rainy snow and they sped backwards narrowly missing a line of parked cars shiny & wet in the snow. It jolts to a stop about ten feet from where the roughnecks are hollering.

One jumps out in front, three from the back. Car idles as the Warlord slides across the front seat, weapon in hand & sits in the open door, giant legs straddling distance, ready to jump back behind the wheel. Two fighters come up on the three men; as they turn, drunk & bewildered, fierce red faces frozen in time lapse, a chain & lead pipe strike two of them; women-fists & feet follow making connections on their bloody mustached faces & knees. The two men counter attack with punches, but they've been weakened by the blows--and the third man is running, away down the street. The last two women fighters converge behind the first pair seconds later in a strike, one with a blackjack--heavy metal wrapped in leather, **WHAM!** **WHAM!** Backhanding with recoil of blows from the first man to the second. The last fighter kicks one mans legs out from under him. He's lost his balance. The remaining man is clubbed into submission. Two men down. They lie, heads spinning, blood spilling out of them. Already the team is called back to the open doors of the waiting car which idles; exhaust flooding gas over the curb. The driver slams on the accelerator, they tear the hell away before a crowd of frightened hangers-on of the street who barely knows what's happened.

Not many miles off, another Warlord comes upon a typical, ugly sight. A derelict in the middle of the sidewalk blocking the passage of passerby's; a bottle in one hand. He had completely twisted his body to the right throwing a punch into space, then a second to the left. At the end of every twist he'd violently throw a punch into the air. Red, green & blue lights of poverty row shops blinked; a semblance of normal life tried to go on beside him. A bus had left off late night pedestrians nearby. The Warlord might have gone on by, but that one of them, an immigrant mother in a shawl & coat & shabby dress, leading a child by the hand tries to pass the man, who suddenly wheels and begins to curse at her, grabbing at both her & the terrified child, causing her to scream and run fast steps necessary to escape.

The man stood, sweaty from drinking so much alcohol; & consuming drugs; a disgusted look on his face. Hawk snarled. **"GET HIM!"** Slams on the brakes, the car jolts to a stop, simultaneously two doors jerk open and the army leaps out; within 3 feet of him they meet the stench of alcohol. Fists & feet strike. Four women attack pummeling, they hit each other in crossfire as the man goes down; sprawled in a stained green jacket, face upon the sidewalk; his red blood pooling into the snow.

Hawk had no pity for this miserable creature.--How many women had he made afraid? As soon as they were in the car, she pulls out of gear, hits the headlights, and races away.

Hawk didn't have to look far for the next hit. Their territory was the West End of the slum strip which incorporated barrio Hispanics, white bums, black ex cons like poison into a fabric of a poor society which struggled to survive. **"AI! ALICIA! MIRA! LOOK WHO IT IS! AI YI YI! *HAWK!* We gotta get him! That no good there!"** As she passed, Hawk got a glimpse of a well-dressed figure standing facing a bush, he wore a long coat. A small arc of piss was coming out from his open coat. **"HE'S THE WORST DOPE DEALER! HE MOLESTS LITTLE KIDS! OH! HE'S THE WORST SCUM!"**

Storm pulls her knit cap down over the thick hair on her head. "I hope the bastard don't recognize me!" Hawks car turned the block, it's nose cut thru the misty & heads back. Now the man is walking on, alone, without witnesses. An easy target.

 Suddenly, the tall gangster looks down at what appears to be four short men surrounding him. As his hand reaches under his coat for a gun; **CRACK!** One woman lashes out with a sort-handled wood bat. From nowhere a chain slugs into his face, its tail end wrapping around his head smashing back into his eyes. **BLAM!** A lead pipe cracks across his forehead. A fist encased in gold colored brass knuckles strikes out a grazing blow, but he is gone, legs bucking out from under him. He goes down hard. **THUD:** human meat, watery, flattening onto the pavement. Alicia kicks the unconscious form; and a cry echoes from the interior of the car, **"COME BACK! GET IN!"** Once inside the safe upholstered interior, as they rolled away thru the night Storm spat, "I don't know if we left him dead or alive."

"Dead I hope." Replied her little femme. Dark eyebrows bristling as her eyes flashed.

The next team came to some raw meat--a gang of anti-social teenagers. Four of them. The women piled out of the car, and again the Warlord slid across the front seat, leaving the car to idle as she trained a sawed-off shotgun converted to automatic fire out the open door. They got more then they bargained for.

The teens, ranging from 14 to 19, red faced, whiskers on their chins, had been drinking. In surprise they were rushed by the four who looked like slightly built men. Arms locked in battle, they began to fight against the dikes who had struck blows with a small crowbar, and another with a Billy club. The advantage of surprise on the side of the women was diminishing as the larger men fought back. A few feet away, back inside the cold wind-filled car, behind the open door, too late the Warlord saw the scales tip, and silently cursed herself for taking on such a big crowd. She stepped fully out of the car; as groans and screams and thuds of fists against flesh assailed her ears; and pumped off five rounds of gunfire into the air. Then stepped forward, gun barrel trained on the melee. Two of the youngest teens had backed off, but one man built like a bull was fighting for his life. He struck out with sledgehammer fists and instantly two fighting women went crumpling down. Another woman struck him with a lead pipe which only seemed to graze off the side of his chest, doing now damage. He ripped out a knife from his jacket & lunged at her, steel blade slashing and she backed off terrified. The man stood yelling in Spanish, waving the knife back and forth in front of him. Lou's shotgun was trained on him all the while, which he did not see. 'Aw, what the hell…' Lou thought. She pumped out 2 bullets, low, that struck his treetrunk size thighs and leg. Immediately the man fell. His partners threw up their hands in surrender, backing off, mouth gaping. 'They're too strong anyway…' Lou finished her thought. Lou holds the shotgun leveled on the cringing teens and hollers; **"LETS GO!"** The women on the ground have staggered back up on their feet, helping hands of their sisters under their armpits. The four women rush back to the car. & the man on the ground thrashes in a pool of blood screaming in terror. Lou walks backwards, holds the gun on them, and sits back in the car, pulls her feet in. Star has slid behind the wheel taking over the driving. Car doors slam. The beautiful butch jolts the car into drive and they speed away leaving a gang of fallen delinquents in shock.

By now 35 minutes had elapsed consisting of driving down streets of snowslush by green & red blinking advertisements of taverns, fast food joints & poolhalls. Scanning loiterers in doorways; those mean punks with dead minds looking for trouble now had become prey themselves. Each carload had tackled 2 or three sweeps. The exhilaration had rapidly grown to a muted weariness, but they had the wild spark of energy to keep going.

A Warlord met up with trouble. At first the men looked like an easy mark. There were 2 of them loitering in the dark. One built on the average size, the other taller and heavier; with a compact frame. The women leapt out, swinging chains and pipes. Rip watched keenly, as she was suppose to do, one foot out the open door, rifle trained on the scene. Finger pressed against the grooved ridges of the trigger until it seemed to melt into her flesh. As they approached, one man reached into his waistband and from her vantage point Rip could see he was pulling out a handgun. Before he could fire, Rip shot off a round. They heard a **BANG!** Saw a flash of white. He staggered a few paces before he felt himself fall to the ground, a carotid artery severed. His last feeling was of being burnt by the increasing gush of his hot blood, before he passed out. **"Shit. I should' a known a big son-of-a-bitch like him would be packing a gun, it's bullies like him that always do."** Her voice echoed over deadened air. By this time, on their fourth hit, the women didn't have much heart left. They'd forgot about Styker, were weary of war. They didn't have the cruelty to keep on with it. There was not much more time. Each Warlord on her assignment paid close attention to the wristwatch on her arm. By the time the police got an idea something was happening, in their precinct, in a bigger connected pattern, they wanted to on the freeway headed home.

So far there were injuries in every car. Blood and bruises and a lot of women scared so the bottom of their guts had turned to jelly & piss trickled down their pants. But they kept on fighting until the end time.

'I'm piling up felony after felony.' Rip thought, disgusted. Looking up into the rearview mirror, watching for cops as she drove. They'd made 4 hits. Only one left to go. Bt she was in fear of the last. Finally the Warlord broke. Pulled into a deserted area, dissembled her illegal automatic weapon & threw it in the trunk. Strode back into the car. Her handsome acme scared face turned to her crew. "Look, I might have killed that motherfucker back there. We gotta go easy. I ain't

288

armed no more. We got one more hit, we vowed we'd do it, all five of us Warlords, so lets find an easy mark. One man alone, just whip the shit out of him, don't kill him, then lets call it a night."

Rip's deep voice rolled over the back seat of the car. They sat like alabaster statues suspended in the moment.

All the women agreed. One by one they nodded their heads or grunted 'yes'. Angel wiped a cold stiff hand across her jaw. She'd seen enough to last a lifetime.

It wasn't to be that easy. They drove 20 blocks up, then over, and no man did they see, but workers hurrying home from late shifts, and ancient madmen asleep like gnomes in doorways. Moonlit bright in a cloudy heaven. White knuckled hands clutched to the wheel, Rip cast her eyes up to the ceiling of the car; **"Aw please send us a man to whip the shit out of him!"**

Making another pass off the spur end of the strip, down 77th street, the crew saw 3 men arguing in a doorway. The car slowed. The sight of them elicited fear. A woman walked by, wearing a uniform of a fast food restaurant visible under her coat. They stopped fighting among themselves and followed right behind her. The car crept up at a distance, its headlights off, unnoticed. She kept walking, and got near the parking lot of her restaurant, turned and watched over her shoulder while pretending to ignore the men. They walked on by. Rip sized them up. One man was a heavy 200 pounder, 6 feet, wearing a sweatshirt with a hood, and thick jacket, white face red with alcohol, & his hair matted and sticking out wild. His friends were smaller, unshaven, men of the streets, who looked like they'd fade away after a single blow. She was positive they had no guns, they were too poor. A gun would have been sold by now to purchase alcohol or even food; or would have been confiscated by the police on a routine stop & search. Rip's gun was gone. It was a relief to go into battle empty-handed. With her prior record, felony assault with a gun would mean the penitentiary.

"We'll go for them. I'm gonna join you. It'll be five of us, and three of them. Go for the big bastard. Bring him down, the others will back off, I'm sure of it."

They parked the car at a distance and waited. Sure enough, in 5 minutes the arguing men swung back thru the wind-cut parking lot and headed down a darkened side street, to piss in the bushes, and drink a bottle of wine. Even as they lurched out of the lot, a woman driver who had gotten out of her car to go in the restaurant & get some food saw the three man gang, and changed her mind, and walked all the way around the building thru the more well-lit sector and went in by the other way.

The night was still, moon shone. The car crept down the street, 'till midway it sped past them, lurched to a stop and five women stormed out. Straight to their target lashing with weapons, kicks and fists. The tall man looked eye to eye with Rip, as a jolting blow of her fist ripped out at him; in a stunned grunt he raised up his own arm in defense, viewing her with terror from his hollow bloodshot eyes. The smaller women followed. Angel clubbed him from the side with a blackjack, and KT pounded him from behind with strikes of two brass knuckled fists. His drunken companions wavered, two bikers held one at bay, one twisting his arm in its ragged sleeve while the other poked his guts with a Billy club; and the other as predicted, faded off into the night. The assault was over in under 90 seconds. As one the gang turned and strode away. Rip hugged Angel, thanking Mother God that was symbolized by the blond butches cleric collar— invisible tonight-- that she often wore. It was over. The five ran back to the car, red taillights in the night. Soon they were back on the highway.

Rip watched the snaky grey highway, then turned to glance up in the rearview mirror, to catch a glimpse of her passengers in the backseat. "I *knew* you'd bring me luck Angel." She confessed. Privately the bulldike thought; 'when we get to Georges' I'm breaken' down my rifle and get her to dump it in the river--piece by piece.'

Aways thru the city, another team was finishing up its assignment. Pale faces in the interior of the car. A small punk dike in a dark jacket, watch cap pulled over her ears. 'Just hit the ones who look no good.' Since fifteen, when she'd been forced to live on the street Jody'd known degenerate males & their criteria. Loitering, fighting, arguing, stealing & harassing people. Females especially because

290

they are weaker in brute strength. As a lot of these special dikes driving thru territories of the night city, her head hurt from being punched, both by enemy men, twice; and once by her teammate by accident. 'Don't forget! Our women can't walk the streets after dark.' Jody recalled the pep talk. The words still tumbled thru her mind in a jumble like alphabet soup. 'If they're drunk, out loitering in the street, making noise, fighting & yelling at women they're asking for it. Don't forget these are the dregs. The ones that raped Stryker. They don't want 'em down there in their country, we don't want 'em in ours. Why do you think they come up here into the States to have their gang wars & run drugs? You never see Spanish doctors and lawyers loitering in the streets? Hell naw! There's all kinds down there in South America; both rich as well as poor. But up here, all you see in the streets is the ones who can't succeed anywhere. And they're full of hate because of it.' The crew's last hit was good. A flashy macho man caught alone. In a snarling response, he lashed out with a one-two punch knocking one dike down, but three more jumped on him. A club across the face, a small 3 inch knife raked down his neck, kicks and more fists from the small army of women. His face and chest covered with blood he lay at their feet, whipped, trying to crawl away. Meanwhile a few blocks down three dikes had two ex-cons up against a brick wall, working them over with fists & boots & baseball bats, until one dove thru them and bolted away, and the other slid down the bricks & lay there escaping into unconscious. The lesbian bikers were laughing. Their voices choked in the wind. Made it back inside the car and sped away. Two more hits, good ones; young mean men. Parasites.

Roy's cadre got one last hit, it wasn't as solid as the mean bastards of the nightbright advertisement-lit strip. Just a bum pissing in public on some poor homeowners flowerbed. The four jumped out. **"WANNA TAKE A SHIT TOO? WE'RE GONNA BEAT IT OUT OF YOU!"** He was a fighting machine rusted by abuse over time. Not as sturdy as they expected. Big, he out weighed any of them by 75 pounds, but it was just the ghost of him left. When four dikes came crashing into his immediate circle he did little. Swung a few wild punches, screamed, & was overpowered. They dumped him on top of his own pool of urine.

291

The last carload drove around looking for one last hit, the hour was past, and they were due to get back on the freeway. At a gas station they saw three giant men, easily 6'5" and 300 pounds. Muscular. Wads of money in their hands, yelling at the attendant. Harassing as they bought soft drinks, cigarettes, bags of potatoes chips, this and that. The three piled into a truck & sped off. Then came another group, with two more into the gas station, yelling gassing up their vehicles, as the five dikes watched. They'd all come off the freeway, as if some sports event had just let out. They were all big, and too many of them. It was frustrating.

Another target proved to be incorrect. As they drove they spied 3 sleepy Puerto Ricans climbed out of the back of a van. The car crept up, & they saw ten more people climbing slowly out being helped by the men, a mother, and grandmother, sleeping infants in their arms. People with no cause to hurt. Themselves victims of the lowlife flotsam around where they lived. The Warlord's car picked up speed. She consulted her watch. They were overdue. The fighter beside her in the front seat, dulled by tension, pain & the impact of blows had begun to fidget her fingers like worms in her lap, nervously. In back the trio was grim, watching thru the chilly windows, holding their bloodied bats & chains.

Down a darkened sidestreet they came to an apartment building. 3 men walked out of its un-lit entrance passing a can of beer between them. The carload of dikes in dark jackets & pants pulled to the side, stopped & watched. The men loitered on the street, illuminated for a brief moment in the headlights of a passing car. Then a fourth came out, joined them, and all four got into a car. Headlights came on. They sat, red embers of their cigarettes shone thru the glass. Then a beercan splattered out of a window, to the ground. "We can't attack them in hand-to-hand combat, they're too big & too many & they might be armed more heavily at us." Spoke the Warlord in a subdued tone. Lifted up her cap, ran her hand thru her hair, then put the cap back on. Looked thru the side mirror as the car began to pull out from the curb. It was a stalemate. 4 dikes in a car, 4 men in another; each enclosed by steel & glass in secret compartments; hiding an unknown factor,--what weapons they might have. **"SHIT."** The Warlord was George, Leader Of The Pack. 'Damn. It was my idea to head back to the house at 1:30. We ain't got enough time to find nobody else!

"FUCK!" George grabbed her automatic rifle, kicked open her door, turned, aimed, in a split-second fired. **BAM! BAM! BAM! BAM! BAM! BAM! BAM! BAM! BAM!** Low, at the tail of the car. The car gave a huge jolt, and men were screaming. George sped away. The night was over. As they gained the freeway, the dikes pulled off their caps, shook loose their hair, and started turning back into humanbeings. "I didn't kill 'em. I fired low. I was mad because there was too many of 'em, too much power and you guys didn't get yer last turn to fight." They were back at her mansion in under 20 minutes. The weapons would be cleaned and stored away for future use.

Upstairs, in apartments over the street, back in the ghetto, people stirred in their beds. 'It ain't nothin.' Just another burst of gunfire in the inner city.

The other cars were already there, sweating heat from their motors in the cold midnight. Several dikes had been hurt bad. One tried to stand, but couldn't. Two others had their shoulders under her arms to hold her up. Blood was all over her face & had spilled down her chest.

In memory, almost every carload could still hear their own rage. That crackling sound of gunfire. Nobody was happy, nor sad--just drained. Spirits even lower then when they'd found out the news about Stryker.

The smell of gunpowder lingered in the interiors of cars. As the vision of blue/white light of crackling gunfire lingered in their minds from those moments in which their lives were in a war zone.

"DAMN! WOW! I ducked for cover when she started shooting!"

"I wanna sleep forever."

"I'm so glad this is over."

"I thought I was dead, but I'm still walken' around."

"I beat the shit out of 'em so much I growed tattoos."

When they got inside, all had similar stories. No one was jubilant. Dull, & very drained emotionally. They climbed single file upstairs.

The series of raids ended sooner then was expected. Time flew fast.

By the end of an hour, 25 raids had been carried off. They'd done enough to put them all behind bars & Daddy George would have reoccurring dreams of herself being strapped in the electric chair.

Most dikes agreed they'd done plenty. Now they had cold feet. "I've had enough. It's crash & burn. Crash & burn. I don't want to be in those men's world anymore. Their streets. And see their ugly, mean, worthless lives. I want to get away from it."

Bruised & bloody, the bikers wiped the slime off their fists.

They got upstairs to the Masterbedroom which was connected to a lavish bath, where Debbie & Georgina waited with towels to shower them down. George strode over their carpeted bedroom in her construction boots, bulk shaking jovially. ***"YUH DONE GREAT!!!"*** She bellowed congratulations with an enthusiasm dredged up with great effort from her flagging spirit. And stooped to pat women on the back, or to take a bruised hand in her mammoth paw for a moment. The weary warriors sat or lay collapsed out on the kingsized bed, or hunched on the rug, backs against the walls. They sprawled out on several stuffed chairs. A sigh went up collectively in response. They examined busted knuckles that were streaked with grime, snow & red crimson blood. They weren't going home, solitary riding motorcycles that night, it would be dangerous. They were too worn. As planned, Georgina & Debbie and some other biker ladies had fixed up the 3 spare bedrooms with plenty of blankets, quilts, pillows & some extra cots. And there was food for anybody who cared to eat. They picked listlessly at the platters of cold cuts, --ham, turkey, beef, & cheeses, garnished with olives & dates, as they waited their turns to shower.

The master suite of George's house was as large as many apartments dikes lived in. Thirty feet across. The bath held a tub, two sinks, a toilet and a large pit shower with two showerheads, one at each end for butch/femme simultaneous showering. Georgina's firm hand ushered the bikers in naked 2 at a time. Those waiting peeled off their bloody, grimy clothes & handed them to Rips wife. Debbie was serious and busy. No makeup. A simple pair of jeans. Spike heels elevated her, to show a delicate turn of ankle--which was the only sexy thing about her tonight. Her curly Puerto Rican hair was brushed back severely into a schoolteachers bun. Clouds of steam arose in the tiled room. Young bodies paraded past, pink, tan, brown & ebony. Firm tits & bottoms. With a grim expression Debbie threw their dirty clothes into paper sacks & hastily wrote the bikers name on it with a marking pen. Georgina and Saundra would do their laundry & have it back at the cloubhouse next week. Bodies glistened pink and brown. Water beat down from the shower to their cries of **"OHHHH!"** and **"OUCH!"** Cleansing wounds & cuts. And taking the pain out of aches. When the biker dikes stepped back out from the tile shower and toweled dry, Georgina, prepared in a pair of latex gloves dabbed alcohol on wounds. Applied salve and antiseptic medication. Each was handed her clean clothes from the fresh sack they'd brought earlier that evening. Then they filed out, and went down the hall into one of the three bedrooms & got their blankets, to bunk up for the night.

When the processional of nude lezzies was finished, Georgina sat a moment with George, wiping a ringlet of hair from her sweaty brow. "Have fun?" The Queen asked, with just a hint of sarcasm.

George's face had collapsed into flabby wrinkles, of a pasty white color--from weariness. She replied in a deep but strangely subdued tone. "I shot up a car full of 'em, & I had to get out and drag a man off one of my fighters. I banged my rifle butt into his skull, grabbed him by the collar & kicked him, and he went out like a light... Some of the fuckers were really scared. They mock women's fear, and make fun of us, but by God, when they're really scared men always scream like women do--except louder." 'It's always the same.' George thought, thick fingers interlacing on her lap as she sat beside Queen Georgina. The bulldike was weary of the sound of screams.

"So yuh had fun." Repeated her wife.

George smiled, a cold sadistic grin. And nursed a big lump on one knuckle.

There came the sound of bikers down the hall whooping in a feeble attempt at a pillow fight, before they'd fall into restless sleeps.

George says nothing. Just grins.

"Our benefit party will be *more* fun." The ample woman said finally. "The gals are gonna bake mountains of cakes in our double oven. Angel's lady is making 5 Angel Food Cakes. The kids really like Angel Food. One of the black gals is baking 10 Peach Cobblers.--Isn't that nice of her?"

The rose & gold wallpaper stretched around the huge bedroom. Furniture of the finest quality. "Well, yuh got to see all the cute butches naked in the shower. All their thin sweet young bodies." Sez George.

"I wasn't in a state of mind to notice tits & ass." Replied the Queen.

The wave of terror was over. 15 men had been beaten senseless. Dozens of others had gone running away into the night in fright. A few visited the hospital, and they left one near-death.

Sun came up. Blood was spilled on a dozen pavements.

Chapter Twenty Five

George opened her eyes and saw the bottom of a cat leaping over her head. It was Georgette, who came to rest on her stomach and began massaging her with his front paws.

But hearing the clanking of dishes, the black feline bounded off the bed and ran down the carpeted steps towards the kitchen.

Not long after, came a great howl from downstairs.
"GEORGETTE! WHY ARE YUH UP THERE!" Queen Georgina
was trying to fix breakfast, and the cat was pacing the ledge above her
head, knocking down a tin of spice. **"I HATE YOU! I HATE
YOU! YOU'RE SHAKING ALL THE DUST DOWN ON MY
PLATE! I HATE YOU! I HATE YOU!"**

"MILK! MILK!" Cried a voice from the bedroom, like a big
brat, from a resonance in her great chest. The desildikes head was
reeling from last nights events.

**"THERE AIN'T NO MILK IN THE REFRIGERATOR! THE
KIDS DRANK IT ALL UP!"** Her wife's voice echoed back upstairs
to where George sat up in bed, laying against a ornate gold
headboard.

Queen Georgina pounded one large hand **SMACK!** on the counter
top so all the plates rattled. The cat only blinked down from the
ceiling with yellow eyes, & did not budge. Soon came the sound of a
clanking breakfast tray as Georgina mounted the carpeted stairs.

It was late morning. The trey had a plate of five eggs, scrambled
yellows & whites in chunks, & a quantity of bacon. Plus pate, brie &
caviar left over from last nights snack for the gang.

Daddy George lived the life of a king. Was served her plates of
food--ten in all,-- and needed a picnic table to eat them off of, seated
on the bed with a pile of leopard skin quilts thrown over her girth.

She had earned the right.

After their house had been cleared of bikers, Queen Georgina could
be more succinct. Slipped under the pokadotted fake animal skin
cover beside her husband; waited until she was midway thru the plates
of her gargantuan meal, and then began. "Yuh ought to get down on
yer knees 'n pray! That's a terrible thing yer doin' George!---Cleanin'
up the streets of the city of those derelict men! Yer gonna get caught
and we'll loose everything!"

"Everything's in yer name, --since the last time." Sez George, munching crisp strips of bacon.

"Whadda if one of them girls goes to the police? The legal fees will eat us alive!"

The Bible says to enter heaven and see God, you have to be as a little child, & Daddy George did it to the max.

As Georgina continued the tirade, George stared into the new day with coal-color eyes. It wasn't an easy matter to withstand that hard gaze of her wife. So she averted her glance up into the top of the room. The gold gilt wallpapered ceiling. Put down the spoon and began diddling her huge fingers in her lap like she didn't know whatever Georgina was talking about.

Now it was true. It was times like this Daddy George did want to reach into heaven, tear open the cloud curtain and see God; because there were few other sources to which to turn with the heavy load of problems she carried on her immense bulldike shoulders.

So, she had developed a way to cast off the worries of the world.

It was like a prayer.

They sat side by side on the lavish king-size bed. Carefully George picked up the trey, and set it on the floor.

Anyone else would have flung themselves on the ground before the Lord in Her Majesty,-- crying out for forgiveness. But George sez; "WELL, IF YER LISTENING, *AND I KNOW YOU ARE:* THEN THIS IS WHAT I'M ASKEN' YUH TO DO!" Laced her fat fingers over her stomach; baring her soul, eyes turned up to the heaven-like ceiling of her palatial home. **"DON'T LET NONE OF THEM GIRLS TALK TO THE POLICE!** *SPARE US!* **AND WHEN YOU GO ON SWEEPS LIKE YOU DO, KICKING ASS, PASS OVER OUR ASSES, WILL YUH!** *SPARE US !* **AND WHILE YER AT IT, KICK THE ASS OF THE RICH SO THAT THE PEOPLE CAN** *LIVE!"*

Once in Oils The Leader had made this remark; "Sure it's a game. Everyone's on a ladder. People are going to be dominate to somebody and submissive to somebody else. When I go home if I do a scene, do you think I fantasize I got tremendous power? Huh? With all these people running up to me with their heads bowed politely telling me all these problems?"

In her private life, it would not be unusual if such a Leader was extremely submissive. It would not be a surprise at all.

George did run the club. It was a cold sexual arena in which she could indulge herself. So much power was given to her. Also, so many trials, struggles, & problems with the gang. It was hard for them, living on the bare extremity of the world known as The Edge. Walking The Wild Side. The Leader had become hardened by the whole thing. The only compassion she had left channeled thru her in infantilism. A strange phenomenon, but a manner in which she kept her heart & remained in touch with her humanity.

The Leader rolled over & went back to sleep briefly. Later, she got up, spoke to her wife & left the room.

When she returned, the 6' 3" tall 350 pound dike was naked. Tuffs of pubic hair shot over enormous pale thighs. Huge tits hung on an iron-hard muscled chest. And carried a large cloth. Lay back ontop of the bed, where Queen Georgina wound the cloth around her mammoth waist & between her thighs & back over her buttocks. When she was finished, it was apparent this contraption was a huge diaper.

The diaper size was 54"; it fit Daddy George comfortably. She sat on the rug next to the playpen and flailed a toy bear against the bars. There was also a toilet seat on a box made of plywood about 3 feet high, conspicuously placed up against the wall of their playroom in the basement. Often those who'd been in the room would make jokes and point at it; 'what's this for ?' Not knowing it was the chief toy of pleasure she had among all the racks, whips, piercing needles, handcuffs & chains in the dungeon.

Daddy George was a practitioner of infantilism. Few knew this.

Georgina had slipped into a mumu of yellow with golden sun flowers; painted toes of her bare feet stuck out on the bottom-- like a Goddess. An Earth Mother. Her bare arms donned with golden bracelets enfolded the huge baby. "NO, LITTLE GEORGIE WON'T GO TO THE 'LECTRIC CHAIR, MOMMY WON'T LET HIM! MOMMY'S IN CHARGE! GEORGIE IS SAFE WITH MOMMY!"

Thoughts of the nights events weighed heavily on her head; possible entanglements with police. Guilt. Two girls had had to be taken to the hospital.—Suppose the doctors got suspicious...

"Mmmmmmmmmaaaaa Mmmmmmmmmmmaaaaaaa Mmmmmmmaaaaaaaaa Mmmmaaaaaaaa Ma Ma! Mama!" George had thrown down the toy, and lay in her Queens arms---now become Mother.

"GEORGIE! LITTLE BABY!" Georgina held the young George. "MOMMY LOVES BABY!"

"MAMA!" The baby kicked it's huge chubby arms and legs.

During the scene flashbacks occurred to her. She'd been a large kid, worn bluejeans, gymshoes, and plaid shirts. Played only with boys. "COME ON YUH GUYS! WE'RE GONNA PLAY BOUNCE OR FLY!" A baseball bat in one hand. **CRACK!** The sound of wood as it hit the ball. Memory. The cornfields of her youth, wild flowers, deserted lots overrun with weeds; the alley behind the houses--that had been their playground. She was bigger then the biggest boy. Back, when she/he was a growing child & still didn't know the ways of the world. The adult, pensive dark eyes stared up into space, laying in the enfolding arms. The adult mused; 'Wouldn't it be nice if we could be a human race again? Not men against women. Fems against butches. The Coloreds against the rednecks?' Thoughts bubbled to the surface.

She wanted to go back to childhood. Wanted to be taken care of. Wore the diaper. An adult who wanted to go back to being a baby. To be fed and rocked to sleep. With no responsibilities. If baby is bad, spank the bad baby, and it's done. No worries.

300

Daddy George lived in a rough & tumble world of fighting. A cold climate of society which viewed her kind in dismay, thru cutting eyes. As a kid had played with the boys only, and, as she grew experienced a sense of camaraderie missing among females.

When they'd first moved into the neighborhood of her youth, there was established a pattern of dominate boys in a loose knit fraternity. They knew George was a girl, but she was big and scared them. Daddy George was meaner then they thought. In a few months she'd whipped all the biggest boys, and assembled them into a real gang. And they remained a gang even into adolescence.

Uneasy lays the head that wears the crown.

So many worries, she had to blow off steam. And did this one scene the others would never see.

It was full infantilism. Some lovers coo like babies to each other, and talk baby talk in each others ears, but don't put on diapers & drink from a bottle with a rubber nipple. There was no really big division for George. Sometimes she got more into it--when her stress was great. Sometimes less into it.

Georgina combed baby's short black hair with her red manicured nails. "Want me to nurse baby? Do you want to suck my big tits?" And cuddled her. "Yer such a big baby, and yer really sweet. Wanna play with your toy bear some more? Does baby want Mommy to read him a story and rock him to sleep?"

Baby George wiggled her naked arms & legs and cooed. "Does baby want Momma to give him medicine to make him feel better?"

"YA YA YA YA !" Screamed the little baby.

Momma Georgina went to the bathroom and returned with a cup of 'medicine', actually a Coca Cola, and gave it to him in a spoon.

"YAH! YAH! YAH!" Baby George was getting cold & uncomfortable; naked but for the big diaper around his bottom. The baby gave a loud shriek, and spit the medicine right back out at her.

"GEORGIE!" Cries Momma in a big commanding voice like an Alto Soprano. Georgina had only begun to call George by the title 'Daddy', a few years ago, after the club's SM scenes had begun. "Shall I spank George for being a bad baby?" Mused Momma. One red fingernail tapped her lower lip in thought. "I shall indeed." Said Mamma. "I have to spank baby, he's been bad. Just like when he spit his carrots up halfway across the room, and ruined all his lovely baby clothes." The couple had contemplated the idea of building a big adultsize crib that George could actually get inside of--an immense play crib.

So, what would follow was a spanking. --Light taps. And a great nursing scene from Mama's big tits.

It was the one shred of humanity she had left--so it seemed when times got rough. And, to go downstairs to the dungeon to go to sit on the toilet seat with Mamma to hold her hand. What a relief!

A big smile on her face, playing Baby in an infantilism scene.

Daddy George had all the qualities of a leader.

Daddy George had all the trappings of a sex addict--in control. Got a wife. Had mistresses. And slaves when she needed them, at any time. And, unlike alcohol or drugs in which a substance abuser could spend a whole day alone at the bottle, frolicking in her vice; it was multi-dimensional. Her addiction involved people. It involved scenes with different personalities and types of women. It was her life touching on theirs.

Some of Daddy George's dicks were sculpted like the real thing. Others in the shapes of fish & corn. And created in a variety of materials. Jelly-like vinyl which was firm but flexible. Hard plastic with molded ribs for extra stimulation. Resilient Silicone. Colors pink, peach, black, & purple.

To end the scene, the robust Mamma got down on her knees on the lush carpet, Baby stood, and Mamma threw her arms around Baby's knees in a hug, then undid Baby's diaper. Out spilled the female scent of a grown bulldike. And a dildo of purple vinyl quivering in a harness out of a nest of pubic hair.

Baby spread her legs wide, one huge bare foot planted on either side of Mamma. Mamma took the cock firmly in her hand, pushing its base steadily into Baby's clit, while sticking the tip, --a bulbous dickhead into her mouth, and began to suck. Erotic, the vision of Mama swallowing half the purple dick, while rubbing Baby's clit with it's base, hard & fast, jerking & sucking. Finally Baby could stand it no more, and, wanting to orgasm in a different position, grabbed Mama, by the shoulders and roughly threw her to floor, with her hot mouth preformed expert cuninlingus, working her to a red hot fever pitch, then mounted Mama to finish the job.

Mama lay on her back, raised her knees, getting in position. The lights in the ceiling revolved as wild solar systems, or so they seemed, in her excitement.

Baby was a good dike driver and drove dick for 45 minutes-even tho she was age 52. With a strap on she'd go to town, working herself into an orgasm at the same time, while giving the ladies all they craved. Gave it to them right between their legs where they wanted it.

Baby George fucked to a grand climax.

Chapter Twenty Six

'Well', Crystal had said; 'If you have to go find somebody & play, ok, but just tell me! Don't run off and do it with her and get emotionally involved! I don't want us to break up!'

The curly head blond was the toast of Oils; the subject of a lot of bikers fantasies; she had been fought over by quite a few butches. But, she wasn't a play girl. Crystal was a wife.

Crystal was pretty. Shapely hands & feet, nails of both painted a demure pink. Trim, her belly was flat, downed with blond hair. Big firm breasts with pink nipples. Her pussy was pink inside.

Even married to Angel, now as she sat at the bar in Oils, Crystal got plenty play. "Who is SHE ?" A novice might ask.

If a biker was around to inform her, "that's Angels woman", her face would fall, and she'd try to forget about it. If no one advised an admirer of Crystal of her marital status, a slim young biker in teeshirt, motorcycle jacket & leather chaps, cap brim down low over her eyes might strut down the bar and approach her, slide their butt up on a red vinyl barstool and ask to buy her a drink, to which ladylike Crystal'd reply, "I'm taken. But you can buy me a ginger ale."

None she'd seen could compare to her Angel.--Big shouldered, sturdy, yet feline and smooth. A real woman and a real butch all wrapped up into one.

As she sat amid the clamor of the nightly party going on in Oils, Crystal had thoughts. 'Let her fuck another woman if she's got to. Especially if its at home with me, I won't be as jealous. I know she's not hiding something from me and planning to run off with the girl. That's how a lot of bikers do it...' Tapped her nails **click, click, click** on the wet bar, and wiggled her foot. One leg was crossed over the other, swinging in unconscious time keeping to the rhythm of the red & gold jukebox. Just then a nice song came on over the sound system. An old soul tune, a favorite of Ross, the grey haired stud friend of the proprietor. It was a black woman singing with a lot of bells and drums. **"YOU MOVE LIKE THE DESERT WIND. MAKE ME LOVE YOU AGAIN AND AGAIN!"** Then another soul tune came on.

Crystal got up from the vinyl covered barstool between two attentive bikers, to go find her mate and ask her to dance.

Heading down the bar, around its smooth laquored wood curve, at the dance area, she was surprised to see Angel and one of the black lady bikers pressing the full length of their leathered bodies together, in a slow, hip grinding dance.

The femme was curious. So she went around behind the couple to see her face. Caught sight of a brown hand resting gently on Angel's shoulder; & straightened hair, colored orange, glistening with oil; a pair of African lips planting a kiss on Angel's thick white neck. Then she saw her face; it was Saundra!

Dumbfounded Crystal moved back away from them, so as not to be seen, tho both had their eyes closed. The black walls of Oils were warm & enclosing. A few other romantic couples swayed together to the rythematic music. Angel & Saundra's thighs were locked together, and the femme pressed her delicate hand in the middle of Angels broad back, pushing the butch closer into herself. The blond got hot watching. 'Saundra always did like Angel. She liked her even before I got together with her.' Crystal hurried out of the dance floor, fast; short jacket pulled over her full breasts, elegant boots moved at a fast clip; jingling expensive jewelry. She reflected confidence, and inside felt secure with her love, but somewhat surprised.

'Well.' She thought, once situated back on the barstool, as simultaneously the two butches turned, each first glaring at each other, to try to engage her in conversation; 'I'd rather have her do it where I can keep an eye on them, then behind my back.'

Saundra was a lady, so, in the course of the evening, came to Crystal to talk. She was shy. 'I'm not sure what you think Crystal, but if the idea bothers you, I mean, if you're mad at me, or don't want this, please, please, --I really mean it, just tell me, & I won't. I can't stand to hurt you, we're getting to be friends. We've done stuff together. We're gonna be cooking cakes and pies and dinners for the Benefit, like sisters, like we're suppose to be, *sisters.* Outlaw women. If you are gonna be upset, secretly, inside, you've got to tell me, and I promise I won't! I'll tell Angel I can't. I really mean it.'

And Crystal told Saundra, it was ok. That she had confidence in her relationship. About how Angel had fought Hawk for the right to take her and be her man, & how Angel had been with her last woman

5 years. And how, like a lot biker women, Angel had this need to share sexually with more then one partner.

And Crystal had a question for Saundra, 'how will you take it? Going to bed with Angel and, well, I know you're single, after you go home alone, are you gonna be ok?'

And Saundra said, yeah, she'd thought about that and yeah, she'd be lonesome. A few dikes liked her, but they weren't her type, and she'd been alone essentially, but for a few one-night-stands, for over a year. And yes, she could handle it. It would be a relief, to be in the arms of someone who was nice. And then the brown woman looked shy, gazed down at her lap, then over the bar into hazy space, dark fingers toying with a lock of her orange hair, then turned to glance at Crystal, and spilled it out, 'Uh, oh... well... I guess Angel didn't tell you?' And music's pounding out behind them, and the jostle of bikers, and the two butches who'd been admiring Crystal are watching them hungrily, one having gotten up to give Saundra her seat; "Uh, I guess I should tell you, well, actually, the way we'd thought it was going to be, was the *three* of us. Me, uh, *you* and Angel." Crystal was dumbfounded. Her jaw dropped open a moment. And then Angel comes striding over thru the crowd, broad shoulders pushing past the sea of black leather fish, blond hair long under a motorcycle cap. And in a moment she's pressed up to Crystal looking down into her face wearing a grin.

"All three of us honey?" Crystal giggles.

"Yeah. *Tonight.* At our place." Sez Angel, nonchalant, pretending to examine her fingernails—while hiding her excitement. "I want to be with Saundra, and I want to be with you. I don't want you to be lonely."

Crystal fixed her with a gaze, a slight smile played over her lips. "You want to be with two women at once, don't you. Ohhhh. Sneaky thing!"

"Yeah. The idea turns me on."

"Oh." Crystal turned to Saundra. "She's a typical butch. She thinks she can handle two women."

They made their negotiations together that night along side the bar rail. They planned everything. The two lonesome butches slid off into the night, to hunt for female companionship elsewhere.

Once again Saundra & Angel danced, bodies pressed together. "I'm so glad yer coming home with us." Angel whispered into the delicate brown ear like a seashell just below a tuff of orange hair To Saundra it was the sound of honey.

"Yuh want anything to drink?" Angel offered solemnly, after they returned to their barstools. Moved her long blond hair aside from her face that was flushed with heat, with a motorcycle gloved hand. "We can have some liquor, get a little high and loosen' up a little."

"No." Saundra was shy. Shook her head and smiled. "I don't need anything."

Privately, the butch was nervous. She'd have to prove her masculinity & satisfy both women, plus cum at least twice herself. But, for the desire raging inside under her shirt & under her leather trousers, it was worth the effort.

Gold lights blink from the ceiling of Oils. In a beeping heartbeat, red illumination spins out of the jukebox in time to the tunes. Saundra & Crystal both wear short skirts that show shapely legs. They sit knee to knee, engrossed in conversation.

As Angel gazes at the ladies, knowing they are hers for the night, that she will undress them, unfasten their bras, slip off their panties & make love to them, her clit gets hot. It throbs under leather pants, until her crotch is wet. Angel feels like a real he-dike. 'I'm gonna fuck 2 women in my bed. Gonna fuck 'em until I don't need no more.' Smiles satisfied to herself. And begins to strut around the club.

Angel confided in Comancho. "Guess what man!" Leans over, a superior smile on her lips, blue eyes half closed, languidly; "I'm taking home another woman. The 3 of us are going to make love tonight."

"Yeah man?" Comancho had a toothpick in her lips, thick hair in braids, Indian style; sat beside her blond showgirl wife Frosty on a sofa.

Frosty giggles. She asks; "Who? You and Saundra and Crystal?"

"Yeah!"

"All three together?"

"Yeah."

Frosty giggles. Comancho slaps Angel on the back. "What a he-dike! Congratulations!"

At the end of the evening, the three got to know more about each other. The blond couple found that Saundra was poorer then they imagined. That the room she rented in a ghetto neighborhood was so cold; & she was so poor she couldn't afford much heat, & when she got up in the morning from under a pile of blankets she had to immediately put on her coat.

Saundra was bouncing on societies safety net right now. Free medical aid from the State, Food Stamps, gas & electric bill paid by the Salvation Army for one severe winter month. One more bounce and she'd be in the street.

Inching along on minimum wage. It was hard for the more affluent couple to believe, but the $20 monthly Outlaws Club dues seemed to be a mountain almost too steep to climb. Yet, the pretty brown woman didn't want to weaken and take on a female lover who she didn't love, just in order to have security & be able to pay the bills. A woman who might eventually abuse her physically, or disrespect her. Or who might have drug or alcohol problems. So, Saundra had tried to keep her standards, and her independence, and live alone. "My rent's killing me girl, how much is your place?"

When Crystal told her she was amazed. "Well, with the two of you working…"

Thru months of their 'relationship, even Crystal had come to appreciate the big money Angel earned illegally from the fraudulent telemarketing scam, at her long hours on the phone. Saw how much better they lived then the Strykers and the Saundra's of the Club. They always had cash to spend. Wherever they went--wither it was to shop for clothes, to eat in a restaurant, Angel would throw down a $100 bill. Stop in a fancy tavern, have a few softdrinks & listen to some mellow music, have a dinner there, drop $50 and not miss it.

The evening had wound down. Bikers stomped across the wood floor boards heading out. The jukebox was unplugged. The three sat on barstools pulled together. "There's no reason for anybody in this country to be in pain! ---If they are it's a lack of money. That's what the Charge Nurse told me at the hospital. And she should know. And all the times I've been in pain & couldn't get medicine. And there's so many unwanted babies being born, and folks with no job. And that all happened *yesterday*, and this is almost tomorrow, and they need help *now!"* Sez Saundra. "The rich people who run this country, they're so cheep! They won't give up the gold--not even to people who are trying! Like me! I mean I'm really trying! I go to work 40 hours a week, every week, basic; and most times 50, even 60 hours, when I work on weekends, or work double shifts. I work hard, I'm honest, I'm good to my patients, and they still won't pay me nothing, --$4.50 an hour. I can't live on that!"

The three went outside, & shivered under the sky. Stars whirled silver upon the black tableau of night. The streets were slushy with snow & Angel was secretly glad she'd driven Crystals car to the club, it was so fiercely cold; & the ice was dangerous on a motorcycle. And it made it perfect to drive them all home. The blond blew steamy breath into the chill, as they walked she had thoughts; 'This horrible place called earth, it could be a good earth. If people just had enough cash. But even if you don't and all these abusive straight people hate us, and all these unfair rules and denial & anti sex, yet, it still can be a good earth, if your life is in order, and you have somebody who loves you and you feel the presence of God.--All problems can be solved. And you can find the happy end.'

As they drove thru the night all three together in front, they talked about the raids in hushed tones. The blond butch had had a lot of sobering thoughts about it. 'Life blows like the wind, hot & cold, east & west. One problem, you take care of that, then there's another situation. It never ends.' Her profile faced the road ahead, solemn. Saundra sat in the middle, crossed one leg over the other, her thighs showed under the short miniskirt, with a glimpse of red lace under; counterbalancing the harlot-effect, she also was wearing a pair of tights like a proper lady. She spoke; "You were nice on the stage, when you gave that speech. Very impressive." Crystal laughed. Tossed her curly head. "The Leather Preacher. That's what some of the gang is calling her."

"It's a compliment."

The three came to a consensus about the raids. None of them felt good about breaking the law. "Everybody in society should get together, and hunt jerks like that out, and hang 'em from a lamppost until they die. Society needs to do it together, so it would be legal."

They took the elevator to the 13th floor.

Saundra saw the couples room for the first time. Looked around. It was the size of her place, but had a private bath, and the neighborhood was much nicer. Looked out the window at the view. Angel stood beside her, and pointed into the distance, over flat roofs of lower buildings into the snowy mist at the general direction of the Club where they'd just been.

Crystal turned on a small heater, & soon the place was warm. Saundra came and sat on the bed. Angel stripped off her motorcycle gloves and jacket, stood in her shirtsleeves looking down at the two ladies who sat on the bed. Then she lit some candles. When the flames grew strong, giving a bright light in a small halo around each, she turned off the overhead bulb, then came to the bed.

Angel touched Saundra's shoulders, gazed down, and the femme looked up into her eyes. Crystal sat back against the headboard, bare feet on the covers, & watched. With short-nailed white fingers, Angel

310

carefully unbuttoned Saundra's blouse, and the brown woman helped her. They pulled off the frilly garment, and beneath it was a lacy slip, red. Her full breasts poked out the slip, sexy; her round belly and hips rounded out the rest. Slowly Saundra wiggled out of her mini skirt, kicked off her boots, then took down one strap of her slip, the other, and her full breasts spilled out, yellow-brown faded skin that seldom saw the sun, with dark brown nipples. Next the red slip came off. A pair of scanty panties peeled down her legs showing a thick nest of tight curly pubic hair. Scent of female aroma mixed with perfume. Angel sat beside her on the bed, still dressed in a shirt & leathers; began to stroke the woman's delicious tits, cupping them, petting the nipples 'till they grew erect.

As Angel petted Saundra, her woman Crystal got up from the head of the bed, and came to sit next to the butch, snaked her arm thru Angels, and unzipped her pants, then began to unbutton her shirt & remove both articles of clothes. Soon the blond butch was stripped to her teeshirt and Jock and jockey shorts. Angel was embarrassed, "I don't have my cock on." And rose to go get it.

"We got time." Interrupted Crystal. Milky discharge was dripping down Angels legs, in excitement from stroking Saundra's luscious tits. She bounded across the bed to the nightstand & pulled out a cock still stuck in the silver ring of a harness. The brown woman's cunt was wet. As the candles flickered on the dresser, making the room seem warm and romantic, Crystal stripped off her skirt & blouse. In barefeet tiptoed to the closet; contemplated,--then threw over her alabaster body a black negligee. Came back to the bed where Angel & Saundra were entwined. She placed her hand between the butches thighs. Her crotch was hot and wet, sticking to her underwear. Angel turned, from where she lay on the pillow in Saundra's arms, and her femme Crystal is leaning over her unstrapping her own bra. Her cleavage spills out, big round pink breasts with reddish nipples. Immediately Angels thumb and forefinger of each hand begin to play with the breasts as they hang over her. Crystal smiles, and moans. Then she backs off, and slips on the negligee, provocatively.

Angel turns to Saundra, and begins to lick her tits, cupping one in each hand, and moving her mouth from one to the other, licking with short feathery movements of her tongue, then sucking deep and hard, drawing the nipple up into her mouth. One hand reaches down into the woman's curly haired nest, deep in, so her fingers are wet, penetrates her with a finger up to the second knuckle. Saundra's eyes flutter closed, her mouth parts in a tiny gasp, her hands reach around Angels broad back, and her thighs open in surrender. Angel fucks down into her soft pungent cunt to the last knuckles, in & out; fucks her in hard fast motions using now, two fingers, while her tongue licks Saundra's hard nipples.

Candles flicker. Crystal sits close to Angel, and caresses her butches back rippling muscles under the teeshirt with pink fingernails. She thought back over her history as an Outlaw. Why she'd chosen the Outlaws over the Avengers she'd never know. To become Hawks mistress--it was a mistake. To go live in her fancy upscale home, with its huge mortgage payments; and the major drugs the Warlord had to deal in order to pay the bills. The cruelty she experienced at Hawks hands.

Crystal pressed her warm womanhood against her lover. Angel was on top of Saundra, fingers going in and out of the brown woman's cunt fast, and Saundra was humping up from underneath to receive the fucking; moaning. Angels clit presses up to Saundra's leg; and she was moving too, getting hot. Silently, Crystal chuckled to herself, as she pressed her big breasts in the negligee into the butches back. If the leader of the Avengers could see her in bed with a black woman... Crystal laughed out loud and covered her mouth. "What?" Angel turned, questioning; eyes heavy lidded, body swimming with the rhythm of passion.

"Nothing baby." Crystal replied.

As if drawn back to the reality of having two women, Angel pulled out of Saundra's pussy, fingers sticky and flavored by pussyjuice, and turned, laying down on the pillow and pulled Crystal over her. Expert hands undid the black negligee, so her beautiful alabaster body was bare. A sweet sight. The butch felt her clit grow hot. It was swollen from having rubbed against Saundra's thigh. Now Crystal was pulling Angel's jockey shorts off down her legs. Angel straightened up; athletic body moved like a panther. Muscles of iron flexed in her thighs. She pulled her teeshirt off over her head, a pair of full breasts

312

bounced out. Saundra moaned at the sight; leaned over the sexy butch, brown skin against white, and began kissing her breasts in long circular sucks & licks of her full mouth. And Angel felt, simultaneously, her woman Crystals lips, red hot on her sex. Curly blond head between her legs; as her own knees raised up, opening her pussy, a pink tongue licking in that fuzzy nest; probing her cunt lips, sucking the nectar of her womanly flower.

Crystal knew how to get Angel ready for hot action.

In moments, the butch was wreathing under the touch of her two lovers. Torso rolling from side to side under Saundra; hips thrusting up to drive her clit into Crystals lips. Flesh to flesh. Both women moaned, wrapping their arms around their particular part of the butches body, chest & and ass.

They moved as one animal, warm, in the embrace and human warmth and female scent. Did what their bodies felt naturally.

Soon, the butch couldn't stand anymore. Was going to shoot her wad into Crystals mouth, or, make it last longer. Both strong hands grabbed her lovers curly head and pushed her away. Her full, hot lips parted from Angels cunt just before the final roller coaster rush of orgasm caught her up, thrusting involuntarily. But in mid hump she stopped, cool air flooding into her crotch in the place Crystal had just vacated. Saundra sat up at the side, round curves of her brown hips and ass, full breasts heavy, wanting for more of the butches fingers, her sucking mouth.

Angel fiercely wanted to feel her clit up against a woman's wet pussy.

At her instructions, the two women lay next to each other, on their backs, knees bent, up, thighs spread, for her to take her pleasure. After questioning them, and receiving a giggling reply, it was Crystal she mounted first. Angel's broad back covered her lover, legs between her legs. Spread her pussy lips with her forefinger and thumb and lowered herself down, so their cunts met, wet and dripping. Angel began to hump fast, her clit pressed into the hot meat of her woman. Her clit & Crystals cunt fit so perfectly together.

313

Strong, raised up on her arms, palms of her hands on the mattress, one on either side of Crystal, their pelvises locked together. Angel's clit rolled around in her woman's open pussy, thrust in and around in her hot full pussy lips, it felt so damn good. Felt her cunt as she rode in her smooth wet pussy, hot, hotter. She rode her like a seesaw horse, up and down, dripping, humping & thrusting, as pleasure mounted in her nerve endings, and thrills shot down her spine. Beneath her, Crystals curly blond head turned & tossed. Her mouth opened in a deep groan; Angel's rubbing clit against her own was bringing her desire to the threshold of orgasm too. Faster Angel humped. Her toes dug into the bed sheets. Her hips buried between Crystals thighs in the rhythm of two familiar lovers who knew each others style well. Crystals arms wrapped around her, drawing her tight. Thrills hot & cold proceeding orgasm shot thru her body, sweat beads glistening on her back, her clit was a fiery sword, her pelvis let go in molten liquid, humping strong, in fluid motion with involuntary lunges as she cum, cunt dripping female ejaculation; their discharge wet the sheets, ass moving up and down between her woman's spread thighs.

Angel lay in Crystals arms until the rapid pounding of her heart slowed.

Candles in the dishes burnt dripping wax down their sides. Making flickering shadows over their cozy den. The heater had given the room a comfortable warmth against the winter night outside.

Then Angel turned to Saundra over the space of the bed. Gazed into her brown eyes. Reached out with white stubbed fingertips to touch gently the woman's orange African hair. Crystal had reached into the nightstand drawer, and came out with a dildo in it's black leather harness decorated with silver studs, and found the lubricant. Soon, after her racing breath grew even, Angel strapped it on, and rolled a condom down over the 8" shaft. Bouncing the full and heavy dick in her hands. Saundra lay back on the sheets, knees spread waiting for her entry. Angel held the dick at it's base, and ran the simulated real-appearing dickhead over and over Saundra's clit. Her brown flower of sex opened, pink and tan. Crystal reached between the two females with the lube, poured it's translucent liquid onto the cock, and Angel worked the cock up and down first over her clit, then down to the opening of her vagina. With each motion, the base of the

314

cock rubbed against her own stiff clit, & she could feel the new stirrings deep within her groin, of desire. Of another orgasm building, as thrills of hot passion came in waves, one upon the end of the first. Angel sat up on her knees between Saundra's brown legs, held her dick & worked it up and down. Saundra's face began to contort, and a moan escaped her lips. The butch knew she was ready. Thrust her dick up into her pussy, driving it in to the hilt, slow, but firm, hard. Her body came to lean over her, and Saundra's arms wrapped around Angel's hips. As butch Angel lay on top of Saundra, she loved the feeling; of being in control. Now thrust her hips in and out with precise thrusts. Saundra gasped as her pussy accepted the hot greased dick; her thighs spread wider and her hips humped up. With long powerful strokes the butch was bringing them both to orgasm. Now it was Crystals turn to watch, her fingers lightly stroked Angels back, increasing pleasure. Angel drove her hips, ramming the dick deep into Saundra's cunt, and Saundra rose up to meet her, with the arc of her spine, so their bellies slapped together, brown & white; hips pumping. Her motion of repeated thrusts of her cockshaft in & out of Saundra's willing pussy rubbed the base of the dick against Angels clit, in growing fire. The two women thrust their hips to each other, fast, faster,

Saundra came; **"OHHHHH AHHHHHH AHHHHHHH UUUUHH AAAAAAOOOO0 AAAHHHHHHEEEEEEEE !"**
While Angel's still fucking, fucking, then Angel cum. Ejaculate, clear liquid ran down the sides of the dildo, over their thighs.

At the prime moment of orgasm, she rocked up and down like a sea saw horse; tail in the air.

Braced up on her arms, tits hanging over Saundra, the butches stomach muscles went taunt, loose, then taunt again. Then it was over.

Angel collapsed down between Saundra's legs, in her embrace; and lay on top breathing hard--having shot her cum for the 2nd time. A double orgasm.

She had ejaculated down the sides of the dildo, over Saundra's cunt. And Angels thighs were sticky with lube & kinky pubic hairs from Saundra's mound were interwoven with her own fair straight ones. Angel, weak with fucking lay half way off Saundra. Panting. Soon gained her breath. Blond hair splayed over her sweat-wet alabaster shoulders. As she lay on her new lover, wearily, felt her wife Crystals hand unbuckle a strap of the harness. Angel stirred, rose up. Her body stuck to Saundra's, then separated. Crystal took the harness loose from her legs, as the butch was too exhausted; got it & the dildo and threw them on the floor. They were finished with it. Angel lay on Saundra a while, feeling her delicious womanly warmth, then, knowing she was heavy, pushed up on her strong arms and flopped down on her belly between the two women. In a moment she was asleep.

The two women looked at each other over the sprawled naked body of their sleeping Angel. Blue eyes met brown. They were satisfied. And laughed like cohorts in a secret play. They talked.

Moon shone in the window. Cold frost laced the panes. Inside, the heater casts its pleasant glow. The quiet time of the late night city outside, below.

The two women gazed across the butch, who was now in a deep sleep. Privately the curly blond thought how she'd just seen her lover's ass humping Saundra, bedsprings creaking, moments past. Crystal had seen her trick with sluts at the sex parties, but this was the first time she'd brought someone home with them.

And Saundra reached out, brown hand touched the side of Crystals face. The blond smiled, she felt wicked--to play with another femme. She reached back in return & touched Saundra's hot flesh with her warm fingertips; caressing her large brown breasts, traced pink painted fingertips down the round curves of her hips.

The slender blond felt she was on an exciting adventure. Arose from her side of the bed, climbed ever the snoring body of Angel, and, as Saundra moved to make room for her, slid her naked body in between the curvaceous dark skinned female and her butch. Their probing fingers touched each other, as they kissed, tongues swirling into each others mouths. After she'd cum, Saundra was big and loose inside, and her cunt was insisting for more. Crystal put two fingers against the nest of kinky pubic hair, and felt into her smooth wetness. Saundra embraced her tight, Crystal could feel her hot breath against her neck, and heard a little sigh; "Ohhhh," as she pushed inside of her soft pussy. Saundra ran her hands over Crystals back caressing her with feathery soft touches, that grew stronger and more passionate, as Crystal pushed harder into her cunt, using 3 fingers now, giving all that the woman's cunt demanded. Crystal didn't suffer from lack of smoothness. Careful, but firm, her hand took the woman hard. Saundra's pussy didn't want to let go of her fingers; it kept sucking them back in, and soon, her whole hand was inside, balled up into a fist, fucking Saundra, whose splintecer muscles tightened around her wrist.

The blond fem fisted the other woman expertly. As Angel slept, warm beside them.

Angel slept thru the whole scene, the pounding and groans and missed the act of love Saundra in return preformed on Crystal— orange hued head between her legs, sucking her off into a mighty orgasm, Crystal's lean torso twisting, and her white ass pounding up and down into the mattress.

In about an hour she awoke. Saw the two women lying together arms around each other. Just heard the tail end of a conversation and; "Uh, I think she's waking up." Accompanied by some giggles.

The blond butch sat up in the bed, covers over her legs. "How long I been asleep?" Rubbed her eyes, then turned to gaze at the two fems. They looked so sweet, so womanly. Immediately she climbed over Saundra, to get in the middle again, between them, to be the star of the show.

"Saundra came twice." Sez Crystal. But not revealing the information about just how she'd come the second time--or with whom.

Angel felt proud, pushed a strand of blond hair off her face. "Most of it's about touching and feeling. That's why I started by massaging her toes." Sez Angel. The two looked at each other & giggled sharing their private secret.

317

Night was cold outside, frost. Homeless huddled in doorways.
100 of them would freeze to death over that long winter in the streets
of the eternal city. if the black woman had been at her home across
town, there'd be no heat. She'd spend the night in a restless chill
under layers and layers of blankets and quilts. She would have been
alone. The building she was in wasn't safe, tenants inside had fallen
prey to criminals; and she slept with a butcher knife under her pillow.
Tonight, with friends it was good. Comfort. Safety. Fun. Peace.
Sexual satisfaction. But in the back of her mind she longed for a
woman of her own. Just like the couple had.

"Hmm." Said Angel looking at Saundra's body in the flickering
candle light.

"What's wrong?" Saundra asks.

"You have no hair on your legs, or arms."

Angel was downed-with pale blond hair. "You're hairless." Sez
the butch.

The 3 of them lay in bed & compared bodies. "I hate these stretch
marks on me." Saundra had discolorations. Lines that were darker
brown then the rest of her skin. Some more yellowish brown. "It's
from loosing weight." Both Crystal and Angel were alabaster
pink/white. They didn't show a mark. But for the butches temporary
bruises & scuffs from the fight last week.

"That's 'cause you got pigment in yer skin." Sez the butch.

"Yes, but she's got such a pretty brown color." Sez Crystal.

They hugged, all three, warm.

It had been a loving experience.

A night of passion.

Candles had burnt to stubs floating in a sea of wax in saucers. Light flickered in the room. It would be day soon.

Next morning, Angel felt on of the world, after her great conquest of fucking two women. 'I'm great!' She thought.

Later, bundled up in coats, they stepped thru a fine layer of new snow to the car.

On the drive to take Saundra home, they began to talk of higher things.

"Faith is something that people keep telling you to have when your broke, and unsuccessful, and don't have a damn thing." Angel said solemnly, gloved hands commanding the wheel as she drove, watching the silvery metallic fish of traffic on the freeway. "Faith is like hope. I like to tell people about evidence. I know God has changed my life, because of an actual miracle that happened to me. Women don't want to hear about faith, or hope, when they've given up; they laugh at you, they spit on the ground and tell you to shut yer face up, and they walk away. But an actual miracle, that interests them."

"I know!" Saundra exclaims, brightly, a chord of gold ripples thru her being, as if strings have been played on a fine instrument. She turns in the seat, from a profile to face Angel. *"I BELIEVE!"* She cries, in a strong voice.

By the time they'd arrived into the miserable ghetto where she lived they three had arranged for their next time together--Saundra was going to take them to her church. A black, predominantly gay church, which had been situated purposefully outside the parameter of the ghetto, where most of its members lived, right near Oils in the semi-gay, semi-artist colony that was springing up there amid the once-desolate warehouse, factory, & cheep poverty housing, in a gaily painted & renovated building.

Chapter Twenty Seven

"How yo' feelen' this mawen' Miss Thang? Ain't got no hangover?
Nothin'? 'Cause yo' was full of it last night!" Came a voice over the
telephone line.

"EBONY! You know I don't drink!" Replied Saundra. Sat up in
bed, pushing her wild orange hair back from her face. Bed jacket,
nightgown and numerous blankets covered her in the ice cold room.

"Aww! Don't fib! Everytime I walked by I seen you liften' a glass
sister!"

"Just one beer! Then I switched to Coca Cola!"

"I saw yo' leave with Angel & Miss Crystal! What yo' all get
into? A late night Outlaws party?"

"Yes."

"Have fun?"

"Yes."

Ebony was a big butch, fat, but big and tall; dike football player
size. Ebony had lived up to her name--having very dark skin. It was
the name her mother had given her at birth as a symbol of pride.

Still preoccupied with the pleasing events of the previous night,
Saundra half listened to the voice as it rambled on & on thru the
phone, supplying 'yes', 'no', or 'I guess' at what seemed the
appropriate time. Her mind still danced with remembrances of the
three of them, their lovemaking. She huddled under the blankets,
goosepimples on her brown flesh. 'I'm gonna dye my hair more
orange.' She's thinking.

"Ain't yo' heard? The crackers are having a ho-down." Ebony
declared with sarcasm, referring to a scion of the Club that enjoyed
Country Western dancing. "Swing yer paaaartner round 'n round wit'
the roll call. That shit. Lou's gonna call."

"Warrior Lou?"

"Yeah, she's a Warlord. The hillbilly, who always be wearen' jeans? The po' one, yo' know, *Country Lou.*"

"A ho down?" 'Saundra's mind went blank. From exhaustion.

"Yeah. That mean the ho is down." Sez Ebony.

"Don't be crude."

"Well, wuz you invited?"

"No." Saundra said.

"See!" Sez Ebony.

"Well I don't *like* Country Western, everybody who knows me knows that!"

"You get my point." Ebony sez.

"Well! I don't know a sister who does--or she's too ashamed to admit it! --With all these judgmental people having opinions about it!"

"See! They leaves us out of everything!" Ebony continues, ignoring the remark.

"Maybe they just don't invite us to things they know we don't like--especially after KT and some of you all made so much fun of the Country songs on the jukebox at the Club--you know what big mouths some of us have got--not mentioning any names, 'Oh, nobody can dance to this! Turn it off! Turn it off!' Those kind of remarks!"

"I'm paying $20 a month membership, I should be able to go to all the events, like everybody else do!"

"Well you ate that much worth of food at the last party Ebony! You sure got your moneys worth back then!" Saundra's mind wandered, as the voice on the other end grew loud; procrastinating.

She had an appointment with the beautician to have her hair straightened & styled, one of her few, small luxuries. Maybe a deeper hue of orange... it blended pretty with her skin color. Right now her hair was done up for sleeping, up in pigtails.

"What yo'doin' today?" Ebony finally wanted to know.

"Getting ready to go to bed."

"GOIN' TO BED! IT'S 4PM IN THE AFTERNOON!"

"Yes. We didn't get much sleep."

"DAMN! DAMN ME! AIN'T I A FOOL! Huh! LATE NIGHT OUTLAWS PARTY HUH! Shit! Them white girls give yo' a good work out honey?"

"Yes." Saundra smiled so big her teeth showed thru full lips with traces of worn off lipstick. "And I've got to get to sleep I have to be fresh for church tomorrow, we're going to the 11oclock service."

"So what's Miss Angel like? I never talk to her much."

"She's as bossy and obnoxious as you! It must be genetic! It runs in butches! We went to the store to buy some food and I saw how she talked to Crystal. 'GET OVER HERE NOW! WHAT BRAND IS THAT? GET THE OTHER BRAND! PUT THAT BACK!" I can't believe it, it's *just like you!* She's a big bulldagger, uh, uh, uh. A big one! *OH! I CAN'T STAND IT!* Crystal is so lucky! OH! But she orders poor Crystal around, and Crystal just goes along with it because they're in love.

'We're going to church tomorrow. I'm taking them with me ."

"Well go ahead girl! Now I see! Now I see! You wasn't out partyin' last night, yo' was out doing missionary work among the non-believers! --Yeah! Uh huh! Miss Thang! ---In the *missionary position!* Well shut my mouth!"

322

"Actually they believe *already*." Saundra spoke after a peeved pause. "That's why they want to go."
to go."

"I AIN'T GOOD ENOUGH FOR YOU !" Ebony howls.

"DON'T START THAT AGAIN, OR I'LL HANG UP!"

"Ok, I'11 be good."

"An' we're gonna pray for Sister Stryker."

"I know yo' likes white women. But try a sistah fo' a change." Ebony cooed. "Yo' know what they say, the blacker the berry, the sweeter the juice."

Chapter Twenty Eight

One evening a few nights later after the raids, a lesbian biker was standing outside the gay boys dungeon in the warehouse district. Some girls from another scion of the gay community were giving a leathersex party; quite a few Outlaws were in attendance.

Snow spun thru the night air, & the moon was waning.

The biker leaned against the brick wall of the entrance,--mind a million miles away. An unmarked police car cruised by. Suddenly it turned on spotlights, throwing beams of light, glaring into her face. A policeman jumps out. **"FREEZE! STAND WHERE YOU ARE! PUT YOUR HANDS UP OVER YOUR HEAD! RAISE 'EM UP NOW!"** And aimed a silver .45 automatic pistol at her.

More law-enforcement vehicles flooded the street, cruisers with red emergency lights spun flashes thru the falling snow against the wall.

A police team entered the doorway with a court order, and met inside with an undercover team of officers that had done their job. As witnesses, & decoys, gathering evidence.

By morning, the Gay Community found this drama had been played out in a dozen sexclubs & taverns of notoriety throughout the city. Oils, which was almost exclusively female had been spared. It was the bold gay males who were the most obvious targets.

50 arrests were made. Players of SM games.

The Tops were charged with assault.

No one outside in the neighborhoods where the dungeons were situated had complained. The slaves didn't complain. It was the cops who made the charges.

Photographs appeared in the daily news, of slaves being held in captive in chains. Some had black hoods over their faces and gags stuffed in their mouths. Some were being whipped. The sight was too appalling for straight society.

All 50 were released on bail, and a trial date was set. To begin in spring. The gay community was in an uproar.

A female biker caught in the raid testified: "He looked like a cop on the edge! --A cop whose loosing his mind! He's like a lots of cops in New York City! He's like a cop trying to redeem his soul!"

Where she'd stood on the street by the dungeon, every squad car in the precinct must have been there. 11 squads, 4 paddy wagons, 3 unmarked police cars and a crowd of passerby's talking & pointing, as 28 police; both in blue uniforms & undercover cops led a file of hooded, chained SM players out of the building onto one section of the snowy sidewalk to put them in the police vans & take them downtown to jail.

"It's voluntary! The slaves choose to be handcuffed! They enjoy being whipped!"

The judge said;   "That's no excuse."

Chapter Twenty Nine

Two figures, a female & a bulldike sat on the bed in Lou's shabby room. The one in bluejeans large, large, rawboned spoke. "I want yuh to be good to the girl. God knows she's a mess."

"What I wanna know," Cookie replied, "is why you don't want me yourself! I wonder why it's so easy for you to give me away to somebody--even if she is sick & almost dead!"

Cookie was perplexed. Face lined in worry. A sad clown; eyebrows plucked & cosmetic pencil-sketched back in, dark, in arches.

Her plump body, obviously femme, a blue workshirt, --one of Lou's, tied under her bosom, showing a bare skin stomach, and bubbly round tits spilling out on top.

"Aw, Cookie." Lou grimaced. Her hands folded behind her head. Feet in construction boots on top of the blanket.

"Why do you wanna get rid of me?"

"I always got girls. I'm a Warlord, remember."

"WELL! I always get butches! I'm a femmy fem! I'm a pretty girl! *Remember!"* She shook her tits under the lowcut plunging neck of the open workshirt. Hands on her hips. Her redlipsticked mouth pouts.

The two lay on top of the bed. It's original broke down mattress had been replaced by a nice one--king size. It wasn't a bad hotel, seedy, but no loud rough people. Few kids. Older people. Quiet. Who cooked dinners on hotplates. A cut above a welfare hotel. Lou could afford it because of the extra income she received under the table, from being a leader in the Outlaws gang.

"Well, if yuh wanna know, George is buying you from me for a few weeks."

"Yeah!? How much you get! How much do I get?"

"I'm using it to fix the car. And get some stuff for the bike. You always need something to pick you up and take you somewhere & you won't use the bus."

"How much Lou!"

"$400. --$200 a week."

'$200! Debbie get's $5,000 to spend a week with somebody! That ain't fair!" She went off on a boat with this man once! She spent a week in a mansion on an estate somewhere with somebody! **It's two weeks out of my life!"**

"Well, yuh ain't doin' nothing with yer life noways." Lou said casually, chewing gum like she'd chewed straws back down home on the farm.

"$400! We should get $4,000!"

When Stryker was ready to get out of the hospital, it was decided Cookie would spend the first few weeks with her--in bed as her love companion. There'd be shifts of bikers taking turns doing shopping & laundry and any nursing necessary. It would save the little dike from having to be put in a nursing home.

"It'll be easy. Yuh already like her, everyone's seen you two together."

"I don't like her as much as you."

"Well, I expect not." Lou drawled. A pleased expression crossed her broad white face. A deep sigh came out of her chest under a bluejeaned shirt. Toes wiggled in the construction boots.

The room was big, and bare. A TV, seldom watched. Racks of his/her clothes, that's all. Wallpaper from a bygone era, & a private bath. It had antique faucets & fixtures from the 1920's. The two

326

dikes spent less time here. More, in the whirlwind of bike runs, parties, other girlfriends houses, Oils, and other gay bars where Lou enjoyed Country Western dancing.

"And don't mess up like the time with that doctor!"

"It wasn't my fault Lou!"

"You bitch! I'll never forget that look on her face when she came back out of the room."

"It was her fault!"

"NAW! All yuh had to say was 'I WANT YER LOVE! GIVE IT TO ME!" --The moment she was gonna cum. And what did you say to her? Huh?" Lou lowered her voice in the dusty echoes of their hotel as footsteps shuffled by outside. "All you could say was, 'COME ON HONEY! HURRY UP! I GOTTA BE DOWNTOWN BY 6PM!!!'"

"BUT I DID HAVE TO GO! AND SHE WAS TAKING TOO LONG! ALL THAT GROANING AND MOANING, AND THEN SHE WOULDN'T COME! IT WAS RIDICULOUS!"

"I'll never forget it." Lou said. "You went out with that old dike, a doctor.--We had it rehearsed. What she wanted, how she wanted yuh to be. She spent $300 on you."

"It was just $250."

Cookie sat up in bed, the perplexed look hadn't left her face. Big tits poked out her half-opened shirt, skirt short & tight over a spread of hips. Long bleach lightened hair fuzzy like a wild horses mane. Then the look of worry turned to happiness. A girlish youth shone in her 40-year old eyes, as Lou pulled Cookie back into her strong arms. Took her in a loving embrace; burrowed her head of short mannish hair under Cookies thick blondish locks, and put a love bite on her neck. "I'm thirsty." Lou said finally. "I'm going out to the store on the corner to get a sparkling apple cider."

"No you aren't! Yer gonna buy a lottery ticket and waste our money! You can't go unless I go!"

Shadows crept over their room. The place was lifeless, but for their heartbeats. If they walked out and left everything it would be of no consequence. It wasn't a home. But, they had each other. Blank walls stared down at them.

"Go ahead and do it. Make the kid feel good... While you're with her I won't have to worry about you."

"Where will you be while I'm with her? Holed up in this hotel room for two weeks?"

"Maybe three weeks."

"AW!"

"I won't be with nobody."

"LIAR!"

"Just think about the $400. I'm gonna buy you a coat, or a dress or maybe even some boots."

"I ain't no hooker Lou!"

"Nope. Yuh ain't."

"That's right! If I was I'd be liven' in a big house up on the hill with Debbie and Rip! Not in this crummy dump!"

"Would I be liven' up there with yuh babe? With my feet kicked up on the dashboard of a luxury Cadillac like Rip's got?"

"'Course."

"Aw, shucks. This place ain't so bad. It's safe. Anyway, when was the last time you spent the night here? Two nights this week? Yer always out."

"All my things are in your closet."

"Yeah, and all over town too."

"At *Ladies* houses. Deb's. Dena's. Frostie's. Stella Dallas! Not *Butches* houses !"

"Yeah, except the few butches we won't mention."

Cookie shook her wild hair, and changed the subject. All them fancy clothes Deb got! All these years I ain't even had my own mail order *catalogue* of fine clothes to *look at!"* Cookie pouted.

"We're so poor, it's cause we're dikes, that's why."

"You could have built yourself up like George did! George worked real jobs!"

"George is 14 years older then me!" Exclaims Lou. I'm 40, she's 53! The steel mills started closing years ago, and the factories have been moving out of town! And that's where she got her start. She built up seniority at the union. Now there's a waiting line at the union hall 8 months long. --Just to get a days work! Things are different now! There ain't a lot of jobs if yer unskilled! I'm too mannish to work in an office!"

"Angel works in an office!"

"Angel is a convicted felon who works breaking the law in an office."

"She flips hamburgers."

"She ain't flippen' hamburgers all the time. She's a telephone con artist too. How do yuh think she can afford to keep her lady in leather skirts and pretty jewelry?"

The couple wrestled on the bed, tossing the plaid cover & pillows about. Lou got on top of Cookie, pinned her down in a typical butch style, to show who was boss. Finally, they lay together side by side, the fem stroking her fingers thru Lou's short brown hair.

Lou's gaze drifted to the cracked dusty ceiling, her mind wandered back over the day's events. "They were fingerprinting today at the welfare office." Lou sez. "A skinny woman, white; she's got on a straight black dress down to her ankles, but with a slit in it, like a nun & a stripper rolled into the same body. She's the Work Fare Coordinator. She's got a doctors degree from college. Welfare's getting' mighty fancy these days. We got fingerprinted and then she spoke to us. She sez; "We don't share this information with any law enforcement agencies." And points her finger up to the ceiling; "We have our *own* law enforcement--right up stairs. And if they catch you they just walk you right across the street to the police station. We have our own District Attorney and Police. We'll call the police to come down the elevator and pick you up & that will be *it.* " They're trying to catch people whose collecting welfare in more then one county at the same time."

Later, as evening shadows fell across the room of their hotel, and lights of advertisements began to blink in the snowy evening outside, while they waited for the taverns to open, Lou did slip out to the grocery store & played the lottery.

Lou had a problem. Gambling made a hole in her pocket. Came back with $1 missing from the $20 which was all they had to enjoy themselves that night--including a restaurant meal. They might need that $1 later. In itself it was small, but in computation with all the rest, over the 25 year span of her adult history, it had trickled away a fortune.

Bluejeaned Lou had felt the teeth of gambling bite down on her. In its wake it leaves poverty. One less dollar to spent on food. Nothing left over for a treat. It causes the inability to spurge on a luxury item--it *is* the luxury. It leaves empty pockets.

As of late, her gambling fever had quelled. Been 3 years since Lou'd been to a racetrack, and lost her money on worthless nags. At times old pals would see her, remember, and ask, 'Yuh' been out to the track?' And Lou would just shake her head, no. But this lottery was tempting. It was available everywhere, & cheep. It was a momentary high that made the lesbian woman feel ten feet tall.

A familiar story of women dikes like her who wanted to be celebrated as heroes. Who wanted to BE somebody.

And who was depressed because she felt small.

"You looked so miserable, you were pouting. You looked like you were mad when you were walking down the street. Are you mad at me?" Cookie had watched her butch from out the hotel window as she went to the store.

"Naw. 'I have thoughts when I'm out alone in the street at night. Wild thoughts. I see the lights of fancy places. I see the strip joints where there's pretty women... And I think about buyen' a long fine car, and runnen' away somewhere and spending my life in luxury; in hotels with swimming pools, and fine restaurants & fucken' a lot of partygirls, a different one for my every mood, in my bed every night. But I gotta get a lot of money first. And I look down at my loosing lottery ticket and tear it up, and then I feel like nobody again. Like I'm two feet tall."

Cookie & Lou had been thru a lot together.

Once the couple'd had a ferocious fight. Blows had been struck, & blood spilt on the sheets. Lou'd been drinking a lot more in those days. She passed out, when she awoke and with a shaky hand felt over to Cookie's side of the bed, it was empty. She was gone. 'So soon she leaves me. Ain't even here 3 days and one fight and she leaves me. I'm gonna go in the kitchen and get a shot of bourbon, take 2 Seconal pills, go down to the bank & withdraw my last $200; and go find a lady somewhere--there's one out here in the streets walking, looking, just like how I met Cookie. I'll take her home with me, I don't care if she's 15 or 50. We'll ball. We'll eat take-out Chinese food & drink more bourbon, then take a taxi to the track & bet on the Daily Double & the Exacta. I'll do all this so I won't get my gun and kill myself instead.' Finally, Lou had drug herself out of bed, stormed into the kitchen for whiskey--and **WOW!** There is a

331

note propped upon the table next to the sugar bowl written in huge child-scrawl by the illiterate Cookie:

BABY! I got up erley. I promis yuu I wont be lazey so yuu wont hav to beet me no mor. I kno it waz for my own gud. I gon fine a job. I gon go to ech restrunt in this town un till I git a waterest job. Hony I love yuu. Tank yuu for beeten my ass and shown me rite frum wrong. I be bak layter.
Yur Loveng Lady COOKIE

Grey wall cracks meandered in a puzzle-jumble and warped baseboard scuffed by time were the box that contained the two women.

Nestled in Lou's arms; the plaid bedspread pulled over them, Cookie asked about the raid. Lou's face got serious. Ran stubby fingers thru her hair. Then replied in this manner; "On the farm, it was my job to kill chickens. There was these 2 roosters they went after a hen. Her legs had gone weak & she couldn't escape. And they were out in the barnyard taking turns fucking her into the mud. I wuz mad and took them two by the neck and yanked 'em out of there, got my hatchet, chopped off their heads and threw 'em to the dogs. The dogs smelled the blood and tore them two roosters apart. They were brothers, home grown, they banded together. We wuz gonna fatten' 'em up, I was suppose to save 'em 'till they got some meat on their bones. They wuz worthless like they wuz---scrawny & young, no meat on 'em. And it was a waste. Our family was hungry. They were just bones & feathers. The dogs ate everything but the claws and the beak. That's how I think about those guys out there, who do stuff to women, they're worthless, they're all feathers & bones. They ain't good for nothing.

Pigs are smart, cows are smart. Sheep are stupid. & Chickens are brainless. Ducks are very smart. You can train a duck to sit on a chair and eat dinner off a plate, I know 'cause I had a brother who did that. He kept a duck as a pet. Now, likewise, there's nothing more stupid and ornery and mule headed as a humanbeing. That's why they got gas chambers & electric chairs to get rid of 'em, just like you do with livestock, --with a hatchet. You keep bulls in a pen, same reason you gotta keep some folks in jails. They had it coming, at least all the guys my team took. I scoped 'em out good first. They were all worth less then shit.   Not just harmless wino's & fools, but bad news jerks too mean to live."

Night overtook the room. Cars rode by in the street outside playing music; leaving a few notes behind to pronounce themselves, before disappearing into air. Noise of a toilet flushing on the floor above.

Before the two lesbians left to go hang out at Oils they made love.

Cookies bleached hair streamed over her shoulders & beyond, wing-like. Knelt at the side of the bed as Lou stood up over her, naked. Cookies head went between the butches thighs, face tipped up into that nest of pubic hair. Cookies pink tongue probed into the wetness of Lou's cunt.

She wrapped her pretty arms jangling bracelets around her bulldike lovers thighs, pulling his/her hot cunt full into her red lips & licked the clit with the tip of her tongue, while sucking simultaneously; producing fire of growing passion. Back and forth her tongue licked, while sucking Lou's clit, drawing it into her mouth, giving expert head.

Lou thrust her thighs forward into that hot mouth, in hungry jerks, jacking her clit up & down in it. Thrills of fire-hot desire rushed up & down her spine, pounding down in her groin. When Lou couldn't stand anymore, & was about to give up her cum, in a juicy, orgiastic release, she shoved Cookie away. Obediently the fem got up off her knees, got up on the bed & lay on her back.

Cookie had a big girth. Really spread her thighs wide. --Acquired from straddling all those motorcycles; arms wrapped around the leather backs of their drivers, and surrendering her love to all those butches, a history-long parade of them, arms wrapped around their naked shoulders as their lower parts moved together, and they drove her down into the mattress.

"Come on, lick my neck!" Gasped Cookie.

333

Lou got on top, wiggled into place, so her clit met Cookies wet cunt.

"Do my neck!"

Lou paused to run her tongue up and down the side of Cookies neck as the woman hollered in pleasure.

Then they screwed. With the conformability of old lovers who are familiar with each others style. Wet juices mixing in cunt to cunt grinding action.

Lou held herself back, until she felt Cookie was ready, and then both were cuming, moving, squirming, pelvis thrusting as they let go, their loins melting into one.

Chapter Thirty

Angel awoke, blond hair tousled, in a pair of rumpled pajamas, with red & white stripes. Lay, blue eyes registering their room around her; groping to where she had wandered in her dreams.

Alarm rings on the bedside stand. Soon the couple is dressing, preparing to drive over to Saundra's, have breakfast at a restaurant & then go to church.

It's miserable. It's cold, and it's wet. It's winter.

God was so invisible & so far.

'All this illegal stuff. I been doing it all my life.' Angel thinks to herself, as she zip's up the back of Crystals leather mini skirt. The butch wore black leather of course, but it was strange, the one place she dared not wear her cleric collar was the church they were going to attend; so she wore just the black shirt instead. Thoughts pulsed thru her mind. 'I got into it from the beginning because I didn't want to work, I was lazy. Society made it easy to be a criminal, --to justify my actions; because they wouldn't accept me being gay.' Crystal was dressed, now. Pert, her reflection gazed back; legs crossed, she sat in the mirror teasing out locks of her curly blond hair. A silver necklace glittered on her bare chest, above the leather top which plunged to show much of her bosom. An expensive leather jacket completed her outfit. 'Women won't go with you if your broke. Crystal begs me to work this job at the donut shop and quit the phony police scam, but if I'd been poor and lived in a rundown place & couldn't afford a motorcycle & was flippen' burgers when I met her would she have been attracted to me? Money does strange things to people. It makes you look nice, it makes you popular. I gotta start all over again at this salary, on the bottom rung. I couldn't make our bills alone. I'll need her income too, so I won't be independent. It's hard, being a cook. Rush hour is hell. That's the time I could run away and just leave them redfaced customers holleren' at me, 5 deep across the counter. Eunice, the manager she likes me a lot, because she says the other employees steal and they hate the job. The reason I don't steal is 'cause I'm stealen' more at my job as a scam artist and I don't need to steal from her. And I like the job ok because I only gotta work there part time, not full time goin' crazy like the other employees. Eunice says I should have her position if she ever leaves and they send her to work at another store'.

The trio had a delicious breakfast of ham, eggs, toast, waffles, bacon, orange juice, tea, coffee & milk. In a counter-culture café surrounded by weird people like themselves. Artists, gays, interracial couples, and freethinkers.

The church was situated outside of the African American ghetto. They had had to abandon their homeland and start the ministry instead in the new twilight zone, ozworld of the industrial landscape of yuppies renovating houses, and gays; that was a place of more education and consequently greater toleration. It was a wise move. The black female minister was a prophet without honor in her own country. The black religious sphere was so narrow minded it barely tolerated a woman pastor, --much less a lesbian.

A few heads turned in their pews inside the primarily all black gay church to see Saundra that Sunday morning, as she walked down the center aisle in her leathers, flanked by two visitors; leatherdikes jangling chains & marching in a fast clip in a staccato of boot heels; and were shown to their seats by a butch usherette.

Saundra wore a tasteful long leather skirt, black leather boots, & a jacket, --of an imitation material resembling leather. A broach sparkled as diamonds over her heart; gleaned from a thriftshop. Dark red lipstick blended with the reddish tone of her brown skin. The two visitors were hard, obvious motorcycle dikes. Black leather, chaps, chaps, skirt, silver zipfront jackets, caps on top of yellow-blond hair contrasting vividly to their outfits.

It was a unique church for black society, in that the female minister had built up a congregation that was 95% percent sissies, studs & he/she's. Plus most of the female studs wore trousers. A great no-no to the black ecumenical customs of that era. Angel & Crystal's pink faces looked around them at the ocean of black, brown & tan faces, here in the inner city; where the women are strong and the men are pretty; and they felt right at home. They sat; Angels leathered arm around Crystal, in the pew.

A Deacon, a black sister with shiny tight curly hair went about singing; ***"PRAISE THE LORD !"*** into every microphone--testing them to make sure they worked so that later during the service the **Hallelujah's** could roll out unencumbered.

In an antechamber behind the pulpit, the Minister was having a fit.--A Holy Fit. The Minster was a black dike, heavy bodied from good eating; wore her hair in a crew cut; decked in expensive rings which glittered on each finger. She was struggling to squeeze her plump body into the Liturgical Robes. Citing scriptures in a loud voice as she heard a seam pop open.

Angel was to say later, after the experience, in her Thank You to Saundra. "I really can't be a part of your church, 'cause your Minister is calling God a father, and She ain't. It's very revolutionary, being in a homosexual church, and all... All............ those ..... lesbians.... and sissies who are black and tan... it's beautiful. We'll probably come back to visit a lot. I love the singing & when they get up and dance in the Holy Ghost. And the preaching is really mighty. But I got my own ministry.

I look at God as a Woman, more. Definitely not a man. And this is important to me. In fact, wither God is anything or not that's a sexual role, means very little. What's vital is that this brainwashing about men being superior--when it's a lie, has got to stop. The center of the earth is female, and to me God is a Mother God. That's vital to me, and I guess it will be to the women I'm trying to reach."

For about an hour the Preacher shouted, sang & inspired souls to spiritual highs. She waved her arms in the air, flowing robes billowed, her rings sparkled, as did her eyes; **"GOD CAN MAKE THE BLIND SEE AND THE LAME WALK! IT'S THE SAME TODAY AS IT WAS YESTERYEAR!** *ALL THINGS WILL BE UNCOVERED FOR THOSE WHO ASK!"*

The pews rocked. Sissies & studs jumping up and down for Jesus. Angel felt the ache in her soul be removed, in it's place a wild freedom of inspiration, from true knowledge of a real God, a real Heaven, a real Miracle Place that, like molten lava was active, and working thru her life. It was quite a bit like the massive Cum-Togethers they gave at the Club; --the part with everybody jumping up & down in the pews, united as one, with tears streaming down their cheeks.

The two blond visitors in black leather & chains in the 3rd row, pink glowing faces, clapped wildly out-of-time to the music. 'Going forward now, I felt I was chained to a horsedrawn chariot of my choosing. And I wouldn't let go--not for the world. Not for all it's gold & powers. It was spirit I was holding on to. No longer flesh. Something great to believe in. Higher then club Oils and it's members. Better then the church and it's congregation where we were.--Something not of human flesh, but Spirit. I wanted to go with it. Nothing could stand behind me & pull me back. Not this, or that to tempt me, to turn me aside.'

Chapter Thirty One

A large grey cloud with a platinum white edge towered in the sky like the ghost of the later day Saints.

A bright dazzling sky--silver.

All those hateful faces in the street; mean straights, violent men, that they must pass to get there; those, totally non-gay and adverse to it. Those humans from all different ethnic groups, but none of them artists. No kindness. No free souls.

They had a common enemy who at best would exclude them, and at worst would do them bodily harm.

The dikes arrived from all parts of the city.

Guests came, even incognito, some of the Avengers, (their hated rival gang), whose feelings towards the Outlaws were more neutral, & who loved a party.

Streamers decked 'the front of Oils, pink & blue & yellow, and clusters of balloons bobbed in the chilly winter scene.

BENEFIT PARTY FOR OUTLAW MEMBER STRYKER was painted on a huge sign. The little dike was not present, still recovering from her battle wounds.

An incident happened in the area where women were parking to get in the club.

For any major events, the redbrick street outside Oils would become congested with motorcycles, cars, & trucks. Unlike the members of the biker club who primarily drove cycles, a lot of guests drove cars which took up more room. By the time the party music had begun to blast into the air, partygoers would have to park further and further away, as much as 5 blocks down, just to find a space.

A trio of lady bikers was negotiating the High Damn Road towards Oils. A truck they passed on the Road contained four ugly, violent passengers. A grizzly tall white giant, gaunt, leaned out of the cab of the truck, ends of his frayed jeans jacket flapping in the wind and yelled at the helmutless bikers as they drove by: **"AW BITCH I KIN DRIVE THAT CYCLE BETTER THEN YOU CAN!"**

The rest, ugly redneck hoodlums hooted and jeered at them. **"YOU CAN'T DRIVE THAT CYCLE WORTH SHIT! GODDAMN! YER PROBABLY ON THE RAG!"**

"ARE YOU LADIES OR WHAT!"

The last dike in the pack tipped her face over her shoulder and yelled at the snaggle tooth grizzled beard bums: *"AW GO FUCK YOURSELF YUH LOUSY REDHEAD OKIE NECKER!"*

And she made them eat the dust of her spinning tires.

But the hoodlums were following the same route, and when they caught up to them at the red traffic signal, the loud berating began again.

At the switch of the light to green, the pack took off down the damn road headed into the city streets, the last biker flipped them the **F.U.C.K. Y.O.U!** sign, she popped the clutch, shifted it into gear, let out the throttle and accelerated to a speed where she thought her hair was leaving her head, but here the fools came right behind her. They were about ten blocks from the club.

A good thing about George was her sense of justice and fair play. It just so happened she had come out of the tavern to go to her van which was parked right outside, since, as Leader a place was reserved for her. They'd been there getting the party set up, since early afternoon. With a couple of teen bikers in tow she had opened up the van's back door to pull out some cases of soda pop when a dike ran into the bar on short fat legs and screams *"SOME WOMEN ARE BEING ATTACKED DOWN THE BLOCK!"*

Without a word, Daddy George put her motorcycle booted foot up on the lip of the van, with huge muscled arms in leather pulled herself inside, stormed thru the lavish interior, which violently shook it's bucket seats, rattling tables; fell to the floor with a grunt, yanked up a secret panel from under the carpeting and produced a automatic rifle. Threw a blanket over it as camouflage, jumped back out of the van, and began to run, joining the crowd.

Racing cycles thru the streets towards the sanctuary of the lesbian tavern, they'd picked up a trailer. The women had dismounted, & huddled in a group for defense, knives drawn, fearfully watching as the wild-eyed criminal men had skidded to a stop, flung open the doors of their truck and lurched out, leers on their grizzled faces & hate in their hearts, preparing to give them trouble.

A gang of dikes spills out of Oils, and without waiting to confer about what to do, they run down to save the women from being beaten. As she ran after them the chains over George's left shoulder slapped & clanked. In a parking area blocks away from the club they find the four women huddled between some cars and a factory wall; only two are armed with knives which they wave in front of them. The grizzly ape-males have left their pickup truck and surrounded them taunting & jeering, but afraid to come too close because of the steel razor sharp blades which the women brandish, threatening.

The gang of dikes numbers over 20, and stragglers are rushing out of the mouth of the club to join them. The crowd of women stretches out over several long streets; and when they arrive at the scene the male attackers look around to see an ever-coming sea of women charging them. They leave off their harassment and rush back towards their truck, but the gangs of women overtake them. Tackle one on the curb and knock him down on his ass. Two others are leapt upon and many small hands grab their ragged clothes and punch & strike, bringing them down also. One man makes it back to the truck, guns up the motor, but as he shifts into reverse ready to escape, by driving into the crowd of women to get out of the metal trap of cars & trucks parked around him, Daddy George runs up, puffing for breath, spit flying from her mouth, breathlessly the bulldike yanks the blanket off her rifle with fat fingers, struggles thru the crowd of females to get a clear shot, and there as the man shifts the gear and jolts backwards she breaks thru the front line blasting the bottom of his truck full of bullet holes, crippling its tires. The horrified man leaps out the passenger door,--into a crowd of raging women. The gang punches and kicks the man. Jubilation. The outside streets ring with victorious yells. After beating them black, blue & bloody, the men are allowed to crawl back into their truck. Their pimply and whiskered scared faces no longer snarl; their expressions just reflect terror. Their macho is gone. They are reduced to being just human. Scared for their lives.

Like themselves, the truck is crippled, but the men drive it anyway; limping and flopping down the streets of the factory district with a gang of females hollering curses & throwing bottles at them. **BANG! CRASH!**

When the scene clears, the dikes back off; stand strong in their boots. A mans bloodied figure lies in the sidewalk. Three dikes pull his limp body up off the pavement, drape his arms over their shoulders and drag him into a car. "DUMP THE STUPID PIG DOWN BY OUTLOOK DRIVE IN THE WOODS. IF HE WAKES UP BEFORE YUH GET THERE, KNOCK HIM OUT AGAIN!"

Of the whole gang, Daddy George was not the most decent, not even the most brave. But had elements of these qualities, and also had charity, and some wisdom, and unlike many of her contemporaries who were queer but not being queer; who'd slid by on the sly, dikes but not dikes, existing on the borders of straight society, George was a bulldike who'd lived the life.

George was now 53 years of age. A bulldike female she got periods, although a lighter flow then when she was young. Inside Oils the gay music pounded. Wild lights danced. And gay girls played. From her efforts, George felt dizzy. Mind in a daze. Felt her body moving in slow-motion across the dancefloor inside it's encasement of leather. Bloodclots and crimson menstrual blood now soaked into a pad between her huge thighs. Very tired, and forgetful. George wanted to rest & to be babied, but the party must go on. The pill she was taking now, washed down with a strawberry soda pop would take away the pain of cramps. And she'd get high on sheer hormones.

George had a Lion heart.

Lights were dimmed inside the clubhouse. Long haired women laughed, hugged, & jumped up and down. Platters of food sat on the tables by the wall, and on the bar. At $10 per head, the club would benefit, and Stryker would have her needs taken care of.

Rip, George, Georgina, Ross and Kelly sat at the bar. With them was the Queens fairy fag friend Selby.

They were having a discussion about their cats.

The immense woman was directing the benefit, a tiara sparkled on the crest of her black hair curled in ringlets, she'd paused to take a breather, & sit on a barstool & join her older friends. "It's not a *She*, *He's* a neutered male." The Queen is saying.

"Oh well, what the hell." Replies the grey haired proprietor Kelly. "Everybody's changing their sex these days anyway."

Selby was a fag to his eye teeth. Tho, being from an older generation & conservative he wore a mans suit, in the old fashion way. --It did show flowery lace cuffs, and collar. His hair was styled very feminine, and his limp wrists and hands with manicured nails & bedecked with jewels and his ultra feminine body language marked him as a total fag.

Rip's pockmarked face turns to her pal George, says in a low droll, "Just got the heater in my Cadillac fixed. Now it works just like it always did. And it should. It's a Cad. We only drive the best. Most everything else on the road's a piece of shit."

The incessant beat of the music was like humanbeings impatient to walk on the moon. In engineer boots they stomped around Oils in black leathers, and cap brims pointed in the direction they were going.

Of course dikes throughout the tavern wore black mainly. And the old owner Kelly recounted a tale to the group of older dikes & fags seated beside her. She talked in a confidential tone.

"Well, yuh know one time, there was this foreigner come to visit, a some such somebody, a big muckety muck from a third world country. Somebody not even gay, but who was visiting *everywhere,* and seeing *everything,* 'cause there was a big political deal in town... Well she's decked out in tribal robes like a rainbow, and got bells on & God only knows what. "Well," She sez; "Well..." ---and she's got

342

this crisp English accent, yuh know, how the educated ones talk? "Well, now I know it est not such a terrible thing." Yuh see that girl over there?" Kelly indicated with a gnarled hand one of the shaved head young bikers bounding around with youthful enthusiasm. "Well the Dignitary had asked what happened to her."

"'It's just a fashion statement.' Somebody tells her.

"Well, dis is a different land." She says. "You know, in my land, people do dat when somebody *die*. You know. Dey do dat when dey mother *die*, or when dey sister *die*, or somebody *die*. Dey shave dere head. See, she's shaved her head! And dat one, wearing the black! And dat one also wearing de black! So many wearing de black!"

"A lot of people do that here in America!" Says somebody.

"Dat is terrible!" Sez this Dignitary. "Why she done it?" She asks, about the woman. So they tell her, it's a style, a fashion, a trend.

"Well, it's OK, we're in a different land; OK, she's cool. I will just remind myself. Because, well, in y land, dey shave dere head, den dey put a scarf over it. Dey are in mourning! De wears de black! Oh! I'm thinking! So many mourning! Has it been a disaster in your country?"

And Kelly's laughing, and George & Rip are howling with laughter at Kelly's impersonation of the foreigner. Selby flounces a lacy wrist and titters behind his lacy handkerchief; while Queen Georgina's bulk ripples in gasps of mirth. Ross is sputtering with laughs, and droll Kelly herself even cracks a smile at the reminiscence.

A band of merry dikes was rollicking, having a Longest Tongue Contest, measuring with,--for germ control, -- a tape measure dipped in liquor.

A voice cut thru the air protesting in tremuletto, "but I'm not **into** that kinky stuff! I'm just into **motorcycles!** I'm very clean cut! I'm not into this kinky business!"

"CITY CYCLE! WING NUT CAPITOL OF THE WORLD! YER' SPINNING OUTTA CONTROL!" --Roars Lady Jane.

"Has George got high blood pressure?" Whispers Ross to Kelly. "She's acting dizzy."

"Might have had too much to drink."

No, it was her monthly period. George felt woozy. The lines of grim reality and euphoria merged. Felt disorientated, like the world was falling out of orbit; its polar axes melting down, its right become left, and east become west. Dikes dancing past, music system pumping tunes; it all blended into one.

The faint fuzz of a moustache showed on her sweaty upper lip. Her epaulets glistened with chains. She wore the title PRESIDENT OUTLAWS MOTORCYCLE CLUB on the silver pin on her chest.

Grim faced biker butches had a discussion. "There's this little device, it removes the valve stem from tires, so the tires go flat." The others nod, serious. "We tiptoed around and removed the valve stems from 10 different choppers and a couple of their cars; 'n we left the little rubber seal in place, so yuh can't tell which ones we hit." Referring to a raid on the Avengers in bygone times.

Suddenly, thru the blue & pink haze and party tinsel, the Leader hears a sound. An audience crying **"PUSSY! PUSSY! PUSSY!"** At the top of their lungs. Some female stood on top of the bar, George caught a glimpse of pink flesh, nearly nude, in only a silver bra & G-string, ignored it and went back to the conversation of her wife & friends where she sat.

Selby's lean male body was draped over the bar. He wore female undies, pink, under his perfumed suit, and lacy shirt. He was a polite sissy of a gentlemanly era. Angular, body hair of a male, but an infinitesimal quality that was so feminine it transcended his sex. The dignity of a lady with which he carried himself. A quiet, sustained dignity.

"I've lived a hard life I must confess, I've been a mean woman." He was saying to his old friend Georgina. "Now that I see it might be over, I've had a lot of thoughts, as you can well imagine. I look to the mirror, --in it is a graying, aging, slightly matronly older woman, (well we can dream, can't we?)" Selby sat next to the Queen; tossed his head, flicking his styled hair over his neck. "I see this aging woman, look back at me. Each morning is a confession. I go to the graveyard every week or so, find where her home is to be and put flowers on her place, and just sit there all day and dream. I'm sure there is life after death, but I do want a nice grave spot. –Right by the rest of the family, by the mausoleum. I do so want her to rest in peace." Selby flipped his manicured hand, finger nails painted with just a hint of pink mixed into the clear polish. –Clear, which was still acceptable for a cultured gentleman. Around them the wild din of dikes in punk hair and leathers grew to a frenzy. "For *years* I've always claimed that you've been more like family or an adopted *(older)* sister Georgina, because I certainly do consider you to be a Grand Humanbeing and a very close Dear Friend. Why should we feel like outcasts, or be neglected thru no sins of our own in this world which dishonors us for our homosexuality? We must carry on with our lives. I care about you and our friendship. It's quite possible that I will meet our Maker soon, and I wish not to have that sin on my soul.--Guilt. Over something I've never chosen, but which was handed to me before birth. Probably by that same Creator. It's quite possible that I might die. I feel sympathy for this member of yours, this lesbian that your wonderful Benefit Party is sponsoring. It's quite possible that she might have died on the operating table during the abdominal surgery. Possible death on the table is a distinct possibility. How different it is for the young! At least I can say I've lived a long life. I'm no spring chicken. Dearest Georgina, if I do succumb to this horrible malady, this AIDS virus, I do hope for a visit in hospital from my very best friend. Can I hope for one visit a day? I reverently hope this wish won't seem irresponsible or immature."

The flowery Selby and his lifelong companion Spencer, a short, flaccid straight appearing man who wore a business suit had dined with Marlin & his fag escort Leslie at a fine restaurant, then had attended the ballet. Now the quartet had wound up at the Outlaws clubhouse to finish of their evening with Georgina & George, having been driven there by a chauffer in a limonene. Here they sat, in luxurious fur lined coats, expensive watches & male jewelry, $500 silk suits, amidst the bawdy, roaring, drink guzzling, food-throwing lesbian queers. This was a party with numerous guests, including men & was expanding the coffers of their treasury with the purpose of aiding it's members-in trouble in the future.

At the far end of the bar where it curved into the back, the audience was crying: **"PUSSY! PUSSY! PUSSY!"** So finally, the inquisitive George got up off the barstool & like a lumbering bear pushed herself a path thru the crowd to see. A probe of lights illuminated a silvery/pink figure light as a cloud standing on the bar above the biker women's heads. She caught a glimpse, could see it was a man.-- George had been around long enough to know a transvestite, or so she thought. She/he was tall, lanky, posing in a pair of stockings, bra, & G string. Then rolled down one stocking & tossed it into the crowd of screaming, applauding women. The dikes seemed to know this person--calling her by name, clapping their hands in time to the music, and 'OOOOHHHing' and 'AHHHHing!'to her gyrations, loudly urging her to **"TAKE IT OFF!"** --That last vestige of silvery costume, the G string; for the bra too had been hurled away to show budding small hormone-induced tits, by a scrawny arm in which tendons were pronounced, and hands too big to be a biological female. Several dikes held their hands over their eyes, afraid to look if he/she did.

George's biker cap brim could be observed as it zig zagged over the crowd of shorter women, cap with a silver chain around it, eagle's wings, and dotted with silver studs. Pointing directly at this person who was dancing on top of the bar, the cap came to a stop. The Leader gazed up--just in time to see the G string come off. Instantly the pink figure was nude, revealing pubic hair and no dick. "He's probably got it tucked back between his legs." George muttered. Pissed. Oils was a women's club, not a male strip joint. The performer threw her G string out into the audience and shook her hips to the right, and to the left with Vengeance. **"PUSSY! PUSSY! PUSSY!"** They screamed back at her.

Then the transsexual lifted one leg and they caught a glimpse of furry wet pussy--it was the real deal. She got down on the stage on her skinny ass, spread her legs and showed it. A brand new cunt. A

346

perfect pussy. The crowd cheered. Women jostled George; dikes in biker gear shouted, excited. One was saying, "It's our first member who's a sex change into a female." The club was welcoming her. George was amazed. Things were happening fast, she could barely keep track--maybe it was the pill, or the affects of hormones, or the brief brush with violence outside Oils several hours ago... Or too much work preparing for the Benefit… A dike was yelling emphatically; "AS LONG AS IT LOOKS LIKE THE REAL THING AND FEELS LIKE THE REAL THING, I'LL FUCK IT." Another testifies, "I wouldn't fuck a sexchange that's no good." So immediately a brawl broke out.

When a weary George returned to her red vinyl barstool; Selby was looking miffed. Brushed the wave ripples of his elegant grey hair back with a pale, fluttery hand. Aquiline profile raised a notch higher into the air with a delicate pride. He was old. He was a mess. His T cell count was down. He was due to insert a suppository into his rectum as needed for anal bleeding. Lean, silvery haired, the 60 year old fairy male looked thru the crowd at the young transsexual star with a kind of bitterness. He'd never had such an opportunity in his youth. But also, he had an inner serenity of being as much a gentile lady of that world as he could have been.

Georgina swivels a degree on her barstool, turning to look at George; ample, white face powdered & painted red with rouge & lipstick. "How does my face look Georgie ?"

The Leader stared at her blankly.

"I'm serious!"

"It looks fatter."

"Fatter???"

"Well what do you want me to say!" Growled the beefy George.

"How does my face *look!* Do my eyes look more pronounced? Do I look like I'm wearing make up?" Queried Georgina.

347

"What do yuh want your face to look like?"

"I'm tryin' out different things.... Not as many blemishes? ... Hah? …How does my eyebrows look?"

"FINE!"

"Do they look darker?"

". . . . ."

"ANSWER MY QUESTION GEORGIE!"

"………."

Georgina produced some cosmetics from a tiny jeweled purse, dabbed on rouge & made a few strokes of eyebrow pencil. "HOW DOES MY FACE LOOK NOW!!"

"ASK SELBY! HE KNOWS MORE ABOUT IT THEN I DO!"

Then George turns on her creaking barstool to Rip; the he/she whose lanky form is stretched out, relaxing, boots planted on the silver bar rail. "Another thing about ladies, they always get in the mirror ahead of you. Yuh can't see if yer' hair is combed right!"

Then memories drift, George is back at the Union Hiring hall--15 years ago. Makes a downward motion of her heavy hand. "Yeah, this gal, she looks as hard and mannish as I do--then she puts on two little earrings in her earlobes & thinks she's passen' herself off as a straight woman. **Sheeeesh!** One place I worked, they had nothing but Spanish down there. They called me El Gordo..." And Georgina butts her head in, and talks:

"We were so poor then, walking and taking the bus. That's all I remember, the walking. We'd go to a party to be with other gay kids, no money for a cab. It was a nightmare. Then George got her first big job carrying steel at the steel yard, and then we rode in cabs. They were nice. Comfortable. We got more and more money."

348

Then Georgina turns to her left & strikes up her conversation with Selby. George tells Rip; "Yuh know she's a big woman. The only way to stop her would be to smash her, 'n I love her, so I can't." The Leader recalled; "many times we were so poor. A young gay couple buying our first house together, with $600 monthly mortgage payments, and I only took home $800 from the Union job, and her earning $200 a week as a dancer--when she worked." George thought about the places, some of the girls weren't refined. She'd put tips in the strippers little G strings and try to touch their nasty little cunts. And would have liked to pull them down off the stage and fingerfuck them & suck them good. And she's saying; "but Georgina would have castrated me right there, with that little knife she carries." Hormones raced thru her body, gave The Leader total recall. She saw in her minds-eye the ruined face of a hooker who'd worked the streets and had met Deb in a bar and wanted to work for Rip. Like a submerged ship it rose up out of the sea of memory. "Remember that wench yuh had?"

"Yeah. She lived at the house and caused more trouble then she was worth."

For a while George had seen them, all three together at the club. "What happened to her?"

"Some man had beat her face in."

"I remember something like that." -- Even then George had wanted to Do Something about it. "When she was working for you?"

"Hell no. She wasn't with us then. It was before we met. And she wasn't working. No, she was just minding her own business." George made a growling sound, and turned back to her strawberry pop and a plate of food which Georgina had set before her on the bar. When she saw women who'd suffered like that, she was glad, glad they'd done something, tho it wasn't enough.

The sound system pumped out music with a strong beat.

George made her rounds, overseeing the Benefit; black leather jacket & pants; at 6' 2" cut quite a figure in the clubhouse. At 350 pounds was awesome. The dikes looked to her for guidance & leadership.

George thought, 'Life's like a game of chess, it can be compared repeatedly. When yer' beginning, yuh don't realize it's a game of win or loose & strategy & luck. Yuh don't realize every move yuh make may cost you.--At the start yuh have a lot of options and chess pieces and *time*. Then, yuh got less and less chess pieces, and less and less time. So yuh got to do what you got to do! Do it now! One day, yer' life's over--yuh see it. The Game's ending....

She just wanted-to ride. **RRRRRRRRRRRRMMMMMMM!** On her bike. But times like these was drawn into racism, arguments about persons of color in their club. Into sexism, with men who were changing into women wanting to join. And old members who'd been female now shooting hormones & growing beards. Vendettas against lawless men.... She just wanted to ride her cycle, but it seemed all this baggage of the heart had come along with the territory...... To feel the wind thru her short masculine hair, and be The Leader. Play life's scene as a Dominate. Just as she had in the boys club of her childhood. 'I could always depend on the boys. Girls were mostly confined to the house; trapped by their mothers doing girl work. They were slaves. Ironing, cleaning, helping to cook dinner. The boys were free..... Unless they were Outlaw girls with no mothers to supervise them. Moms too sick, or old. Then they were free too.'

Chapter Thirty Two

It was spring.- First green shoots appearing under blankets of wet dead leaves turned to mulch. Cranes appeared everywhere in the City as they uprooted buildings in ceaseless destruction & reconstruction.

Stryker sat up & stared into a new future from her special hospital bed, they'd rented for her room, back in her hotel. She was healing from the abdominal surgery caused by the self-inflicted gunshot wound.

Members of the gang were with her continuously, or she'd have had to go into a convalescent home for the duration. –A depressing grey barracks populated by ancient dying elder humanbeings who society has all but forgotten and shoved away under a blanket, out of sight. The Indian, Comancho sat by her bed and told her of the plans to move her & some homeless members in to a commune together. To set up a house for them, that the club would rent, maybe even purchase, with pooled resources. "It's adopt a Jew." Stryker said feebly from her bed. "Adopt a Jew fer' Jesus." And Angel smiled.

8 flights down on the street; a woman climbs out of a battered old car and walks along the brick wall corridors formed by ancient hotels interrupted by glass & steel of modern skyscrapers.

Long bleached brown/blond hair halfway down her back; femmy black leather jacket; carrying a Chinese parasol over her head because it was cute; bluejeans & boots, the 40-year old Cookie made her way to Stryker's.

The pasty white dike looked ill. Weeks of confinement had added to the pallor of her complexion. Between various dosages of medicine both for her body & for her mind she wondered if it was possible to find a few moments of peace squeezed between the hours of torment of life. But she struggled. There were reasons she kept on living. Things like her poems. Art. And sex. The love of a woman.

The Indian wore a bluejean shirt, collar open, beads & feather warrior necklace against her brown skin. Thick black hair held back by a headband. Butch. Solemn she peered at Stryker who lay under the blankets, chubby arms on top still showing bruises from her ordeal. "Stryker, ever see a flock of birds sail thru the sky? Yuh never see one bird alone but that it's flying on its way to be with its flock, or get to its nest with a mate. Yer' all alone in this room going crazy & it's part of the reason you tried to kill yourself.

351

"Maybe I'll get more popular." Sez Stryker.

"Daddy George sez yuh don't got to be popular to be in the Outlaws, jest pay yer dues. And everything else good will happen."

Angel opened the door when she heard footsteps in the hall. Cookie had buzzed downstairs in the lobby. She floated thru the drab corridor, a straight shot to a dusty fire escape with EXIT written in red letters on white; over a threadbare carpet, leaving a trace of perfume in the air. Cookie brought a womanly life into the dreary hotel. "Well, does she want me?" Cookie gazed over the room at the pudgy butch lying in bed.

"She wants you." Comancho whispers.

"No she don't." Says Stryker, peevishly.

"Yes she does!" Declares Angel.

Cookie crossed a few paces to her bedside. Touched Stryker's arm, and sat down, making the bed creek. "Come on baby." Cooed Cookie.

"NO." Said Stryker with a little pout.

"YES." Said Comancho & Angel in unison.

The butches patted their butch buddy's leg under the covers, winked knowingly to each other and said their goodbyes.

After the butches left and they were alone, Cookie pulls off her shoes & jacket and climbs into bed next to the dike.

"I know Daddy George made you come here." Stryker sez. "Her & Lou made some kinda bargain."

"Yeah, yuh know a lot don' t yuh, big brain. Huh. Nobody makes me do nothin'."

"Yeah, well I don't believe it." Sez Stryker, but she's trapped in the bed with the woman, who feels warm and soft. Cookies red lipsticked mouth opened and the best words she could think of spill out.

"I'll be yer' woman for a while, because you've been so nice to me. And I see how important that is. I'll stay with you until you get better, & we'll see each other after, until you find a lady of yer' own."

"That's nice Cookie. I would have considered it before I was dead. But now that I'm dead, at least I should be dead, I see how totally unimportant this nice stuff is."

"What stuff honey?" Cookie sez, and her soft hand has found the little butches arm, & is petting it. Then turns over, so her soft big breasts press up against Strykers side. "Yuh ain't dead. Yuh ain't a cold corpse, so forget that funny business! Cookie don't sleep with dead corpses. Cookie ain't a neckrowfillyack. She's a lover of butches. *Live* ones. "I'll be yer' woman and I'll make love with ya...
...Whatever you want me to do. We was doin' it before this all happened."

"I'll just be a pain in your ass." Stryker complains. "I'm not all that nice like everybody makes out now that I'm hurt. I been running with the Outlaws for the last 2 years, they are bad girls and so I learned a lot of things I didn't know before... But I still ain't bad enough. I ain't strong enough to get a pretty woman like you on my own merits. I ain't got the style or technique or nothing."

"Yuh just need a few minor adjustments, that's all. Yer' too polite. Yuh sound too nice baby... Yuh need to put some base in yer' voice and a swagger in yer' walk, then you'll get some results."

"That's just superficial stuff! There's more wrong with me then that!" Sez Stryker, indignantly. "I know for one, that I can't satisfy you... You and Lou do a lot of things... I wasn't butch enough when I fucked you before."

"It helps honey, but not everybody's a manly butch like Lou. Sometimes it's nice to have a change. Somebody cuddly and warm like you are. Like a Teddy Bear. But do whatever you want. You can ignore me, but I'm gonna stay right here next to you. I mean it. Or you can play with me. Whatever yuh want goes, baby. I'm yours."

"It'll just hurt me, after you leave!"

"I won't leave! Not till yer' better & can go out to the club and find more women. And we'll still be friends & we'll be together again, after. That's how I am, I can't be with just one butch."

"I might not ever get another woman! And I'll see you in the club with Lou, **UGH! PLEASE!** Don't hug her & kiss her, at least not in front of me where I can see!"

"I won't! I'll hug you!"

Spring breeze blew around the windows in rivulets of air. The two lesbians snuggled under the covers. Downstairs, the city clamored thru it's work day, pounding & building & planning blueprints. And it's artists dreamed dreams & figured ways to sketch them into reality. And a few good people still struggle along trying to pick up pieces of the world.

"I can make love gentle. That's about it. I can't be hard. I ain't got a tough personality; tho I try and try. I scrunch up my face and get in my motorcycle costume, try to think mean thoughts, but it won't work." Stryker sez finally.

"Give it to me hard as you can then, Stryker. That's good enough."

"Cookie, I still think you're a Madonna. The most beautiful Madonna I've ever seen."

"Oh Stryker!" The perfumed Cookie clapped her hands in happiness; bent over and kisses her on her chubby lips.

They lay on the special hospital bed with it's folding mattress side by side, caressing. 'I haven't got it in me to order her around like Lou does. I'm not strong enough to beat up men to protect her or even myself. I haven't got it.' Stryker thinks.

"Stop feeling sorry for yourself." Sez Cookie watching the miserable expression that plays over the butches face.

"I'll try to be different when I get well."

Cookie plants another red lipstick print on Stryker's mouth. "I like yuh the way yuh are. You have something Lou and the others don't. And I appreciate somebody whose been good to me."

"Yeah. Whatever in the hell that was." Said Stryker but buried her face in Cookies bosom, and inside began to feel the golden glow of being cared for. Of being humanly close.

Chapter Thirty Three

So this book is events in the lives that surrounded them. A single series of exploits from that period of Fall 1993, to Spring 1994, in the Outlaw Chronicles.

The gang went on and on.

The highs and lows. The Saundra's, Strykers, and Daddy George.

There are currently 120 Outlaw members.

Racism is history, now many new bikers are 3rd world; including Latinas, blacks, and a few Asians.

And the first male member had become a woman.

George, it's founder shook her head in amazement. The club was growing out of control. Bigger then she ever dreamed it might.

Many of the Outlaws during that timeframe had been dwarfed by cataclysmic events. Their individual lives seemed swept along by a huge whirlwind beyond their personal comprehension. So, also, felt their hurts had been assuaged by acts of their Club.

The chastised Punk & Jody had made amends. Embarrassed for the wrong they'd done in their drunk rage, and told Saundra they were sorry.

All wasn't well with the world --but at least the globe was still spinning and the Outlaws were still a band together. Of women strong.

After her obnoxious behavior amid the club in times past, involving her ex-woman Crystal, one of the five Chiefs, Hawk was restored to warrior glory by the manner in which she'd taken to heart Strykers cause, going into battle & leading others with courage.

They were lesbians because they desire women. Wither or not they strap on dicks. Nothing can replace the touch of a woman, her scent, her feelings, her cunt in their lives.

In the end, somebody takes the covers off. The wrapping is off the mysterious Christmas gifts of green & red & gold—at last. The curtain goes down, -- playacting is done. And the theatre lights come up. We see who is in the audience. Who we're sitting next to. The real players are unmasked.--We see who is of flesh. Who has a heart. --Even a tiny pitiful heart like Daddy George had, which was more then enough to sustain her & her friends thru life. And who is demonical. No longer human. Heartless. With no soul.

They had made it thru the wintry yuletide season. Thru the cruel winds wild lament & the bitter weather; to seize the prize.

The devil was defeated, driven back to his dark realm. The criminals had been stopped with their own guns.

Sometime courage is this tiny spark of love. –Driven by the heart. Other times courage is not caring; just letting caution go, and fight for the helluva it.

Angel had found a key. It was, to be renewed by the spirit in your mind, not by what comes thru the world. Renewed by the Spirit of God blowing thru your mind. What comes thru the world hurts. It beats us down. It's moments of success get us charged and moving once again--but this success doesn't always last.

'I'm going for joy. Wild horses can't drag me from it.' Angel was so hungry for love. So hungry for sex. So hungry for God.

They made lesbian love. It was normal. Even joyful.

A rush of golden kisses from the sun.

The Preacher was on fire with the Holy Spirit; "Know that this God of ours is an incredible Task Master, She drives us, drives us, drives us almost to the breaking point.--Because, we live in a world we've tried to create. With all our own abilities, and securities. And She wants us to break loose out of that and see what we are truly capable of. What life truly is. We worship in our tiny homes with safe white picket fences, and property lines, 'God just give me this, get me that and I'll be happy.' Asking for a bowl of gruel, a piece of stale bread, when God would give us Paradise, and make us Great. But we got to shake loose the securities and the chains."

The acts of God are pure. All others are the compromise of this world and its half lies.

It was near the end. Angel felt she was on a clear channel of victory.

While she washed the floor with a grey string mop, Angel flipped the radio knob and out of the Donut Shop's speakers spilled strong notes of classical music. Her spirit soared. Soon everything seemed clean. All was right with her world.

What she felt at the end of her journey was peace.

'And I was moving thru the wind with the Power God gave me. Forward, making my way to the Heart of Christ.'

The new job had resulted from this method.—Nagging.

Angel & Crystal were both Christians. Every night they said their prayers. About this time,--in the wee small hours of the morning after a wild bout of partying at Oils with their biker sisters,--all Angel wanted to do was romance Crystal a little; stroke her warm sides and tits & thighs, work her hand between those sweet wispy-haired pussy lips until it got wet,--then strap on her cock and climb up on Crystal and take a quick fuck.

But nearly every night recently, when they were at prayer, on bent knees by the side of the bed holding pale hands; right in the middle of "GOD OUR MOTHER WHO LIVES IN HEAVEN", Crystal's voice would die, she'd stop stone cold, turn to Angel, interrupting the sacred prayer and ask some crazy question, like: 'Angel how can you believe in God and ask Her for all these things and still go down to work at 8 o'clock each morning and call yourself Officer Anglin from the Metropolitan Police Department over the phone, soliciting money for a fictitious charity which has paid you $40,000 over the last two years and only $6,000 of it actually went to any crippled children, --if that. And we are praying the same God to buy a house and have kids of our own and to have a good life and be healthy and you're doing this?" –Thereby shattering the prayer scene.

Now the dick in its warmer being heated for use of female pleasure was just minutes way. Time was ticking. Angel was worn down by the nights events & didn't feel like arguing. Angel wants to turn Crystal over and make love, and thinks; 'I should tell her anything she wants to hear, 'Ok baby, I'll quit that crappy scam job you hate so much'--then say I forgot about it the next morning—'I must have been talking in my sleep.' Next to her, inches away, the curly blond is thinking, 'I should tell her, 'no, no, no'. No sex until she quits and gets an honest job, regardless of what it says by biker code that I gotta give it to her when she asks.'

After a sweet tongue lashing to the exasperated Angel, Crystal submits. –And what a lovely submission it was, as the cock glided in and out of her hot pussy lubricated by natural juices & warmed lube.

Somehow, by God's mysterious ways, these scenes of prayer & penance had worked.

Angel couldn't believe it was her.--In fact, thought it must be somebody else in a cooks white hat, flipping hamburgers on a grill, taking orders behind a glass window. It had to be some character in a play--but not her.

Since Angel had gone legal she no longer had to worry about police busting in the office door and arresting the crew. Had got an honest job, and took a drastic cut in pay, from $600 per week--with no taxes deducted,--tho it had been a grind, working the phones 8am to 8pm—to earning just above minimum wage; $5 per hour for slaving over excruciating hot ovens. The hours were a lot shorter, and the stress was the less, except at the lunch hour rush. With Crystal's income in Window Display of a major Department Store, together they cleared $400 per week.

The blond butch was always in a hurry. Floating behind her, smell of men's cologne with which she doused herself because of sweating at the grill. Hung her black leather jacket on a peg in the employees room in back, chopper parked outside in a special area of the lot.

Hair in her eyes, flipped it back with grease spattered fingers. Got orders mixed up. **"SHE ASKED FOR A CHEESEBURGER!"** Hollers the frantic cashier. The blond cook tosses a substitute onto the hot splattering metal surface of the grill and flips a bun from between two hotdogs with brown grill stripes burnt into them, throws a blackened patty & slice of cheese into it.

"Take this one!" And it comes apart.

The donut shop wasn't Caviar, but she could dream. White walls, a list of prices painted on it in red letters. Pots of chili bubbling on the stove. Eunice, the cashier, flying fingers totaled up the tab; the registers sounding bells & clanging as the cash drawer opens and shuts. Angel's sales pitch for the fraudulent charity was on an old tape, tucked away in the recess of her mind. After the job was the tunnel vision thru which she looked homeward --to be with her wife. When the little insults of the day turned to joy.

Angel saw more police officers now that she was a cook flipping hamburger paddies & pouring coffee then she ever had on the run, racing down back stairways to avoid a raid. Or slouching past red light district taverns and gay clubs incognito while inside officers arrested her unfortunate sisters & brothers and led them to awaiting paddy wagons. The cops in blue uniform came in off the beat for coffee, and looked at Angel as a respectable worker on a job providing food. What a reversal. No longer was she a salesperson begging, demanding, & intimidating people to contribute. Now, customers came to her with fistfuls of money; they came in a rush, money spilling out of their wallets, in a hurry to be fed the greasy fast food burgers & donuts.

Angel felt no guilt about her new job, as she had before. No longer felt like slime. Customers looked at her as an ordinary worker, like themselves. The law was on her side. A cook giving out food, coffee, and filling the sugar shakers so they could get their adrenaline fix.

A lot of bikers hung out in the Donut Shop when Oils wasn't open. Common women who listened to funky music of the jukebox. The latest hits. Cozy in the cold of a frosty spring, amid the sizzz of hamburgers frying in grease on the grill.

Eunice has given Angel the nod; wiping her hands on her apron the cook swings around the end of the cooks stand with a loping gait & goes to join a pal, Comancho the Indian, on her break, out in the customer area. Seated at picnic benches on the whitewashed floor, legs sprawled out, the tow butches confer. The Indian wears a feather stuck in her native style headband. A pair of expensive slacks & matching shirt. They discussed their new jobs. "Yep partner. Technicolor's the only place that ever took me back. –Quite a few times. I've done some stuff on some jobs before. Talk about the wayward daughter returns; I'm the waywardess of wayward." Muses the Indian, chewing a toothpick. Red & golden jukebox pounds songs building a lush invisible environment around them. "Now if I can only get back into good standing with this company, maybe they'll actually give me a raise. I want to get back to be their pet dawg. I may not get out of the yard, but I can get out of the dawg house."

And Angel's saying something like; "Well, if yuh worked here at The Donut Shop, yuh'd eat hamburgers morning, noon & night. I tell yuh, worken' at this hamburger joint, I'm gonna get very sick of burgers 'n donuts,--after 2 years. Only after 2 years mind you. It takes 2 years to stock up on 'em. Get my fill of 'em."

It was an evening in April; Angel's standing at the grill, toes of leather boots, and ends of bluejeans visible under a white apron; cooks cap on her head. Had become a world philosopher, observing human behavior in her long hours in which she had to deal with the public. Customers came in, hungry, dollars clutched in their hands, hungry, running in for a lunch break off the job...

Angel wondered what it would be like, an age, futuristic, a science fiction time when money was no longer a problem for anybody. And human beings who grasped to earn money, to invest, to save money over a lifetime, she wondered what they'd be wanting then? What would be their quest ?

Grease splattered the steel hood of the range. A plastic counter, orange color. Freezers of patties, frozen buns. Shelves of jars of pickles. Relish. Ketchup. Mustard. She had time for many thoughts here. Her Journey To A Woman was complete. Had found Crystal. Life's bitter cup was sweetened. So where would she go now? In her journey thru this earthly timeplane?

Quite often her buddies from the Club hung out with Angel when she wasn't busy. Draped over the counter & they'd philosophize. Comancho was one of these. The Indian spoke, "The human race is like sheep on a string. They're constantly lost. Somebody has to pull 'em back when they get to the end of their rope. Give 'em a tug, and try to lead 'em home where they'll be safe."

"Like we did for Stryker."

Angel had been told by the management not to wear her cleric costume on the job, but still put it on at the club, where she was developing the nickname The Leather Preacher. Her black motorcycle jacket hung back in the storage room, a comforting reminder to freedom, which lay a few hours off, around the clock. She'd wipe her hands on the apron, throw it into the laundry bin, slip on her jacket, punch the time clock, slam the door, go into the blast of cold outdoors, as the hot steamy inside of the hamburger joint shut back up behind in closing, swing one leg over her motorcycle, and flick the ignition with her wrist, and ride.

So, sometimes she'd ponder on the job, as stars swum in the night sky, silver against basic black; as a philosopher, 'that can be my work. I got a new job, this material employment as a cook, but I can have a spiritual one as well.' Angel thinks, 'My job could be to lead them out of the shadows. Lead them out of dead ends. Like I was led. To lead them out of the shadows into the light where they can see God.

Just as I was saved, and my life spared, so I can give something back. It's only what they already know, I'll help them find it. They just lost it for a moment. It's inside us. In the collective unconscious of humankind. To lead them out of a shadowy world into a place as bright as heaven.' Where, as I said; I was going somewhere fast. Harnessed to a great energy, going to see God The Creator, with God. Left behind the problems. The never-ceasing problems of this earth. Out of the $125 per week hotels & drunk girls and the red light districts, and loitering men of the street to be feared. Out of the coldness of women and the lack of fun. I was on my way. Out of the partygirls and sex-yens, and the one night stands following night after night of lonely lesbians looking for a female lay. Out of lovesick junkies looking for a fix.

What better place for the touch of the hand of God (Her Most High Holiness). To preach the good news from the most desolate place. To fall but at the end of things --as creatures reach the end of their rope struggling & straining, going hot & cold & mad, as it must have been in the beginning, in a baptism of fire, in the volcanic bowels of the earth, as the soil within us, to be born.

She might make a good preacher. And a good leader. Not too big & bossy. A person who can understand the more unfortunate because they're not so strong themselves.

Angel was thankful for the work begun by George; the club had given her a home, friends & a wife. The ideas of the big bulldike, that women need to be free, and proud to express themselves as they did as girls, before they become subjected to the burdens of women. That

362

they should stand up and fight, protect themselves & those they love, functioning as a team. That they should keep pushing on, even tho it hurt. Keep trying, tho it seemed of no use. Keep struggling for a better day. Keep on fighting back. —"**Daddy George was the Leader Of The Pack. She rode a Harley, and she wore black.**"

www.ingramcontent.com/pod-product-compliance
Lightning Source LLC
Chambersburg PA
CBHW060413030726
47495CB00003B/560